Joythïéf

BRENDA J. PIERSON

Joythïëf

Crimson Fox
PUBLISHING
TURNER, OREGON

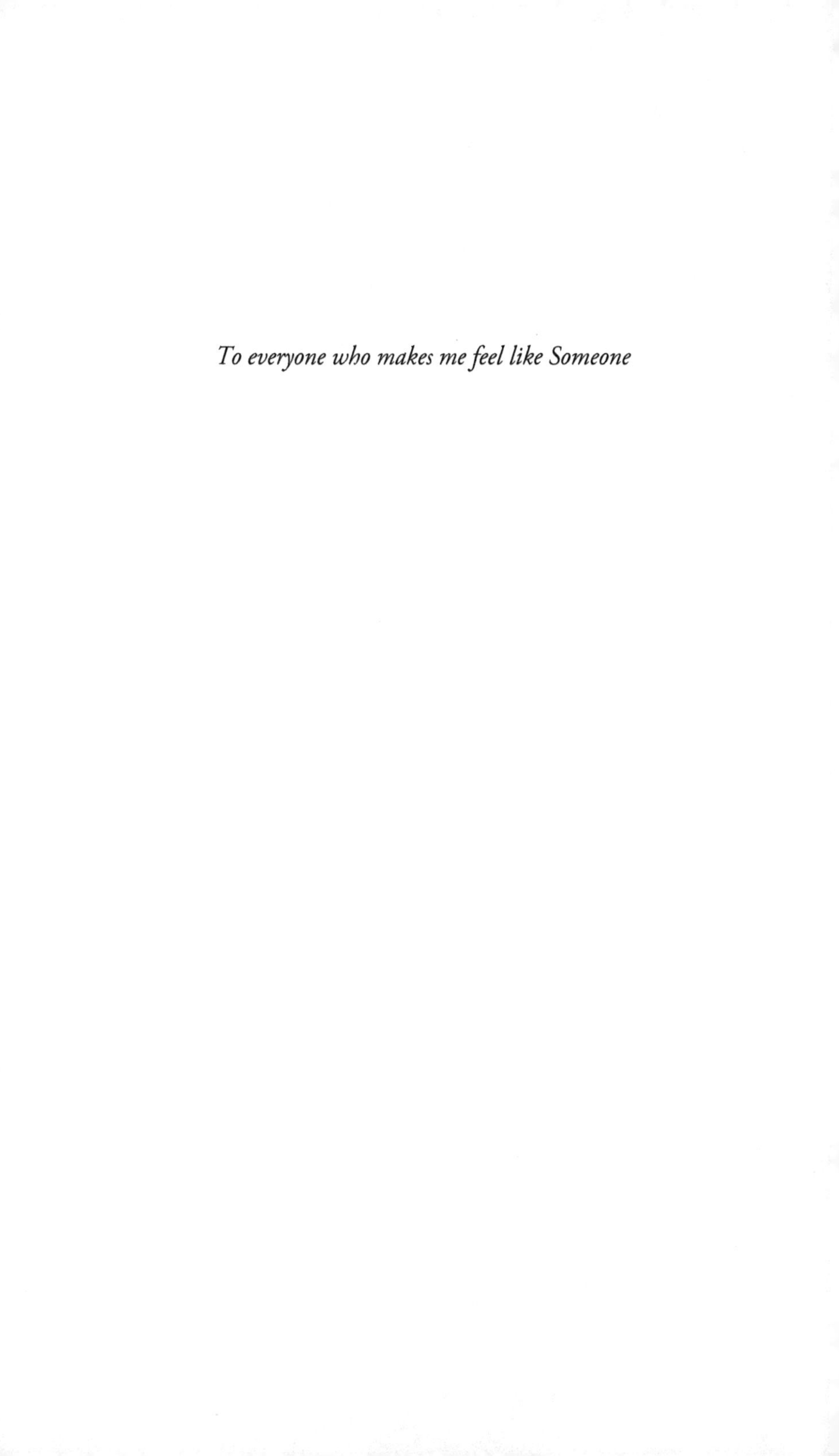

To everyone who makes me feel like Someone

BRENDA J. PIERSON

Joythïef

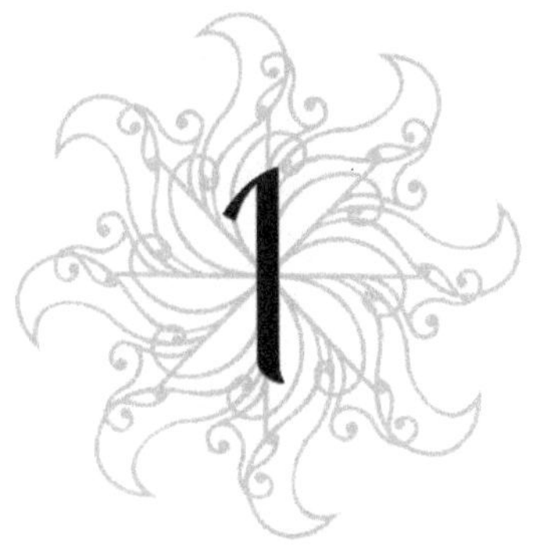

ost people wouldn't consider clinging to the outer wall of the palace, swaying in the cold night breeze, an enjoyable activity. Mariq could think of nowhere else she'd rather be.

The risks were almost too great to count. If anyone saw her, she'd be shot from the wall. If her fingers slipped on the cold marble, she'd plummet three stories down. The palms and small ponds in the sheik's garden might cushion the fall enough for her to survive, but the guards who would investigate such a ruckus wouldn't be nearly as lenient.

But if nothing went wrong, Mariq would sneak into one of the most heavily guarded buildings in Kuriza and no one would be the wiser.

She paused with only her eyes above the windowsill, surveying the room beyond. The grand library of Tufe Kolam Meidani, Sheik of Kuriza. Compared to the rest of the kingdom—bland, ordinary, virtually lifeless—this room was an explosion for the senses. Scrolls lined the walls, each in their own individual niche. Rarer, more expensive leather tomes decorated large tables inlaid with gold and ivory. Bronze censors filled with spicy incense smoked in the corners. Each tile on the mosaic floor shone with colors vivid enough to make a sunset jealous.

Everywhere she looked treasures lay about. Casually, almost distractedly. As if this great wealth was little more than a trinket to set aside and gather dust.

Spider-thieves across Kuriza whispered of this room. Dreamt of the prestige entering, and escaping, would gain. Mariq could slip away with a single tome and earn the respect of every thief in the Scorched Lands. Not to mention enough money to live in comfort for the rest of her life.

But Mariq didn't smirk at the thought, nor did her imagination swirl with greed and excitement. She wasn't here to steal.

She peered into the shadows, opening her ears for any hint of movement. The library was deserted.

Now she smiled.

Mariq Ashai Meidani, daughter of Sheik Tufe Kolam Meidani, clambered into her library. She took a moment to resettle her sarong over the knives, lockpicks, rope as thin as spider-silk, and harnesses for stolen goods strapped to her legs. Another moment to smooth her hair and calm her breathing. Finally she turned her attention to the tight sleeve on her right arm.

Even more than her thieving equipment, this was her most essential tool. It had taken months and a considerable amount of gold to get the fake tattoos, only reaching from wrist to halfway to her elbow, drawn on the sleeve. They named her a servant girl—not a slave, as the requisite hole through her forearm would be impossible to fake—with no title or heritage to speak of. It was a marvel, a treasure more rare and valuable than anything in the famed library. It erased her true heritage tattoos so thoroughly Mariq often wondered if it was magic.

She shook her head. Magic was gone—purged from the Scorched Lands long before she'd been born. Anything that could do the impossible, that could not be explained, had been destroyed and was better off that way. Or so she'd been told. She still found herself wondering about it more often than not, despite being told over and over to stop asking so many questions.

Then again, she'd never been good at obeying what others told her.

Mariq peeled the sleeve from her arm, revealing her true heritage tattoos. They crawled from palm to shoulder, inked in indigo and gold, far more intricate than her serving girl's disguise. They proclaimed her daughter of the wealthiest kingdom in the Scorched Lands and a prize many nobles sought for their sons. When she married, her husband's station would be intertwined with her father's. Most women in Kuriza would kill for tattoos that spoke of such value. Mariq would have been content with the fictional serving girl's, if only her worth was placed in who she was rather than what she could be traded for.

She hid the sleeve in her thigh holsters beside her treasure for the night, did one final check of her appearance, and grabbed a book from the table. A history of the Night of Bloody Sands. She'd read this story many times before, how generations ago the people had defied their evil rulers and taken control of the Scorched Lands before they could be destroyed. Her family had stood against darkness and triumphed, and therefore—according to her tutors, at least—they were blessed to rule. Mariq figured it had more to do with holding absolute power and squashing anyone who dared to think otherwise, but her opinion didn't matter much.

She opened the book to a random page and walked out of the library, as if she'd been so absorbed in the content she'd lost track of the hour. The servants knew she was prone to these distractions and wouldn't question her being up so late. If any of them were still awake.

It was, after all, closer to dawn than dusk.

She navigated the marble hallways and staircases by memory, small potted palms rustling near the open windows. The breeze smelled of salt from the sea to the west and hot spices from the desert to the east. The hallways felt deserted and peaceful, just the way Mariq liked it. During the day far too many leering sycophants and unsavory characters working for, or with, her father and brother lingered around the palace.

Mariq moved to turn the page when a sound reached her ears—quiet and easily overlooked, but years of training with thieves and assassins had taught her to recognize it in an instant. A blade sliding from a sheath. A knife, from the way it cut off so abruptly.

Mariq dropped to a practiced crouch, cringing as the priceless book fell to the ground beside her. A cluster of palms cast the corner in shadow and she dashed under them, pulling one of her own knives from its sheath on her calf. Her heart pounded, but her hand was steady and her thoughts clear. Half a lifetime of practice served her well.

She scanned the shadows. A shape stirred, too dark to be normal, moving against the wind. Soft footsteps echoed in the expansive marble hallway. If she hadn't been searching for him, she'd never have noticed him. He was good.

But she was better.

Mariq shifted forward, allowing the fronds hiding her to rustle a bit more than normal. The shadow paused. An instant later something heavy thunked into the wooden banister beside her. An ebony knife, its handle waggling from the force of impact.

Her blood chilled. Any spider-thief would recognize that blade, but she pushed her dread and shock aside. She couldn't afford to lose focus now. Ebony knives always came in pairs.

The shadow advanced on her. No doubt hoping that first knife would distract her long enough to close the distance and strike with the second.

Her stomach roiled. She was a thief, not a killer. But she couldn't evade the assassin—he would be trained in her arts of hiding and stalking just as she had been trained in his. Trying to run now invited a knife in the back. She had to kill or die.

Mariq flung her ivory-handled dagger before she could reconsider.

The man attached to the shadow fell without a cry.

Mariq stayed silent until she was sure their confrontation had gone unnoticed. Then she rose on shaky knees and approached the assassin's body, scanning his heritage tattoos. Son of a merchant, fairly wealthy for the working class. Not married, for which Mariq thanked her luck. Leaving a man dead was horrible enough. Creating a widow or orphans would have been more than she could have stomached. Nausea already burned her throat as it was.

Mariq turned to face the knife in the banister. Its ebony handle, exact opposite of her own specially made ivory ones, made her shudder. She didn't need to cut his palm and see the blood well in his scars, revealing the hidden knife-star that marked the members of the Star-Blade assassins. This weapon was proof enough.

The Star-Blades. The same guild that had trained her as a thief, given her an identity that had nothing to do with being pawned off for political gain. Among the Star-Blades she was a woman, an accomplished thief, a person rather than a treasure. She had worth that went deeper than the circumstances of her birth. She valued that gift more than anything her father's grand palace could offer.

But the ebony dagger mocked all that. Only the highest-ranking members of the Star-Blades were given those weapons. No one who held those blades would take a contract that breached the rules of the guild. And their rules left no room for debate: other members of the Star-Blades were off-limits.

So why did a member of her own guild try to kill her?

Mariq could spend the rest of the night puzzling over that. But first, she had to get out of sight. No one in her father's household knew she was a spider-thief. She could hardly afford to be exposed the very night a body was discovered in the palace.

She retrieved her knife, wiping the man's blood from the blade and returning it to her sheath. She took his Star-Blade daggers as well, scooped up the discarded book, and dashed up the stairs to her rooms.

The scents of cinnamon and sandalwood permeating her chambers didn't calm her as they usually did. She felt too full of energy, too overwrought to relax. The ebony knives seemed to burn her. Why had they been aimed at her? What had she done to deserve such ire? She was a princess, yes, daughter of the wealthiest and most powerful sheik in the Scorched Lands, but that should have deterred an attack like this, not invited one. She was much more valuable as a pawn than a corpse.

She laid the knives on a pillow, staring at them as if waiting for them to speak. No, this couldn't have been a political attack. This had to be personal. Someone wanted her dead, someone rich or powerful enough to turn her own guild against her. But who? Before today she'd have sworn such a person didn't exist. No one could subvert the Star-Blades so thoroughly.

But they had, and the assassin below wouldn't remain undiscovered for long. If her father discovered who he'd been after, he'd begin asking uncomfortable questions. Questions Mariq couldn't afford. She had to make sure no suspicion could fall on her.

She turned from the knives and knelt before her ornate jewelry table. Gold and precious stones winked at her in the dancing light of her oil lamps.

Ignoring the vast wealth arrayed before her, Mariq reached beneath the table and pulled a wide, flat box from the shelf hidden below. A fairly ordinary piece for Tufe Kolam's palace—built of semi-precious stones and somewhat common woods rather than gold and mahogany—but Mariq treasured this more than anything in her chambers.

She lifted the lid and gazed into the interior, pride swelling in her chest. Her extra thieving tools lay in pristine condition, and she unstrapped her gear and knives and set them in their places. Then, from the depths of the hidden pocket in her thigh holster, she retrieved tonight's treasure.

The square of pinkish clay looked like garbage, a piece of detritus swept to the side of the road and forgotten. But it held far more value to Mariq. She hadn't plucked it from a trash heap on the street—she'd pried it from the roof of the third tallest building in Kuriza. A challenging climb for even a spider-thief, known for their skill at clinging to walls and ceilings like their namesake. After a moment it joined the small pile of similarly unimpressive-looking stones. Clay, rocks, a few small mosaic tiles.

She had one for almost every notable building in the kingdom. Proof of her skill and courage. Proof she was more than just the delicate princess everyone expected her to be.

Then again, she doubted anyone would care. Even though her audacity would scandalize her father's court, her skills abhorrent for someone of her station—let alone a woman—what was the worst the people of Kuriza would muster? A scolding? Polite shock?

They were her people, yet Mariq had never understood them. They walked through life as if nothing in it could interest them. They lived and breathed but they might as well be dead. Their emotions, their vitality, never surfaced. She saw it more and more with each passing year—colors grew a bit duller, people smiled more rarely, they never got angry or happy or anything other than melancholy. Even the children had stopped running and playing, trudging after their parents with eyes far too sad and dead for people so young.

She'd never figured out what was wrong with them, or why she wasn't afflicted. Nor were her father or brother, for that matter. A few scattered people managed to keep their vitality while it drained from everyone else. As if the whole of Kuriza had fallen ill and only they were immune.

Yet another mystery, more thoughts to whirl through her mind on a night when she already had too many. Why did they have to come all at once? Why couldn't she just shut her mind off once in a while and enjoy some peace instead of being plagued by curiosity and imagination and *desire*? Desire to live, to act, to accomplish. To *do*. It drove her mad sometimes, even as it sustained her in this often-suffocating life.

She closed her box of treasures and stowed it. Soon she was pacing, and a moment later she once again stood before the ebony knives.

The black blades mocked her. Damned her. Offered her a thousand questions, but no answers.

"I'd expected to find those in your back, and you slightly less alive."

Mariq spun toward the voice, the knives practically leaping into her hands. A man stood on her balcony, a cloak of the most profound black rendering him invisible against the darkened sky. Not even a glimmer of his features could be seen. It may as well have been woven from the night itself.

He knew she'd been a target tonight. Which meant he had a hand in it. She flung one of the assassin's ebony knives at the block of shadow. The man sidestepped with surprising speed, catching the knife in a fold of his cloak as it trailed behind him.

"That's hardly a polite way to begin a business arrangement." His voice seemed familiar, full of the arrogance that came from a lifetime in command. She heard it in her father and brothers' voices every single day.

"Neither is an attempted assassination," Mariq spat. "There wouldn't have been much negotiation had he been successful."

"You'd not have been worth the effort if you hadn't bested him."

"You mean this was a test? To prove myself worthy to negotiate with a man who'd ordered my murder?"

He took a few steps forward. Even in the light of her oil lamps and candles she could see nothing of his face. "Call it what you will," he said, sounding bored. "But you will do as I say."

"I won't work for you."

"You say that as if you have a choice." Again, he sounded bored. As if this was nothing but the required tea and social niceties before the real negotiations could begin.

"What makes you think I'll do anything you say? You have no power over me."

"You may find I have ways of persuading you, princess."

Mariq shivered. She did not want to find out what those ways entailed.

He continued as if she hadn't argued. "Sheik Zahra of Hatife is looking for a new bride. You will be called upon to fill that position. You will, of course, accept."

Another shudder. If her father had indeed arranged this, she wouldn't have an option to accept or refuse. It would simply happen.

Hatife was the closest thing Kuriza had to a rival. If her father could ensure peace by giving its ruler his daughter, he wouldn't hesitate. He would consider it a good deal—after all, whatever price he'd negotiate for her hand would be worth far more to him than she was. Even if she would be Sheik Zahra's, what, fourth wife? Fifth?

"Why do you care what arrangement my father makes for me? Do you want me to steal from him?"

"No, princess. I want you to kill him."

Mariq's stomach plummeted. The knife in her hand suddenly felt like an abomination. "I'm not an assassin. I'm a spider-thief."

"I beg to differ. You just killed a man trained by the best assassins in the Scorched Lands. By right of victory in battle, his title belongs to you."

"That was different! I was defending myself."

"He is dead by your hand. That makes it murder." The man in the cloak stepped forward, and Mariq raised her remaining dagger between them. "You've done it once, you can do it again. Whether you like it or not, that is what you must do."

"You can't force me to kill anyone." Her voice shook even more than the knife in her hand.

In response the man moved, his cloak blending with the shadows so seamlessly Mariq couldn't track him. She spun, scanning the room, but saw nothing.

A heartbeat later he grabbed her from behind and pinned her against his chest, a dagger of his own held at her throat. Mariq struggled against the grip, but his arm tightened and the blade pressed against her skin. She froze. She had no doubt he would use it if he thought it necessary.

"I told you I had ways of persuading you," he whispered into her ear. He lifted the dagger just enough for her to see the liquid shimmer on its blade. "Do you know what this is?"

Her heart thumped painfully in her chest, and her legs grew weak and watery. Star-Blade poison was universally feared, and for good reason. The guild's alchemists were second to none and very creative in their work.

"This is a special blend. It won't kill you—at least, not the way you'd wish it would. This poison kills the part of us we love the most. Do you cherish your beauty? You will shrivel into an ugly old bag before the month is out. Do you treasure your courage? You will soon cower in terror before the gentlest kitten." He paused for a moment to allow the implications to sink in. "So, princess, what do you value most?"

Mariq trembled, a sheen of sweat coating her skin. She knew

exactly what the poison would target—everything she'd learned from the Star-Blades. Nothing was dearer to her than the strength of body and mind they had taught her, the identity her accomplishments had earned for her. Without that, she was nothing. One treasure among many in her father's palace, to be bartered off for the greatest gain.

"Poison me and you could lose the skills you're demanding I use for you," she said.

"Oh, don't worry. Carry out our wishes and you'll never feel its bite. Refuse, and it won't matter what you lose. You'd be useless to us anyway."

"I'll find an antidote," Mariq said, though she didn't sound nearly as confident as she'd wanted.

"Even the Star-Blade alchemist who created this poison could not find one. A single touch of this blade and you will never again be the woman you are. Face it, princess. You've lost. Your only way out is to obey."

Mariq didn't have to fake the defeated slump of her shoulders. She'd always dreaded the day she would be married off, and now it had come. What kind of life would await her outside Kuriza? No more thieving, that was almost certain. No more freedom of any kind was more likely. She would become an ornament in another rich man's palace, one of many. Allowed nothing but tiny distractions to keep her busy while her life passed by without her.

The looming threat of the poison only made it worse. She didn't want to become an assassin, but if she didn't, she would lose everything she'd fought for. Then she would be nothing, and her guilt would destroy whatever the poison left intact.

The man chuckled again, clearly enjoying Mariq's misery. Her grip tightened on the knife she still held, pinned against her body by the man's arm. Useless now. But that didn't stop her from imagining it disappearing into the shadows of his hood.

"I knew you'd come to see reason," he said. Mariq did her best not to stumble when his weight suddenly disappeared from behind her.

She spun, extending her knife as far as she could in hopes of catching the man. But he was already gone. Melted into the shadows as if he'd never existed. Mariq could still feel the dagger against her throat, though, that lurid poison resting against her skin. She ran a hand over her neck. No cuts. No poison—not yet, at least. But it had been close.

Just the thought made her heart fall into her stomach, as if her insides had been hollowed out. Her entire body started trembling. The knife dropped to the floor.

Mariq followed a heartbeat later.

arly the next morning, before the sun had proper time to broil
the desert, Mariq received a summons from her father.

She waited until the servants had left before swearing and climbing out of bed. Her delicate princess persona would have been shocked to hear such language come from a lady. But Mariq had learned to swear with the thieves and assassins of the Star-Blades. She could make any delicate princess faint with a few choice words.

Bone-deep weariness clung to her. What little rest she'd gotten had been plagued by nightmares. Not the best preparation for a meeting with her father—especially one announcing her upcoming marriage.

Mariq took extra care with her appearance, donning her favorite purple-and-gold sarong. Sleeveless, of course, to show off her elegant heritage tattoos in full. The silk was smooth and cool against her skin, and the cut made her feel beautiful and feminine while still allowing her to move.

She waved away the servants who returned to do her hair, needing the calm actions to keep herself from panicking. She combed her hair and let it fall down her back, held away from her face by a band of gold coins around her forehead. More jewelry followed, bracelets and anklets and armbands of gleaming gold and sparkling gems. Mariq felt herself relax as she assembled her outfit. She might be a thief, scaling buildings and stealing worthless chunks of rock, but that didn't mean she couldn't like pretty things. On the contrary—she liked pretty things very much. Most thieves had this trait in common, whatever they actually ended up stealing.

Appearance assembled and delicate princess persona firmly in place, Mariq had no more reason to leave her father waiting. She'd already taken longer than prudence called for, but still she hesitated, looking over herself in the polished glass. Finding nothing to fix but searching again and again anyway.

She took a few deep breaths, stroked the silk covering her legs to calm her hands, and left her chambers for the meeting with her father.

Mariq was almost surprised to see no sign of the assassin at the bottom of the stairs. Her father had been most efficient at erasing the evidence of a threat in his palace, especially since emissaries from Sheik Zahra would no doubt be present for today's meeting. He couldn't seem weak before his rival, after all. Mariq knew better than to think the matter forgotten. His spies would be hard at work asking questions and tracking down hints until they found the one responsible. She didn't envy the man's fate once he was brought before her father.

But to anyone who didn't know, nothing had happened. There was no body, no blood, not even a scuff on the marble floor. She almost could have convinced herself it had all been a dream. How desperately she wished it had been.

She paused once more before entering her father's library, took a few deep breaths. She couldn't do anything about the shaking of her hands. She'd just have to hope no one noticed.

The dry scent of parchment and leather welcomed her back to the library. Mariq kept her eyes away from the open window she'd crawled through last night, kept her fingers from checking that she no longer had the tattoo sleeve covering her arm. Otherwise she might be tempted to leap out, climb away to freedom and never return.

She had to pretend this was all normal. Nothing suspicious. She was just a delicate princess here to do her duty.

She turned her attention to her father. He sat at one of the low mosaic tables, an emissary across from him and her brother at his right hand. Lookan glanced at her, his expression a contradiction to itself. His mouth sneered in disdain, but his eyes held a twinkle of encouragement. Even after twenty years she'd yet to figure him out. In private he urged her to push her boundaries, to not allow her father and the stigmas of their culture to keep her in her role. But if anyone was within sight or earshot he treated her with as much disregard, as much animosity, as her father. He did both so convincingly she could never tell which was the truth and which a façade.

She half-turned as a servant entered, bearing a tray of tea and spiced cakes. Mariq took the tray with a small nod. She knew her place here. Princess she may be, but with guests of such stature she took on the role of servant. A subtle way for her father to show her off. *See how obedient she is? She will make a good wife—for the right price.*

She felt their eyes on her as she knelt beside the table. The small gold coins fringing her sarong clinked and her many bracelets and anklets chimed with every movement. Usually the conversation had resumed by this point, but today the men were silent. They just… stared. She felt like a pig being traded at market.

Only her intense training kept her hands somewhat steady as she poured cups of tea and placed them before the men. Once finished she settled back on her heels, waiting for a command. It was almost a relief to kneel there, half-bowed in submission. At least now they could only see the top of her head.

The silence stretched to awkwardness. Was there a problem? Did the emissary disapprove of her? She darted her eyes up as much as she dared, catching a glimpse of the men at the table.

Her brother sat stiffly, scowling deeply at the emissary. Anger simmered in his eyes, but why? He held no love for Sheik Zahra, being a threat to the kingdom he would inherit, but this seemed far too personal for that.

But if her brother was angry, her father was *fuming*.

He seemed relaxed, but Mariq knew the subtle signs that showed her father struggled to restrain his temper. He kept his hand closed around his teacup, leaned back extra far from the table, and his toe tapped out of sight. His jaw clenched and unclenched repeatedly. What about this man irked him so much? Mariq cast her eyes toward the emissary's arm, to see who they dealt with.

Her gaze landed on bare skin. Not a marking in sight.

Mariq couldn't believe it. Even the lowliest beggar, the most trodden-upon slave, had a tiny ring around their wrist, stating their name and place of birth. But not this man. The unmarked skin proclaimed him to be No One, from Nowhere. Owner of nothing. With no honor to call his own.

The only thing on his arm was a finger-width hole pierced between the bones of his right forearm, a few inches above his wrist. Slave. A chain wrapped around his wrist, looping through the hole, claiming ownership of him. Mariq had never seen this particular chain before. Sheik Zahra's? She had no way to know, but her stomach churned at the sight. What kind of man could claim ownership of another with a band of barbed wire? Tiny, needle-sharp spikes dug into the man's wrist every time he moved it. Scabs and dried blood crusted the skin around it, and beneath that white and red scars crisscrossed his wrist, so many layered upon each other it was amazing he could still use it.

The emissary broke the silence at last. "Look at me." Not a harsh command like she'd expected, but a request. She obeyed.

He couldn't be more than five years her senior. Strong shoulders and a competent demeanor made him more handsome than he would have been otherwise. No emotion showed on his face, no signs of anything but stoic obedience to what he'd been told to do. Mariq could almost think him heartless, but his eyes betrayed him. Deep brown like thick, rich coffee, they held such a world of pain they broke Mariq's heart. There was a man in there, but the barbed slave-band and naked arm locked him away from the world as effectively as a stone wall.

"Mariq, this man is here on behalf of Sheik Zahra," her father said. He spoke slowly, as if to a dim-witted child. "He is here to take you back to Hatife for a *bardiya*. Do you understand what that is?"

Of course she knew. He'd been telling her to expect one since she was three. "One season in Hatife, for the sheik to decide whether he wants to proceed with the marriage," Mariq said. She was grateful for that, at least. Being carted off for a *bardiya* was much preferable than being taken directly to a marriage bed.

"Good girl. Your servants are packing your things. You leave for Sheik Zahra's palace in Hatife at first light tomorrow." *Good riddance,* his tone said, as if she and the nameless slave couldn't get out of his sight quickly enough. He stood and left the library without any of the customary pleasantries. A subtle insult, as much as the slave's presence had been to him.

Just like that, she'd been sold. Become property of a man twice her age who she'd never met.

Mariq couldn't begin to sort out her thoughts. She'd expected to feel horror or terror in the face of an imminent marriage. Or perhaps saddened by the thought of leaving Kuriza, the only home she'd ever known. But they weren't there. Hints of them, she supposed, if she searched deep enough, but a strange numbness filled her heart. As if she floated through a dream, not allowing anything to affect her because sooner or later she'd wake up. But this wasn't a dream—no more than her encounter with the assassin or the man in the nighttime cloak had been a dream.

She arrived back at her chambers with hardly a memory of getting there. She stood in the doorway, watching servants scurry about her rooms. Trunks laid open everywhere, half-full of her beautiful silks and treasured ornaments. Two servants wrapped her jewelry in velvet. Several more hauled furniture out of the rooms. She had to step aside as two men carried out one of her tables. Mariq watched it go, a stab of pain shattering her numbness. Her father didn't even have the decency to wait until she'd gone. It was her last night here, and she'd have to spend it among packed trunks and an empty room.

MARIQ stood on her balcony, back to her bare room, long after the last of the servants had left for bed. There would be no sleep for her tonight. If she had one more night in Kuriza, she would make it worthwhile.

Besides, she still had one more treasure to collect.

Mariq pulled the sleeve from her holster and tugged it on over her heritage tattoos. She wasn't a princess any longer. She was average. Invisible.

Free.

She reached into the potted palm to her right and pulled out a rope, spider-silk thin like the ones in her harness. She looped it around the railing, tested her knot, and swung over the edge, out of the dim candlelight and into the night.

The darkness didn't frighten her. Nor did the silence or loneliness. Mariq was a spider-thief. These were her comforts. Her home.

You'll never get anywhere if you wait for others to lead you. You have to make your own path. She never failed to remember Lookan's words when she snuck out like this. She'd been so young and already feeling trapped by her station. He'd shown her a way out—or at least, gave her the push she needed to find her own way out.

Of course, when she'd tried to make her own path in front of her father, Lookan had been the first to condemn her for it.

In a matter of heartbeats she landed on the ground and raced toward the walls of the palace. A few more brief moments and she was up and over, with no more thought or energy expended than a hare dashing in and out of a garden.

Not for the first time—or even the first hundredth time—Mariq considered never returning. It would be half a day or more before she'd be missed. How far could she get in that time? With that much of a head start and no witnesses to mark her passage, even her father's guards would be hard-pressed to pick up her trail. She could steal what she needed to survive and she would be more free than ever before.

But that would mean running away. Admitting defeat. Lookan would be so disappointed if she did that.

Only cowards run away, he used to tell her. *Facing your problems head-on is the real mark of courage. Defeating them is what makes people heroes.*

The words stuck with her, even now. She knew Lookan didn't believe in heroes, but he'd known she did. And he'd taught her to keep fighting. She would be a hero, if only for herself. She would rise above the role her father had carved for her. She would defeat it. Which meant she could never allow herself to run from it.

Mariq crept through the silent streets, grinning each time a patrolling soldier passed without a glance in her direction. While most children had playmates, Mariq had the soldiers. She'd played games with them for years—how close could she get without being detected; how many times could she pickpocket, and return, an item from a single guard; how often could she make them deviate from their paths without catching her. Even now she'd pause and play with them just for the practice. They were some of her greatest entertainment, and they had no idea.

Tonight, though, she had no time for games. She had a treasure to collect, and only a few hours to do it in.

Out here in the darkness Mariq could forget about the poison, her marriage, the ultimatum that might drive her to murder. Only she and the darkness existed, she and the tower that held her final treasure. Out here she wasn't a princess or a pawn. She was a spider-thief. Every action she took, every decision she made—and yes, every consequence of those decisions—lay solely with her. For a woman with no control over anything more substantial than what color she would wear that day, that meant everything.

It didn't take her long to reach her target. Mariq paused at its base, rolling her shoulders and bouncing on her toes. While she stretched, she looked up. And up. She craned her neck as far as it would go and only then could she make out the top of the minaret.

The tallest building in Kuriza. One of the few buildings she hadn't scaled yet. She needed a roof tile for her collection.

Time to practice the *spider* bit of being a spider-thief.

Excitement buzzed through her entire body, energizing her like nothing else could. She kept looking up to the top of the minaret as she rolled and tucked her sarong until the silk rose past her knees, exposing her knife sheaths and far more skin than she ever would have in public. Propriety be damned. She had climbing to do, and a silk skirt clinging around her ankles was hardly conducive to that.

The minaret had been built of sandstone, and decades of driving winds from the desert had pocked it with innumerable holes and divots. Mariq slid her fingers into one, testing her weight on it. Not the most solid hold, grainy and a little too shallow, but sufficient for being so low to the ground. She found a small hole a few handspans from the ground and stuck her toes into it.

One more breath, then Mariq straightened her knee.

And she left the ground behind.

Her cheeks ached with how wide she grinned. She never tired of this feeling. Clinging to a wall like a spider, nothing but her strength and determination keeping her aloft. Making use of a lifetime's worth of training to do something truly remarkable. Something no one would have suspected her capable of.

Mariq focused on the wall before her, scoping out holds and climbing with slow but steady progress. The wind picked up as she crested the roofs and walls surrounding her, whipping her hair across her face and her sarong against her legs. She didn't let it distract her. She kept her eyes on the wall, her focus on holding steady and continuing to climb.

Sweat crawled down her body despite the cool night. Her muscles ached, then screamed at her, but Mariq reveled in it. Almost to the top.

More climbing, more sweat, more fatigue. Mariq had never felt better.

Her heart raced in her chest as she pulled herself onto the roof of the minaret. A narrow lip at its edge allowed her to sit in relative comfort. She rested for a few moments, breathing in the crisp night air, looking up at a sky so filled with stars the entire thing seemed to glow. The desert below was no less beautiful, dark curves of sand dunes reflecting the starlight in streaks of silvery light and black shadow. Behind, the sea shimmered like molten metal, stretching into infinity.

This was what it felt like to be alive. Atop a building few had ever scaled, looking down on Kuriza like a bird in flight. How many people had ever seen a view like this? How many could say they'd watched the sun rise over the desert, illuminating Kuriza bit by bit like a gift being brought to light? That they'd done something so amazing, so unique, it defied everything they'd ever thought possible? How could anyone say they'd even lived if they'd never done something that surprised them?

The demure princess Mariq pretended to be had never lived a day in her life. Mariq the spider-thief had lived more than most people did in a lifetime.

And this is what the poison would take from her. The freedom, the exhilaration of being a spider-thief. She would lose these views. These experiences. It was more than just a skillset for her. It was her life.

Mariq stared over the desert, her view obscured by tears she refused to let fall. She couldn't run from this any more than she could run from her marriage. She would defeat it. She'd find a way.

She had to.

Mariq extracted an ivory knife and dug at a nearby tile. She pried it loose and weighed it in her hand. Dull, ordinary clay, nothing special. Not even worth a second glance under normal circumstances.

Mariq held up the tile, looking past it to the expansive desert and endless sky behind it. These were far from normal circumstances.

She clenched the tile in a fist. This would join the others as her most valued possession. A great treasure.

And possibly, she feared, her last.

3

Mariq had barely arrived back in her rooms before she was fetched and loaded into her palanquin. Her father didn't bother to say goodbye. He'd shown more emotion sending off a caravan of gold and silks than he did at sending his only daughter to another kingdom, likely never to return. She tried not to let it bother her.

"Good morning, sister," Lookan said, the slightly nasal tone of his voice exacerbated by the early morning. He parted the silk of her palanquin and climbed beside her without so much as a pause. The impropriety alone made Mariq stutter. "Relax, I just have some things to speak to you about. We'll be in full view of the servants at all times."

"What are you doing here?" she asked.

"Did Father not tell you? I'm to be the arbiter of your *bardiya*."

Mariq closed her eyes, breathing deeply to calm the sudden rush of emotion. "There should be no need for an arbiter this soon."

"Father thinks you may need one sooner, due to your… failings."

Failings. That's what he called her independence, wit, and temper—the few times she'd shown them in front of him. Imagining the horror in his eyes if he ever found out about her Star-Blade training filled her with dread and amusement in equal measure. "You have encouraged me to pursue those *failings* for my entire life," she said. "Despite how much you scorn them in front of Father."

"I can't let him know I'm ruining one of his best pawns," Lookan replied. "I still want to inherit his kingdom, after all."

Pawn. Not daughter. She should be used to it by now.

"Besides, I don't think you regret my actions over the years."

Regret? No. Lookan had been the one to instill this independence in her. He'd helped her sneak away from the palace her first time, had taught her a love of adventure and action. That, in turn, had led her on a search to make a life for herself. In a way, she'd become a Star-Blade because of him. She wouldn't trade that life for anything. "I used to dream that you were making me strong so we could rule Kuriza together," Mariq said, a tiny smile emerging at the memory. "You were teaching me to be smart and independent so I would never have to be anyone's pawn again. We would be great leaders, working together, the way our mother used to rule with Father."

She immediately knew she'd said the wrong thing. Lookan never liked talking about their mother. Mariq used to pester him to tell her stories—being older, he remembered her better—but he would always scowl and scold her for being weak and sentimental. That, at least, hadn't changed in the last twenty years.

"Our *mother*," he said, spitting the word like a curse, "left us. She betrayed Father and Kuriza and we were better off from the moment she disappeared. She does not deserve the lingering love you and the peasants have for her."

Mariq knew she couldn't win this argument and kept her objections silent. But the people *had* loved her mother, and for good reason. She had always been kind and loving toward everyone, but especially her children. As Mariq grew older and looked back on her memories or listened to the stories, that picture had grown into a soft-spoken yet determined woman, quietly confident and never willing to bend for anyone. A woman who fought for what she believed in and never let anyone—not even a sheik—cow her into submission. Mariq hoped her father saw her as a failure because she reminded him of her.

Lookan shook his head and *tsked.* "You need to let her go, Mariq. She's nothing but a weakness. People like us have to be strong. Especially where we're going. Sheik Zahra has an interesting reputation to say the least, and if we're to make the most of this situation neither of us can get distracted by emotion."

If only he knew how right he was. Mariq couldn't afford any distractions right now. Not with the weight of the poison hanging over her head. *All I need to do is find a way out of this mess. And if I can't... I'll just have to get it over with.*

Their caravan left a short time later, making its way through the streets of Kuriza before most people were out of bed. Mariq tried to settle back and enjoy the journey—after all, the pillows were comfortable and the layers of sheer silk screened out much of the rising sun. They tinted the light a strange, brilliant color, pleasing to the eye but impossible to name. Heat still seeped inside, the air stifling, but it was better than walking unshaded like the servants. At least her father had accorded her that small courtesy.

Within an hour she could no longer see the glittering line of sea along the horizon. Dry brown grass lined the caravan trail, waiting for one of the all-too-rare rain showers to turn it lush and green for a few days. Short, squat trees and shrubs dotted the hills around her. She inhaled, juniper and sage and dry sunshine spicing the air. She feared she would never smell it again.

The farther they got from Kuriza, the more her desert—the Desert of Plenty—became just another desert. The trees tapered off, leaving scrubby bushes in their place. The grass dwindled until they trekked over little more than sand. Hot sunshine, more intense and unrelenting than she was used to, pounded down on them. Even the distant mountains seemed to shudder under its blinding heat.

Uneventful, boring days merged with cold, vulnerable nights. Mariq longed for the freedom to stretch her muscles in her knife drills, but outside her cramped palanquin privacy did not exist in a caravan such as this. The best she could hope for was a couple moments to slip away to take care of necessities, and even then she couldn't guarantee every eye had been averted.

At long last they approached the border between Kuriza and Hatife, and the caravan slowed enough that Mariq peeked out of the palanquin to make sure they hadn't run into trouble. The servants and guards looked relaxed, if a bit wide-eyed and slack-jawed. Most glanced forward and backward several times, comparing the sights. Mariq didn't even try to quash her curiosity. She leaped from the palanquin to see for herself.

Several of the men tried to escort her back into the shade, but she waved away their concern and matched their pace. Unwilling to disobey the princess, let alone lay hands on her, they let her walk beside them in uncomfortable silence.

At first Mariq couldn't see what had amazed them so much. The desert looked the same as it had for days, endless sands and sunshine with almost nothing to break the monotony. But as she walked small shifts caught her eye. A glimmer in the air here, a spot of intensely bright sky there. Rather than grow tired trekking through shifting sand, she felt energized with each step. Every breath felt fresher, cleaner, more full of life than the last.

She glanced back and finally understood the awed expressions that had brought her out here in the first place.

The desert behind them looked empty in a way that had nothing to do with foliage or wildlife. Colors seemed washed out and weariness set in just thinking of heading in that direction. The sands behind them seemed no more lively than a dull, flat painting.

Mariq looked back toward Hatife. Vibrant colors, vivid scents, energy. The servants and guards chatted with one another, smiling. *Laughing.* Moments before they had been dour and bland like the desert behind them. Like most everyone in Kuriza.

Mariq hurried forward to the caravan drivers. They seemed to expect her because one look at her face and they chuckled to each other. "First time leaving Kuriza?"

She nodded. "What is it? What's making everything change? It's like…" She fumbled for a proper word.

"It's like magic, eh?" They chuckled again like it was some private joke.

Mariq hesitated, instinct telling her to reject the term, but she paused instead. Yes, it almost was like magic.

"Sun's 'bout to reach peak," one of the drivers said, shading his eyes and glancing toward the vibrant sky. The brightness hurt Mariq's when she lifted them. "Best the lady gets back into some shade. We'll make it to Hatife proper in a day or so."

She had a thousand more questions she wanted to ask, but she returned to the palanquin. Another day to reach Sheik Zahra's palace. Maybe then she would find some answers.

TRUE to his word, the caravan reached civilization late the next day. Mariq felt ready to go mad from inactivity and curiosity. She parted the silk beside her and watched as they crept up on Hatife. First they passed a herd of goats and their lone keeper; next palm groves with small, agile children scampering up to the fruits; and then the great city nestled in the sheik's power rose before them. It wasn't as grand as her father's palace by the seashore, but this place was… majestic. No other word could describe it. Buildings sprouted from the dunes, colored like the sand and complementing rather than detracting from the horizon. The palace itself rose above the other buildings, nearly as tall as the minarets surrounding it, full of graceful curves and colored with thousands—maybe even millions—of brilliant glass tiles. A peacock amongst dun-colored quail.

Their procession wound through the narrow streets of Hatife, likely the only thing to interrupt the bustle of the suq since the last monsoon. Cinnamon and cardamom scented the air, the haggling of the merchants flavoring it just as strongly. Mariq peeked out from the palanquin, staring at the commotion in wonder. These people were boisterous and intoxicating in their sheer vitality. They shouted, gestured, laughed, smiled. Mariq had never seen anything like it.

Kuriza was a calm, quiet, dead place. The people were never furious or passionate or overcome by grief. They were upset, or at peace, or unhappy. Their emotions did not stretch further. But here, Mariq saw a riot of emotions she'd never dreamed possible.

Long before she was ready, her palanquin passed through the gates to the sheik's palace. What little happiness she'd found as she marveled at Hatife evaporated like a puddle under the sun. In mere moments she would enter her new home. What would the sheik be like? She'd heard rumors of his character, but knew better than to trust them. Rumor spoke of her father as a wise and benevolent ruler. She knew him in truth, cruel and uncaring and hungry for power at whatever cost. She would believe nothing about Sheik Zahra until she'd met him for herself.

Her palanquin halted and Mariq parted the silks, blinking at the full brightness of the sunshine. She stood to exit and met the gaze of the handsome emissary she'd met in Kuriza, approaching to escort her inside. She hesitated for an instant at his outstretched right arm, pierced with a barbed slave-band and naked of all tattoos. No One, from Nowhere. He must have left Kuriza immediately after the negotiation and ridden hard to beat them here. "Welcome to Hatife, princess," he said with a bow. That monotone voice, empty of all emotion, was about as warm and personable as the statues behind him.

She took his offered hand and emerged from the palanquin. It felt good to stretch her legs after sitting so long. She'd have liked to pause for a moment, get accustomed to the light and sounds and smells of Hatife, but the man turned and began leading her into the palace. Mariq had no choice but to follow.

"Where is Sheik Zahra?" Mariq asked, looking around. Plenty of people filled the courtyard, but they were all workers. No members of court waited to greet her. Mariq couldn't say she was disappointed— she welcomed any delay in meeting, and subsequently killing, the sheik, but to arrive with no official welcome felt like another insult.

"He was called away on urgent business. He apologizes for not being here to greet you but asked that we make you comfortable in his absence. As soon as he returns he'll arrange for a more proper welcome."

The man bowed and gestured her forward. She should have expected the sheik would have more important things to do than wait for bride number four to arrive. Or was it five? Receiving a new wife had likely lost its thrill long ago.

Pulling herself from the thoughts, Mariq followed No One into the palace.

A stunning foyer greeted her, vibrant silks lending color to the expanses of gold-veined white marble. Palms grew by the large windows, blowing gently in the hot desert breeze. A fountain of cool, clear water dominated the middle of the floor. A treasure indeed! This much water was unheard of so deep in the desert.

Another servant approached, a woman this time. She was about Mariq's age but much shorter, only coming up to her chin. Short hair also, somehow still feminine despite being cropped boyishly. Modest tattoos revealed nothing special about her heritage. She smiled at Mariq but avoided her eyes. "Welcome to Hatife, princess. Please allow me to show you to your rooms."

They left the emissary behind and the girl led her through corridor after corridor, each as grand and graceful as the last. She pointed out directions or explained the history of the palace as they went, and Mariq found herself relaxing at her chatter.

"What's your name?" she asked.

The girl stopped talking and looked at Mariq. Her eyes, brown so dark they were nearly black, looked much older than her face. "My name is Ehra, mistress," she replied.

"Please, just call me Mariq."

Ehra smiled that same distant, sincere-yet-doubtful smile, then turned a corner and opened a tall door bedecked with gold leaf. The rooms the sheik had granted Mariq were no less spectacular than the rest of the palace. Massive windows opened onto a balcony overlooking half of Hatife and the vast desert beyond. Expansive pillows lay everywhere, sheathed in silk and fine, soft cotton.

"Is there anything I can get for you, mistress?"

"Mariq. And no. I'm sure everything I could ever need is here somewhere."

"I'm sure you're right," Ehra said. "The sheik has been importing things into these rooms for over a month. I'd imagine you could outfit an entire army by now."

Mariq smiled. *An army of harem girls, likely.*

She wandered around the room, taking in the luxuries, searching for a way to keep the conversation going. Now that Ehra had completed her task, she seemed… caged. She stood in the middle of the room, touching nothing, as if trying to take up as little space as possible. She clasped her hands in each other and moved very little. Mariq got the distinct impression she was holding herself in. But why? She'd seen other servants make these kinds of motions, but servants—like No One—who had been beaten and were terrified of upsetting a volatile master.

Ehra raised her eyes, meeting Mariq's. They weren't the eyes of someone afraid for their life. Intelligence shone from them, steady despite a lingering sadness.

Ehra bobbed her head. "Will you be needing anything else?"

Mariq shrugged. She felt a kindred spirit in Ehra. A girl, trapped by her station, but so much more than she was allowed to be. "Just a friend."

Ehra ducked in something not quite a bow, smiled once more—a bold, genuine smile this time—and left the chamber.

Mariq lost several moments just staring at the room. The sheik had done well. Tasteful and elegant without being stuffy or pretentious. Mariq hadn't dared hope for anything half as wonderful.

She sighed, shivering against the threat looming over her head. No matter how wonderful this place proved to be, it still lacked the one thing Mariq longed for most. Freedom. Until she could escape the threat of the poison, even a beautiful place like Hatife would be her prison.

Whether she liked it or not, she had to start planning her first assassination.

A persistent scratching woke Mariq. She forced her eyes open, trying to wipe the haziness from her mind.

No hint of daylight shone in the sky, only a low-burning oil lamp on her desk and the moon outside illuminating her chamber. Black, unfamiliar shadows clung to the room. She eyed them suspiciously, though she saw nothing sinister about them. Just a new room, with new furniture.

She heard it again. The scratching, coming from near the window.

She grabbed an ivory knife from under her pillow and sat, shivering a little as the blankets fell away. Her light robe provided no defense against the chill desert night, but she pulled herself out from the covers anyway. She might need the mobility. How embarrassing would it be if she left herself vulnerable because she was hampered by bedsheets?

A man rose from the railing around her balcony, lifting himself over it and onto the tiles. Mariq kept her eyes on him as he crept into her room. He moved with a strange awkwardness, as if his mind knew how to skulk but his body could not execute the motions. He seemed unaware that Mariq had no trouble following his movements.

She cleared her throat. "I could have hit you with a knife a dozen times by now," she said quietly. No need to alert anyone—not yet, at least. Mariq could handle a single trespasser well enough.

The man froze, his body gone stiff. A second later he deflated and stepped away from the shadows. "I thought I might be out of practice."

That voice… Mariq had heard it before. She reached behind her and snatched the lamp. She could just make out his features in the weak light. And his naked right arm. No One, from Nowhere. "You're Sheik Zahra's emissary," Mariq said. "The one who met me in Kuriza, and who escorted me into the palace."

The man nodded.

"What are you doing here?"

He shuffled from foot to foot. "Our, uh… mutual employer… sent me to check on you."

Mariq drew a sharp breath between her teeth. Mutual employer. She glanced down at the barbed slave-band. Not Sheik Zahra's then. The man in the nighttime cloak's. Somehow it didn't surprise her the man who would blackmail her into assassination would force something so cruel upon his slaves.

Her hand gripped the handle of her knife so hard the blade shook. "You're an assassin," she hissed.

"You could say that, though it's not as if I have much of a choice." His arm twitched, emphasizing the barbed slave-band wound around his naked wrist. "Besides, scorning me for being an assassin is a bit hypocritical, don't you think?"

"I'm not an assassin. I'm a spider-thief."

"You're no less of an assassin than I am."

Mariq narrowed her eyes. Had he just admitted he was guilty of the title? Or had he, like Mariq, been forced into it somehow? Cold and distant he might be, but he didn't seem like a killer to her. Plus with that horrid slave-band binding him… who knows what a master like that would force his slaves to do. "So neither of us is completely innocent. But if you aren't just an assassin, what are you?"

He paused, looking confused, as if the question was far more difficult than it should have been. A long, uncomfortable moment passed while he flexed his wrist, scraping new cuts into his skin from his slave-band. "I am whatever my master demands I be."

Mariq lowered her knife. "And today that entails slinking through the shadows of my room?"

He shrugged, but seemed more dejected than regretful. "I had no choice. My master commanded I make contact with you. This seemed the best option."

"It's not a very good option when it's that easy to spot you," Mariq said. Then she cringed. The poor man suffered enough from his enslavement. He didn't need her scorn as well.

The man eyed her, his expression blank. "Cendim is going to like you."

Cendim. Sheik Zahra? "Why should that matter? If you have your way he'll be dead before we marry."

"Far sooner than that," the man said. His voice was empty of inflection, as if reading a proclamation. "Our employer gives you a grace period of one month to get accustomed to the routines of the staff and the sheik. After that, he'll expect word of the sheik's death."

Mariq's blood ran cold. "One month? You can't be serious!"

"I am. The sheik must die, as soon as possible."

Mariq stared, dumbstruck. She'd known murder had been demanded of her, but it had never felt more real than it did at this moment.

No One seemed to notice her hesitation. "Are you afraid?"

She took in a sharp breath, ready to deny the accusation on instinct. But when she met No One's eyes, full of sympathy rather than contempt, her stubbornness dissolved. She hated how frail her voice sounded. "Of course I'm afraid. I've been threatened into assassinating a man. If I fail this job, I could lose the one thing I truly value. But if I succeed, I'll have an innocent man's blood on my hands. How could I not be afraid?" Her fear threatened to choke her. She'd need to go climbing tonight just to calm down and work off the terror roiling through her gut.

When he replied, his voice had gone soft, as filled with compassion as it had been emotionless before. "I'm not your enemy, Mariq. I know what it's like to be trapped in a hopeless situation."

Mariq couldn't keep her eyes from falling to his naked arm, the slave-hole threaded with barbed wire. No One, from Nowhere. Owner of nothing, yet owned by someone who clearly saw him as property. Even more so than Mariq was viewed as property. "Who did this to you?"

No One cocked his head, as if he didn't understand the question.

"Your master. Who is he, to force this on you?" She reached for the barbed slave-band, but hesitated before touching it.

"I don't know," No One said. His voice sounded choked and small, like a frightened child's. "I've never seen his face. He's a Star-Blade, a high-ranked one. That's all I know."

"Then what are you doing here?"

"I'm a diplomatic trade. A peace offering, you might say. I still belong to the Star-Blades, but my orders are to obey Cendim as if his word were my master's."

Mariq raised an eyebrow. "And gather valuable, and sensitive, information while you're here?"

He didn't reply, but he didn't need to.

What a terrible position to be in. No family, no friends, and not even a face to go with the man who owned his life and traded it like cattle. How alone this poor man must be. "What's your name?" she asked.

The man stiffened. He blinked at her, stunned for a moment, before recovering. "What?" His voice stammered on the simple word.

She looked up again, met his eyes. "Your name. If we're going to work together, I'd like to have something to call you other than No One."

He cocked his head at her. "No One?"

Mariq felt heat flush her cheeks. She should have learned to keep her mouth shut by now. "No One, from Nowhere. It's…" She gestured toward his naked right arm. She no longer dared to look at him.

The man glanced down at it. She couldn't tell if the statement amused or saddened him.

"Please. I'd like to know your name."

He seemed… amazed. As if no one had ever stopped to ask him such a question before. She saw something soften in his face, a few of the hard lines easing away. A bit of the tension released from his shoulders and he let out a breath. "Turien."

Mariq smiled. "Turien. It's nice to meet you." She hesitated, letting out a breath of her own. "It's nice to have an ally in this."

Mariq could feel Turien pull away in his silence. Retreating from the intimacy of friendship, of even the hint of forming anything more personal than what was required. Cold formality infused his voice, his posture, his entire being. As effective a wall as anything constructed from stone. "Alliance notwithstanding, we still have work to do."

Even understanding why Turien pushed her away—at least in part—rejection still stung Mariq's heart. Would he rather be No One? Perhaps it was easier for him that way.

She might have an ally, but she would still have to face this alone.

WHY had he told her his name?

Turien berated himself all the way back to his small room in Cendim's wing of the palace. She'd have learned it soon enough, from another servant or even Cendim himself. He couldn't remain anonymous forever.

But he'd told it to her. Trusted her with it, from his own lips. Just because she'd asked.

You're getting sloppy, fool.

Nothing would come of it. He'd been ordered to ensure she succeeded in her assassination, after all. They would have to work together at some point. She couldn't continue to call him No One, accurate as that may be.

Yet the way she'd looked at him, asked him who he was, what he was… like she actually cared about him.

Caring was dangerous. Turien didn't dare to care for himself beyond basic human necessities. Caring meant you got invested. You wanted to improve. And wanting to improve got men like him killed.

If he wanted to continue living, he had to be content with being No One, from Nowhere. Mariq had seemed ashamed to tell him this name, but Turien would adopt it. It would help him keep things in perspective. His desires meant nothing. Only his orders mattered.

The fact he needed the reminder was just another condemnation. Coming here, living beside Cendim and his household, had become the most dangerous job he'd ever been given.

It had supposedly been a political trade, to show some measure of trust, or at least no direct violence, between Hatife and his master. Everyone knew what it really was. And yet Cendim hadn't treated him like a spy. Turien had been welcomed into the palace as if he were the most honored and trustworthy servant. He'd been given luxuries he'd never been granted before—a closet full of clothes tailored just for him, his very own room, even a small bathing chamber with a brazier of hot rocks to heat his water. Perhaps most people didn't consider these luxuries, but to Turien they were a treasure trove. He hadn't dared take a hot bath for weeks simply because he had never had the opportunity before.

Cendim Zahra, the Sheik of Hatife, called him by name. Trusted him with vital tasks, like picking up his new bride. Even asked for his opinion on occasion. He knew who Turien worked for. He knew why he was here. Yet he'd made Turien feel valuable. Worthwhile.

Like he was a person.

And now Mariq, Princess of Kuriza, had done the same. Even knowing he had blood on his hands, that his presence meant the eyes of his master followed her. Knowing his orders involved ensuring she murder an innocent, genuinely good man. When she'd looked at him she hadn't seen just a nameless slave. She'd seen a man and treated him as such. Turien still couldn't believe it.

He shook his head. It was improper for him to even think of her. She was a princess. He was…

His master's chain bit into his skin as he flexed his wrist. He had to keep things in perspective. He was a tool for his master to wield as he saw fit. He had no other identity, no other purpose.

He was No One, from Nowhere.

He'd do well to remember that.

Three days later, Mariq was invited to dine with Sheik Zahra.

Her stomach twisted as she read the elaborate invitation—an old-fashioned tradition she hadn't seen in years. Tonight she would meet her husband. Or her first victim. Whichever it ended up being, the thought made her stomach tie itself into knots.

A short message at the bottom of the invitation, in exquisitely precise handwriting, read: *I will be there. You can do this.* A break, then in a shakier hand: *No One.*

Which didn't make her any less nervous. Mariq still didn't know whether he planned to help her *out* of this nightmare or help her *accomplish* it.

She shook the thought from her mind. Turien was the wrong man to be thinking of. At a time like this, she should be focusing on the sheik. Her future husband. Her target.

The servants in Kuriza had long since been accustomed to Mariq's penchant of dressing and styling herself, but here it took much coaxing to shoo the hovering servants away. She needed to calm her nerves before such a meeting, and she had no better way than this. She was fully capable, after all, of matching colors and arranging her hair. Her delicate princess persona owned precious few skills. She might as well make use of them.

She dressed in her most flattering cuts and brightest colors. She bedecked herself with bracelets and necklaces and anklets until she glittered with gold. Last, she strapped her ivory knives to her shins. A girl couldn't go to dinner unprepared.

She took several long, deep breaths. Perhaps that would help keep her hands and knees from shaking.

It was just dinner. With the possibility of murder.

Ehra slipped into the room, silent as ever. At least she'd waited long enough for Mariq to hide her harnesses.

She stood by the door, keeping to herself as always, but her eyes held a world of compassion. "Are you ready?"

Mariq tried to answer, but words failed her. She stroked the silk, letting the smooth fabric slide through her fingers.

"It'll be all right," Ehra said. "The sheik is a good man. You'll see."

I hope you're wrong, Mariq thought. *The thought of killing a bastard is bad enough.*

Ehra escorted her to a large dining hall. One wall opened to the desert, but between the shade of the roof and dozens of palms lining a running fountain, the midday heat was kept at bay. A table sat near the windows, amidst the foliage as if in the middle of an oasis. Tasteful and beautifully decorated, not too pretentious but elaborate nonetheless. Mariq ran her eye over the crystal and silver. The sheik had impeccable taste.

The doors opened behind her and Lookan entered the room. He nodded to her, without obvious affection or animosity, his eyes traveling over the wealth displayed in the room. Mariq ignored him. She was already nervous enough without her brother adding to her stress. At least he didn't force her to kneel and submit to him, even though technically she should.

A few moments later a servant announced the sheik's arrival. Lookan turned, standing straight and arrogant. Mariq slipped to her knees and lowered her eyes, waiting for the dominant man to recognize her presence.

Sheik Zahra exchanged a brief greeting with Lookan, then moved away from her brother. "Oh, don't be so traditional," he said, his rich baritone brimming with mirth. "Stand, my dear. I don't enjoy being worshipped any more than you enjoy doing so."

Mariq didn't move for a few heartbeats, too stunned to react. Lookan sputtered something, but the sheik remained before her. She could feel him watching her, waiting. Heart pounding, slightly off-balance, she rose and met his eyes.

He was indeed older than her, but not as much as she'd feared. He'd reached middle-age without losing strength or grace—he could likely hold his own in a fight with a man half his age. The heritage tattoos crawled from his fingertips to the top of his shoulder, possibly even onto his back. Their design differed from Kuriza's, more flowing and graceful, worked in shades of brown and bronze that made it seem as if his arm shimmered. Traces of black shot through his silvery-grey hair. Very few lines marked his dark skin, and the ones that did made him look distinguished rather than old.

His smile, which spread across his face and made his eyes dance, made him stand out the most. This was the smile of a man accustomed to happiness. No cruelty or malice marred it, the way it did to Mariq's brother and father.

Maybe Ehra is right, Mariq thought. *Maybe he really is different. Damn.*

Turien stood a step behind him and to his left, paying her no more mind than any other stranger would. Smart, given their allegiances and secrets, but her heart still contracted just a bit.

The sheik stepped toward her, reaching for her hand. She offered it, and he bowed when he grasped it. When he looked at her he met her eyes like an equal—an honor very few men had ever given her. Her father was not one of them. "I apologize for postponing this meeting, but I had some… unfortunate business to attend to."

Mariq slid into her demure princess mask. "It was no trouble. I'm honored you made time to meet with me at all."

The sheik made a face like he'd sucked on a lemon. "Enough with the diplomacy, shall we? I kept you waiting, I'm sorry for that, and you have a right to be frustrated. But let's wipe that away and start anew. Would you like some food?" He started for the table without waiting to see if she followed.

Lookan scowled as he followed the sheik to the table, glaring back at Mariq as if blaming her for his casual attitude. Mariq took longer to move. This man ruled the second-largest kingdom in the Scorched Lands, the biggest danger to her father's power. In many ways Hatife was more wealthy than Kuriza—perhaps not in gold or spices, but in artisans and culture Hatife had no rival. She'd expected the man in charge of a treasure like that to be poised, arrogant, self-righteous, and an all-around pompous ass.

Sheik Zahra hovered by his seat, sniffing at each dish and snagging samples like a child pinching sweets. Lookan sneered and sat with rigid arrogance. All the sourness she'd expected the sheik to possess oozed from him. The sheik ignored him, chatting with and thanking the servants by name as they retreated from the table.

It was so absurd, so refreshing, Mariq choked down a laugh.

"I won't force you to join me, but you'll miss a wonderful meal if you continue to stand there." The sheik plopped into his chair and started piling food onto his plate with glee, grinning all the while.

Mariq moved toward the table, dazed. She hadn't known what to expect, but this far exceeded anything she could have imagined. She could hardly make sense of it.

The sheik grinned as she took her seat opposite his. "Lovely. Let's eat. Then we'll talk."

The meal was as stunning as the table settings. Couscous with tomatoes and green peppers, lamb with lemon and saffron, fresh bread, olives, prunes and apricots and sweet mint tea. The sheik ate with gusto, even waving Turien toward the table to help himself. Turien hesitated, a riot of emotions playing behind his stern face. His right arm twitched and Mariq saw his grimace as the barbed wire of his slave-band cut into his skin. He stayed in his place.

Lookan ate each bite stoically, glaring at the sheik as if trying to force him to obey protocol. The few times he looked to Mariq she smiled, not even trying to suppress the mirth in her expression. She couldn't deny it amused her to see Lookan writhe in frustration. She'd endured many meals with the same treatment—about time he felt the humiliation, the scorn, for himself.

When they had finished their meal, the sheik leaned back and sighed. Mariq had never seen a man look so content and satisfied with life. She watched him, as if waiting for the charade to end and the real man to emerge.

The sheik must have seen her expression. "My dear," he said, "I know this must seem strange to you. It goes against everything you were trained is proper, and you haven't a clue how to react."

Well, he was partially right. The demure princess would be at a loss, but the Star-Blade spider-thief knew how to speak her mind. It just wouldn't be prudent to do so.

"You certainly set unique precedence, Sheik Zahra." Lookan's voice dripped with diplomacy.

"I strive to," the sheik replied, the glitter in his eyes betraying how much delight he took in ignoring Lookan's sarcasm. He raised his glass of tea to Lookan, took another sip, then turned his attention back to Mariq. "While you are here, my request is that you be at ease. The traditions of our culture mean little to me. I prefer my companions to be actual human beings, capable of conversations and enjoying themselves. It's better for all of us that way."

"Those who have heard me speak my mind might argue that point," Mariq said without thinking.

Lookan snorted. "That's an understatement."

The sheik laughed, full-bellied. "They're just afraid if they let a woman speak she'll have a wit sharper than theirs. Fear not, my ego can do with an intellectual match."

"In that case, Sheik Zahra…"

"Please, call me Cendim."

"Then, Cendim, if you're looking for an intellectual match, you may find yourself still searching. Brains don't necessarily accompany a quick tongue."

"Truer words have never been spoken!" Cendim laughed again, wiping at his eyes with a linen napkin. "Where have you been hiding this delightful woman?" he asked Lookan, his gaze never leaving Mariq's.

"Wherever we could manage," Lookan muttered into his teacup.

"What a shame. A treasure like her should never be shoved away. A woman who can make you think and laugh with a single sentence is a prize to be cherished."

Heat flushed Mariq's cheeks and she dropped her eyes to the table.

They continued talking throughout the afternoon, Lookan growing more surly as Mariq grew more comfortable. Cendim's charm made their conversation easy and relaxed, as it would be between old friends. Mariq found honesty coming more and more readily to her lips. She spoke her mind, responding with true answers rather than correct ones, and she had never enjoyed a conversation quite so much.

The sun had nearly set by the time Cendim rose from the table. "My dear, it has been a delight. I've not enjoyed a meal so stimulating in many years. I believe your wit has nothing to fear from an old man like me."

"It's been a pleasure, Cendim. The opportunity to speak my mind is refreshing, to say the least."

"I'm sure it is. I hope it becomes a habit."

"I don't foresee a problem. Once I unleash this mouth it takes quite a bit of effort to wrangle it back under control."

Lookan snorted. Mariq and Cendim ignored him.

Cendim took her hand. "You're a welcome addition to this palace, Mariq. A jewel amongst jewels."

She and the sheik smiled at one another. Perhaps marriage to this man wouldn't be so bad. Though she felt no blossomings of love on the horizon, she already treasured his companionship. It was more than she'd dared to hope for. Not a bad way to begin a marriage, all things considered.

If she didn't end up killing him.

Her lovely meal sagged like a stone in her stomach. She'd tried not to believe Ehra, to see through Cendim's mask of pleasantness and find an arrogant bastard she could, conceivably, kill. But she'd failed. There had been nothing in Cendim's character except what everyone claimed—goodness and honesty. She'd been ordered to kill the only genuinely good men she'd ever met.

The knives on her shins burned with guilt already.

She didn't want to kill him. How could she even consider it? He was wonderful, the best man she'd ever met. But what choice did she have? She could either kill him or live out the rest of her life without what she valued most. Live as a boring, demure little princess. Death would be better than that.

Her death. Not Cendim's.

"Mariq," he said, pulling her from her troubling thoughts. "Do you know how many sheiks and kings and rulers I had thrusting their daughters and granddaughters in my face? I even had a shah from beyond the mountains try to sell me one of his own wives."

Mariq didn't know what to make of that. Why would he tell her this? It didn't seem like something to make her feel jealous. She paused, caressing her sarong with her fingertips. "Why?"

Cendim cocked his head at her.

"Why me?" she clarified. "If you had the choice of so many women, why would you pick me?"

Cendim didn't seem fazed. "I've heard much about the beautiful Princess Mariq over the years. Not just beautiful, but strong and intelligent as well. There is much to her that is not recognized or appreciated among others who look down upon her for being a woman." He did not glance at Lookan, but none of them missed the implication. Mariq blushed. "It seemed a shame to let such a rare woman be wasted in an environment like that. Your skills should be celebrated and enjoyed. I thought rescuing you from there would be welcome."

"It is," she said, hoping her gratitude showed in her voice. "And I hope you don't come to regret that decision."

He gave her a meaningful look, one not filled with lust but with something infinitely more wonderful—respect. "I'm certain I won't."

# 6

ariq needed to get out. She had to move, to breathe fresh air and see pretty things to help work out the thoughts cascading through her mind.

Climbing was out of the question, at least until the sun set and she could venture out in relative safety. So she fell back on her second-most favorite activity, the one thing a demure princess and a spider-thief could both enjoy.

It was time to go shopping.

Ehra had seemed reluctant when Mariq asked to go to the suq last night, and even now she paced and fidgeted like they were about to go thieving. The irony was not lost to Mariq.

"Will you need anything else before we leave, mistress?" Ehra asked for at least the fourth time. She'd been fretting over her like a mother hen all morning.

"For one thing, I need you to start calling me Mariq."

"I'm not sure that would be proper, mistress."

"Something tells me no one cares about being proper around here."

Ehra laughed. Her mirth didn't last, replaced by more worry, but Mariq was content to see at least a little happiness from her.

"Let's just go. If we need something I'm sure we can find it at the market." Mariq had to take her by the hand and drag her out of the room to convince her to stop fretting and leave.

Just before they exited the courtyard, Cendim called out. He jogged up to them, grinning like a boy who'd escaped his chores. "Would you ladies mind some company? I have business in the suq and would be honored to escort you until our paths diverge."

"Not at all," Mariq said, covering her surprise with princessly poise. Cendim had business in the common markets? Business he would conduct himself? Her father would have been abhorred had anyone even suggested he step foot outside his pristine palace. Yet Cendim hurried forward as much as Mariq, as eager to be out and about as she felt.

He ducked his head in acknowledgement as he offered Mariq his arm. To her surprise, he offered the other to Ehra. With a lady on each arm, Cendim looked like the happiest man alive. "Wonderful. It's been ages since I've been down to the suq. It's always a joy to see what my people are creating."

As soon as they left the palace, a handful of guards following at a discreet distance, Mariq had to restrain herself from dashing forward. She couldn't wait to see if Hatife was as exciting as she remembered from her brief exposure. She wanted to see *everything*.

Cendim set a brisk pace as they wended through broad, bright streets. He spoke of the history and architecture of Hatife and nodded a greeting to everyone they passed. Enough people seemed unsurprised or even familiar with Cendim that Mariq could tell he made these excursions often.

He grinned wider than ever before when the suq came into view. Even Ehra seemed to catch their enthusiasm, looking around as if she couldn't see enough.

Mariq bounced on her toes as she entered the narrow alleyway between displays of spices, glass, silver, and every kind of trinket imaginable. Beautifully woven sarongs and rugs hung on wires overhead, shading the street and tinting the light in patches of color and shadow. Mariq could taste spices on the air, heavy and sweet and hot. Men and women of all ages chattered and hollered at one another, calling out to passersby or haggling over prices. Laughter rang through the crowd as often as shouts did.

Wonder and amazement settled over her just as it had the day they'd passed over Hatife's border. Colors, sounds, even the people were more vibrant here. Kuriza's suq wasn't half this lively, or this exciting, or this anything. It was quiet and dull, while there wasn't anything quiet or dull in sight here.

The difference between Hatife and Kuriza had never been more clear than right now, being jostled and cat-called and enticed from every direction.

"It's like magic," Mariq muttered, remembering the chuckles and grins of the caravan drivers at her amazement.

"It *is* magic," Cendim said. He inhaled, as if trying to absorb the energy of the market.

They strolled through the alleyways, stopping often to admire Hatife's legendary craftsmanship and artisans. Mariq couldn't turn around without spotting something amazing—intricate weaving, delicate pottery, intensely flavorful cooking, glass in colors and shapes she'd never thought possible. Once again Hatife proved itself the superior. Kuriza's markets held many functional items but very few beautiful ones. Here, so much beauty surrounded Mariq she couldn't take it all in.

While Cendim spoke with a merchant Mariq and Ehra wandered to a nearby stall. "How do they do it?" she asked, turning a silver perfume bottle over in her hands. The metal had been formed to look like vines crawling up a thin glass orb, with the stopper on top a flower of such detail Mariq swore it had to be real. "I've never seen anything so impressive."

The woman behind the display bowed. "My son is very gifted," she said, as if that explained everything.

Mariq held the gleaming silver up to the light, watching colors spin through the glass. "It's beautiful."

The woman bowed again. She didn't look old enough to have a son as a silversmith. Mariq would have guessed she was only a few years older than her.

"How much?"

Before the woman answered a boy parted the curtains behind her and raced up, tugging on her sarong. "Mama! Yasin won't play with me!"

"Yasin is busy, Tahir. So is Mama."

The boy, no older than four or five, turned pouting eyes toward Mariq. She smiled at him, and the boy flushed and smiled back. He stood for a few long seconds while his mother wrapped the perfume bottle, clearly exerting every bit of patience he had, then tugged on her sarong again. "Mama? Is Yasin done yet?"

"I don't know, baby."

The boy—Tahir—turned around, still clutching his mother's sarong. "Yasin! Are you done yet?" he called.

Mariq heard tools clink together, then the curtain was pulled aside again. Another boy, perhaps eight or nine, half emerged. "Not yet, Tahir. I have to finish this one first, then we can play." He held up a lump of silver, the beginnings of a detailed pattern giving Mariq a faint impression of what it would be. A jasmine flower, possibly.

Mariq stared at the boy, calloused fingers gripping the silver. A heavy leather apron was tied around his waist, tools sticking out from multiple pockets. Just like she'd expect from a silversmith. But a *boy*?

She looked around, but no one seemed to think it odd but her. Even Ehra hardly gave him a second glance.

"Are your boys at it again, Nida?" Cendim asked, coming up beside Mariq and watching the children bicker with fondness.

"They always are," Nida replied, exasperation and love in her tone. "Yasin and Hadi were this way, too. Once Tahir gets his gift, they'll calm down."

"Think it'll be silversmithing again?" Cendim asked. "It's run in the family for, what, three generations now?"

"Four, if you count my father's uncle."

Nida finished wrapping the bottle and held out the bundle, but Cendim took it before Mariq could. "Thank you, Nida. Whatever Mariq has purchased, I'm sure she will love it."

The woman's eyes went wide. "Oh! Is this… I should have guessed. My lady, we are honored to have caught your attention."

Mariq nodded, deeper than tradition strictly called for. "It's my pleasure. How much do I owe you?"

"For the bride of our sheik? Nothing."

"Nida," Cendim said, a gentle scolding.

The woman waved her arms. "No. I won't accept anything for it. You give us enough, Cendim. Consider this my gift."

Cendim bowed. "We accept it, with many thanks."

Once they were a few steps away Cendim gestured toward Ehra. "Make sure Nida gets reimbursed somehow. Perhaps an extra shipment of silver?"

"Of course."

Cendim nodded, then turned to Mariq. He cocked his head at her.

"Mariq? Are you all right, my dear?"

Mariq nodded, but so many thoughts reeled through her mind she couldn't sort them all out. That woman had *given* her the perfume bottle—a week's wages at least. And she'd done it for love of Cendim, her sheik, who knew her family, her children, and allowed himself to be known in turn. From the way he waved and greeted people they passed, Cendim had struck up a friendship with other merchants than just Nida.

Mariq glanced back, even though she could no longer see Nida's stall through the crowd. Nida sold the goods, but the silversmith had been her son. Mastering such craftsmanship would take decades—far longer than that boy had been alive.

"I don't understand," she said.

"What don't you understand?" he asked.

Mariq fumbled for a moment. "Anything, it seems."

Cendim laughed. "That, my dear, is not true. You may not be accustomed to the way we do things in Hatife, but I'm sure you'll adjust soon enough." A man gestured toward Cendim, and he nodded back. "That's my meeting. Ladies, thank you for letting an old man tag along. It was a genuine delight." He bowed to them both, then turned and disappeared into the suq.

Mariq watched him go with as much fondness as he'd watched Nida's children. "Is he always this… normal?"

"He loves people," Ehra replied. "The worst thing you could do to Cendim is seal him away in his palace and give him no interaction but 'yes, my lord' and 'no, my lord.'"

"And how about you? What do you love, Ehra?"

Ehra looked around her, deep sadness crawling into her expression as she stared at the colorful stalls and vibrant people.

"Ehra?" She followed her friend's gaze to another shop, this one selling gorgeous lengths of silk. A family sat behind the table displaying their goods, all five of them working on a single large piece. They laughed and talked while they worked, embroidering intricate patterns with lightning speed and only the occasional glance at their hands.

"They love it," Ehra said. "You can tell. There's nothing they'd rather do than that."

Mariq couldn't deny that. Before coming to Hatife she'd only witnessed contentment and joy like this when she used her spider-thief skills, climbing buildings and sneaking through shadows. Looking around here, though, she saw it everywhere.

Except in her friend.

Ehra didn't speak for several long moments. "I love helping people. Healing people."

"Then why don't you do it? I'm sure Cendim would let you work with the healers if you asked," Mariq said. "He doesn't seem like a man who would want anyone under his care to be miserable."

"No, he's not," Ehra said. "But I tried that before and it… didn't work out very well."

"Why not?"

Ehra looked like she'd rather be stabbed than relive whatever had happened.

"No, no. Forget I asked. I don't want to make you miserable, either."

She seemed to relax at that, though her posture still held bowstring-taut tension. "I don't mean to keep secrets," Ehra said a moment later. "I wish I could tell you. It's just…"

"Some secrets are too scary to share," Mariq finished for her.

Ehra nodded. "Though some aren't as shameful as others."

Ehra's tone had changed, taking on a hint of playfulness and smug knowledge. Mariq's heart leapt into her throat. "Such as…?"

"Such as a princess climbing walls and watching the sunrise from the roof of the palace."

Her breath caught and her heart beat painfully against her chest. She'd only climbed up once, right after her first meeting with Turien. She hadn't thought anyone saw her! "I can explain," she started, desperately searching for something, anything, that could do so without exposing her.

"You don't have to. It's not as if anyone is surprised you're more feisty than most women in your station. If you weren't, Cendim never would have taking a liking to you."

True as it was, Mariq couldn't calm the pounding of her heart. That had been far too close for comfort. "You don't think it's strange for me to go climbing?"

"You just walked through the suq with a sheik who acted like a child let loose on a playground."

"Good point."

"Most of us aren't what we seem at first," Ehra said, her characteristic sadness creeping back into her voice. "It's one of the qualities Cendim prizes the most, and something he seeks out in his companions. We all learned long ago not to ask too many questions about what skills people may be hiding, or where they may have learned them."

Now Mariq fell into sadness. If climbing were her only secret, she'd have nothing to fear. But if Cendim and Ehra learned the whole truth of her skills, and her mission here, she would lose them. Perhaps that's what Ehra had meant about shameful secrets. Did Ehra, too, have something she hid for fear of Mariq's reaction? She couldn't imagine it being worse than coming here to assassinate the best man she'd ever met.

They lapsed into silence and Mariq returned to basking in the wonders of the suq. The wonders of Hatife. Cendim's care for his kingdom had never been more self-evident than right here: in the streets, the markets, watching everyday people doing everyday things.

The people prospered and Hatife thrived because of it.

Would this prosperity survive Cendim's death? If she assassinated him, who would take his place? Would the beauty, the joy suffusing the suq die with their sheik? Just the thought sent Mariq's heart plummeting.

They left the market and stopped for lunch and tea at a stall in the shadow of a massive dome. Mariq smiled as she looked up at the pinnacle, rising higher than any building around it. *I'll need a tile from that roof.*

First, though, she would have to figure out how to avoid death and poisoning. Without her freedom costing Cendim's life.

"A MOMENT, Mariq?"

Lookan's voice made her jump. She'd been so busy with Cendim, tours of the kingdom, and meetings with Turien, she'd almost forgotten her brother had accompanied her to Hatife.

They walked side-by-side for a few steps in silence. Lookan seemed relaxed, but she could see the seething anger in his eyes. Likely still fuming over the way Cendim disregarded custom and pushed the demure little princess further away every day.

"Well, my sister, you seem to have done well for yourself." He may as well have snarled the compliment.

"I'd have thought you'd be happy, given I'm to marry a man who appreciates the qualities *you* helped instill in me."

"No telling what he'll do with them."

"You make it sound as if I'm as weak and pliable as Father always wanted me to be. I'm not, and you should know that better than anyone. You would never allow me to be that way."

Lookan smirked, but the expression didn't last. If anything, he scowled deeper than ever. "I don't trust him."

"You don't trust anyone."

Lookan shook his head. "He reminds me of… her."

Ah. That explained so much. If Cendim was like their mother, no wonder Lookan would bristle at him. He'd spent most of his life trying to forget her, to distance himself from her memory. Trying to keep Mariq from abandoning his example to follow hers instead.

"It'll be fine, Lookan. Cendim is a good match for me. An alliance between Hatife and Kuriza will be good for us both." She desperately tried not to think of what would happen if she had to go through with her part in the Star-Blades' threat.

A flash of emotion—hatred? disgust?—crossed Lookan's face. "You think we brought you here for an alliance? You think I came all this way just to broker *peace* between our kingdoms?"

Mariq stopped mid-step, her stomach churning. "You can't be serious."

"You should know our father would never ally with a man like Sheik Zahra. He's weak. Sentimental. Imagine what someone strong could make of Hatife."

"Someone strong. Like you?"

The glitter in Lookan's eye said more than words ever could.

"What happened to wanting to inherit Father's kingdom?"

"I'll have all the Scorched Lands under my control if I can help it."

Lookan's ambition shouldn't have surprised her. It really shouldn't have. "Cendim is a better ruler than Father ever has been. Than you ever could be, if you plan to follow in his footsteps. I thought you were better than that."

"I *am* better, sister. I'm not going to follow Father. I will supersede him."

"By being more merciless, more demanding on your people? By

being *worse* than him? Hatife is a gem because Cendim isn't like that. Taking him away would destroy what makes this place beautiful."

"I thought I'd taught you better than that, sister. Being beloved is a weakness. Leaders should be strong and firm. They should know what they want and pursue that until they get it."

They paused their argument while a servant traversed the hallway. As soon as he rounded the corner Mariq jabbed a finger at Lookan. "You taught me to stand up for myself, to make my own path. To see what I want and not let orders or expectations stop me from getting it. Well I see what I want, and it's Hatife just as it is. I will not let you destroy it for your own ambition."

They stopped and faced each other. Lookan the encouraging mentor was gone. Mariq could only see the arrogant bastard he presented to their father and Kuriza's court. An heir their father—a man Mariq often wished had no part of her life—would be proud of.

"So that's how this ends?" Lookan asked. "After everything I've taught you, you'll betray me for Hatife?" His voice dropped slightly, some of the nasal tone evaporating under his scathing anger.

"If you're going to destroy Hatife just to turn it into another oppressed kingdom to make yourself more powerful, yes."

"You weren't supposed to fight me. We were supposed to be a team. Working together, ruling together, like you used to dream."

"I've grown up now, Lookan. My dreams have changed."

"So be it. Stay here with Hatife and your precious Cendim. Grow weak in your compassion. It'll make you that much easier to conquer." His gaze traveled the immaculate hallway, taking in the mosaic inlays and graceful curves of the doorways. While the subtle beauty put a smile on Mariq's face, it made Lookan grimace. "At least we'll only have to deal with you for a short while longer."

"What do you mean?" Her throat felt too tight to squeeze the words out. His tone made it clear he wasn't talking about her marriage separating them.

Lookan hesitated. "I'm sorry. I shouldn't have said that much. An accident on my part."

She knew he didn't "accidentally" say too much. Lookan was never careless with his words. If he said something, he wanted to say exactly that. No more, no less.

The Star-Blades had sent her here to assassinate Cendim. Now Lookan insinuated Kuriza would take his kingdom from him anyway. What about Cendim had made him such a target? It seemed everyone wished to take him out of power. If she didn't know better she'd swear it was just another plot to keep her from happiness and freedom.

Lookan began to chuckle, and Mariq realized she'd been staring at him, wide-eyed and open-mouthed. Before she could find something to say, he turned and waved a hand at her. "Lovely as always, sister. I'll see you when I return from Kuriza."

Mariq shuddered. She could only hope he wouldn't return with an army at his back.

awn had painted the sky with gold and lapis lazuli, and Mariq was awake to watch it. She'd been awake for the depths of night, too, when the darkness had been so complete she could see nothing but the distant stars. Her bed lay untouched, though a track of empty floor testified to a night of pacing. Worrying. Thinking.

Thinking had become very dangerous.

She'd been in Hatife for nearly a month and each moment she spent here made her love it all the more. She'd dined with Cendim several more times, and after each she treasured his friendship more. Her time with Ehra, and even brief meetings with Turien, had endeared them both to her nearly as much. Hours spent wandering the palace had shown her glorious mosaics and small hidden oases and gardens and sculptures.

Now, more than ever, Hatife had become her home.

And her month-long deadline was nearly upon her.

She hugged herself, though the bitter chill of the night was fast departing before the rising sun. This kingdom had become a paradise because of the man who led it. Cendim gave his people respect and prosperity, and they blessed him for it. What would happen to Hatife if she assassinated him? Would it endure, or would a leader like her brother come in and ruin what Cendim had spent a lifetime creating?

Even if she didn't consider the kingdom, Mariq couldn't kill Cendim. He was more than kind and charming. He'd seen her worth, plucked her from the oppression of Kuriza and brought her here to be the woman her father refused to let her be. Here, she'd been given the freedom to be whomever she wanted. She'd thought a gift like that would be forever beyond her reach.

No. Whatever threat lay over her, she couldn't take the life of the best man she'd ever known.

That left her here, right where the man in the nighttime cloak could find her. If Cendim lived past the next few days he would come for her. She knew better than to hope she'd escape such a meeting unscathed.

What if she ran? She could scale this wall in moments, sneak out of the palace. Sell some jewelry, take a few items from her rooms. That would give her enough money to go somewhere and start a new life. If Mariq couldn't be found, she couldn't be poisoned. She could be free.

Until she was seen. The general public might not know of her Star-Blade training, but many people knew her within the guild. They had already sent one assassin after her. If she abandoned this mission, they would search the entire Scorched Lands for her. And when they found her—not if, there were far too many Star-Blades trained for this sort of thing—they wouldn't just send one. They'd send an army.

And what about Cendim? Another assassin would be sent in her place. One who wouldn't care whether he was a good man or a good leader. Cendim would die as surely as if she'd killed him herself. Turien also, for failing to watch over her.

No, running away would be even more costly than giving in to the Star-Blades' demands.

Ehra slipped onto the balcony with her, saying nothing but offering support nonetheless. Faithful Ehra. Always there at just the right time, without being pushy or invasive.

"I don't know what I'm supposed to do," Mariq said. She crossed her arms before her, staring out at the desert coming alive with the rising sun.

"Can I help?" It was her place to ask, as Mariq's handmaiden, but duty didn't drive this question. Friendship did.

"I'm not sure how you could. It's complicated." And that was an understatement.

"I want to help. Please, Mariq."

Mariq turned to look at her friend. Ehra stood a few small paces away, close enough to show friendliness and compassion, but far enough away to be just out of arm's reach.

She could trust Ehra, she knew that much. She had a feeling her friend wouldn't be scandalized to learn of her Star-Blades training. She hadn't been exaggerating when she said no one was concerned about being proper here. The entire palace of Hatife—the entire city, from what she'd seen—didn't seem to hold to the stigmas Kuriza did.

Ehra stood there silently, closed within herself. As if she kept herself chained, held away from others physically the way Turien held himself away emotionally.

Mariq couldn't throw this on Ehra. Whatever kept her away was more than enough for her to handle. She didn't need to shoulder Mariq's burdens, too.

The only thing Mariq could do was move forward. She could never do that with Cendim's blood on her hands. So she might as well get it over with.

"There is one thing you could do for me," Mariq said. Ehra turned to her, as if eager for any way to help. "I need to see Turien, the slave without heritage tattoos, but I can't let anyone know."

Ehra raised an eyebrow.

"It's nothing like that, I promise. It's... complicated. Can you arrange some way for us to meet? Privately?"

Ehra watched her for a moment, studying her with more intensity than she'd expected. The secrets burned between them. Ehra *knew* there was something going on. How could she not? Asking for a clandestine meeting with a tattoo-less slave didn't scream of innocence.

Oh Ehra, if only you knew the extent of this...

She nodded, accepting that Mariq wouldn't or couldn't explain. She didn't seem happy about it, but she left.

Mariq returned to staring over the desert, now golden in the sunlight and shimmering with heat. Her heart hammered, her stomach so knotted she doubted she'd have an appetite for days. But she could do nothing else.

I hope I'm doing the right thing.

As if she had a "right thing" to do any longer.

EHRA arranged their meeting in the dining room. It would be quiet at this time of the morning. Mariq and Turien would have plenty of time to themselves to discuss their situation.

And Ehra would be there to hear it.

Not that they knew it. She doubted either of them would suspect her of eavesdropping—of spying. But that's why she excelled at what she did. She was well-loved and trusted, which made her innocent.

The thought made her chuckle, though regret weighed on her heart. Ehra couldn't remember the last time she'd been innocent.

She squeezed her eyes shut, fists clenching on their own. Memories flooded her. Memories she wished she'd forget.

She'd been a child. Too young to understand the implications of her power. Too little to grasp the concept of magic, or consequences, or to know that some things should be hidden away and never used.

Too innocent to know the difference between a miracle and a monster.

She'd just wanted to help. Healing was all she'd ever wanted to do. She'd spent hours in the sick rooms, watching the surgeons do their work and asking questions. They'd been all too happy to have her around, to send her to fetch supplies or help when they needed an extra, albeit small, set of hands. Ehra had learned much about healing there. She'd been happy.

But then she'd come into her magic, and the monster had reared its head. She still had nightmares of it. The blood. The lifeless bodies surrounding her, the horror in the eyes of the surgeons as they saw what she'd done.

She'd spent fifteen years running from it. Burying the monster. Pretending that part of her didn't exist. It worked sometimes. Other times...

Yes, it had been a long time since Ehra had been innocent.

Footsteps freed her mind from its torment, brought her thoughts back to the present. Ehra opened her eyes and made sure she was well hidden. The balcony might be invisible from the room below, a marvel of engineering made specifically for purposes such as this, but she still crouched low. If anyone could spot the tiny hint of her presence, it would be Mariq.

The princess entered the room, her poise and grace flawless—the picture of regal perfection. But Ehra could see her scan each corner and every shadow like a nervous hare. She did a sweep of the room, making sure she was alone. Even when she'd confirmed the room was empty she didn't relax. Tension filled her every movement. She stood still, looking out the window as she had when Ehra had found her this morning, arms clutching each other as if trying to hold herself together.

Ehra wished she could tell Mariq how much she knew. She was all too familiar with keeping secrets, hiding the truth of yourself for fear of judgment and being ostracized. They had much in common that way.

But then Mariq would learn about the monster. All of Ehra's secrets, the truth she tried to forget, would be laid bare. Mariq had embraced her wholeheartedly, unconditionally. She didn't look at her with fear or contempt. She let Ehra be whomever she wanted—gave her a measure of freedom those who knew of her monster denied her.

Only one person had ever given Ehra that—her father. And of course he did, they were family. Ehra had never found someone not bound by blood who accepted her this way.

What would happen if Mariq learned the truth? Better to have a friend for who she seemed to be rather than be alone for who she was.

Turien entered a few minutes later. Ehra watched this enigma closely. A man with no history, no station, a slave and a spy. Despite all her research she'd never been able to find out who that barbed slave-band belonged to. An enemy for certain, with at least some ties to Kuriza's court and the Star-Blades. Nor could she determine who Turien might have been. She'd found no records that could hint at his true identity. Did he have parents out there, who'd mourned the loss of their infant son so many years ago? Who could he have been, had the Star-Blades not claimed him so young? A merchant, a leader? It didn't matter. That man did not, could no longer exist. He was a prisoner, never allowed to be his own person. Sent to gather information, a secret dagger in case his master needed one. Ehra understood that all too well, also.

Turien wasted no time. He strode toward Mariq and didn't bother with pleasantries. "This is dangerous, Mariq. If someone should see us…"

"Ehra is the only one who knows I wanted to meet you. She'll keep it secret."

"Are you sure we can trust her with something like this?"

"I'd trust Ehra with my life."

She hadn't even hesitated. Mariq stared at Turien as if daring him to defy her confidence. Ehra had to choke back a sob. Mariq trusted her with her life? What sad irony.

Turien didn't seem convinced. "Even so…"

"I might be reckless at times, but I know when the danger is worthwhile. I wouldn't have called you here if I didn't have something I needed to say." She started pacing now, rubbing the fabric of her sarong between her fingers. A nervous habit she must have picked up as a child, to hide a more obvious show of emotion.

"Then say it. I'll help, if I can."

Ehra watched them closely. They stood together, relaxed, clearly accustomed to each other's presence. They spoke with familiarity. With fondness. This wasn't their first meeting.

"I can't…" She looked around, ensuring they were still alone. Then she sighed, dropping her voice to a bare whisper. "I won't kill him."

Ehra leaned forward to make sure she didn't miss anything.

"You agreed to the contract."

"I had no choice! I never wanted to do this and you know it. How can anyone expect me to kill Cendim?" She stalked up to him and jabbed a finger into his chest. "How can *you* expect me to kill him? He respects you. Can you stand there and tell me to take his life after he's been so good to you?"

Ehra could see the battle take place in Turien's mind. His fists clenched, he drew in a deep breath and didn't let it out for several seconds. He flexed his right hand, as if willing the barbed wire of his slave-band to cut open his skin. "I have my orders, just as you do." It sounded like he was trying to convince himself.

"How can you continue to follow them when you know it'll cost Cendim his life?"

"Because otherwise it will cost me mine!"

The dining hall fell silent. Ehra didn't dare breathe in case they heard her. Mariq and Turien stared at each other, but Ehra couldn't read their emotions. She wouldn't have been surprised if punches started to fly, or if one of them melted into tears.

Turien heaved a huge breath, rubbing his face with his hands. Tiny beads of blood trickled down his arm from beneath his slave-band. "I wasn't sent here because I'm invaluable, or even good at what I do. My master sent me here because I'm disposable. Should Cendim have refused me, imprisoned me, or sent my head back to my master, they'd have lost nothing. If I return with nothing of use, they can kill me themselves and have no repercussions. But if I can prove myself here, I might have a chance to be somebody."

Ehra glanced at his tattoo-less arm at the same time Mariq did. Even from this distance she could see Turien stiffen.

"Of course, I'm not one who should want to be somebody, am I?" His voice sounded defeated, with a hint of burning anger behind it. As if he'd had this argument with himself a thousand times but had never been able to win it. Ehra had never heard such emotion from him before. "Even returning with thoughts of becoming someone would mean my death. I would have been better off had I never come here." He shook his head, flexing his wrist to tear more cuts in his skin. "I'm No One, from Nowhere."

Ehra's heart bled for Turien. He spoke that last like a mantra. Reminding himself of who he was—or wasn't. Ehra knew that way of life all too well. She wasn't a monster. The monster wasn't her.

She almost missed the wince from Mariq. The princess hesitated, looking uncomfortable, then took a step closer to him. "You aren't No One, Turien. I never should have… I'm sorry."

Ehra couldn't tell whether that eased some of Turien's burden or added to it. She suspected he didn't quite know, either.

They were silent for a few moments.

"There has to be a way out of this," Mariq muttered. "But no matter how hard I think about it I can't see one. We both know how futile it would be to run from the Star-Blades. Killing Cendim is out of the question. Could we kill the man in the nighttime cloak before he poisons me?" Turien opened his mouth but Mariq continued speaking. "No, that would be worse than running. That leaves getting poisoned." She sighed, rubbing her neck with one hand. "If only we had an antidote."

Ehra perked up. She hadn't heard this before.

Turien shifted, then spoke like he knew he would regret it. "I might know someone who could try to find one."

Mariq brightened. "Truly?"

"It's a long shot, but… well, Cendim is an alchemist."

Ehra could feel the mood in the room shift. Darkness, hesitation, fear crept into their expressions. Mariq returned to hugging herself. "If we ask him, we'll have to tell him everything."

Turien nodded.

"I can't do that, Turien. I can't admit to Cendim I've been sent here to murder him! He doesn't even know the truth about my training." She hesitated, swallowing several times. "Cendim is one of the only people to accept me for who I am. If he knew all my secrets as well…"

Ehra closed her eyes, exhaling. How many times had she said the exact same thing?

"If we don't find an antidote, you're doomed," Turien said. "My master will not hesitate to use that poison if you don't kill Cendim."

Mariq spoke barely above a whisper now. "I know. But I don't know what else to do."

Long moments passed in silence. Then Turien spoke. "We could go through with the plan." He didn't sound at all happy at the suggestion.

Mariq's head shot up, eyes glaring at Turien. "You can't be serious."

"It's your life or Cendim's."

"You're suggesting we bow to the demands of this demented man and *murder Cendim*?"

"I don't see that we have much choice," Turien replied.

"You might choose to hide your emotions and pretend you don't care, but I can't do that," Mariq snapped. "I won't."

"Mariq…"

"No. I refuse to be a part of something as hideous as this. If you won't help me find a way out, then I'll do it myself. I'm refusing the contract."

"I'm not saying I won't help you. I'm saying I can't."

"That doesn't mean our only option is to kill Cendim!"

Turien didn't answer. He didn't need to. His doubt showed clearly.

"It isn't worth it. I couldn't live my life knowing it cost Cendim his." She paused. "Could you?"

A life for a life. Was every bit of their conversation, their secrets, a reflection of Ehra's struggles? Was she cursed to see herself in every situation, never allowed an escape from the monster even in other peoples' lives? She squeezed her eyes shut, clenching her fists. Her monster haunted her every waking moment, followed her through her dreams each night. Would she never be free of it?

A long pause stretched into awkwardness before Turien spoke again. "I don't know."

Me neither, Turien. Me neither.

Ehra snuck backwards, slipping out of the room. She'd gotten more than enough information—more so than even she'd expected. Cendim would want to hear this.

As for the rest… just more torment from her monster. Ehra had long since gotten used to it by now. She could manage.

She was about to sidle out of the hidden door when a passing shadow caught her eye. Nothing. All was still and quiet, as it should be. But it hadn't been her imagination.

Someone else had been eavesdropping on Mariq and Turien this morning.

8

ariq rubbed her forehead as she walked back to her rooms. Had the meeting been a success? She'd refused the contract and chosen Cendim's life over hers, just as she'd wanted. But her conversation with Turien stuck in her mind. *Cendim is an alchemist… If we ask him, we'll have to tell him everything.*

Just the thought sent Mariq's entire body shivering. She couldn't imagine how that conversation would go. *Cendim, thank you for welcoming me into your home. I'm supposed to be killing you right about now… could you help me counteract a poison so I don't have to go through with it?*

There would be no more secrets after that. Cendim would know it all—her Star-Blades training, the assassination ultimatum, everything. How would he react? He was a good man, not cowed or blinded by the traditions of Kuriza, but how could he welcome a liar, thief, and assassin into his home? He'd be wise to throw her out and never look back.

Still, he hadn't thrown out Turien. But Turien could be useful—by observing the spy, Cendim could glean information about the master. What did Mariq have to offer? Nothing.

No, she couldn't approach Cendim. She'd known the price for her refusal. She knew it would cost her more than she was willing to pay. But if it allowed her to retain the respect of Cendim, it would have to be worth it.

She could do nothing except wait. Go back to her rooms and live her life until the time to pay for her actions came.

"Mariq?" She jumped as Ehra's voice drew her from her thoughts, then slowed to allow her to catch up. "Is everything all right?"

"No," Mariq said. "But I'll manage."

Ehra seemed to understand, because she didn't press the matter. Thankfully Mariq didn't have to find a way to explain. She didn't think she'd be able to.

"Cendim asked me to give you this."

Mariq turned to see Ehra handing her an elegant envelope—another old-fashioned invitation. Cendim wished to dine with her again. Mariq found herself smiling. Yes, she had made the right decision, no matter how hard it may be. Anyone who made her smile simply by asking for her company deserved this sacrifice.

They returned to Mariq's rooms in silence. She wanted to slip into a bath and let the warm water soothe her thoughts. Nothing more. It was only midday but perhaps she could lie down for a few hours and catch up on some rest before dinner.

The man in the nighttime cloak waited in her chambers, a patch of midnight in the height of sunshine.

Mariq froze. Ehra doubled back toward the door, clearly intent on getting help.

A knife spun through the air, thudding into the doorframe before Ehra had taken two steps. "Draw attention and the next blade will find your spine." The speed with which he'd thrown it told them both Ehra would be hit long before she had ducked out of sight. She didn't try to flee again.

Mariq should do something. Draw her knives, move to a more defensible spot, something. Her instincts screamed at her to act. But the sight of him in that pitch-black cloak was a nightmare come to life. The harbinger of the end of her life—at least the life she'd made for herself.

Fear made her immobile. Her stomach twisted and a small voice in her mind started screaming like a child. This couldn't be happening. Not so soon! She'd left Turien less than an hour ago. How could he have learned about her refusal so fast?

"At a loss for a witty comment at last?"

She couldn't think of anything to say. She could only think of the man's poisoned dagger and the imminent loss of everything she held dear.

He strode forward, his pace casual. Ehra moved to intercept but he paid her no mind. An almost lazy backhand sent the tiny girl stumbling to the ground. Her head hit the wall and she lay still, breathing but out of the fight.

Mariq backed up, keeping as much room and furniture between them as she could. He didn't seem the least bit put out by this. "You've refused the contract."

"Yes." Her voice sounded small and frightened, not at all the image she wanted to project.

The man hesitated, faceless cowl staring at her. "You must not wish to save your life, then."

"Of course I do. I just don't want it to cost someone else's."

"This isn't a negotiation, Mariq. You kill Cendim, or I take away your skills."

"I will not kill him."

"If you refuse to work with us, you're the enemy," the man said. "And we never leave enemies alive."

He lunged. No banter, no drawn-out exchange. Only quick, brutal efficiency. The way of the Star-Blades.

Mariq broke from her paralysis and dodged aside, but he had the advantage in every way—his daggers were already drawn, that cloak of his would act as an admirable shield, and he wasn't burdened by emotion. He could act with speed and precision, whereas Mariq's every action would be hindered by hesitation, doubt, and fear. But she couldn't go down without a fight. She would force him to defeat her rather than giving herself to him and his poison.

The man reached her in an instant—or had she stood there, petrified, for one heartbeat too long? It didn't matter. The moment she felt his nighttime cloak brush her skin she spun away, jabbing out an elbow to catch him in the chest. The blow hit, but layers of velveteen cloth muted the impact. She used the momentum to lift her leg and pull a knife from her sheath in one fluid motion, then spun and slashed downward with the blade. It didn't hit flesh, but she did hear a significant amount of ripping fabric.

He cursed as he reached forward. Mariq dashed away as fast as she could.

Not fast enough.

Sharp, searing pain jabbed into her thigh. Hot wetness followed, and on the next step Mariq stumbled. The fall sent a jolt of agony through her. She managed not to cry out—she would not let him see her fall apart like a helpless child—but the man laughed at her nonetheless. "Enjoy what remains of your life," he said, a distinct note of satisfaction in his voice. "If you can."

Damn him. Mariq's jaw clenched. She lifted her head, ready to hurl anything she could at him—fists, knives, scathing words—but he was already gone.

Even as the blood cooled on her skin, a different kind of cold seeped through her. An icy chill deep inside, running through her limbs and settling in her soul. The wound pulsed with each heartbeat, sending more ice through her body.

The poison. No. No no no.

Mariq stared at her leg, details blurring through her tears. Blood welled from her thigh to stain her beautiful sarong. Despite all the anger, the fear, the pain, she could only focus on her sarong. Ruined. Stained. Useless. Just like she would be now. This had been one of her favorites. Now it was trash. Who would want something so damaged? Who could even hope it would ever be the same again?

Mariq stared at the bloodied silk and saw nothing but her own destroyed life. Rage and pain choked her and she cried out, beating her fist against the floor.

"Mariq?"

She choked down her screams, if not the hot tears trailing down her cheeks, at the obvious fear in Ehra's voice. Her friend seemed disoriented, but alert enough to crawl towards her. A large bruise already discolored the side of her face. It had to be painful, but Ehra ignored it as she leaned over Mariq. She tried to staunch the flow of blood, but even though the cut wasn't deep it bled profusely. Ehra swore and piled more fabric atop the wound.

"This is more than I can handle," she said, strain clear in her voice. "Hold this here. I need to get help."

Mariq put as much pressure as she could on the makeshift bandages, though she was already weak and growing weaker. Ehra hesitated for several moments, clearly uncomfortable leaving Mariq alone.

"Go," Mariq said. Her voice sounded feeble, even to her. "I've had worse."

Ehra bit her lip, her forehead crinkling. Then she left and Mariq was alone. Just her and the poison, eating away at her soul.

TURIEN hadn't intended to pass by Mariq's chambers. He'd just been wandering, trying to figure out the best course of action. Now that Mariq had refused the contract, what would happen? He feared telling his master he'd failed, but if he found out and Turien didn't admit to it, his punishment would be even worse. Did Mariq know what a dangerous position she'd put him in? He scraped the barbs of his slave-band across his skin again, not daring to think too much. It didn't matter whether he agreed with her or not. He could not defy his master to side with Mariq. But if she refused to kill Cendim, what could he do?

He was so preoccupied with his thoughts he didn't see Ehra until she had nearly bowled him over. Her eyes were wide and her breath far too fast. "What's wrong?"

She pointed back toward Mariq's chambers, not a dozen paces away. "Mariq. She's been stabbed. We need help. Go make sure she's all right." And then she flew past him, rounding the next corner at breakneck speed.

Turien stood in the hallway for several moments, dumbfounded. It had happened. His master had done it.

He finally got his feet moving and charged into Mariq's rooms. He didn't allow himself time to dwell on the impropriety of the action. He was No One, he shouldn't even consider bursting into a woman's room—a princess' rooms—without permission.

A crimson trail streaked the floor, ending where Mariq leaned against a wall. Her torn, stained sarong clung to the side of her leg, wet with oozing blood. She stared at a hole in the fabric as if she could imagine nothing worse than the ruined material.

Mariq looked up as he approached, her eyes glassy, rimmed with red. She watched him blindly for a moment before recognition kicked in. "Turien." He heard nothing in her scratchy voice but weariness. No pain. Just sadness. "I thought I'd prepared for this. I thought I was ready to face my fate. But now..." A tear leaked down her cheek.

Turien shifted. What could he say? He didn't understand what suffering she endured, what thoughts and fears ran through her mind. She was losing a life she loved, replacing it with one of passionless existence. Turien had known nothing but that his whole life.

What would the poison take from her? It would find nothing to take from him.

In lieu of responding, Turien took the bloodied rags from her and pressed them against the wound. He tried not to stare, but the curve of her leg drew his eye again and again. As if barging into a princess' room wasn't brash enough. He tore his eyes away and concentrated on the wound.

Ehra had better return with a healer soon. Mariq looked awfully pale.

"Will you be all right?" she asked.

"I should be asking that question of you," he replied.

Mariq leaned her head against the wall, her eyes fluttering closed for a second. "I hope your master doesn't blame you for this. It was my decision."

Turien paused. "I hope he doesn't, too."

Mariq reached out and grasped his left arm in her hand. "I'm glad you're here."

Turien redoubled his efforts to staunch the blood flow, trying to find something to say. No one had ever been happy to have him around.

"I'm sorry I called you No One," she mumbled. Turien wasn't sure she even knew she was speaking. "You deserve better."

No, he didn't. He deserved exactly what his masters always gave him: nothing. Believing differently was becoming far too dangerous. And far too easy. Damn Cendim, and Mariq, for making him care about himself. And about them.

"Just stay with me, Mariq," Turien said.

She squeezed his arm in reply, though there was virtually no strength to her grip.

He sat in awkward silence, listening to Mariq's occasional whispered statements, keeping steady pressure on the wound. When he heard footsteps behind him he breathed a sigh of relief. At last he could retreat and try to sort through his thoughts.

He turned, ready to greet Ehra and the healer, and met the cool gaze of Cendim himself.

The sheik took a few steps into the room and stood there, surveying everything with detailed interest. Then his gaze returned to Mariq and Turien, where it stayed. Turien jerked away, cheeks growing hot. He hoped Cendim didn't take offense to him being so close to his betrothed.

Cendim didn't speak for a few heartbeats. When he did, his voice was as cool as his gaze had been. "We'll discuss this in the dining hall as soon as Mariq is tended to. I expect you all to be there."

9

Her leg had been bandaged and cleaned, pain-numbing tea brewed, the ruined sarong discarded. Mariq had gotten that warm bath after all, but it hadn't been nearly as relaxing as she'd hoped. She could think of nothing but the poison. Could she feel it, running like ice through her veins? Was that tremor in her hand the poison already beginning its work?

Mariq managed to walk into the dining room without assistance, though she felt weak and shaky from blood loss and the cut stung with each step. She'd had worse injuries in training. But just knowing the poison lingered there made it so much worse than it should have been.

Ehra and Turien looked nervous as she entered, but Cendim greeted her with his customary smile. As if nothing had gone wrong at all. He ushered Mariq to her seat then moved to take his, motioning Ehra to the place on his right and Turien the one on his left. "Please."

Ehra sat, looking as if she belonged at the sheik's table. Turien didn't budge. "I don't think…"

"Sit."

Mariq had never heard such command in Cendim's voice. It didn't seem as if Turien had either, for his eyes widened as he sat without another word.

"I trust everyone is as well as can be expected, given the state in which you were found earlier?"

Everyone nodded.

"Good. There's no delicate way to broach a subject like this," Cendim said, "so let's just jump right in. First of all, I think it best we make it clear where everyone stands in this palace. Or, rather, who everyone truly is."

His eyes met hers, and Mariq felt a tremor jar her. Was this a bluff? Was he waiting for her to admit it, to condemn herself? Or did he already know?

Cendim nodded, as if confirming something. "Perhaps it would be best if I went first." He picked up a dinner knife and held his right hand out, palm up. Mariq's mouth went dry in an instant.

The sheik didn't even flinch as he cut a long, shallow gash across his hand. Blood welled and flowed into the invisible, unmistakable grooves she'd seen a thousand times before. Even so, she stared at the bloody knife-star on his palm for long moments, as if she couldn't comprehend what she saw. "You're…"

"I used to be. Assassin third rank, personal alchemist to the Master himself." The pride in his voice soured. "A long time ago. Now I'm just Cendim, Sheik of Hatife with a rather… colorful past."

Mariq just blinked at him. Her mouth hung open in a most unladylike manner, but… Cendim was a Star-Blade. Her kind, caring, compassionate husband-to-be, her unfortunate target, was an assassin.

And I thought I was in trouble before.

Cendim hesitated, making sure she met his eyes. "You aren't the only Star-Blade at this table, my dear."

Mariq's heart thudded in her chest.

"You didn't think I knew, did you? Mariq Ashai Meidani, daughter of Sheik Tufe Kolam Meidani, Princess of Kuriza, and Star-Blade spider-thief, first rank. The only woman to ever achieve so high a ranking." Cendim looked at her, and Mariq could see no condemnation in his eyes. No fear, no anger, nothing. "I know who you are, my dear, far better than anyone else. It is why I brought you here."

Speechless, Mariq stared at Cendim.

The sheik smirked, then turned to Turien. "I assume it's safe to say that slave-band belongs to more than just an affiliate of the Star-Blades. A leader for certain, if not the Master himself?"

Turien hesitated, flexing his wrist. But he nodded, emotions Mariq couldn't read flashing across his face for an instant before being squashed behind stone-like neutrality. An expression he'd no doubt mastered at far too young an age.

Cendim nodded. "As I expected. And as for Ehra, here…"

Mariq snapped her attention to Ehra. Her friend smiled, not at all self-conscious or shy, and reached up to tug at her right shoulder. Mariq gasped. She knew that motion—she made it every time she returned from a night of thieving.

A sleeve just like her own slid off Ehra's arm, revealing heritage tattoos as intricate and extensive as Mariq's. Same flowing script, brown and bronze like Cendim's, crawling all the way up her arm.

Mariq looked from her to Cendim and back. Now that she knew, the similarities were unmistakable.

Cendim nodded. "Ehra is not my servant," he said. "She is my daughter, firstborn of my line, with a mind as sharp and skills as dangerous as your own. She is my joy." He smiled at her before turning his attention back to Mariq. "I put you into her care specifically."

"To watch me, in case I put you in danger?"

"Partly," he admitted, "but also to evaluate you. I had to know if you were the woman I'd heard of, and if your temperament was suited to my task."

Mariq looked around. She thought she'd been sent to a place where her skills would get her exiled at best and killed at worst. Instead, she sat at a table with two other Star-Blades and the daughter of one. She wouldn't be surprised if Ehra had some Star-Blade training as well.

"I've chosen my household with care. No one is here by accident. I have healers, alchemists, warriors. Even my wives and children are taught these skills. At a single call, every living being in my palace will be equipped for battle—and capable of carrying it out."

Mariq didn't know whether to be impressed or frightened. "What are you going to do with this private army of yours?"

Cendim leveled such a vehement gaze on her she hardly recognized him. She could see the Star-Blade assassin now, and it terrified her. "I'm going to wage war on the Star-Blades," he said.

Even though she knew he was serious—deathly serious—the notion was so foreign Mariq laughed. "You're going to battle the Star-Blades?"

"Not just battle. Destroy. I'm going to topple them and grind their ashes into the dust. I'm going to erase them from history."

"Ehra didn't exaggerate when she said you were outfitted for an army, did she?"

Cendim just watched her, not a trace of mirth to be found.

"But why? And how? The Star-Blades won't go down easily. You were one of them, you know how impossible it would be."

"Nothing is impossible, if you know how to approach it. Everything has a weakness. The Star-Blades' is their arrogance. The masters believe nothing can touch them. It makes them lazy. Given enough time, and enough skill, we can use that to exploit them."

Mariq hesitated. He was determined to take them down, with or without her. "What makes you think I'd even join you? I'm a Star-Blade too. How do you know I won't fight you for them?"

"Mariq, my dear, I know you better than that. The Star-Blades have trained you, but they have also scorned you. They sent an assassin to kill you and, from what happened earlier, I assume they still hold quite a threat over your head." He quirked an eyebrow. "And you do not associate with them, even in your own mind. The Star-Blades are 'them,' not 'us.'"

Why did she continue to argue? Of course she wouldn't choose the Star-Blades over Cendim. They'd betrayed her, poisoned her, and tried to kill her. They'd enslaved Turien and plotted to assassinate Cendim. Orders like these had to come from the highest-ranking members of the guild—which meant it was rotten to the core.

If she only had a short time left to use her skills, she could think of no better cause than Cendim's.

Yet the thought of going to battle against the Star-Blades…

"I know it's daunting, my dear. But I've been planning this for a very long time, and you're the last piece of the puzzle I needed. With your exceptional skills, I believe we can succeed."

Mariq could sense Turien's attention. He knew, just as she did, she wouldn't be useful to Cendim for long. He watched her, as if waiting to see if she would admit it.

As much as she wanted to deny it, the poison froze and burned in the cut. Her hand still trembled, whether from nerves or blood loss or the poison didn't matter anymore. She couldn't deny it. She was terrified, and couldn't pretend otherwise. Even if she wanted to.

Her voice caught in her throat, choked by a sudden sob. "Maybe once. But not anymore."

Cendim tensed at the despair in her tone. He dropped his voice lower, empathy clear in his tone. "What's happened, Mariq?"

"I've… I've been poisoned. It's killing me, but not in the way you think."

She looked at Cendim's face just as all the blood drained from it. "Tell me," he whispered.

Mariq glanced at Ehra, who looked mournful and full of empathy. Turien sat still and expressionless as stone—she knew now that meant he battled emotions too strong for him to contain. Mariq lowered her eyes, wiping her nose with her hand. "It'll take what I love and destroy it. My thief's skills, my ability to fight… it'll all drain away. The poison will make me useless. How can I give you these skills if I start losing them any day now?" She sniffled, loathing herself for becoming so weak. "Without them, I don't even know who I am anymore."

The silence at the table crystallized, becoming thin and fragile. Mariq looked up. Cendim had frozen in place, an expression of horror painted across his face.

"Do you know what this poison is?" she asked.

Cendim closed his eyes, his exhale becoming a groan. His shoulders slumped, as if he wished the earth would open up and swallow him. "I most certainly do. It's called Joythief."

Even more than wondering how he knew, a single question forced its way to the forefront of her mind. "Is there an antidote?"

"No," he replied, and Mariq had to fight against the despair clawing through her gut. "None that I've discovered. And for someone else to make an antidote would be, except by some miracle, impossible."

"What do you mean, 'someone else?'" Turien asked.

"Joythief is my creation. I developed the poison during my service to the Star-Blade's Master."

"Then why can't anyone else make an antidote?"

Cendim started to speak, falling short of a single word multiple times. "I've known many excellent alchemists, but it takes more than intelligence and skill to create Joythief. Or its antidote, should one exist."

Turien crossed his arms in front of his chest. "Then what does it take?"

Cendim sighed. "Come with me. This will require some explaining."

THEY had relocated to her father's private office. Cendim had left them here to "gather his evidence," as he said. Ehra could only guess what he meant by that.

She'd known of his past as a Star-Blade and an alchemist as long as she could remember. She'd known he planned something big for several years now, that her training as a spy had largely been for this. But he'd never told her more than that, and the revelation of his war against the Star-Blades had shocked her as much as it had Turien and Mariq. She waited for his explanation with as much dread and anticipation as the others.

Turien paced, and Ehra watched him from the corner of her eye. Something about her father's comments had agitated him. His knowledge of Turien's master, unspecific as it was? Or something to do with the Joythief?

Ehra couldn't deny her own curiosity in that matter. Her father didn't speak of his Star-Blades days often. Too many regrets, he said. She had a feeling the Joythief may be one of those.

Mariq joined her by the window, saying nothing. They stood there for a long time, watching the sunset fade and stars appear in the darkening sky.

Her father returned, his arms laden with bottles. He dumped them on the desk and began arranging them, the various powders and liquids a mystery to everyone but him.

"Turien, if you would do the honors?" Turien strode toward the sheik and surveyed the bottles somewhat apprehensively. "I will give instructions, if you would mix."

Mariq and Ehra stood before the desk, watching as Cendim began directing Turien in the making of Joythief. Mariq shuddered, clearly disconcerted by the sight. And why wouldn't she be, given what Ehra knew of the poison? She didn't understand how a poison could kill an attribute, but that was the way of magic. It did things that made no sense to any logic but its own. Sometimes those things were good, miraculous blessings. Other times they were abominations.

The sky had darkened by several degrees by the time Cendim finished his instructions. The murky mixture looked more like the slurry left after a flash flood than a poison to Ehra.

"That doesn't look like it did on the dagger," Mariq said. "The poison was clear like water and made the blade seem wet."

"Every ingredient is there, in their proper proportions," Cendim said.

Mariq frowned. "But that isn't Joythief."

"No," Cendim replied. "Not yet."

He reached toward the bowl, laying his finger on the rim. Ehra felt something strange, like the deep pulse of a drum thumping her heart.

The liquid swirled, all on its own, and began to steam. It cleared before their eyes, from murky mud to translucent clarity. "Now it is Joythief," Cendim said.

Mariq and Turien gasped, and even Ehra had to stifle her surprise. She'd never seen her father's magic at work. Effortless, painless. It hurt no one, cost him nothing. So different than her own.

Life was so unfair. Why couldn't her magic be like her father's?

Why did he have a gift and she have a monster?

No one spoke for several heartbeats. They stared at the poison, as if waiting for the illusion to pass.

"What did you do?" Turien asked.

"It's nothing I can teach. It's a born gift. Most would simply call it magic."

Ehra watched her companions' reactions. This knowledge, this admission of magic, would either make them allies or push them away. It would lead to trust, understanding, or more disdain. She wanted to look away, to not see the horror she feared would come, but she had to know.

Mariq looked shocked, confused, and betrayed. Understandable. Kuriza had taught their people many things about magic—most of which weren't true. It wouldn't be the first time they'd had to reeducate someone on what magic truly was, and what it could and could not do.

But Ehra didn't see the horror, the revulsion she'd dreaded. Mariq, at least, wouldn't push her away because of her magic. Yet.

Tension eased out of her shoulders, and she released her breath. She hadn't realized she'd been holding it.

Turien hid it well, but for a brief instant Ehra had seen disgust written plain across his features. Not surprising, given his servitude to the Star-Blades. He'd have been indoctrinated on the evils of magic more fiercely than most. What followed was much more interesting, though: intrigue. Genuine curiosity. Turien might not be a lost cause after all.

It also meant his life had just become infinitely more dangerous. Ehra knew what price breaking free of the Star-Blades exacted. Her father had been the target of many assassination attempts during her lifetime.

"If you're the only one who can make Joythief, how did the Star-Blades have any to poison Mariq with?" Turien asked.

Her father seemed to age a decade at the question. "I made it for the Star-Blades, like I said. When I left I collected all the samples I could find. But I was a Star-Blade for many years. I made countless batches of Joythief for them. What I could collect or destroy before I ran away would have been a fraction of what they must have stockpiled."

And now they'd come to the root of everything: her father's time in the Star-Blades and the terrible guilt he carried because of it. He rarely let it show, but Ehra knew. It's what drove him to this insane plan to wage war on the Star-Blades. To collect spies and thieves and assassins to him, but for what? To atone for this terrible past he despised?

In the silence that followed Mariq spoke, her eyes traveling over the Joythief but resting on Cendim. "How does it work?" They all knew she wasn't asking about potion-making.

Cendim shrugged. "Some people have a gift. They are remarkable in one area, far exceeding the skills of everyone else. It is more than simple talent—normal people can be exceptional just as easily—but when a person attains the impossible, you can be assured magic is involved." His eyes flit to Ehra, but no one else seemed to notice.

"I thought we eradicated magic," she said.

"In Kuriza, perhaps. But not everywhere. Though the people who possess magic don't advertise it."

"Why not?"

Because some of us are given curses rather than blessings.

"Imagine how threatening a person such as myself is to the masters of alchemy. It took very little study for me to gain the knowledge and skills they had collected over a lifetime. And even so, well before the age they could create a simple potion, I created impossible potions. Things that shouldn't exist. They could devote every moment of every day for the rest of their lives to duplicating it yet they can never succeed. How could they continue to call themselves masters of anything, if a teenager too young for betrothal outshone them?" Cendim paused, but Mariq and Turien stayed quiet. Thoughtful. "People with magic are a threat, and sooner or later those who feel threatened eliminate us. But they can't tell anyone about it, because how could they justify killing an innocent simply because they were better than them? So magic is kept secret. Those with it don't wish to be hunted and killed, and those without it either think it's been eradicated—which is fine by us—or they refuse to bring it to light so they can be free to eliminate it whenever it is discovered."

"That's horrible," Mariq said.

"That's human nature," Cendim said. "It's why the rest of us must fight against it at all cost. We must prove to the world—and to ourselves—we can be better than that."

"But what does any of this have to do with the Star-Blades?" Turien asked.

Of course Turien would be the one to return to the Star-Blades. In his mind this had less to do with humanity or magic and more to do with the people who controlled his every move.

"What do you know of the Star-Blades? Truly?" Cendim asked.

Turien stiffened. The Star-Blades owned him. To speak against his master would mean death. But Turien held no love for them. When he'd first arrived in Hatife he'd been overwhelmed by the way Cendim treated him. Ever since Ehra had seen the war he fought with himself, the fear of his master battling with his growing love for her father.

To fight an internal war was one thing. To verbalize it, though…

"I've known nothing but the Star-Blades," Turien said. "From my earliest memories there is nothing but them. Everything I know, everything I've become—for what little it's worth—is because of them."

"They have formed your life according to their wishes. They've abused you, denied you the most basic of human rights. Yet even after all that, you don't believe they should be destroyed?"

"I didn't say that," Turien said. He sounded more confused than adamant, though.

"Very well. Then let me tell you why the Star-Blades must fall."

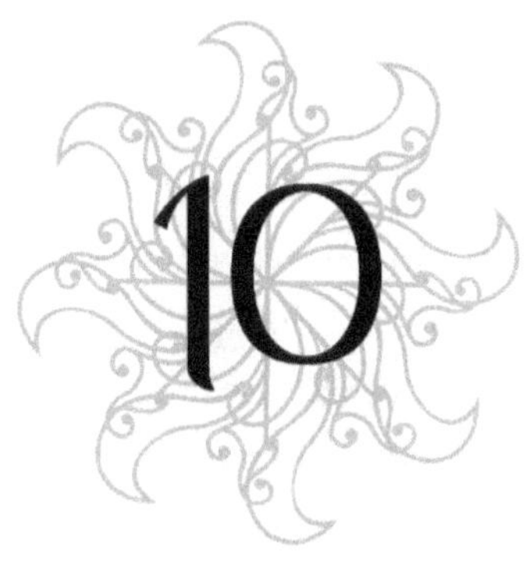

endim stood before Mariq and Turien, a glass of strong liquor in his hand. He paced and drank, mumbling to himself, much like some of Mariq's tutors had done. "You know the Star-Blades as a guild of thieves and assassins. I know them as an order dedicated to eradicating all magic, who would rather see the world destroyed than exist alongside magic-users." He turned to look at Turien's scoffing face. "You think I'm being dramatic. I can see it in your eyes. But tell me, Turien, what is the greatest battle the Scorched Lands has ever endured?"

"The Night of Bloody Sands," he replied. Every child learned about that night.

Cendim nodded. "The night of revolution, when power of the Scorched Lands was taken from the weak and given to the strong." People normally said the phrase with pride, or awe, but Mariq heard something different in Cendim's tone. Disgust.

"Thousands of people sacrificed themselves for the betterment of the Scorched Lands that night," Turien said. "We have had peace and prosperity across the desert since then. How can you condemn the actions of those who did what was necessary if you're determined to do the same?"

Cendim leveled a cool gaze at Turien. "Tell me, Turien, why those actions were necessary. Explain to me just how bad the former rulers were, and why those who took their place were better."

A calm, rational challenge. Cendim sounded as if he genuinely wanted to hear Turien's reasoning. And Mariq could see that Turien wanted to give him a solid, convincing argument.

But he couldn't.

Turien sputtered, his eyes twitching as he searched his memory for a justification. He knew there had to be a reason somewhere, just as Mariq believed, too. But she couldn't recall one. Not a single reason why the Night of Bloody Sands had to happen. Just the information that it had, and the statement that it had been for the best. She'd been told so, and so she had believed.

Cendim's voice was quiet and slow. "Never is the Night of Bloody Sands explained. In all of history, there is no reason for that massacre. We have just been told to accept it as the right thing, and we have."

Turien still wrestled with his disbelief, mute with frustration and stubbornness. Mariq, however, brimmed with curiosity. "So why did the Night of Bloody Sands happen?"

Cendim smiled at her, though his words were grim. "I've already told you. People will do terrible things to those they fear."

Pieces of the puzzle clicked together in Mariq's mind. "The old rulers had magic."

Cendim nodded. "And the new ones feared their power. They believed magic had no place in the world, let alone in a position of power. So they revolted." He stared at his drink for a moment before downing half the glass in a single swallow. "The Night of Bloody Sands wasn't a revolution. It was a massacre."

Mariq glanced at Turien. He'd gone deathly pale and stood as rigid as she'd ever seen him.

"They killed everyone with magic. Even those suspected of having magic were murdered. Thousands of innocents. Children, even." Another swig and Cendim drained his liquor. "Those who escaped death were driven into the Mad Desert. Most died within days, dehydrated or attacked by wild animals. The few survivors formed their own kingdom, a haven of magic hidden in the sands.

"Finally rid of magic, rule of the Scorched Lands was divided between two groups: those who took the thrones ruled in name, while the rest worked in secret to maintain that rule. Thus the Star-Blades were born. They have worked together ever since to keep magic from returning, at whatever cost."

The thought sent a chill down her spine. If the sheiks were that intertwined with the Star-Blades... "Does that mean my father is a Star-Blade also?"

"I doubt it," Cendim replied. "Kuriza has always been more closely tied to the Star-Blades than the other kingdoms—inevitable, given their close proximity—but the sheiks have traditionally been assets to the guild rather than a part of it."

It made sense, but still Mariq fretted. Even if Cendim didn't believe her father to be a Star-Blade, what did that mean for her? For her secret? Surely he couldn't know. He'd never have allowed her the charade if he'd known.

Turien crossed his arms. "Over a hundred years have passed in peace since then. Why do you have to act against them now?" he asked.

"Because," Cendim said, his voice rising in passion, "the segregation of magic and non-magic isn't natural. It's straining the very fabric of the world. By stamping out all magic in the Desert of Plenty, the Star-Blades are throwing the entire world out of balance. And the kingdom of magic in the Mad Desert is no doubt doing the opposite—they're likely working toward a world of magic dominance, which is only putting more pressure on nature."

Mariq thought back to that day in the desert, standing between the vibrant, lively Hatife and dull, dead Kuriza. The difference between the two kingdoms had been painfully obvious. They had, in truth, felt like two separate worlds.

"By purging it from their kingdom, Kuriza is creating a world free of magic. Yet just across an invisible border, magic is allowed to thrive. And farther away, the world is forced into a magic-dominant state. These extremes are wrestling with each other." Cendim held up his hands, palms facing each other, and strained. "Two halves of our world, fighting each other to conform. Yet they are so diametrically opposite they cannot coexist." He flung his hands wide. "Eventually they will not be able to remain in contact at all."

Turien crossed his arms. "How do you know this? The world seems as stable as it's always been. There's no evidence of something drastic happening."

Rather than answering him, Cendim turned to Mariq. "Tell me about Kuriza. What is your homeland like these days?"

Mariq stammered, confused by the question, but gathered her thoughts. "It's… well, it's a quiet place. Not much happens there, and no one gets very excited about anything."

"It feels dead, does it not?"

Mariq hesitated. Then she nodded.

"Kuriza is nearly devoid of magic," Cendim said. "And magic is essential to life."

"It is not," Turien said, his arms lowered, his hands clenched into fists. He seemed offended by Cendim's statement. "Those of us without magic survive well enough."

Cendim shook his head. "I did not say one required magic to survive. I said it is essential to life. This land needs magic the same way it needs water or air or sunlight. Too long without it, and it cannot continue to exist as it always has. People may not be able to use magic, but that does not mean they don't need it. Simply put, magic is life. Magic is passion and energy. Take that away and you get a people who *survive well enough*, as you put it, but they are far from truly living."

Mariq found herself nodding. People did not enjoy life in Kuriza. They did not laugh or cry or experience freedom the way she always had. The way the people here, in Hatife, did. Was that because of magic?

"But Cendim, some of us still have that kind of passion. Does that mean…?"

"Are you magic-users? Possibly. Or it could mean you had magic in your family, passed down from your parents. Even if you can't access the power magic could still be in your blood, strong enough the vacuum hasn't siphoned it from you yet."

Her father had no magical abilities in him, Mariq was sure of that. Tufe Kolam would have used that power to his advantage any time he could, and he wasn't one to keep quiet about his accomplishments. Her mother, on the other hand, had disappeared one day when she and Lookan were children. There had always been something special about her, something that gave her the strength to stand against what most considered a woman's proper position. Mariq liked to think she got her stubbornness from her. And as Lookan had pointed out, Cendim resembled their mother in a lot of ways.

Had that been magic giving her those traits?

While Mariq pondered this, Turien spoke. Mariq could tell he tried to keep the skepticism from his voice, but he didn't sound sure of himself at all. "Suppose what you say is true," he said. "This division could literally tear our world apart."

Cendim nodded.

"Why would they even consider it then? If that happens they'll die as surely as everyone else."

Mariq shook her head, her mind on her brother and father and the many, many others like them. "They won't believe that. They think they can survive anything, because they're convinced they are smarter and better than everyone else."

"Yes," Cendim replied. "And those people often hold the most influence. We can do nothing until they are dealt with. Even if it means we have to force unity upon them, and eliminate those who refuse to accept it."

"That sounds like the same reasoning used on the Night of Bloody Sands," Turien said, condemnation deepening his voice. "People with magic are oppressed, so let's kill the oppressors."

"Don't you think I've tried peaceful solutions?" Mariq had never heard such anger in Cendim's voice. "I've worked for decades trying to make peace. What have I been met with? Assassins. Don't think you and Mariq are the first. How many more times will they try to kill me? While I'm trying to stave off war my enemies are growing stronger. I won't stand for it any longer. If my enemies are so determined to start a war, then I will give them one."

Silence filled the room. Even Ehra seemed surprised by her father's outburst. He glared at Turien for a moment, breathing heavily, before the anger drained from him as if blown away by the wind, leaving him looking small and tired. The depths of sadness in Cendim's eyes struck Mariq like a physical blow. "I'm sorry, Turien. You're right. I know you are. But we must have faith our reasons will outweigh our crimes. I will do everything in my power to prevent as many deaths as I can. I do not relish drowning in blood. Those who are outside this battle will not be harmed, as much as I can guarantee it. But those who oppress magic and perpetuate its extinction must be stopped. The Star-Blades are the worst of them. Therefore, the Star-Blades must fall." He hesitated, pouring himself another glass of liquor. "They committed their massacre out of jealousy and fear. If a peaceable solution cannot be attained and the same methods are thrust upon us, at least we are acting to preserve the greater good."

"I'm certain the Star-Blades believed they were doing the same."

"Enough, Turien," Mariq said. "It doesn't matter what the Star-Blades believed back then. What matters are the facts, and those facts point to Cendim being right. If the Star-Blades aren't stopped, it could destroy everything."

Turien's face screwed up in displeasure, but he didn't argue. Mariq took that as a victory.

"Why are you fighting this, Turien? You of all people should wish to see an end to the Star-Blades' cruelty."

Turien flexed his wrist, blood welling beneath his slave-band. Mariq could see him cringe from the pain, gritting his teeth and sucking in a breath as the barbs tore open his scarred skin. He didn't respond—likely because any answer he'd give would be the wrong one.

"So what do you want us to do?" she asked, turning back to Cendim. "You wouldn't have told us all this if you didn't have a plan."

"Quite true, my dear. Quite true." He settled himself at the desk. "Just as the Star-Blades have worked to eliminate magic from the world, there is another organization committed to restoring it. They have worked in secret for many years, as the Star-Blades have."

"They," Turien said. "You mean 'we.'"

Cendim nodded. "I do. They are my organization. Myself, along with a few others."

"More magic-users in hiding," Turien stated.

"Some. Not all," Cendim replied. "Just because you aren't one of us doesn't mean you can't—or shouldn't—fight to protect us."

Turien suddenly seemed unable to meet Cendim's gaze.

"We've done well enough to keep the Star-Blades at bay, but that's no longer enough. Our spies tell us they're planning something. They were intercepted before we could learn much, but what we did gather tells us we can't be content with stalling them any longer."

"That's the 'unfortunate business' that pulled you away the day I arrived, isn't it?" Mariq asked. "You had to find out what had stopped your scouts."

Cendim nodded. "As much as I hated to miss your arrival, I feared the things they learned were too important to wait. And as much as I wish otherwise, I was right. We must act before they do. That's why I need you both. Turien, I need your knowledge of the Star-Blades and their patterns to help us stay a step ahead of them. And Mariq, I need your skills to retrieve anything that might tell us what they're planning, and to bring it—and yourselves—back safely."

"But Cendim, all of these plans rely on Mariq having her skills," Ehra said. "If she's been poisoned by the Joythief…"

"Yes, that does pose a problem." He hesitated, eying Mariq. Then he stepped forward and knelt before her, silently asking permission to examine her wound. Uncomfortable as the thought made her, Mariq shifted aside her sarong to reveal the red-stained bandages. No one reacted to the exposed knives strapped to her calves, or the hint of thieving harnesses on her thighs. "How long ago were you first poisoned?" Cendim asked, gently unwrapping the bandages.

"Hours."

"So just the one application. And how potent was the dose?"

"I've no idea. But I could see the poison on the dagger. The blade looked wet."

Cendim grunted. Not a good sound.

"How are you feeling?"

"A little shaky. Tired. The wound feels cold—so cold it burns."

Another grunt. Not encouraging at all.

They stayed that way for several minutes. No one spoke. Cendim poked around her wound with gentle motions, but it still hurt. The horrible iciness seemed to spread.

Finally he looked up, his expression grave. "We'll need to speed up our plans," Cendim said. "I can't predict how quickly the Joythief will affect you, Mariq, but I'd rather not risk your skills failing halfway through."

He sat back, preparing to stand, but Mariq caught him by the arm. "Wait. You still want me?"

"Of course."

"There are other spider-thieves, Cendim. Far more reliable than I will be. You can't let all these plans rest on my soon-to-be-gone skills."

"Is that all you think you are?" Cendim asked. "That your only value is in your thieving skills, and without them you're useless to us?"

Mariq's spine stiffened, and she had to hold her breath to keep her heart from pounding out of her chest.

"My dear, you are worth so much more than what the Star-Blades gave you. It's unfortunate your thieving skills are dwindling, for certain, but they aren't the only reason I brought you here. Your mind is just as valuable to me, as is your heart. Even with your diminished skills, I would want no other at my side."

"You'd endanger the entire mission just because you want *me* instead of another spider-thief?"

"It isn't like he has much choice," Turien said. "The Star-Blades aren't just the best at training assassins and thieves. They're the only ones who do it. You may be the only competent thief in all the Scorched Lands who would agree to fight for Cendim's cause."

Everyone glared at him.

"He is correct, of course," Cendim said, clearly unhappy at Turien's bluntness. "But the point remains. I want you, Mariq Ashai

Meidani, for far more reasons than the fact you're good at taking what isn't yours."

Mariq stared at him. She'd known he valued her, but to hear it so plainly made Mariq's heart hurt. Not a bad hurt—it was the pain of having a hole that had stood empty for so long filled.

"I'll do it," she whispered. "Even once the Joythief takes over, I'll do my best."

Cendim grinned at her. "I had no doubt of that, my dear."

By some unspoken cue, they all looked at Turien next. He seemed keenly uncomfortable with the attention.

"And what of you?" Cendim asked. "I know you came to this position by no will of your own. But now that you're here, and have heard and seen what I plan, what will you do?"

Turien looked to each of them in turn, eyes wide like a cornered animal. He clenched his hands into fists, but for once he didn't flex his wrist to tear open his wounds again. "You're asking me to defy my master. Throw away what little life I have just to follow you on a fool's quest."

Cendim didn't so much as pause. "Yes."

"Do you have any idea what would happen to me if I agree?" Turien lifted his right arm, showing off the bare skin and barbed slave-band. As if any of them had been able to forget it. "Without the protection of my master, do you know what this gets me? Nowhere. It means I can't do a damn thing on my own. If I lost this protection, and was unlucky enough to live through it, I'd be on the street without even the credibility to beg for handouts to survive."

"Turien, do you truly believe you have no one in the world who would take you in?" Every word rang through the room despite Cendim's quiet, gentle tone.

Turien froze, as overwhelmed as Mariq had been a moment ago.

"I can't blame either of you for your insecurities," Cendim said, glancing between Turien and Mariq, "but I can tell you both are unfounded in this house. I take in my allies with care, and once chosen I do not abandon them."

Turien still looked unsure, but he didn't argue any more. Mariq thought she could see a shift in him. A little more confidence, perhaps? Or a sense of belonging?

Apparently that was enough for Cendim. "First things first: Our spies told us the Star-Blades have been working furiously, organizing a huge operation and sending out orders to every ally they have. We have been able to successfully intercept a few of these orders, but there is one Star-Blade ally who has thwarted all our attempts at subterfuge." Cendim met Mariq's eyes. "And his instructions are the most essential of them all, for they contain not only the Star-Blades' intention for magic-users, but for the stability of our kingdoms as well."

Mariq caught her breath. Her father's orders. Which he would hold in the very heart of his heavily fortified palace in Kuriza.

"Failing that, our only other option is to learn of their plans from the source—from someone high enough in the Star-Blades to have access to their innermost workings, and a vested enough interest in both Kuriza and Hatife to send a spy to watch over us." He turned toward Turien, who paled to a sickening greenish shade.

"You want me to spy on my master, and get him to tell me what they're planning?" Turien laughed, but it sounded half-mad. "You overestimate my value. They never have, and never would, tell me more than the very basics required to complete my mission."

"I know how dangerous these tasks are," Cendim said, "and I won't force them upon either of you. But we must know what the Star-Blades are planning, and there's no one more equipped to do it than you two. Turien, you've spent your entire life with the Star-Blades. You know more about their inner workings than anyone alive, and your access to the very top of their command chain will be invaluable. Even the tiniest hint of their plans would be helpful. And if there's one person who could succeed in a theft this complicated, it's Mariq."

Cendim's confidence in her was inspiring, but Mariq feared it was ill-placed. Yes, she had snuck in and out of her father's palace hundreds of times before. But that was when she was a welcome sight inside its gates. If she returned now, it would be as an intruder. She would have so much more to worry about than climbing walls this time. She'd have to get all the way in, and all the way out, without being seen by anyone.

Mariq and Turien looked at each other, gauging their reactions. Turien looked as incredulous, as terrified, as she felt. But Cendim was right. What choice did they have?

Mariq ignored her hammering heart, her sweaty palms, the sickness in her stomach. She tried replacing them with confidence, but the best she managed was hardly terrified. "All right," she said, blowing out a breath. "I guess we're off to Kuriza."

"We have no time to lose," Cendim said, nodding. "You must leave immediately. Discover what you can, but do so safely. Return as soon as you can. And luck be with you, my friends."

O f all the places in the world, why did Cendim's missing piece of the Star-Blades' plans have to be in her father's palace? Had Mariq known, she could have brought them with her when she first went to Hatife and saved everyone the trouble of returning. Instead she found herself hunkered in the darkness at the back of her father's palace, features concealed by a widow's heavy black veil, waiting for Turien's knock on the servant's entrance to be answered.

The nights weren't as cold here in the Desert of Plenty as in the dry desert around Hatife, but still Mariq shivered. A handful of days atop a fast-galloping horse hadn't prepared her for a return to Kuriza. What if someone recognized her? What if the Joythief had already stolen her skills? What if she failed—what would happen to Cendim and his dreams then?

"Now is not a good time, Mariq," she chided herself. "Just get in, get the plans, and get out. Overthink later."

If only it were that easy. The plans would be locked away somewhere, guarded by all the security her paranoid father could muster. She scanned her memory for anything out of the ordinary—places her father forbid her to explore, heavily guarded corridors or curiously locked doors. She couldn't remember any. But she knew they were somewhere. They had to be.

Her worries vanished, if only for a moment, when the door opened. Turien said a few words to the servant girl inside, quiet enough Mariq couldn't understand them, then held up his right hand to display his slave-band. A brief, tense pause followed before the door opened farther and Turien entered. He whispered again, and the servant answered. Then Turien motioned for Mariq to follow.

By the time she got to the door Turien stood alone. "How is it you're allowed access without question? And with a stranger in tow, no less?" Mariq whispered.

He closed the door and started leading Mariq through narrow, utilitarian corridors. "My master often meets me here. It's not difficult for a nobleman to bully servants into letting their personal slave into the palace at will, no questions asked."

No, it wouldn't be. Especially since Turien's master gave his slave a barbed band and forbade him the decency of a heritage tattoo. No servant would want to deny a man like that anything he asked for.

Turien led her through the labyrinth of servants' quarters and a few moments later they reached hallways Mariq recognized. A few more turns and she would be back in the grand corridors of the palace proper. Which meant that at any moment she and Turien—

"I have to go this way," Turien whispered, pointing down an opposite hall. "My master uses a small storage room for our meetings. If there's anything to be found here, it will be down there."

—would have to part ways.

She'd known they would have to split up sooner or later. They each had their mission, and Turien's scant training couldn't help him follow the spider-thief paths Mariq would doubtless be taking. Still, she didn't relish the thought of proceeding alone. It felt too isolated, too vulnerable to be in these vast halls with no allies at her side.

It felt far too much like being back home.

Mariq pushed the emotions aside and nodded. "Be safe."

"You too. See you at sunrise, outside the city gates."

"I wouldn't miss it."

Turien almost smiled as he turned away. Mariq counted it as a victory.

The first of many tonight. Hopefully.

She crept forward, pausing in the shadows near a corner. A brief moment to ensure no one waited on the other side, a quick glance at Turien's retreating form, then she emerged into a dark and silent and eerily familiar hallway. Mariq felt as if she'd been gone an eternity and yet only left yesterday.

She crept through the palace, an intruder in her childhood home. She tried to keep calm, to analyze the situation as a spider-thief should. But everywhere she turned were reminders, little bits of her life that whispered memories into her mind. Lookan had first challenged her to defy expectations and sneak away in this corridor, starting her on her path to the Star-Blades. She used to sit in this window for hours, daydreaming. A turn down this hallway would take her to the secluded, unused room where she used to practice knife drills by night.

And here was the staircase where she'd nearly been assassinated, had killed her first man, and gotten tangled up in this mess.

She pushed the thoughts away. She was a spider-thief. Distraction would cost her. She had to focus.

If her father held the plans, he would keep them somewhere close to him—not just as a precaution, but as a trophy. Her father would never let anyone, including himself, forget his accomplishments.

Creeping through the palace, dodging servants and drawing ever closer to her father's chambers, made sweat collect on Mariq's forehead. Her heart drummed in her ears. Her hands hadn't trembled like this since her first real mission as a spider-thief. What was wrong with her? She'd done this kind of thing dozens of times before. So why did she make so much noise she was bound to draw attention?

The Joythief, she thought. *Is it working already?*

She'd been poisoned only a few days ago, but it already felt like a lifetime. She found herself analyzing each movement, reviewing her knife drills and thieving skills over and over in her mind. She mustn't forget. Each time her hands trembled or a memory faltered her heart twisted and her stomach plummeted. Would it happen slowly, losing one aspect at a time until it was all gone? Or would she wake one morning and have nothing left? She hadn't thought to ask Cendim. Perhaps that was for the best.

Then again, with how much she worried and thought of it, perhaps not.

Focus, Mariq. You can't afford to get distracted now.

She closed her eyes and took a deep breath, clearing her mind. Almost to her father's chambers. Three guards stood between her and the door, staggered along the corridor. Who knew if any lay beyond? She'd never been allowed to see the inside of her father's rooms.

Three guards to bypass. If it hadn't been made known she'd been sent to Hatife, she could have just walked up to them and ordered them to do something other than guard the door. But she couldn't risk that now. It would point every finger to Cendim once they learned the plans were missing. If it would have even worked in the first place, which she doubted. These guards would be loyal to her father and wouldn't listen to anyone else, let alone his misfit daughter.

She stayed close to the walls, lingering in the shadows as much as possible. The soft night breeze covered the sound of her breathing and the rustling of the palm fronds helped mask her footsteps. She snuck forward, on the balls of her feet, moving slowly so she didn't draw any attention.

The guards looked right past her.

Suppressing her grin, Mariq crept past the first guard, then the second. They never knew she was there.

The third guard stood in front of the door, facing her. No way to get through without him knowing it.

Mariq just kept smiling. She was a *spider*-thief. The name meant she didn't need things like doors.

Slipping through the tall, open windows, Mariq clung to the side of her father's palace. The mosaic tiles were cold and slick, offering very little to grip. She refused to look down at the marble-tiled courtyard over forty feet below. More than far enough to kill her on impact.

She moved as quickly as she dared, not wanting to be on that wall any longer than necessary. Maneuvers like this were risky. She'd only dared it going in and out of her library because she'd known the path and minimized every risk. Out here, on a path she hadn't scouted, higher than before, without knowing for sure what waited for her on the other side? Sloppy. Risky. Unnecessarily dangerous, especially for one with unreliable skills. Why had she been so eager to take this route?

Focus, Mariq.

She shuffled along the wall, her toes barely finding purchase. Her fingers ached and trembled from the strain. She tried to calm her breathing, willing strength into her limbs. Weakness and terror flooded her entire being instead. *I'm a disgrace to the title of spider-thief.*

She had to suppress a deep sigh of relief as she slipped back into the palace.

Her father's chambers were opulent to the point of being

grotesque. Her searching eyes couldn't land on anything that wasn't gilded, bejeweled, or covered in silk. There were more riches in this room than in the treasury. And Mariq would know—she'd tested her skills by sneaking into that vault more than once.

She crept through the room, careful to return everything she touched to its exact position. She couldn't leave any evidence she'd been here. If they were lucky, her father wouldn't have need to access their plans for a while. By the time he went looking for them, this could all be over.

She cursed her clumsiness as she tripped, almost breaking a mosaic vase worth more than her life. Anger and despair battled in her. Mariq hadn't been clumsy since she'd started to walk. Part of her wanted to sob, the other wanted to find the man in the nighttime cloak and introduce her knives to his gut.

Mariq spotted a door on her left, ornamented with gold and jewels like everything else. She nearly passed it over, until her eye caught the complex lock buried among the riches. She knew, without being told, that the only key would be carried by Tufe Kolam himself at all times.

Luckily Mariq didn't need a key.

She slipped a thin set of picks from her sarong, inserting them into the lock—no, wait, the other one goes in first—and began fiddling.

A few minutes later she realized she had no idea what she was doing.

Oh, she knew the *theory* of the thing. Align the slides so the lock will open. She'd done it a thousand-thousand times in her training. But now that it mattered most, her hands were awkward and stiff and she made more noise than a rampaging elephant while making no progress whatsoever.

Mariq muttered curses under her breath, damning the man in the nighttime cloak to the worst her imagination could conjure. Still the lock refused to open.

Concentration, prayers, more curses. Nothing helped.

She could do this, damn it! She knew she could. It was part of being a spider-thief, part of being *her*. The Joythief couldn't have stolen everything from her. Not this soon, not this suddenly! She had to have some skill left. Just enough for this. *Please,* she pleaded, ignoring the tears streaking down her cheeks. *Just enough for this.*

A tiny click sounded from the lock.

Relief drowned Mariq. She was, for now, still a spider-thief.

Her heart hammered as she eased open the door. She had no clue what to expect on the other side. A hidden chamber? A vault filled with mounds of gold? A corridor leading to some long-forgotten part of the palace?

Or an unexpectedly plain closet. Mariq was almost disappointed.

Unadorned wooden shelves lined the top half of the rather small closet, and a utilitarian desk filled the lower half with drawers and cubby holes. Papers and scribing equipment lay on the desktop in painfully precise order. Tiny notations identified each individual niche, some written out, others in code.

Mariq scanned the notations she could read. Day-to-day functions of the kingdom, tax records, a few reports that seemed interesting but nothing to do with the Star-Blades. Not that she was surprised. This closet may be a secret, tucked away in Tufe Kolam's private chambers, but only a fool would clearly mark evidence that would damn him as thoroughly as orders from a guild of assassins and magic-destroyers.

Despite her rank amongst the Star-Blades, Mariq knew very little of their codes. Each specialty had their own, and the command structure was said to have codes within codes so thick they required an entire chapter of Star-Blades dedicated to deciphering and creating them. The clustered symbols on these letters meant absolutely nothing to her.

If only Turien could have come with her! He had to have at least some knowledge of these codes. Or did he? Just because the master knew didn't mean the slave would.

Turien's knowledge aside, Mariq was still caught in the same problem. What scroll amongst the dozens here contained the information they needed? And how would she know it when she saw it?

She could just take them all and sort through the information later, but that would cause huge gaps in the closet's filing system. The theft would be immediately apparent the second Tufe Kolam opened these doors. Cendim's plan required stealth, and alerting the Star-Blades that their plans were compromised would lead to disaster.

Should she pick one at random, maybe something hiding near the back that wouldn't be noticed? She could take one of these empty sheets and curl it into the missing scroll's place so it wouldn't be obvious until it was removed. That was a good plan. But which one? How could she possibly guess? The odds of her bringing any useful information to Cendim with that plan were slim at best.

Then again, standing here wasn't going to get him any information either. Especially since Mariq's time was running out.

Mariq swore under her breath. Another slip-up. She never should have stood here debating for so long. She should have been gone already, grabbing whatever was available so the theft—however valuable it may or may not be—wouldn't be detected. Information was critical to this mission, certainly, but so was not alerting their enemies. Instead she'd stood here, paralyzed by indecision, while precious time had slipped by. Escaping this room would be tricky enough if the guards and shadows remained where they had been. By now everything will have changed, and Mariq would be blind to her enemies' locations and the suitable hiding spots to avoid them. She now had to retreat and hope for the best, risking both her information-gathering and stealth objectives. Her masters would be ashamed of her.

As they should be, she thought. She was ashamed of herself.

Mariq grabbed the scroll with the most intricate-looking coded label, rolled some blank paper, and stuffed it into the cubby. She swung the closet doors shut just as a slight creak and the subtle movement of air signaled the chamber's door was opening.

Mariq dashed away, seeking the first cover she could find. Fear set her heart racing and threw her thoughts into a whirlwind. She had to find a way out. If the guards caught her, her father would have no mercy. Cendim's plans would be discovered, and everything he fought for lost.

She could not be the cause of Cendim's downfall.

Heavy footsteps entered her father's chambers, moving through a methodical search. Had they heard her? They must have—what other reason would they have to barge into the sheik's bedchamber?

They might suspect something, but they didn't know what. Or who. She could still slip out and get away, if she was careful.

There were plenty of shadows for her to cling to, thanks to the torches held by the guards and the abundance of shiny, shimmering things to reflect the firelight. She crept on hands and knees, moving far more slowly than she'd have preferred, inching her way to the door. Only long practice allowed her to keep her panic under control and not make a mad dash for freedom.

"What's this?" one of the guards said. Mariq froze as the guards moved toward the far end of the room. *My picks.* She'd left them in the lock.

No time for caution now. She leapt to her feet and raced out the door, just as the guards began hollering about a thief.

urien didn't hold much hope of finding anything in the small room his master used for their meetings. There was little more than a cupboard and a few racks for wine barrels against the walls, and his master never brought any kind of paperwork with him. But it was his best bet for finding something to bring back to Cendim. Perhaps something would be there, waiting for him to discover.

He didn't expect it to be his master, standing in the exact middle of the room, radiating menace from the shadows of his cloak.

"Close the door."

Turien obeyed with limbs that felt far too watery to properly manage the job.

"You return to us, without word of Cendim's death and with no intelligence to offer. You didn't even alert us to your return. I pray, for your sake, you have a satisfactory explanation."

Turien tried to stop himself from shuffling. He had no reason to be back and no progress to report. If anything, he had a string of minor disasters he could name. But that was even more likely to get him killed than silence.

"Something is troubling you." His master sounded curious. It disoriented Turien for a moment. The voice that came from the depths of that shadowcloak was always impassive, as the man's whip had "encouraged" him to be.

"It's just… Cendim…"

"Ah," his master said. "The sheik has been talking."

"Yes, Master."

"Words have always been his preferred weapon. One he's most proficient with, I must admit." He paused for a moment. "Tell me what he's said."

Turien dove into his explanation immediately, and not just because he'd been ordered to. He needed to get this off his chest, to hear what his master had to say about Cendim's statements. Would his master's version of events make as much sense as Cendim's?

"The Night of Bloody Sands," his master said once Turien had finished. "Is that what has you so conflicted?"

Turien nodded.

"You think those magic-using leaders were innocent?"

"I… fear, Master."

His master laughed, leaving Turien speechless. He hadn't believed the man could muster that much emotion. But even so, it sent a chill down his spine. The cruelty Turien knew he was capable of tainted the sound, twisting it into something harrowing.

"They were as far from innocent as possible. They made a weapon—one to force magic into people, to punish others by taking their magic away."

"I've never heard of anything like that before."

"Of course not. Do you think they'd be stupid enough to leave it around for someone to find? A criminal always covers his tracks. When the cowards fled, they took the weapon with them." A brief pause, and his master's voice grew sour with condemnation. "Given their way, they'd have forced everyone to become a magic-user or die."

"So instead, you forced every magic-user to flee or die. You justify your actions by stating you had to do what you did to prevent the other side from doing the exact same thing," Turien said. He couldn't believe he defended the magic-users. When had he started taking Cendim's side in all this?

"Do not forget whom you serve, Turien," the man snapped. His voice had turned icy and dangerous, and Turien knew a wrong step now could cost him his life. He'd seen it happen before. Far more often than he cared to remember.

"Of course not, Master," he said, pouring all the sincerity he could into his voice. Sincerity, he found, which was far from genuine. "But…"

He couldn't believe his own audacity. Contradicting his master? Questioning direct orders? He must have gone mad. Or contracted the same bold, loose tongue Mariq possessed.

His master's voice was cold, humorless, and deadly. "Yes?"

No turning back now. He likely wouldn't leave this room alive—he might as well try to get some answers before he died. "What about Cendim's other claim? That the division between magic and non-magic is going to tear the world apart?"

"If something isn't done, yes. Which is why we're working to correct this imbalance even now."

Turien knew all too well the Star-Blades' method of correction. It would be drastic, irreversible, and leave a lot of people dead. "How?"

Long moments of silence followed. Turien expected to die in every single one.

"The magic-users aren't the only ones who have impossible weapons. If they can find a way to infuse magic into people, we can find ways to remove it."

The Joythief, Turien thought, his heart racing. He kept his face impassive. *Cendim said he'd only recovered a fraction of what he'd made.* But this sounded like it would function on a widespread scale. Could something like that—mass Joythief—exist? The thought of the Star-Blades wielding a weapon like that made his blood run cold.

By removing magic, they would save the world—accomplishing the goal Cendim worked so hard to achieve. But at what price? If Cendim spoke the truth, the entire world would suffer without magic. People would live, but never thrive. They would become cold, distant, uncaring. Like his master.

And if there were more people like his master, there would be more people like him. Enslaved. Given no chance to live for themselves. Hundreds, thousands of No Ones, from Nowhere.

"You disapprove?"

Turien jumped and wiped the scowl from his face. A fatal mistake, to let his true feelings show. He bowed his head and took a step back, radiating apology and remorse and fear with every drop of sweat that fell from his brow.

His master didn't reply. He stood there, dark and brooding in his shadowcloak. Turien could feel the man's eyes on him, could almost taste the rage in his aura.

They passed several minutes this way, though it may as well have been days to Turien. The wait was a torture all its own.

"Be very grateful," his master said, his voice deathly quiet, "that you have so ingratiated yourself with Cendim and his household. Were you not indispensable to him, I would make you wish for death a thousand times over before ushering you to it."

Turien bowed lower, not trusting his voice. Relief spread through him, leaving him lightheaded and exhausted.

"Cendim has pushed his cause too far," his master continued. "He's hardly a threat to our plans, but the man is dangerous nonetheless. If you had done your job and ensured he was dead, we would be ready to move against his allies and squash their little rebellion before it ever starts." Turien could feel the weight of anger and disapproval on his shoulders. "But Cendim must die soon."

"Yes, Master." What else could he say that wouldn't reveal how much his heart pounded and his throat constricted with fear and doubt?

"Once he's eliminated, we will show the magic-users just how innocent their revered ancestors were on the Night of Bloody Sands. They will feel the power they tried to levy upon humankind." His master chuckled again. The sound was like a greeting from Death himself.

Turien didn't say a word.

"Leave this place, Turien. The next time you return there will be news of a death to report—either Cendim's, or your own."

Turien bowed, resisting the urge to race out of the room. Any time he left his master's presence with his life, he considered it a small victory. This time he felt like he'd won an impossible war.

Still, his master's orders left a bitter taste in his mouth. His response to Turien's doubt had eased some of the conflict in his heart. Only he hadn't expected this resolution.

Turien had never been more certain. Helping Cendim, and Mariq, was the right thing to do. He would smile as they destroyed his master. And Turien would be right there beside them. Holding the knife, if it all possible.

If he survived until then.

MARIQ didn't dare re-enter the palace, despite the multitude of inviting windows along the way down. The guards inside would be swarming the corridors, on high alert for any hint of her presence. It was too risky, even for spider-thief.

Then again, climbing down four stories of slick, cold marble wasn't exactly the safest option either. The guards out here hadn't raised an audible alarm just yet, but that didn't mean they were unaware. It just meant they didn't want her to know they knew. Even now they could be scanning the walls, bows at the ready, just waiting to see an out-of-place shadow…

Damn. Now her shoulder blades itched.

It felt like an eternity before her feet reached solid ground, and her muscles screamed at her to rest. But she couldn't stop now. She had to get out of the garden, over the wall, and meet up with Turien. And the first rays of dawn were already starting to lighten the sky.

She welcomed the uneventful escape and trek to her meeting point that followed. After such a fantastically botched job, it was nice to know something could finally go right.

Turien waited for her at their rendezvous with obvious impatience. He paced and fretted enough even the horses were nervous. The moment he saw her he rushed to her side, flushed with so much emotion she hardly recognized him.

"Thank the stars, Mariq, I thought you'd been captured. We have to get out of here. Now." He grabbed her arm and began hauling her toward the horses.

"What happened?"

"No time to explain. But Cendim was right, we're out of time to stop the Star-Blades. If you hadn't gotten those plans, you have no idea what they could have done. We just have to hope we can stop it in time."

"We just have to hope I actually got the plans in the first place," Mariq said, wrenching her arm from Turien's grip so she could retrieve the hopefully-helpful scroll. "I couldn't decipher the codes, and there were so many, that I had to grab what I could."

She handed the scroll to Turien, who paused just long enough to peer at it in the still-dim morning light.

"Can you decipher it?"

He shook his head. "We can only hope Cendim will be able to, in time."

In time. Time is exactly what they didn't have.

"It's useless," she said. "We have no way to know if I found anything helpful. And worse, I tipped off Father's guards that we're here. I'm a miserable spider-thief."

"They know?" Turien's voice edged toward hysteria. "If they know, we have to get out of here. Right now."

"Maybe I can come back," Mariq said, fully aware of how foolish, and desperate, she sounded. "There has to be a cipher somewhere. I could sneak back in, see if I can find a book of codes or something…"

"Mariq, you don't understand! My master knew I would be here. He questioned me about Cendim. Worse, he seemed to *know* Cendim is planning something and that I'm involved. But he didn't seem concerned about it. He's up to something. I don't know what. But I know the Star-Blades are going to act, and they're confident they can't be beaten. And now that they know you were here too, they won't waste any more time. They'll act *now*, before we can do anything to stop them."

She didn't want to believe him. But the pure terror his voice compelled her to listen.

"We have to get back to Hatife, Mariq, before anyone can catch us here."

CENDIM hunched over a table covered in papers when they arrived. He glanced up and the entire room seemed to warm. "Welcome back. I need some good news." He stood, groaning as if he'd sat there for far too long, then met their eyes. One look at Mariq's and Turien's expressions wiped his fragile hope away. "Tell me everything," he said.

Mariq summarized as quickly as she could. The faster she got this over with, the better.

She handed over the scroll. "I did manage to get this, but I have no idea if it's even close to what we're looking for. Everything in the closet was coded, and the guards started investigating before I could figure out which scroll was the one we need."

"Were you identified?" Cendim asked.

"I don't think so, but I can't be sure." She shook her head, no longer trusting her voice. "I think the Joythief is taking hold. I fumbled on the climbs and could barely pick the lock."

Cendim nodded, his eyes fixed on the indecipherable scroll and his face set in a deep scowl. "I'll set my spies to this at once. We just have to hope they can break the code, and find some useful information, quickly." He looked back to the table as if the information on those pages was a physical burden. "I must admit I hoped for better results. If Hatife has ever needed a stroke of good luck, it's now."

"What happened?" Turien asked.

Cendim looked to Mariq when he answered. "A messenger arrived from your brother yesterday. He'd ridden hard through the nights to bring me this." He reached back and plucked a sheet from the table, handing it to Mariq.

She scanned it, horror making her heart clench. "A declaration of war." So Lookan's warnings hadn't been a bluff after all. Kuriza really did mean to subdue Hatife, diplomatic marriage notwithstanding.

"We're by no means defenseless, but it's clear the Star-Blades mean to use this very genuine war for their own purposes. They'll divide our resources and force us to defend Hatife, clearing the way for them to finish their plans with no interruptions." Cendim sighed, the sound heavy with regret. "We're desperate for help and, potential clues notwithstanding, are no closer to finding a way to stop them."

"I wouldn't say that," Turien said. "It isn't much, but I did glean some information from my mas... *former* master."

Cendim turned to Turien. "What did you learn?" Mariq didn't dare breathe for fear of destroying the fragile, tentative hope in his voice.

"After he berated me for my failures and ordered me to ensure you were killed as soon as possible, my old master mentioned the Night of Bloody Sands and a weapon the magic-using leaders had created. Something about taking magic out of people, or forcing it into them. He also alluded to something else that sounded a lot like Joythief." He gulped and paled. "He said as soon as you were dead, they would use these weapons against the magic-users."

"That isn't possible," Cendim said. "There's no way to remove, or implant, magic."

Turien cleared his throat. "My master knew I'd report what I heard back to you. Why would he have told me this if he wasn't certain it existed?"

"Misdirection?" Mariq replied. "My family are experts in that."

Turien shook his head. "It's not the way of my master. He uses fear, and once one threat is found to be false there's no weight to any other. There is much more to fear in truth than in lies."

Cendim furrowed his brow, clearly troubled by the prospect. "I agree with Turien. My experience has never led me to believe the Star-Blades would seed false information in hopes of cowing an opponent.

Especially ones with personal history in their ranks, such as us. We must assume this weapon, whatever it is, actually exists." Rather than falling into despair, like Mariq felt sure would happen to her, Cendim seemed bolstered by the information. "Our path is clear. We cannot allow the Star-Blades to use this weapon. Therefore we must find it and take it before they can do so." As if it were that easy.

"But Cendim," Mariq said, working to keep her voice reasonable, "we have no idea what this magic-altering thing is, or where it could be. How are we supposed to find it before we run out of time?"

The sheik turned to Turien. "Did your former master say anything else? Anything that would give us a clue where to begin our search?"

"He said those who survived the massacre took the device with them when they fled."

Cendim grunted and began pacing. "I was afraid of that." He wrung his hands, an uncharacteristic gesture of nervousness that set Mariq on edge. When he turned back to them, his eyes were shadowed and haunted. "My friends, I'm sorry. I should have anticipated this. Had I known where this would send us, I would have hesitated to bring you in at all."

Mariq looked at Cendim curiously, but beside her Turien gasped. "The Mad Desert?" he asked. He seemed as shaken as Mariq suddenly felt.

A chill went down Mariq's spine. The Mad Desert... no one went there voluntarily. Those few who came back were never quite the same again. "I've heard that place is haunted," she whispered.

"Not haunted," Cendim said. "Just overrun with magic."

Her face must have shown her confusion, because Cendim explained. "After the massacre in the Scorched Lands, the remaining magic-users had nowhere to flee except the deep desert. Over the generations such a concentration of magic-users has infused the desert with power. As empty as Kuriza is of magic, the Mad Desert is full to bursting with it. Magic in concentrations like that can affect people in… unexpected ways." He turned to Turien. "And if they have a device like your former master described, it would be even more overrun now. Dangerously so."

And we have to plunge headfirst into it? Mariq felt weak at the thought. Hatife had proven to her that magic wasn't evil, as Kuriza declared, but Cendim's tone regarding the effects of too much magic made the horror stories from her childhood feel a little too plausible.

Turien nodded solemnly. "If my old master doesn't already have people on the way to retrieve this device, they will leave soon. We have to get there first."

"Agreed. You must leave at once." He waved to a servant and began giving quiet, precise instructions.

"Are you sure sending us is still the best idea?" Mariq asked, gesturing to Turien and herself.

Cendim paused, looking at Mariq. "Who else could I send? No one is half as qualified for this as you are."

"But I'm hardly a spider-thief anymore, Cendim. I'll be worse than useless. I'll fail and put the entire mission at risk if I try to use my skills again. Send someone else."

"There is no one else, Mariq. We can't let it be known what the Star-Blades are up to. It'll cause panic, unplanned strikes. Chaos and anarchy will reign. And what will they do with it? Use that as an excuse. They'll tout this as the reason magic-users must be oppressed—they're dangerous, volatile people who need to be controlled." He paused, placing his hands on her shoulders and looking her in the eye. "Mariq, if that happens, the Star-Blades will get exactly what they're after. And all of Kuriza will rejoice for it."

"But there must be someone better suited than me! By the time we're ready for me to steal this thing I'll be no better than some beggar off the street!"

"I doubt that," Cendim said with a smile. "You're smart, capable, and even if your body fails, well-trained. You might lose the physical skills, but you have the experience. You have knowledge. And intellect will beat brawn any day."

He smiled at her, full of trust and fatherly love, and continued making plans as if she'd never objected. "Once in the Mad Desert, you'll need to find your way to Temhet-Sakh. Our scouts report it is a great city of magic. That would be the best place to begin your search." He paused, seeming reluctant to continue. "Take Ehra with you. She has navigated much of the deep desert before, and I have no doubt her skills will prove most valuable to you.

"Find whatever the Star-Blades intend to use and deal with it however you must. Retrieve it, destroy it, whatever needs to be done. I trust all three of you to judge what's best in this situation." He paused, the weight of his responsibility heavy in his voice. "I wish you better luck this time around. We're going to need it." Cendim turned back to the paper-littered table. "By the time you return, I fear Hatife will be at war."

Turien entered Cendim's alchemy lab, his heart pounding. He hadn't been this nervous about facing Cendim since his initial arrival in Hatife. "You asked for me?"

"Ah, Turien. I did," Cendim said. He had his back turned, so Turien couldn't see what he did with his hands. For some irrational reason, that made him even more nervous. He resisted the urge to flex his wrist, instead rubbing and scratching at the skin. The slave-band chafed in a way that had nothing to do with barbs and blood.

Cendim fiddled with whatever he worked on for a few more heartbeats, then turned to face him. He held five tiny vials filled with bright blue liquid. "Here. I've been preparing these for you."

Turien took the vials gingerly. They were so small he feared he'd break them. "What are they?"

"A special brew of my own making. It's a similar composition to

Joythief, surprisingly enough, except that… oh, never mind. You don't care about the details. What matters is that they will give you access to the powers of magic. For a short time."

Turien forgot to breathe. With magic at his beck and call, he would certainly be somebody. Perhaps even somebody enough to escape this life of No One. "I thought you said magic couldn't be implanted."

"I did. These won't give you magic. They'll just open the pathway for you to access it. It's the potion's magic doing all the work, using your body as an outlet. A fine differentiation, perhaps, but an important one."

Turien looked from the vials to Cendim. "Why?"

"The people of Temhet-Sakh revere magic as strongly as Kuriza despises it. There may come a time when you'll need the status of being a magic-user in order to proceed."

"Or we may get into a situation we can't find a way out of, and the magic might help."

Cendim nodded. "It might."

"How long will it last?" He found his eyes glued to the glowing vials.

"An hour, perhaps," Cendim replied. "I can't be sure, however, since I cannot test it myself."

"And once I have the power of magic? What happens to me?"

Cendim shrugged. "I cannot guess. The magic chooses how it interacts with a person. For some it amplifies the abilities they already possess, but for others it gives them a new persona. There's no way to know what you will become until you use one."

Turien glanced at the vials in his hand. He wanted to take one now, to taste the power of magic and find out what it would give him. Would he become like Cendim, and be able to make impossible potions? Perhaps he could develop an antidote for Mariq if that happened. Then again, the magic might make him a fighter, an assassin, a brawler. Or it could do something useless, like make him a musical savant or a genius chef.

Cendim placed a hand on his shoulder, drawing him out of his thoughts. They locked eyes. "Be careful with these, Turien. Only one vial per day. Any more, and the magic will consume your life-force. Remember that whatever you do while under the effects of the magic, you will still suffer the consequences afterwards." He paused, and his voice grew quieter. "I'm not sure if I'm giving you a blessing or a curse with these. But they're the best gift I can give."

"You said you made these for me," Turien said. "Why?"

"I already told you," Cendim replied.

"Not why. Why *me*?" Turien paused, brow furrowed. He placed the vials on the table before him. His eyes remained down, locked on his bare skin and the barbed slave-band wrapped through the hole in his forearm. "I'm a heritage-less slave, owned by those who would use me to destroy you. You had no reason to trust me, yet you do." He pulled his eyes from the slave-band and met Cendim's. "Because of you, I can never go back to life as I knew it. You've destroyed me with your kindness."

Cendim didn't answer. Instead he shuffled flasks and liquids around his table until he found what he was looking for: a knife. This he handed to Turien, handle out.

Turien accepted the blade, though he had no idea what Cendim expected him to do with it. "What is this for?"

"It's an opportunity for you to decide what to be, for yourself."

"I don't have a choice in that matter," Turien said flatly. His heart raced, though he didn't know why.

"Of course you have a choice, Turien. We always have a choice, even when it seems we don't." Cendim hesitated, then seeing Turien didn't understand, gestured toward the knife. "You are a man, Turien, and no man should be property."

Turien opened his mouth, but no sound came forth. Cendim couldn't be suggesting…

But he was. The sheik of Hatife watched him with gentle, sympathetic eyes—eyes glinting with defiance. Cendim dared him to do the single stupidest, most brash thing a slave could ever consider. An act that would brand him as a traitor, a deserter, a man to be killed for his insolence.

And Turien was considering it.

He stared at the knife and his slave-band. The sharp blade would slice through the thin wire easily. A quick tug, a moment to unwind the barbs from his forearm, and Turien would cast off his enslavement. He would declare himself free. And the Star-Blades wouldn't hesitate to kill him the moment they found out. If they were that generous. There were worse things than death for a man of his status. Or lack thereof.

"You said it yourself, Turien. The Star-Blades are no longer your masters. They hold no power over your thoughts or emotions. They should not hold power over your body."

Turien stared at the knife. He could start over. Build a life of his own. Follow his dreams.

The fluttering in his heart turned to a painful, speeding beat. His stomach clenched, his hands started to shake. So many options, so many decisions… and he hadn't the first glimmer of a clue where to begin. Who would he be? He didn't know. What would he do? He had no idea.

He'd become this man because he'd been ordered to. Everything he'd learned, everything he'd done, was at the command of the Star-Blades. Every piece of him had been crafted by his masters, given to him whether he liked it or not. It had never occurred to him to ask for anything else. He was No One, with no right to things like desires or dreams.

But Cendim offered him exactly that. Rights. Dreams. Choices.

Turien put down the knife.

It was too much. He couldn't handle that much responsibility. He couldn't build a life now, after a lifetime of mindless, unquestioning servitude. This was his identity. No One.

"I can't," he whispered.

Cendim picked up the knife, holding it out to him again. "You can."

Turien did not reach for the knife. He stared at it, held steady in Cendim's outstretched hand. The sheik was giving him everything he'd never dared to dream for.

He lifted his eyes to meet Cendim's. It took him a moment to form words. "My question still stands. Why me?"

Cendim sighed. "Is it so hard for you to believe you deserve to be free?"

Yes.

Cendim must have seen the answer in his expression, because he put the knife down next to the vials of blue, magic-gifting liquid. Close enough that Turien didn't even need to stretch to reach it. "I can't make this decision for you, my friend. But I can tell you it's one you should make for yourself."

With that, he skirted around the table and left the room.

Turien didn't move. He stood, arms at his sides, eyes locked on the vials and knife. Two gifts. One that might kill him, one that might give him more life than he'd ever imagined possible.

If only he could tell which was which.

The knife called to him. He reached out his hand, resting his fingers on the cool blade.

It might spell his death. But would it be worth it? Would a short time as his own man be worth the years he could lose?

Empty, miserable years. Turien had learned and experienced more in the few months he'd been here than in his entire life before that.

Started thinking of dreams, if not actually dreaming them.

Cendim had taught Turien how to live. Perhaps Turien should learn to accept those lessons.

He didn't allow himself any more time to think. To argue with himself. He scooped up the vials of magic-gifting potion and tucked them into a hidden pouch on his belt. Then he grasped the knife's handle in his left hand, feeling awkward, and raised it to his right.

The slave-band stared at him, encircling his wrist, twined between the bones in his forearm. A mass of scar tissue surrounded it, thousands upon thousands of miniscule cuts. A lifetime of flexing and slicing, daily reminders of his place in the world. Of his role as No One.

No more.

Turien slid the blade between the band and his flesh. He didn't care that he cut the skin. He didn't care how badly it would hurt. He just knew he had to get it off.

The barbs dug into his muscles as he tugged on the band. Shots of lightning-sharp pain jolted up his arm from the hole between his bones. That hole would never close, would never stop hurting. He didn't care. It would be better than having the barbs of his slave-band threading through it.

He pulled the blade against the band, gritting his teeth against the pain. Blood dribbled down his arm, dripping onto the floor. Turien didn't cry out. It would hurt to be free, but far less than it hurt to be a slave.

The slave-band snapped with a *twang* and Turien stumbled from the sudden release of pressure. He dropped the knife and pulled at the wire, sucking in a breath as the barbs sliced their way out of the hole. He let the bloody slave-band fall to the floor. He stared at it. Then he crushed it beneath his boot.

He'd done it.

He was free.

He fell to his knees and vomited.

DESPITE Mariq's exhaustion, her doubt, and her lingering sense of failure, the next sunrise found her, Turien, and Ehra mounted atop a trio of Cendim's sturdiest camels. Horses would have been faster, but they needed hardier mounts to survive the harsh conditions that awaited them. Mariq didn't mind. Something about the camels' stoic nonchalance and stubbornness felt comforting for a journey into the Mad Desert.

She still couldn't believe that's where they were headed. She'd say they were mad for even considering it, but if rumors were true, the real madness waited farther east. That did not bode well for any of them.

Then again, none of them were in the best condition to begin with. Turien had arrived with a bloodied bandage where his slave-band should have been. She'd known, without having to ask, that no barbed wire hid under the bandage. Turien had done the most daring, foolhardy thing a slave could do. He didn't look like he quite knew how he felt about it. He kept clenching his fist, flexing his wrist, then looking surprised and squeamish when it didn't cut his skin. A moment of pride and excitement would flash across his face, only to be replaced with sullen horror. The poor man looked more lost than Mariq had ever seen him.

Ehra had retreated even further into herself, speaking only when spoken to and sometimes not even then. No hint of the vivacious energy in her eyes remained, little more than hollow sadness left in its place. She kept her camel away from Mariq and Turien, offering to scout ahead and forage for additional supplies, even volunteering for watch duty that night. Anything to put distance between her and her companions. Mariq wished she could talk to her, maybe find some way to help, but Ehra wouldn't even let a conversation get started. It broke her heart, but she could do nothing to help her friend.

And as for her…

The Joythief continued its work. The cut had nearly healed, but she could feel the poison's icy touch whenever she tried to utilize her skills. Sometimes it would let her function as if nothing had happened. Other times it made her feel as if she'd never held a knife in her life. Out here, that unreliability would be worse than having no skills at all. If she knew she couldn't fight she could run or hide. If she thought she *could* fight, though, and it turned out she couldn't, she would be dooming them all.

And they would encounter a threat sooner or later. This desert might be barren, even by a desert's standards, but that didn't mean they were alone out here. Rattlesnakes, jackals, scorpions, hawks… and maybe more. Perhaps it was the rumors of this place playing with her imagination. Perhaps it was her anxiety over the Joythief, or a simple matter of a body and mind exhausted by a flurry of events. But she swore some other danger awaited them here, something even worse than the normal desert vipers.

Less than half a day from Hatife, and Mariq already felt the Mad Desert growing stronger around her. Growing more *alive* around her. Her eyes saw nothing but dune after dune of powder-fine sand, heat shimmering above the horizon, but she felt the desert brimming with… not sentience, but life nonetheless. This desert wished to consume them. If they stayed here long enough, it would devour them.

Less than half a day. And Cendim had said their destination, the great city of Temhet-Sakh, was two weeks' travel into the desert? Deep in the throes of magic, while this little spit of desert barely dipped its toe in the current?

The thought sent cold shivers down her spine and turned her bowels to water. Now Mariq understood why people who entered the Mad Desert were never quite the same again.

Is that why Ehra looked so distressed? Why she pulled away from her friends, as if even the thought of conversation was too much to bear?

What price had the Mad Desert exacted from her the first time she'd come here?

Mariq spurred her camel forward, receiving an angry bellow in return, to catch up with Ehra. "Can I ask you something?"

Ehra glanced at her, hesitating for half a heartbeat. "Sure."

"Your father said you'd traveled here before."

She nodded. "It was... a sort of pilgrimage, I guess."

Pilgrimage. Mariq had never thought to ask, but now it made sense. Her father had magic, after all, and he'd said her skills would be useful. Mariq had a feeling he meant more than just fighting or tracking. "You're a magic-user, aren't you, Ehra?"

Ehra's face fell. "Yes," she whispered, shame and pain and longing in her voice.

"What does your magic give you?"

She clamped her mouth shut, eyes staring far into the desert. After several long, uncomfortable moments Ehra whispered, "It turns me into a monster."

Mariq's stomach twisted at the haunted look in Ehra's eyes. Whatever her magic did, Mariq was glad she didn't have to bear it. From Ehra's reaction and deep sadness, she wasn't sure she *could* have borne it. "I'm sorry," she said, at a loss for anything better to say.

Ehra's silence felt heavy as a funeral shroud. Mariq knew better than to press for any more explanations.

"Why does this place feel so... hungry?" Mariq asked. She hadn't intended to ask such an ominous question—she'd only wanted to try pulling Ehra from her misery—but her own spinning fears had pushed it out before she could stop it.

Ehra's eyes scanned the desert, not focusing on anything specific in order to see as much as possible. Her shoulders were tense, ready for battle. "There are… *things* in the open desert. Some of them used to be men, but the deep magic has changed them."

"Changed?" Turien asked. Mariq hadn't noticed him ride up beside them, but she was glad he'd come. This didn't seem like a conversation she'd be eager to repeat.

"Magic emphasizes a person's most fundamental nature. A person who can use magic finds their deepest passions, desires, or most driving needs are enhanced by it. My father loves alchemy more than almost anything—and his magic responds to it, gifting him with the power to make impossible potions."

She paused, looking around at the desert once more. "Out here, though, the entire desert is saturated with magic. It flows too freely, and anything that spends time here drowns in it. It begins to change them, bringing out their basic natures. For some, that is a gift—intelligent people become geniuses, creative people become savants."

"Cendim told me it can give people different personas," Turien said.

"Different personas than what they show the world, perhaps," Ehra said, her tone sad and brimming with the kind of depth that came from personal experience. "Just because a person is kind and gentle doesn't mean they don't have a brute inside them. It just means they're hiding who they really are."

Turien nodded, and Mariq sensed depth in his motion as intimate as Ehra's had been. "So intelligent people become geniuses and kind people become saints. But if a person's fundamental nature is more primal…" Turien's voice trailed off as he shivered.

Ehra nodded. "People like that are overrun by those desires. Those who desire control, power, sex, lose their humanity. They become animals, predators, hunting for anything to sate those primal natures."

Now Mariq found herself watching the sands, too. Her fears

regarding the desert and its consuming hunger felt too imminent, too oppressive. Too *real*.

"So these…" Mariq trailed off.

"Beastmen. As a group we call them the Feral."

Mariq nodded. "The Feral… are we in danger from them?"

Ehra's eyes remained locked on the desert. "Yes."

"What do we do?" Turien asked.

"There isn't much we can do," Ehra said. "Stay alert, watch for danger, keep moving."

"And don't go mad," Mariq whispered.

Somehow, Mariq felt her odds on that weren't so good.

ariq had long since lost track of how many days they'd passed in this place. Ten? Twelve? The first day alone had felt like weeks, and each day after that had been worse. She no longer smelled the stink of camels or felt the sand abrade her skin. Nor did she acknowledge the dancing mirages anymore. Nothing existed out here— no puddles of reflective water, no domes rising from the dunes. There was only sand and heat and misery, and any reprieve she saw from the corner of her eye was bound to be nothing but a disappointment.

Except for the Feral hounding their heels. Those, sadly, were no mirage. Ehra had first spotted them on their fifth day in the Mad Desert, and they'd rarely been out of sight since. The all-too-real threat kept their distance, but watched them pass with predatory intensity. Never wavering. Never losing sight of them. Just following, and watching, and waiting. It made Mariq nervous. Being stalked grated on her sanity far more than the deep magic they traveled through.

And the magic wasn't easily ignored, either. It was a subtle irritant on her subconscious—like a gnat buzzing around her ear. She could feel it suffusing her, soaking into her essence like oil into skin. She hadn't noticed any significant change to her actions or thoughts—and they had all been watching each other like hawks, just in case—but the feeling wouldn't pass. What would it do to her? The Joythief had already changed her once. If the deep magic tried to change her again, would she even recognize herself anymore?

Too many thoughts swirled through her mind. Too many changes, too much unknown. Mariq wished for solace more than anything, for peace and rest, but she knew none of that would come while they lingered in the Mad Desert.

Another mirage shimmered into existence before them, a wavering grove of glistening minarets. Mariq hardly took notice. The deep magic was making the mirages more and more strange the farther they ventured from Hatife.

But this mirage wasn't passing.

Mariq blinked and rubbed her eyes. Usually the mirages only lasted a few seconds. Clear the vision, change perspective, and they evaporated like rain in the depths of the desert. Yet there they stood, dozens of minarets against the far horizon, looking as ethereal as everything else Mariq had glimpsed these past days.

She glanced to Turien, then to Ehra. Both had their eyes locked on the same spot.

She returned her gaze to the minarets. They wavered in the ambient heat, tall sinuous spires that shone like crystal rather than sand or stone. They looked unnatural, somehow, as if they defied the very laws of physics. Nothing that thin, that delicate, could possibly stand so tall. Could they?

"That isn't a mirage," Ehra whispered. "That's a city. A real city."

"Is that Temhet-Sakh?" Turien asked.

"It must be," Ehra replied.

"How could people have built something like that?" Mariq said, reverence in her voice she hadn't purposely put there.

"Maybe they didn't," Turien said. "Maybe it's a natural structure, and they just adapted it?" He clearly wasn't convinced of his theory any more than the others were.

"However they did it, it's beautiful," Ehra said. Her voice was wistful, her eyes wide with wonder.

They must have stood still, transfixed, for longer than any of them knew. When Mariq was finally able to tear her sight from the spires, movement across the dunes caught her attention. Or had the movement itself been what had snapped her back to her senses? Her training, today, seemed to still be present after all.

She didn't unsheathe her knives, but she did reach down to feel their reassuring weight on her thighs as she scanned the horizon. There, on the left—a dark line of men, galloping toward them with inhuman motions. "Feral incoming."

Turien leaned forward. "They aren't just stalking anymore. That's an attack."

All of them stiffened. Mariq saw Ehra look toward the Feral, then back to the city. She knew what her friend was thinking. They would never reach the safety of Temhet-Sakh before the beastmen were upon them.

As one they spurred their camels forward. What choice did they have? Mariq didn't have to be told being caught by the Feral would be worse than death.

They raced toward the shimmering spires of Temhet-Sakh as the beastmen charged. Horrible, half-human war cries followed them. Terror drove Mariq forward, her belly hollow and icy with dread. She pulled out a knife, trying to seat it properly in her hand. Did she still have the skill to throw it with any sort of accuracy?

A sharpened bone flew overhead and embedded itself in the sand just behind Turien's camel. It snorted and bellowed and shot forward with more speed than Mariq had thought a camel could muster. Several more crude arrows followed, their narrow misses setting Mariq's heart racing. Losing their humanity had not affected the Ferals' aim.

Mariq's head whipped to her right as she heard a cry. Were there Feral on that side as well? Had they been surrounded? Sweat greased her already loose grip on the knife. Her other hand, on the reins, clenched so tightly her knuckles shone white.

Mariq could almost see the gates of Temhet-Sakh now. She prayed they would be open.

She glanced left. The beastmen were close, far too close for comfort. Mariq could see crazed, bloodshot eyes and lines of frothy saliva on disturbingly human faces—the only lingering sign of their origins. Nothing else about these Feral hinted at a trace of humanity left.

A shout ahead drew her attention. The gates of Temhet-Sakh opened and men poured out, the sun reflecting off polished armor and bared weapons. They approached fast, but not fast enough. The beastmen were almost upon them.

Mariq looked to the right. The people there grew closer as well, nearly in time with the beastmen. She still couldn't tell who they were, though—she could make out little more than moving spots on the sand. Friend or foe? She had no idea. But she did know those ahead were human, coming to their rescue, and Mariq spurred her camel faster toward the sanctuary of the city. The guards had almost reached them.

The Feral made it first.

A huge beastman—close to seven feet if he stood upright—leaped straight for Ehra's camel, a massive bone spear ready to plunge through its neck. She dodged, and the beastman tumbled through the sand before bouncing back to his feet and swiping at the legs of Mariq's camel.

His weapon struck home. Her camel bellowed, a heart-wrenching sound, and crashed to the ground. Mariq flew free at the last moment, landing hard against the sunbaked sand. Dizzy, aching, yet knowing to lay still was a death sentence, Mariq scrambled to her feet. Her knife had been lost in the fall. She unsheathed her other knife as she settled into a fighting stance.

The massive beastman loomed over her. His shoulders were more than twice the width of Mariq's, and each leg was as big around as her waist. Compared to his six-foot-long spear—she didn't want to think about the kind of animal a bone like that had come from—her tiny knife might as well be the stinger of a bee.

The beastman didn't wait. He swung a two-handed overhead chop down at her, all predatory instinct and no grace. She rolled out of reach. She could never parry a blow with so much strength behind it, and a single hit from that bone would finish her off.

She kept moving backward as the sound of hoofbeats grew in her ears. A heartbeat later one of the Temhet-Sakh guards came up behind the beastman. One strike from the guards' sword and the beastman staggered. He turned away from Mariq, showing her a line of blood across his shoulder blades. It enraged him enough he left the easy prey behind and chased after the guard.

Chaos consumed the desert, making it hard for Mariq to keep track of details. The battle broke itself into dozens of small fights, two or three opponents engaged together, melding and breaking apart as they wove in and out of each other. Being the only person on foot, a single knife to defend herself with, made her both impotent and vulnerable. She had to get free of the crushing hooves and swinging swords. She had to find a way to get herself and her friends to safety.

If she could find her friends in this melee.

Mariq dodged through the battle, one frenzied step at a time. It was like dancing with a drunken partner—she never knew which way to go next, stepping to one side only to dash back the other way before her weight had even settled. In this mad scramble, one wrong move would cost her life.

All around her people screamed, weapons clashed, bodies fell from horses and camels. The sand drank copious amounts of blood faster than she would have believed. The liquid made it sticky and crunchy, clinging to her shoes with each step.

The terrible hunger of the desert's magic seemed to grow with each drop spilled.

Mariq could see the gates of Temhet-Sakh, open and inviting, just a brief run away. They promised safety, sanctuary. She had to get there, to help her friends make it.

Something hard and sharp slammed into Mariq's side. Her breath was stolen from her before she could even cry out. Time stopped as she stumbled to a halt, hand grasping at the bone spear that had impaled her side. No. It couldn't end like this. Her friends, her entire world, were still in danger.

She fell to her knees as her vision went black.

THE confusion of battle made Ehra's thoughts heady and full of fog. The fight unfolded as if in a dream. In moments like these, she felt so alive she never wanted it to end.

But that was the monster talking.

Mariq fell, a spear thrust deep into her side. Hot, red blood gushed from the wound, with a hint of black tar seeping through. Her kidney had been punctured. An agonizing, and mortal, wound.

Ehra raced to her side. She leapt from her camel at full speed, rolling as she landed. Sand flew from her skid, showering Mariq and peppering her wound. Ehra didn't let that worry her. She just tried to keep her eyes from the red, red blood pulsing with life and soaking the hot sand under her knees.

Ehra looked down at her friend and felt her vitality slipping away. It wouldn't be long. Her life was weak, a bare mist of spirit clinging to the body. In just a moment, it would be lost. Unless Ehra took hold of it…

No. She could not let her monster take over. Ehra struggled to silence it.

But this was Mariq, her friend. And she was dying.

Ehra had to do something.

Another wounded lay close by. Blood covered his face so thoroughly she couldn't distinguish any of his features. He looked like a corpse already, except for the barest hint of breath moving his chest. His life force hung above him, holding onto its body by the thinnest of tendrils. No matter what happened, this man would die.

Cringing, tears for Mariq and herself streaming down her face, Ehra answered the call of the monster.

She reached out to the man's life force, grasping the misty threads in her hand. They were soft and warm against her skin, the strength and power of life itself making her woozy. She could feel it seeping into her, infusing her blood with new life. For a moment Ehra was invincible, all-powerful, stronger and faster and better than any human in the world. She could conquer kingdoms with a smile and erase them from existence with a swipe of her hand. It was an intoxicating, carnal pleasure, and one Ehra longed for with every fiber of her being.

To give it up would be excruciating. It might as well kill her.

She turned her eyes back to the woman. Her life was as weak as the man's she'd just taken. Ehra could take that one, too, and become more than superhuman. She could become a goddess.

But her magic had a different purpose. It gave her the power to heal, to mend body and life and magic. That this miraculous gift required a sacrifice—she couldn't create magic from nothing, after all—was bad enough. Hoarding the power for herself would be inexcusable. It would be nothing short of murder to take someone's life and not restore another's.

Ehra pushed the monster aside, forcing her way back into control. The monster didn't give in easily, but Ehra had a lot of practice shutting her up.

She took the life in her hand, praying the man would forgive her, and mingled it with Mariq's misty spirit. She merged the two together, coaxing the new life into Mariq's body. Once enough of the power had been fed into her Ehra reached down and yanked the spear from her side. More blood gushed out, but not as much as one might have expected. Mariq howled and cried out, but then the pain and fear faded into silence and relief.

The blood beneath Ehra's knees had already begun to cool. There were no more wounds to continue its flow onto the sand. Mariq moaned, weak but very much alive.

The sounds of battle had stopped, but Ehra only now noticed. She heard the suffocating silence of a hundred breaths held, felt the burden of a hundred gazes locked on her.

Scuffled footsteps approached, and Turien threw himself to his knees before her. His eyes locked on Mariq, his expression twisted by anguish. The relief when he saw her living overwhelmed Ehra and lightened the darkness in her heart.

Then he looked at her, and her heart grew cold and dark once more.

She knew what he'd see. Ehra kneeling in a pool of blood, her hands covered in it to the elbow. A dead man to one side, a pale and impossibly alive Mariq on the other.

Ehra turned her eyes down, unable to meet the awe and horror she knew she'd see in her companion's face. He would be grateful she'd saved Mariq's life, of course, but how could he not also be horrified that she'd taken another man's life to do so?

Sometimes she still couldn't tell the difference between a miracle and a monster.

THE Temhet-Sakh guards cleared away the last of the Feral and exchanged a few angry words with the third group, but Turien didn't pay much attention to them. He dedicated his focus to Mariq and Ehra, his thoughts spinning as he tried to make sense of what he'd just witnessed.

Mariq had been dead or close to it. He'd seen plenty of mortal wounds in his days serving the Star-Blades. He knew what corpses looked like. Mariq had the same waxy skin, the same flat eyes.

Ehra had done... something. He still couldn't wrap his mind around it. But then Mariq was alive, with no sign of the injury that had stolen her life heartbeats ago. And the man beside them both was quite suddenly dead.

He'd known magic existed, had grasped it had immense power, but he'd never expected anything like *this*.

Several guards started herding them away from the battlefield toward Temhet-Sakh. One lifted Mariq, unconscious but breathing steadily, and carried her away. Turien scrambled to his feet to follow. Something about the way he held her, more like a diseased corpse than an injured woman, made him wary.

Another guard prodded him in the back. "Let's go." He had a strange accent, clipped and short unlike any Turien had heard before.

Turien glanced back, but the guard kept his eyes on the gates of Temhet-Sakh.

He tried to catch Ehra's eye, but yet another guard—this one huge and wearing a more elaborate uniform, with heritage tattoos that screamed of his importance—helped her to her feet. She didn't even reach to his shoulder, and his arms encompassed her body wholly. His motions were tender and caring, but possessive in the way he kept his arm around her waist to support her and ugly lust in his eyes. Turien clenched his fists. He'd seen men like this far too often amongst the Star-Blades: men who were bigger and stronger than the rest and wielded it like a weapon. Whenever they saw something they liked they claimed it as their own, daring anyone to stop them.

His steps had slowed as he watched the guard guide Ehra away. The guard behind him gave him another shove forward.

Can they sense we don't have magic? Cendim had said they revered magic as strongly as Kuriza despised it. Is that why they're treating us this way while Ehra is escorted like a queen?

His hand inched toward his belt, where the vials Cendim had given him still rested in their hidden pouch. If he could drink one of those, it would give him access to magic. Would it be enough to convince these guards to treat them well? But he couldn't drink one of the potions without the guards noticing. And Mariq… he couldn't get close to her, let alone force a glowing blue potion down her throat without the guards taking note. That would only make their situation worse.

Turien forced his hand away from the pouch.

He had grown up in Kuriza and spent the last year in Hatife, the two richest and grandest kingdoms in the Scorched Lands. Temhet-Sakh, however, dwarfed them both with its gates alone. Tall enough for the largest of war elephants, they were half a man's height thick and almost perfectly clear. Rather than impressing a visitor with huge contraptions of metal and jewels, this astounded with its simplicity. It spoke of confidence and power in abundance—*we don't have to follow the other leaders' examples. We'll simply do the impossible and let it speak for itself.*

An equally elegant courtyard greeted them inside the gates. Paving stones and walls melded with the surrounding desert, sleek and smooth as glass. A few hardy desert plants were arranged in tasteful patterns, a hint at prosperity without screaming of greed or gaudiness. If the people had been half as pleasing as the architecture, Turien might have felt at ease.

The guards fanned out as they entered the gates, subtly blocking their exit as well as further entrance to the city. The huge guard stood in the middle beside them, an arm still around Ehra's waist. She didn't seem to notice—her eyes were huge, her mouth open as she looked at the beauty of Temhet-Sakh.

Mariq was half-dropped to the ground beside Turien. He glared at the guard, but the man didn't look back as he took a place among the others.

The huge man stared at Mariq and Turien for several heartbeats, a deep scowl in his face. "What are you doing here?" he asked, a clear accusation in the question.

"You brought us here," Turien replied. He didn't dare say more. The man's gaze had turned dark, the same way his master's voice had before he pulled a weapon.

"We would never allow a magic-user to fall to the Feral," he said. His hand tightened on Ehra's waist. "Those without magic, however, rarely come to our gates. You do not belong here."

Strong hands clamped onto Turien's biceps, holding him far more tightly than required.

The man looked back to Ehra. His voice grew gentle when he

spoke to her. "You are magic. You are welcome inside these walls." He turned away, pulling Ehra around with him.

She hesitated, her head swiveling to look back at Turien. "What about my friends?"

"Don't worry yourself about them," the guard said, his tone equating "them" with vermin or an infectious disease. He tightened his arm around Ehra, turning her until she had no choice but to look away. "They are not worthy of a magic-user's attentions."

He turned a corner, pulling Ehra out of Turien's sight. A moment later everything else disappeared as a bag was shoved over his head and punches rained down on him.

15

Gherrim had rarely, if ever, welcomed such a beauty to Temhet-Sakh. Sojourners were rare, more so now than in the past, but often those who made it to the crystal gates were worn and dirty and hardly acceptable for their pristine streets. But the woman beside him, tattoos speaking of wealth and status, body petite and beautiful as magic itself, was the kind of person Gherrim loved to escort into Temhet-Sakh.

And speaking of magic…

He'd seen her display of power during the battle, had felt the magic wash over the desert as she'd saved that woman's life. While he couldn't approve of her choice in companions, the magic she'd exerted had set his entire body alight. Even being this close to her was like standing in sunshine, like the skilled hands of a woman soothing sore muscles.

He inhaled, not smelling with his nose but with his magic. He'd long since come to rely on this skill. Magic never lied, after all. Magic was true. Pure in a way nothing of this world could be.

The magic wafting from this tiny woman belonged to a titan. It made Gherrim's heart pound. Power. Strength. Pure, potent magic the likes of which he'd only felt once in his life.

The kind of magic one did not relinquish easily.

"Don't hurt them."

Gherrim glanced down at her. It took him a moment to realize she referred to the others she'd arrived with. Those without magic. "I told you not to worry about it."

"They're my *friends*. Maybe you don't understand what that word means?"

Gherrim smirked. The small ones were always the fiercest. "I understand well enough. But their fate is out of your control now. You've already done enough by saving the woman's life."

He felt her tense, trying to draw away from him. He kept his hand on her waist, guiding her, keeping her near. Close enough to touch. Close enough her magic washed over him like perfume, delicious and invigorating.

"You're in Temhet-Sakh now, greatest city in the world. Here your magic will find a home more suited to someone as powerful, and lovely, as yourself." He flexed his fingers, soft fabric and curves beneath his touch.

She squirmed and broke free of his grasp, pausing to glance around like an animal ready to bolt. The guards surrounding them deterred her and kept her close. "Where are you taking me?"

"All new magic-users who arrive in Temhet-Sakh are brought to the sultan," Gherrim replied. "So few make it through the Feral and raiders to reach the safety of our gates. He likes to welcome them in person, in order to place them quickly."

Before she could say anything else they reached one of the massive city squares. Gherrim watched her as she gasped, stopping in the middle of the street. Temhet-Sakh had that effect on newcomers, and Gherrim never tired of it.

Temhet-Sakh was a wonder. Streets like molten glass, buildings rising seamlessly from them in all colors of the desert. Cactus flowers, brilliant in their shapes and shades, bloomed from planters at every corner. Clear water trickled through irrigation troughs. And through it all magic thrummed, tantalizing.

Magic filled everything here. Everyone. Most peoples' power prickled against his senses, a faint scent amongst thousands of others. Stepping into a crowd like the one gathered in the square was a caress, a lover's kiss.

He put his arm around the woman beside him again. Her magic thrummed stronger than all of these commoners' combined. Gherrim couldn't find words for it. Consuming. Intoxicating. Pleasure incarnate, life itself.

She didn't stir as he sidled close to her. She stared into the square, awe clear in her features. Gherrim grinned as she closed her eyes and breathed. He felt her skin prickle just like his did in the presence of such magic.

"You can feel it," he said. "The magic calls to you, does it not?"

"Yes," she whispered.

"How does it feel?"

She took another breath, eyes still closed. "Wonderful." Her voice sounded as full of pleasure as he felt. Magic did that to those with strong power.

Yes, this woman would be right at home in Temhet-Sakh. Gherrim would make sure of that.

EHRA could hardly believe what her eyes showed her. The impeccably clean streets reflected golden light from the sky above. The buildings on either side towered over them without blocking the blueness of the sky or the brightness of the sun. They shimmered with subtle colors as she walked past, orange and rose and purple like a sunset. Each building was distinct, with unique architecture and color palettes, yet blending together like an artist's dream. Ehra felt as if she walked through the very heart of the desert—the beauty, heat, and grace all molded into physical form.

People milled through the area, laughing and talking without a care in the world. Their heritage tattoos varied in style, extent, and even color—magic clearly ran through many of them. Competitions were held in the streets, people played with their powers as if it were a game. Couples lounged about in various stages of passion. Plenty of guards lingered around, but even they seemed more inclined to indulgence than maintaining order. Ehra didn't know whether to avert her eyes or drink it all in.

And magic coursed through it all—a river of power, a heartbeat pulsing through the city. A lover's touch caressing her. Begging to be used. If blood didn't still cover Ehra's hands, a gruesome reminder of the price of her monster, she might not have been able to resist.

The guard moved closer to her, his arm brushing hers. His tattoos were extensive almost to the point of royalty, varying in shades from deep navy to bright sky blue. Threads she couldn't read intertwined in the pattern: along with birth and rank, it held hints of his place within the structure of magic.

He noticed her attention and spoke, gesturing slightly at her tattoos and then his own. "This city was made for people like us. It is an extension of us, and we of it. Here we are home like we have never been anywhere else. People like us belong here." He paused, ever so slightly. "Together."

Ehra's instinct told her to recoil. She'd seen the way he treated Mariq and Turien, and his arm around her felt more controlling than welcoming. Even now he pulled her through the streets, dictating her moves, not allowing her to slow or detour. She should push him away before he got the idea she accepted his advances. But each time their skin touched she could feel his magic. Each spark sent a little jolt of pure joy through her, the same kind of exhilaration she felt when she embraced her monster and used her magic. Yet his touch was harmless. It didn't destroy anything. It didn't take anyone's life from them.

Most magic-users could experience this every day of their lives. They could sit in a marketplace, embroidering with their family, and revel in the magic. It was a right of every magic-user, and Ehra's monster had denied it to her.

She could endure this man's control for a moment longer, if it meant she could enjoy his magic. Just another moment.

They walked in silence while Ehra drank in the beauty of the city and the intoxicating power pulsing from the buildings. They passed a market full to bursting with goods and groups of children playing in the streets, open doorways advertising every kind of pleasure imaginable and some Ehra had never before dreamed of. With each step deeper into Temhet-Sakh, the magic grew stronger until she couldn't take a breath without feeling power tingle down to her toes.

Focus. Remember why you're here. Mariq and Turien need you. Father needs you.

Ehra struggled to grab hold of her thoughts, focusing on details and what few plans she had to keep from losing herself to the magic. She looked back to the guard. "You said something about the sultan placing new magic-users."

He nodded. "Temhet-Sakh is a city of magic. Everyone who enjoys her benefits must contribute to her upkeep. It would be worthless to put a mage somewhere their skills cannot be used. Everyone's magic must be used to its fullest potential in order to maintain our beautiful Temhet-Sakh."

Ehra looked around at the glass-like walls. "So everything is constructed with magic?"

"Of course," he replied, seeming confused by her shock. "Magic is not a tool, like the shovels or axes used by those without magic. Magic is a servant, at the beck and call of those powerful enough to control it. Why should we not allow it to work for us?"

"Don't you worry about balance?" Ehra asked. "Using this much magic all the time is dangerous, isn't it?" Snippets of conversations raced through her mind, magic and non-magic tearing the world apart, but so much power fizzing in her blood made it hard to think straight.

The guard laughed. "Magic is an eager beast. You'll see. It leaps to our command. It wants to be used. How can there be harm in giving it what it wants?"

His tone spoke of several meanings to that innocuous question, but Ehra ignored it. Her thoughts felt foggy from the intense magic, her reactions sluggish. She could feel it around her, in her, longing for her to command it.

That's because there's too much here. The balance is off. This is what we have to fix.

The sultan's palace was a marvel of artistry and magic. Warm orangey-pink stone, polished like glass, rose effortlessly from the ground. Streaks of purple and blue like sunset and sky swirled up the walls in enchanting, mysterious patterns. It stunned with its simplicity and inspired awe more than any building Ehra had ever seen before—even her father's immaculate palace in Hatife.

The interior walls held the same colors as the outside, but sunlight shone through them to make them glow. Desert flowers bloomed from miniature oases sprinkled throughout the palace. The place didn't scream of wealth, it whispered of elegance and sophistication. Ehra felt as if the most precious aspects of the desert's beauty had been encapsulated just for her.

She was so astounded by the palace she didn't realize she'd already been brought to the sultan. He was a young man, no more than a decade older than Ehra, not handsome but not ugly, either. Plain in a way rulers seldom were—except for his heritage tattoos. They glowed—literally *glowed*—in every shade the desert could conjure, crawling from the tips of his fingers up his arm, the side of his neck and face, and disappearing into his hairline. The mysterious threads tantalized her, pulsing with magic and secrets she couldn't unravel.

"Good afternoon, Gherrim," the sultan said to the guard. "What do you have for me?"

"We met a group of sojourners outside the gates, majesty. This young lady was among them."

He pushed his hand gently on her lower back, urging her to step forward. She did so and bowed to the sultan, low enough to show respect but not so low as to designate her one of his subjects. She was royalty herself, after all, not even half a step below this man's power.

The sultan stared at her, not cruelly but most definitely calculating. He seemed to be evaluating her worth, eyes darting from her face to her heritage tattoos to her very soul, it seemed. Ehra's confidence fled under that stare and her gaze fell to the floor. She didn't like her odds of being found worthwhile, especially in the eyes of such great magic-users.

After an uncomfortable moment, he smiled at her. "What brings you to our sanctuary, Lady…?"

"Ehra," she answered. "Ehra Zahra, Princess of Hatife."

"You honor us, my lady."

"Hardly," Ehra muttered.

"What brings a princess here? Do you act as an emissary from Hatife?" Ehra couldn't ignore the twinge of nervousness in the question.

Ehra clawed her way out of the heady magic, grasping at the thoughts flitting through her mind. Strain on the magic. Star-Blades' plans. The device they so desperately needed to retrieve. "I am here on my father's business, but not in an official capacity. It's a personal matter."

"Not so personal it cannot be shared, I hope?"

Ehra paused. How much should she tell this man? He ruled this city, so if anyone would know where to find the device it would be him. But if it was as powerful as rumors said, it would be beyond precious to Temhet-Sakh. To walk in and demand its location would make them guard it closer, and then their work would be exponentially more difficult. Better to glean hints than scare away all answers. "Temhet-Sakh's power is renowned even in Hatife. Magic is an academic interest of my father's, and he wishes to learn more of it."

"Ah, yes. We do indeed have quite the store of magic here. I'm sure we can arrange for some tutelage."

Ehra nodded in thanks. Not a bad place to start. Besides, the prospect of learning more of magic, of practicing it, made her guts squirm with longing.

"What can I do for you in the meantime, my lady?" the sultan asked.

"My friends," Ehra replied. "They were taken as soon as we entered the city. It seemed to be under… less than ideal circumstances."

The sultan's eyes flicked to Gherrim. When they returned to Ehra, she could see he already knew all he wanted to know of the situation. "My guards are trained to protect this city from all threats. And here, that includes more than simple bandits or thieves."

"I don't understand," Ehra said. "My friends aren't a threat to your people."

"They are not magic-users, correct?"

Ehra paused, her heart racing, before shaking her head.

"Temhet-Sakh is a city of magic. Those who cannot use magic are vagabonds. They become leeches on our society. Eventually they become bitter, useless, and angry. Violence follows. It's better for all if they are kept from our city." Ehra opened her mouth to argue, but the sultan continued before she could speak. "I promise you they will be treated with all the respect they deserve."

Ehra didn't like the sound of that, but she could tell nothing would change his mind. Pushing too hard would make people suspicious of her, make it more difficult to find Mariq and Turien. Ehra had better ways of learning things she wasn't meant to know. As much as she hated to leave them any longer than necessary, Ehra accepted the sultan's answers with a silent nod.

Magic brushed her skin, whispered in her ear. Begged to be used.

"However… you, Ehra, are a very powerful magic-user. Your magic beats through this place more strongly than any I've seen in years. You would be most welcome in my court, princess."

A place in the sultan's court. Ehra knew better than most the best place to gather information was among those seeking favor from the powerful. She could never refuse an opportunity like that.

Besides, the magic here was so… Ehra couldn't even find a word for it. The magic here was everything.

She met the sultan's eyes. They seemed to bore right through her, seeing everything she'd ever tried to hide from the world.

"You would find Temhet-Sakh to be a most accepting community. No one can understand a magic-user like another magic-user. Out there, we are feared and misunderstood. Often ignored, even more often unloved. Here, you would find a home."

She had a home, in Hatife, and a father who loved her. He'd never been anything but good to her. But to have a home within the magic…

Of course, if she stayed the magic would consume her. It would eat at her until she couldn't control it, and then she would use it. And she could never allow herself to do that. No matter how much she wanted to.

"No," the sultan said, understanding dawning in his eyes, "it isn't love or acceptance or appreciation you crave. You already have that, while most who come here don't. What you crave is purpose."

She nodded without even realizing it.

"You have talents and passions you can do nothing about in the non-magic world. But these talents are a part of you, and denying them is denying the truth of who you are." He leaned closer, so close Ehra could barely focus on his face. "I can help you. I can give you a purpose and let you use your magic to be who you really are."

Ehra's voice was as fragile as glass—as fragile as her hope. "How? When I use my magic I become a monster. It's too easy to hurt people instead of help them."

"Do you believe you're the first to come to me with a dangerous power? My dear, there are thousands of individuals in this city, each with their own unique gift. Not everything can be harmless. In fact, I find those who are most useful are those with the more dangerous gifts. A person who can create a flame from an empty oil lamp is both economical and prudent. But a person who can incinerate a building with a gaze can heat boilers for an entire city, defend their home from attack, and much more. Their power makes them dangerous, yes, but danger and power often come hand-in-hand. And great power makes for great purpose."

Ehra's heart raced. She couldn't control the trembling in her body. Could it be true?

The sultan grinned. "You didn't realize those who recognize that spark in you will use it, did you? That we will fan it until it is more than a simple spark, but a flame one cannot ignore? I see your potential and I intend to make it blossom. That is what it means to be in my court. There is no one whose skills are ignored, whose genius is unnoticed. We are a city of artisans, of talent exposed and wonders achieved. Everyone has something uniquely theirs to give the world— something beautiful and, yes, sometimes terrifying—that only they can offer. To reject that gift is a crime against the person and the magic that gave it to them. I never reject a gift from the magic that sustains us. Even one like yours, Ehra Zahra."

Ehra remained still, afraid to move for fear of disturbing this perfect dream come true.

"I don't demand a decision right now. Stay for a while, let Temhet-Sakh take care of you. See how we live. If this lifestyle suits you, then we can discuss a more permanent placement for you."

Ehra didn't even think about it. She nodded.

"Excellent. I hope you find Temhet-Sakh as pleasing as we are sure to find you." The sultan smiled. "Gherrim, if you would give Lady Ehra a tour of the city, and find a place for her to stay?"

Gherrim returned his hand to Ehra's lower back. "I'm sure I can find somewhere for her." She didn't resist as he led her from the palace.

The day passed in a blur of mind-tingling wonders and intoxicating magic. Gherrim showed her the city, the desert, the people of Temhet-Sakh, and Ehra took it all in. She felt giddy, as if drunk. As if she'd wandered into a dream.

When darkness fell and the night grew cold, the buildings lit the streets with a gentle glow. It shimmered in warm shades of white and orange. Ehra had never seen anything quite so beautiful.

Gherrim led her to an elegant guesthouse and made arrangements for her. He walked her to her room, easily as grand as her chambers in her father's palace. Only here the low, sensual thrum of magic pulsed through the walls. The place could have been a refuse heap, but with that power in the room she would have preferred it to anywhere else in the world.

Tomorrow she would begin looking for Turien and Mariq, start combing the sultan's court for information on the device her father needed. Tomorrow she would be princess and spy and friend. Tonight, though, she would revel in the magic and sleep in its pleasurable embrace.

ot, humid air suffocated him. Turien coughed and ripped the bag from his head. Every muscle in his body protested the action.

He could barely see anything through the darkness. He seemed to be in some kind of cell, large enough for two or three paces in either direction at most. But he couldn't find the door. Cold, seamless glass covered every surface, a solid wall in each direction. He did, however, find Mariq huddled in the corner opposite him.

He shuffled toward her, checking her over as well as he could. She didn't seem injured and she breathed normally. Her clothes were saturated and sticky with drying blood, but none of it was fresh. He sighed deeply in relief. Ehra's miraculous healing hadn't been undone by the guards' cruelty.

Turien sat back and leaned against the slick wall. He didn't know how long he sat there, mind numb. Minutes. Hours. Not like it mattered. There was little else to do inside a prison cell.

He unwound the bandage on his right wrist and rubbed his hand across the innumerable scars, circling the hole between the bones in his forearm. Forever a prisoner. Removing his slave-band hadn't changed anything. No matter where he went, no matter what he did, he would never be free.

He'd been a fool to believe Cendim. He'd never had a choice. He never would. At least the Star-Blades hadn't thrown him in a tiny cell. With them, he could breathe fresh air and converse with other people. Even if they didn't allow him an identity of his own, they allowed him a life. Far better than what these sorcerers of Temhet-Sakh had given him.

He banged his head against the wall behind him, cursing his gullibility and Cendim's ridiculous ideals and the hope that could very well have cost him his life.

Mariq stirred. She moaned and grasped her head, her waist, anywhere she could as if expecting to have to hold herself together. Turien was by her side in a heartbeat. "How do you feel?" he asked.

"I should be dead," Mariq said, her voice hoarse but surprisingly clear. She sat up, moving as if she'd just woken from a restful night's sleep. Only her eyes betrayed the horror of what she'd been through— even in the darkness she looked terrified, haunted, and she clung to Turien as if afraid she'd return to death if she let go.

"You should be. But you aren't." When Mariq didn't calm Turien took her chin in his hands and gently made her face him. Her eyes locked on his and refused to let go. "You're all right, Mariq. I promise."

Even in the darkness Turien could see her brows furrow. She watched him for a moment, then nodded. Turien released her, but she stayed close. She looked around at the tiny, featureless cell. "Where are we?"

"The magic-users' prison. Where else?" he replied, not bothering to hide the dejected tone of his voice.

"Why?"

"Why not?" Mariq didn't reply, so he sighed and thumped his head against the wall behind him again. "Because we aren't like them."

"You mean we don't have magic, so they threw us in *prison*?"

"Seems so."

Mariq searched their tiny cell again. "Ehra…"

"She has magic. They took her."

They both grew quiet at that. They had known of Ehra's power. But the magic she'd exhibited… Turien still couldn't wrap his mind around it. Mariq had been dead or close enough, and Ehra had taken another man's life—or spirit, or whatever he wanted to call it—and put it into her.

It didn't make sense. Cendim had said magic enhanced a person's skill—in his case, alchemy. What could have given Ehra such power over life and death? A skill at healing? But that didn't make sense either. Bringing someone back from the dead, manipulating the force of life itself? Impossible.

But that's what magic did, wasn't it? It gave a person the power of a god. It meant the world held no boundaries for them. In that one area of their life, 'impossible' did not exist.

Even raising someone from the dead.

What would the people of Temhet-Sakh do with her? That kind of power wasn't something just anyone should control. Turien wasn't sure *anyone* should control it. He knew all too well what it was like to have a disposable life, knowing it could be taken from you on a whim. If the wrong person got ahold of that power, it could alter the face of the world.

Given that he and Mariq were imprisoned simply because they had no magic, Turien was certain Temhet-Sakh held quite a few of the wrong people.

He couldn't stay here and wallow at his misfortune. They had to get out of here. Not just to save their own skins, but to keep Ehra's terrifying power away from the rulers of Temhet-Sakh. They'd have seen her display of power as clearly as he had. They knew what kind of weapon Ehra could be. If they held such contempt for those without magic, Turien could guess where they'd try to point her power first.

He couldn't let anyone enslave his friend the way he'd been enslaved. He had to get Ehra away from the people who would use her for her magic.

And he could do none of that from inside a prison cell.

How could they get out? The walls were sealed, no doubt with magic. Ordinary people like he and Mariq could never escape this place. They'd need magic to even have a prayer of getting out of here.

Magic.

Turien paused. His heart beat wildly. He reached into his hidden pouch and pulled out one of the vials Cendim had given him. It glowed in the darkness, enough to illuminate his and Mariq's faces with liquid blue light.

"What is that?" she asked.

"It's a gift from Cendim," he replied. "Or a curse."

"A gift or a curse. Which one is it?"

"I won't know until I try it." He stared at the potion for a long moment. "Once I take this, it'll give me the powers of a magic-user. But I don't know what form those powers will take. It could be something that will help us get out of here, or it could be something worthless."

"So try one. What's the worst that could happen?"

"I only have five," he said. "What if I need them later?"

"What if we die in here because you refused to use the one thing that might help us, just in case you needed it in the future?"

He blinked at her. "Good point."

He glanced down at the potion once more, hesitated for a moment, then drank the entire thing in a single gulp. It tasted, strangely, like sweet mint tea.

Several heartbeats passed. Was it even working? Would he know it when it did?

Mariq gasped. He looked at her, able to see her face clearly for the first time since he'd woken. Where was that light coming from?

He looked down and froze. He glowed. The blue light that illuminated her came from *him*.

Cendim's magic allowed him to make impossible potions. Ehra's gave her the power to manipulate life itself. Turien's… he had no idea what it did. Streamers of blue light, like glowing rivers, swirled around him. He reached his hand into one and felt the power in it like lightning coursing through his arm.

"What are they?" Mariq asked, awe clear in her voice.

"I don't know," he said. "I'm not sure what I'm supposed to do now."

Breathe.

He pulled in a lungful of air, choking as the streamers of power flowed into him as well. He could feel the power mingling with his blood, writhing under his skin. It sliced through him like a jagged knife. It was changing him somehow, and Turien's fear turned to revulsion.

Accept.

The magic felt alien. It crawled through his body like maggots through a corpse. He wanted to expel them all, refuse it, but something deep in him demanded he not. He struggled against the horror, trying to relax as the pain built to mind-numbing levels. He stopped fighting and refused to think about what the potion was doing to him. He let it happen, even though every one of his instincts screamed at him for it.

Devour.

Ravenous hunger assaulted him. He inhaled again, sucking an impossibly deep breath in through his mouth. Blue streaks of magic flashed toward him and disappeared into him, but he wasn't satisfied. Not by a long shot. He kept taking it in, never stopping to exhale, never slowing in his meal.

Turien devoured magic. Gobbling it up, sucking it from the air and into himself with abandon. It hadn't given him access to the powers of magic. It had given him access to magic *itself.*

Cendim had said the composition was similar to Joythief.

This potion made Turien into living Joythief.

Turien continued to inhale, continued devouring the ambient magic as if nothing else could sustain him. As if he could never be satisfied.

This couldn't be good. He'd meant to help Cendim and Mariq restore the balance of magic, not destroy it like his former masters wanted! He tried to stop, to hold his breath and cease feeding on the magic, but he might as well try to stop a monsoon. It kept pouring into him, no matter how hard he fought it.

A deep, shuddering boom shook their cell. Turien tried to turn toward the sound, but the magic locked him in place. He could only catch glimpses through the corner of his eye as the glass beside him resonated with the sound, growing thinner and more transparent with each heartbeat that passed. Blinding white light saturated their cell, silhouetting several burly men preparing to enter.

As soon as the wall dissolved, they charged into the cell. Turien was powerless to defend himself as they rained punch after brutal punch on him, knocking him to his knees and then his belly. Mariq screamed. He hoped the dull thud that followed wasn't her head being smacked against the wall.

The streaming flow of blue magic started to slow, granting him

movement—only now shock and pain left him unable to make use of
it.

He could feel the magic inside him, slowly dissipating. Could he
find a way to use that? Their cell was open. If they could defeat these
three—four—no, five men, they could make a dash for freedom.

A heavy punch to his cheek brought stars to his eyes and bile into
his mouth. He spit, choking on blood and vomit, and escape seemed
out of the question. It took everything in his power just to remain
conscious.

Strong, merciless arms hauled him to his feet. He couldn't focus his
eyes through the dizziness and pain and blood. He tried to fight back,
but the guards dragged him away before he could even summon the
strength to consider doing something.

He caught one final look from Mariq before they pulled him
outside. She looked terrified.

He held her gaze as they resealed the wall behind them. Only then
did he give over to the blackness crowding his mind.

MARIQ had curled herself into the far corner of the tiny cell as soon as
they'd left with Turien. She hadn't moved since. Unless she counted
the uncontrollable shaking that had wracked her body for what seemed
like hours afterward.

The image of him standing there, surrounded by rivers of light and
color, still hung before her eyes. It had been a dazzling sight. Even
through her terror, Mariq could hardly believe the beauty of it. And
then fear had turned to awe as she saw the walls around her begin to
dissolve. The flat, featureless glass had… words failed her. They didn't
break, or shatter, but were *unmade*. They melted into the blue light

flowing into Turien. For a moment she'd hoped they might fall—they'd been rebuilding themselves, but Turien had unmade them even faster.

Then the booming had started, and guards poured into their tiny cell. A blur of violence and motion and terror followed, and then they were gone, a beaten and bloodied Turien pulled out with them. The wall had reformed, and darkness had fallen upon her like a shroud.

Hours had passed since then. She might have slept—she couldn't be entirely sure—and a meager meal had been dropped off and ignored. Her head still ached from the slap the guard had given her. A warning to stay out of the way when she'd tried to get to Turien.

Waking up and finding herself imprisoned had been horrible, but sitting in prison *alone* was worse. At least she'd had Turien before. Without him, the darkness seemed more sinister, the silence more ominous. Her mind was a terrifying and lonely place to be.

At first, she'd thought the faint sounds were just her imagination conjuring a new level of torture. As they grew louder and more distinct, though, Mariq started to pay attention. She pressed her ear to the walls, searching for the source of the noise.

She felt the vibrations first. An entire wall pulsed, as if from massive blows on the other side. It wasn't the guards returning—they had come from the opposite wall. Where their entrance had been dramatic, this felt more violent, more sporadic. Clandestine. She could hear the hesitation before each pulse, the long pauses between where she could imagine whoever made the noise checked to see if they'd been heard.

Her heart raced. Was this a rescue?

She heard footsteps, muffled conversation, and then a clear female voice called out. "Stand back!"

Mariq scurried to the far wall and pressed herself against the glass.

The vibrations in the wall grew stronger, the sounds more intense, until Mariq felt each pulse in her skull. She could feel magic in those blows. Just like when Turien had unmade the walls.

A final pulse, one last blow, and the wall shattered into a cloud of dust and shards. Mariq shielded herself as best she could, but a thousand tiny, stinging cuts sliced open her skin.

Two figures wrapped in concealing dun-colored robes strode into the room. The one on the left stepped forward, handing Mariq a bundle of cloth. "Put these on," she said. Mariq nodded and started covering herself with the heavy fabric. "Be ready to move. Follow us closely and whatever happens, do not lose sight of me."

"My friend, Turien," Mariq said. "They took him away after…" She couldn't bear to continue the sentence.

"We know. He is being retrieved as we speak."

Relief threatened to choke Mariq's voice. "Thank you." When she'd steadied her voice again, she asked, "Did Ehra send you?"

"I don't know anyone by that name," she said. Before Mariq could ask further, the woman shushed her. "I must listen for the signal."

Cursing herself for her stupidity, Mariq stood still. Of course they couldn't chat. A rescue like this would require many components, much like a well-planned theft. The first rule of an operation like this never changed: don't let anything distract you. And Mariq had been here, doing her best to distract the one person who could get her out of this place.

She hoped the stress of her imprisonment and the excitement of release had caused her to forget, but she feared the Joythief had taken even more of her training from her.

A sound, barely on the edge of hearing, tickled Mariq's ear.

The woman nodded to her partner. "Your friend is safe," she told Mariq. "Are you ready?"

"Yes."

"Then run!"

The women sprinted through the smashed wall. A few tunnels and shattered glass openings later, they emerged into the city. The light blinded her, and Mariq stumbled behind the woman. She couldn't make out much of her surroundings—a few buildings, a street or two, but it was mostly a blur of sand- and desert-colored blocks.

Within moments, they were outside the city and sprinting through the raw desert. She focused on the dunes before her and ignored everything that could be a distraction to her footing.

Through the chaos of their escape, Mariq caught a brief glimpse of Turien. He was indeed safe, as the woman had said, but he seemed far from sound. Both eyes were blackened, one swollen shut, and he didn't seem to be moving much under his own power. Their rescuers hauled him to safety like a sack of grain.

A thick band of silver, inset with a huge gem as black as night, circled his brow. It looked like a crown, but Mariq found herself more troubled by that addition than any of Turien's other injuries. Whatever horrible things they had done to him, the sour feeling in her gut told her this was by far the worst.

17

Two days and Ehra had found nothing. No hint of where Mariq and Turien had been taken and even less on the device. Her search had taught her much about Temhet-Sakh, though, introduced her to so many people their names and faces and magic—more important to a person's status than their birth—all blended together. She was left with a montage of meeting people, of brief conversations and quick laughs or scoffing arrogance. Her awe at their casual use of magic and excitement at being welcomed by them had yet to dim. In fact, with each new acquaintance she felt more at home, more at peace than ever before.

Hatife had been good to her. Her father had never blamed her for her monster, had never ostracized her. But others had, until Ehra had been forced to adopt a different persona, the quiet girl who rarely spoke and never had fun, just to avoid their attention.

Temhet-Sakh, though, promised far more than that. Here Ehra could be herself, if not free to use her magic. The monster would never allow that. But she met with no condemnation here, no judgment for her power. Just acceptance and understanding. And, of course, magic. Magic was *everywhere* in Temhet-Sakh, from the ground she walked on to the air she breathed. It was everything here.

Gherrim called on her shortly after breakfast, as he had each morning since she'd arrived. His obnoxious behavior and possessiveness chafed at her, his assumed control of her every move sitting uneasily in her stomach, but fighting it only made him hold her more tightly. Besides, the magic suffusing the streets and sparking between them helped smooth some of his rough edges. She couldn't step out of his too-intimate touches when the magic made her warm and giddy like strong liquor. She couldn't push away his clinging presence when his doting attention sent a flush of pleasure through her. She loved how he made her feel, so she chose to ignore just how much she didn't like him.

He placed his arm around her waist as he led her outside, but not toward the sultan's palace as he normally did. "Where are we going?"

"The sultan has found a place for your magic to be used," Gherrim said. "We're going to the sick rooms."

Ehra's heart thudded in her chest. Her fingers tingled and went cold, but did fear or excitement cause it? "We can't... being around sick people is so dangerous..."

"You have to be around them, if you're going to heal them."

Heal. He couldn't be serious. All Ehra had ever wanted to do was heal, to cure people of their sicknesses and ease their pains. Her monster gave her that power, but at a price she could not bear to pay.

"You saw what it took for me to heal Mariq in the desert. You know what it costs for me to heal."

"Everything will be taken care of," Gherrim said.

"But…"

"Don't worry about it," he said, more sternly this time. "I told you it will be taken care of."

He wouldn't allow more arguing after that tone, so she swallowed her lingering doubts and focused on the positive. It was too good to be true. She was going to help people. She could put her magic to use and do something good for a change.

She was going to heal.

Gherrim stopped them at a large building, just as graceful and beautiful as the others, and pushed open the door. The sight inside sobered and intoxicated her. Sickness and pain permeated the room while families cried and healers scurried from bedside to bedside. The smell of herbs and chemicals laced the air, poorly masking the odors of vomit and blood and sickness. Still, Ehra breathed deeply. She could smell the life leaking out in here.

"I'm sorry, but if you're not ill I must ask you to come back later," a healer said as he strode over to them. His wild hair looked as if he'd been running his hands through it for the last several hours. Deep, bruise-colored circles hung beneath his bloodshot eyes. "Terrible accident out in the desert, I'm afraid. Far too many injuries to address and not enough time to waste on anyone who will live through the day."

"Healer, this is Princess Ehra Zahra of Hatife. I'm sure the sultan told you she would be here today?" Gherrim's tone held a mild reproach, as if insulted he hadn't recognized them on the spot.

The man's eyes brightened. "This is her, yes? Oh, welcome, princess. You couldn't have come at a better time."

"The pleasure is mine," she replied, smiling at the harried healer. "Where can I start?"

"Follow me," the healer said, ignoring Gherrim as he led her into a closed-off section of the sick rooms. The smell of blood thickened in here, and Ehra felt her monster stir. "These are the most serious of the wounded. We've done all we can for them, but they are beyond our help now."

Ehra knelt beside one of the beds. The man in it was hardly recognizable as one any longer. Deep scratches—likely from a jackal—ran down his mangled face and the length of his chest. She could see his heart beat through one of them.

She let her monster out just enough to see the mist of life hovering over him. It was thin, much of the red of life bled out to gray. "I could heal him, I think," Ehra said, "if I had enough to draw on…"

"You misunderstand, princess. These men aren't here for you to heal. The sultan said you would need life to feed upon in order for your magic to function. This is that life."

She looked back at the doctor, horror and hunger warring in her breast. "You're suggesting I kill this man to heal another?" She hoped he didn't notice her salivating at the thought.

"It isn't as monstrous as you believe," he said, as if able to read her thoughts. "No matter what we do, this man will die. But how many could you heal with his life?"

Ehra looked back at the mist. She could heal two, maybe three people with this, as long as their injuries weren't too extensive.

"He was in agony, screaming until his throat bled then choking on the blood as he continued to try. In order to calm him, we had to give him several doses of sedatives." He cleared his throat, as if the memory pained him. "He will not wake from that heavy of a dose. He is already dead, princess. But you can put him out of his misery, give peace to his family, and restore life to others in the process."

A tear slid down Ehra's cheek. How could she do this? Yet she found herself poised and ready—eager, even—to do it. She kept the monster buried because of this. It was far too easy to juggle the lives of others in her hands.

But then again, the doctor spoke wisdom. If this man would never wake, why bother to preserve his life? It could be used for others. And in his own, mundane way, even this ordinary healer held lives in his hands every day and made decisions that would allow them to live or die.

Besides, the dead man's life looked so appetizing.

Ehra released the monster and grasped the misty life hanging before her. Soft, warm power coursed through her, setting every inch of her body alight. The sheer strength of life and magic made her toes curl.

It would be so easy…

She bit her tongue, hard, bringing the monster back under control. She could feel the strain, though, and knew she wouldn't be able to hold onto her sanity for long. "Who am I healing?" she asked through gritted teeth.

Holding her shoulders, the healer guided her to a bed just outside the dead man's room. A woman lay on it, pale and sweaty, a blood-soaked bandage encircling her waist. Ehra grasped the woman's life-mist, resisting the compulsion to take it in and mingle it with hers. She threaded some of the man's life with the woman's, knitting her muscles back together and restoring her depleted life.

Ehra rocked back on her heels, and the healer steered her to the next bed. This man had cracked his skull and broken both legs. Ehra gifted him the rest of the dead man's life, feeling the power drain from her body as she crashed to the floor.

The room fell silent as every conscious person stared in awe at her.

Ehra knelt, panting, weak and dizzy and giddy. "More," she whispered. "I need more."

The healers burst into motion, separating the room into those who would sacrifice their lives and those who would be healed. The loved ones of the wounded clamored for Ehra's attention, begging for their spouse or child or brother to receive her gifts. Those who were refused wailed and beat the healers with impotent fists, while the others fell to their knees and praised the gods for the miracle they'd been granted.

All of that faded from Ehra's awareness as she fell into a rhythm of taking and giving, of death and rapture and life and loss.

Time passed. Ehra knew it but neither cared nor tracked how much. Lives came and went. She doled out the magic as she was directed, then as she saw fit. The monster purred, already craving more. It was always ravenous. Ehra no longer tried to stifle it.

A new life was brought before her, and Ehra reached for it. Something made her hesitate, causing the monster to howl inside her. "This one is not like the others," she said. "He is weak, but his life is not failing."

The human before her twitched, his eyes traveling wildly as he wrung his hands. "Uh… no, princess, he's not. It's just… you've already taken all the men who were going to die, so the sultan had us bring you some prisoners."

Ehra cocked her head. The word struck a chord on her, bringing memories—and her struggling humanity—to the surface. "What?"

"There's still a lot of people who need your help, princess. These are bad men. The only thing they are good for is to save the lives of others more worthy."

The prisoner shook, his life quivering with terror. "Please, no. I didn't do anything wrong. I can't use magic, that's all. It's not my fault. Please, please don't kill me!"

Ehra couldn't tear her eyes from the man's life. It was stronger than any of the others she'd taken. A full meal when she'd been feeding on nothing but crumbs. The tiny, human part of her mind screamed and fought against it, but the pull of the life was too strong. Ehra reached out her hand, grasped the man's life, and pulled it to her. It flooded her body, intoxicating and empowering her in a way the others never had.

The goddess laughed and ignored his screams.

She saw the big guard standing in a corner, watching her intently. His life pulsed strongly, red with strength and power and lust. His blood coursed as he looked upon Ehra's magic. As it should. She was a goddess, her magic incomparable. Of course he would want to take her. Who wouldn't want magic like hers for their own?

She granted a thread of the life within her to a wailing child. A gift from the benevolent goddess. That child would now worship her, as she deserved.

Time was inconsequential as Ehra took and gave life as she willed. None dared to step in her path, except to bring her more offerings. The petty humans scurried to do her bidding.

Only one particular human didn't. He stood before her as if expecting *her* to bow to *him*. As if the goddess of life should bow to anyone.

"What have you done?" he screamed at her, his face red and his life throbbing with rage.

"I have taken and given life as I have seen fit," she replied.

He blinked at her, pausing for a moment before shaking his head and continuing in a more rational tone. "I don't care about this healing business. I meant the prison. Where are your friends?"

Now it was Ehra's turn to blink. Her friends, in prison?

"Don't play dumb with me," the sultan said. "Your friends without magic were in prison this morning. Now they are gone. What have you done with them?"

Ehra's heart stopped as she caught her breath, crashing back to sanity. She looked around the room, at the trail of bodies left in her wake. Men and women she had killed with impunity. Bile rose in her throat, even as the memory sent a shiver of pleasure through her body.

Had one of those prisoners been Mariq? Or Turien? Had she killed her own friends in her madness? She hoped she'd have recognized them and stopped even in the throes of her monster, but she couldn't be sure.

"I don't know what you're talking about," she said, her voice—her entire body—trembling. She blinked and shook her head, trying to clear the monster from her thoughts.

The sultan stared at her for several moments with the same intensity he'd shown before. Finally he grunted and turned away, not even bothering with apologies or farewells.

Every eye followed him like moths drawn to a flame, and Ehra used the moment to slip into one of the private rooms in back. The loss of the power, of the pleasure, had left her feeling hollow. She wanted, needed to fill that emptiness, but to venture back into the magic so soon would be disastrous. She couldn't do that again.

She sat on the cot—which had so recently been the bed of a wounded man, a man she'd killed—and wept. Hot tears poured down her face and deep sobs wracked her body, but she didn't try to stop any of it. To deny the horror and sadness her actions caused would be to lose her humanity.

She was already far too close to that.

Gherrim entered the room and closed the door behind him, but didn't approach her. He just stood there, staring at Ehra as if he could still see her consumed by her monster. She feared to look into his eyes, to see the horror and rejection in them, but she had to face it.

She steeled herself for the worst and met his gaze. He focused on her like a predator, ready to pounce at any second. But anger or fear didn't have him locked on her like that. Hunger did.

Ehra sniffled and dried her eyes, trying to compose herself. He still stared at her as if she was the most alluring woman in the world, but she had no idea why. "What?" she asked, trying to smooth her hair and look like she hadn't just murdered dozens of people and then mourned their loss.

"You were magnificent," he said, his voice thick and his eyes glazed. "In the throes of your power… gods, I have never seen a more delicious sight."

She shivered.

"Ehra," he whispered, lifting her to her feet and crushing her to him, "let me take you home. Right now."

She squirmed in his arms, but he didn't give her even an inch of room. "I'm a monster, Gherrim," she said, breaking out of his embrace only to wrap herself in her arms. "You saw what I did out there. I killed so many people without a second thought. How could you want to be with me after that?"

He took her face in his hands, forcing her eyes to meet his. "I want to be with you because you're mine. You've been mine since the moment you entered Temhet-Sakh." His fingers caressed her cheeks. "Don't you feel it, Ehra? Your magic calls to me. It makes my blood boil. I need to have it—to have you—like I've never needed anything else."

"Gherrim, after everything, I'm just… I'm not ready for…"

He crushed her in another embrace, kissing her so deeply she couldn't resist. She should stop him, should push him away and just go home. She needed to be alone. She needed space, she needed to get herself sorted out before…

Gherrim flicked his tongue against her lips, and she opened her mouth to accept it. She could *taste* Gherrim's magic, hot and passionate. The power flowing through her, between them, made her dizzy. She shouldn't be doing this. Not now. Not with Gherrim. But the magic dragged her down, just as it had pulled out her monster. She couldn't fight it. She couldn't stop herself.

He crushed her to him, his hands everywhere. Ehra didn't want this. But she needed it. She needed more. If she couldn't have the monster, her own magic, perhaps she could just have this.

Most people didn't know of Ehra's monster. They only knew the person she pretended to be. And those who did know… no one had ever seen her monster and still treated her like a human. The only people who loved her were those who knew nothing of who she really was.

Gherrim knew. He'd seen her lost to the monster and still wanted her. He might be the only one in the world who would accept a murderous beast like her. Could she quibble over a few character traits? This might be her only chance to be loved for herself. Wasn't Gherrim, overbearing and obnoxious as he could be, better than nobody?

Gherrim broke the kiss, keeping his face close to hers. His eyes were dilated, his breath short and erratic. *This is a mistake,* she thought. *I should stop this before it's too late. Like I should have stopped my monster.*

"Come to my bed, Ehra. Let me make you mine." He kissed her once more, and his hand slid beneath her sarong. Magic sparked through her, deliriously pleasurable. "I won't take no for an answer."

She didn't try to refuse him again.

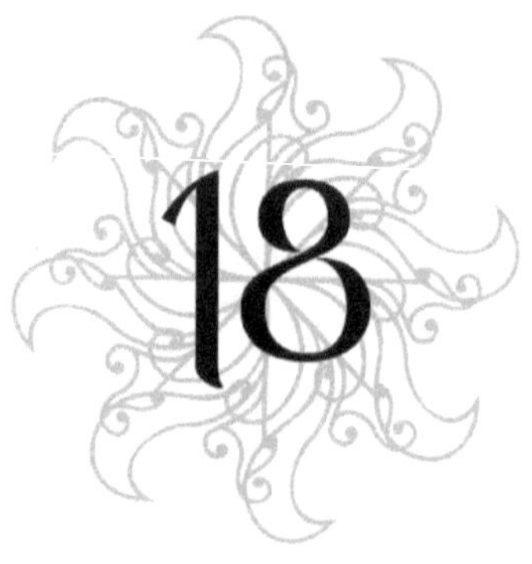

usk approached and still Mariq ran after her rescuers. She could feel nothing but pain and exhaustion, her mind numb with the effort not to drop to the sand. Her entire world was the next step. Just one more. Breathe. Run. Ignore the pain. Breathe. Don't close your eyes. Run.

Shadows stretched from dune to dune, washing the sand in darkness and treachery. Mariq's rescuers didn't seem the least bit fazed by it. They traversed the dunes with surprising speed, agility, and confidence. Mariq was far from clumsy, but she was grateful she hadn't fallen or broken an ankle by now.

Her rescuers slowed. Mariq stumbled as she tried to match their pace, moving from a run to walk and then to stillness. Her legs felt awkward, gangly like a newborn's. Her heart raced, her breath coming in such short gasps she felt lightheaded and nauseated. Standing still was harder than moving—it took all of her willpower not to collapse.

The woman who'd given Mariq her robe placed a gentle hand on her shoulder. An insignificant weight, but Mariq sagged under it. "Sit," the woman said, and Mariq crumpled to the ground without conscious thought. "We have a few moments. Recover your strength."

Mariq focused on her breathing until the dark spots in her vision lessened and she could sit without having to concentrate. She noted Turien lying in the sand nearby, unconscious or nearly there, his breathing shallow but steady. It took more effort than climbing the minaret in Kuriza, but she managed to crawl to his side. She couldn't do anything for him, but at least she could sit beside him. Perhaps he'd take comfort in that, even if he didn't wake to acknowledge it.

He was a mess of dried blood and bruises. That horrid black stone on his forehead drew her eye, as if pulling her very essence to it. Mariq shuddered. She forced herself to look away.

It shouldn't have been so hard to do so.

A few stars had begun to glitter in the darkening sky. Their rescuers milled about the area, talking. None of them seemed as exhausted or out of breath as her.

After a few moments the woman returned, handing her a canteen from which Mariq drank greedily. A slab of something that looked like dried nut paste followed. "We're going to camp here for the night," she said. "We don't want to risk a night run with someone who's not accustomed to it. Don't fear, we're far enough from Temhet-Sakh to be safe. And we know how to avoid their scouts should they extend this far."

Mariq was too exhausted to argue. She munched on the mealy food and drank the lukewarm water. Her heart started to resume a somewhat normal rhythm. Her limbs ached and quivered, but she stood and stretched. It wouldn't do to wake in the morning with cramped muscles that refused to answer her commands.

She didn't remember lying down to sleep, but the woman shook her awake as dawn erased the stars above. The dunes were awash with pinkish light. "It's time to go," the woman said.

"Where are we going?" Mariq asked. Exhaustion and pain made her voice thick. "Who are you people?"

"We'll answer all your questions in time. For now, we must run. We have only a few more hours before we reach Haven."

Only a few more hours. Mariq sat up and groaned. The woman might as well have said they only had to run back to Kuriza.

Turien had fallen fully unconscious now, the bruises and cuts on his body making him look less like a man and more like an abused slab of meat. One of their rescuers—Mariq had yet to see any of their faces—fashioned a kind of sling from some extra material and lashed Turien to their back like an overgrown baby. They took a slower pace today, for which Mariq thanked her lucky stars. Her sore, stiff legs felt like they'd fail with each new step.

The same routine started all over again. Breathe. Run. Don't trip. Run. Breathe.

The sun rose above them, the desert heating until Mariq felt as if she were roasting. She lost track of time, distance, everything. Only pain, exhaustion, and running mattered.

Mariq nearly missed the signs they approached the end of their torturous journey. She saw only the faintest trace of the scouts, heard the whistled signals as an afterthought. Only when they came to a stop once again did Mariq realize they were there.

Wherever "there" was.

The dune they stood upon looked just like the dune before, and the dune before that, and the dune before that. They stood in the middle of the most vast, desolate nothing Mariq had ever imagined. No sign of civilization or humanity. Not even a handful of tents or a rogue piece of cloth caught by the wind.

She didn't have the breath to speak, and her brain felt too foggy to think of a proper question anyway. She just panted, staving off dizziness and exhaustion, as their rescuers led them to the edge of the dune.

Suddenly Mariq stared down into a crevasse filled with greenery. Palms and shrubs and more vegetation than she'd seen since the palace gardens of Hatife. A cool breeze escaped, smelling of moisture and life. Mariq even caught the glint of sunshine reflected off water—and out here, where not even cactus dared grow wild, that was a marvel in and of itself.

She finally found the breath to speak. "What...?"

"Welcome to Haven," the woman said.

Mariq didn't know what to say. The sight before her was like a mirage, the stuff men dream of when they're lost and delirious. But this was better than a mirage. It was real.

The woman chuckled and gestured for Mariq to head down a path she hadn't noticed before, narrow but gentle enough to not be treacherous.

She couldn't take her eyes off Haven. With each step more of the crevasse revealed itself—Mariq saw a shaded area that looked like a park, with several people enjoying picnics; something that looked like a suq hugging the far wall; even a waterfall where a dozen or so children splashed and bathed. The entire area rang with laughter and voices and the sound of water. It was like a dream. In the middle of the desert, these people had built an oasis. No wonder they called it Haven.

Once they reached the bottom, their rescuers paused to unravel the yards of fabric covering themselves. Mariq did the same, grateful to be free of the stifling cloth.

Fresh, moist air greeted her as she removed the hood. Heat broiled the desert above, yet down here a cool, refreshing breeze blew. She tried not to stare as her rescuers revealed themselves to her—many of them were women, and all of them had identical heritage tattoos. They spoke of common value, naming everyone equal in this place. Mariq had never dreamed of something like this. In her world everyone knew where they stood, and standing meant everything.

One of the women approached, streaks of gray in her hair, her face rough from sun and wind. Sternness lined her features, but her eyes were kind as they met Mariq's.

She led Mariq along a path through grasses and between tall palms, over streams and ponds that glittered like diamonds. Mariq couldn't take it all in. "How is this even possible?"

"Through a careful partnership between our community and the desert," the woman responded.

"I don't—"

"We will explain everything you wish to know later. For now, we must get you and your companion to the healers." Mariq started to protest, but the woman stopped her before she could get a word out. "Time spent in Temhet-Sakh's prison is always more trying than one would suspect. Be patient. Each moment away from that wretched place will help you recover."

Mariq glanced backward, toward the large man carrying Turien. "Will you be able to fix him?"

Concern creased the woman's face. "We will do what we can."

She ushered Mariq through crowds of people, each as lively and vibrant as any she'd ever met. When she'd first arrived in Hatife she'd thought those people were alive in a way those in Kuriza had never been—here she saw what life was intended to be.

Mariq felt her tension drain away as the woman guided her into a cool, darkened room. Cots lined each wall, most of them empty.

Turien collapsed onto one as soon as his rescuers released him, and Mariq followed—more gracefully, but not by much—as soon as she could. She was determined not to sleep until she knew more about these people, her surroundings, and Turien's state, but her eyes betrayed her and drifted closed.

She woke to soft voices and gentle touches. Part of her knew she should be alarmed, but they were so soothing, Mariq couldn't work up the strength.

"Good afternoon," a woman said. Mariq vaguely recognized the voice. "Move slowly. Your body is still trying to recover from your ordeal."

She struggled to sit, finding the task far more difficult than it should have been. The woman waited at her side, helping her up with practiced strength.

"Feel better?"

Mariq nodded, regretting the motion as it set her head spinning. The woman stepped away, returning a breath later with a cup.

"It's good to see you return to us. Since you arrived you've been delirious and in and out of consciousness." She inclined her head in a shallow nod. "My name is Nirta. Welcome to Haven."

Mariq would have returned the bow, but thought better of it. She preferred to remain on the bed. "Thank you for saving us."

"It is our duty to reclaim what Temhet-Sakh mistreats," she replied.

"How long have I been here?"

"We arrived at Deepening, day before yesterday."

"Deepening?"

"The time of the leaving sun, when the darkness Deepens and the magic strengthens."

Nirta refilled her cup, and Mariq drained it. "Where is Turien?"

The woman's face grew a shade darker, and Mariq's heart raced. "Your companion?" Mariq nodded. "It may not be wise…"

"Please. I need to see him." Mariq could hear the frailty in her own voice, and it scared her.

Nirta looked at Mariq for a moment before nodding. "Very well.

Are you strong enough to walk?"

She nodded. She would be, if it meant she could see Turien.

Her legs wobbled and refused to take her weight at first, but she did not let herself fall. Tentative steps, more of a hobble than an actual walk, would have to suffice. When she'd gained a bit more strength, Nirta led her outside

Painfully bright sunshine met Mariq's eyes. She squinted and swayed while she let her eyes adjust. The blur came into focus as the most beautiful sight she had ever seen.

The walls of the crevasse stretched high above them, so high she could see only a narrow sliver of bright blue sky. But instead of dry sand, greenery coated the walls. Balconies crisscrossed back and forth, plants of every description winding around the rails and growing up the walls. Moisture saturated and cooled the air until she could almost believe they'd left the desert altogether. The buildings were modest yet welcoming, and contentment filled the air as much as the moisture did.

Some people they passed had dreadful black stones on their foreheads like Turien did—Mariq turned away from them before their pain made her weep.

Nirta led her to a much smaller building a few doors down from where she'd been. Somehow Mariq knew this place saw sorrow often. Her heart clenched. If Turien was here, she had to prepare herself for the worst.

Dim light made it hard to see, especially after the brilliant sunshine. Mariq could only make out the rough outlines of a few cots and some tables. Troubled breathing to her left alerted her to Turien's presence. Emptiness, physical and emotional, filled the rest of the room.

Mariq moved to his side and sat on the edge of the bed. The only sound was Turien's breath as she waited for her vision to return, and for the terror choking her to subside. She reached for his hand, only to find it wrapped in thick plaster. What had they done to him?

After long moments, she could make out his face. Swelling from multiple hits distorted its shape, and even in the dimness she could see several horrific bruises. Blood crusted his lips. A soft sheet covered most of his body, but she could tell he had more injuries underneath it. Just the thought of what he'd gone through made her stomach churn.

That awful stone still clung to his forehead. She reached over to grab it, but Nirta stopped her. "Do not touch it."

Mariq couldn't identify what emotion coursed through her at that. Anger? Fear? Perhaps both. "Why not?"

"Do you not know what it is?"

Mariq shook her head.

"That is a voidstone. It is a thing of pure evil. Nothing good can come from contact with it."

She could identify *this* emotion. Definitely anger. "Then why is it still on his head?"

"The voidstone cannot be removed. It is rooted onto him. If we attempt to separate him from it, he will die." Nirta paused. "Come. It's time you returned to your rest. You can do nothing for him when you're half-conscious yourself."

Nirta moved to guide her from the room, but Mariq remained on Turien's bed. She stared at his broken form for many silent moments, her heart aching. The few people she'd seen with voidstones on had made her heart weep. Seeing this one on Turien, though, somehow seemed worse. "What will it do to him?" she asked.

"It will siphon his magic. He will be unable to use it as long as the voidstone remains."

"Turien isn't a magic-user," Mariq said.

This time, Nirta froze in her steps. "He isn't?"

"No. He had a potion that allowed him to access magic for a brief time, but that's all. He's never used magic on his own."

Nirta was silent for a long, torturous moment. "I must take you to our patriarch," Nirta said, sounding shaken. "If what you say is true, he will wish to hear it from you in person."

"You never answered my question," Mariq said. "What will the voidstone do to him?"

Nirta shrugged. "If he truly has no magic, there's no telling. They have never been used on those without magic before."

"Take a guess, then."

The woman stared at Turien for a moment. "Perhaps it will do nothing. Perhaps it will drive him mad. I wish I had a better answer for you, but in truth I have no idea."

19

espite Gherrim's insistence, Ehra hadn't gone back to the sick rooms since releasing her monster a few days before. She hadn't been able to face what she'd done. Gherrim tried to soothe her with compliments and caresses, but Ehra couldn't erase the image of all those bodies strewn behind her. Lives she'd sacrificed without a second thought. Gherrim couldn't understand, didn't try to understand. He said her magic was beautiful, her power intoxicating. She still saw it as a curse.

Worse still, she didn't know what had happened to Mariq and Turien. She hoped their absence meant an escape, that they were safe, but she couldn't be sure. No one had seen anything. Even the palace gossips had precious little to say about it.

She chatted with a lady she'd come to know rather well, an elegant woman born in Temhet-Sakh with the power to create water—a treasure in such a dry land, which alone explained her high position in the sultan's court—when Gherrim came up behind her, his hand resting on the curve of her hip. "Excuse us," he said to the woman, pulling Ehra away before she could object.

"You could have let me finish our conversation," Ehra said.

"It can wait. I have something to show you."

"What is it?"

"It's a surprise."

Fear clamped Ehra's heart. "You aren't taking me back to the sick rooms, are you?"

"No. Though you should go back. Many people owe you their lives, and your magic was astounding to witness." His hand slid lower, as it often did when he talked about her monster. Ehra's sick feeling only intensified.

A young guard fell in behind them as Gherrim started up a large staircase. Ehra knew better than to ask his purpose and followed mutely, climbing until her legs ached.

They reached the top of the stairs and a small trapdoor in the ceiling above them. Gherrim opened this with a key from around his neck and climbed up a short ladder onto the roof. Ehra started up after him, and once she was within his reach he hauled her up beside him.

Delirious, heady pleasure would have made Ehra swoon, if Gherrim hadn't been there to catch her.

It took her long moments to recover her senses. The magic was so thick up here she could hardly breathe. Her head spun and her limbs trembled from the overwhelming strength of it. She closed her eyes and inhaled, giddy with power.

Finally she opened her eyes and stood on her own feet. The sights from this high were almost as intoxicating as the magic. Temhet-Sakh was a mural of glass and color spread before them. Outside the crystalline walls, the desert stretched in waves of heat and sand and magic. Ehra could almost *see* it out here.

Still, the beauty of Temhet-Sakh couldn't hold her attention for long. The source of the magic hung in the center of the roof, tantalizing and alluring like nothing Ehra had ever felt before. Interwoven brass circles formed an open sphere, the entire thing hovering more than Gherrim's height above the roof. Glowing tendrils of light and magic danced about the roof, curling in and around each other until spiraling into the sphere, forming a dense ball of magic about the size of a man's head. Each thread pulsed with color and life and power. She could feel the magic in it, the sheer power and subtle grace of it. Just standing in its presence made Ehra dizzy and giddy. "What is it?" she asked.

"That is the teshneh," Gherrim said. His voice sounded as dreamy as hers. "It's what makes Temhet-Sakh possible. This is the heart of magic."

She'd found it. The device her father had sent them here for. A wealth of power. The person who controlled this magic would control the whole of the Scorched Lands. The entire world would be laid at their fingertips.

No wonder the Star-Blades were after it.

She'd never imagined something so small could hold such a vast amount of magic. It enchanted Ehra. The teshneh drew her to it, as if it had been missing all her life and now it longed to reclaim her. Ehra desperately wanted to go to it. She would never be whole without it.

Gherrim's strong hands kept her rooted in place. "Stay out of the magic. See those streaks of light? Standing in one is like standing in a sandstorm. A brief encounter might sting, but even a few moments of exposure is enough to kill. That much magic can consume a person."

For a moment Ehra didn't care. She *needed* that power. That magic made life worth living, and she'd been denying it to herself for her entire life.

"It's wonderful, isn't it?" Gherrim asked. "Most people don't even know it exists. I pity them."

Ehra forced herself to look away from the teshneh. "If it's a secret, how do you know about it? How did you get us permission to be up here in the first place?"

"Haven't I told you? I'm not just any guard, Ehra. My job is to guard this."

She stared at her lover in astonishment. That explained why he had the ear of the sultan, and the freedom to do pretty much whatever he wanted in Temhet-Sakh. "Why you?" she asked, blurting out the question before she could think of how it sounded. "I mean, everyone in Temhet-Sakh is placed based on their magic. What does yours do, to give you a responsibility like this?"

Gherrim pointed to one of the mysterious threads in his heritage tattoo, such dark blue it was almost black. "I'm a magic tracker. I can find anyone, or anything, from their magic alone. I can sense the teshneh anywhere, at all times. If someone has been in its presence, I can tell."

Ehra traced the line up and down his arm, wishing she could read this particular pattern. What would it tell her about the magic? "Is that how you always know where to find me? You can follow me by my magic?"

He nodded and kissed her. "I could follow your magic to the ends of the earth."

Ehra fought down giddy giggles. "You still haven't explained what we're doing up here."

"Right." He gestured to the guard who'd followed them up. Ehra had almost forgotten he'd come. He looked like little more than a boy, his eyes wide and limbs trembling as he stared at Gherrim in terror. "I wanted to conduct a little experiment."

Gherrim drew his sword from the sheath at his side and approached the young guard. The boy didn't move as Gherrim rammed his blade through the boy's gut. He grunted and crumbled to the ground as bright red blood flowed from the wound.

Ehra crashed to her knees beside him and tried to staunch the bleeding. "Oh gods! Gherrim, go for help!"

"You don't need help, Ehra. Heal him."

Hot, delicious-looking blood covered her hands. "I can't. I don't have any life to take."

"Take the magic."

"It doesn't work like that, Gherrim!"

His voice was cool, as if he wasn't watching one of his guards die before him. "Doesn't it?"

She glared up at him, but her eyes caught the swirl of powerful magic instead. She reached for it on instinct, releasing her monster to grasp the magic and save this man's life... only the monster didn't respond. Ehra remained herself, holding the magic in her hand. It felt just as soft and warm as a life did.

Cautiously, in awe of her actions, she mingled the pure magic with the dying boy's life. The cool blue power merged with the pulsing red mist, the two intertwining in a beautiful piece of artwork before the magic *became* life. It turned red and Ehra pushed it back into the boy's body.

He convulsed, coughing, as his life returned two-fold.

Complete silence engulfed Ehra, as if the entire world had stopped to gape at her power. She'd just taken pure magic and given it as life to a dying man. And she hadn't needed to become a monster to do it.

"I did it," she whispered, staring at the seamless flesh where moments before blood had gushed onto her hands.

"You did," Gherrim said. "And how do you feel?"

Ehra took a breath. "Wonderful. Powerful. Like... like some of the magic I used to heal is still in me."

Gherrim grinned. "I knew it."

She looked at him, overwhelmed by the flood of emotions raging through her. How could she control them? She needed to scream and cry and dance and make love, all at once and all right now.

Her joy doubled and threatened to drown her as the boy stood and patted his stomach. He smiled, the expression more haunted than joyous, then turned and walked away. More completely healed, more quickly done, than she'd been able to do with anyone.

She still stared after the boy when Gherrim sat beside her, wrapping one of his giant arms around her waist. He seemed proud, like his prized puppy had just performed a complex trick. Ehra's excitement calmed as the facts caught up with her emotions. "You risked that boy's life, just because you believed I could heal him with pure magic."

Gherrim nodded. "I did."

"How did you know it would work?"

"I didn't."

She stared at him. "How could you have done that?"

He looked back at her without a trace of worry or concern. "I can sense your power more keenly than even you can, Ehra. You're far more powerful than you think. I had faith that if tested, you would find that out for yourself."

"You shouldn't have done it. If I'd failed, you would have murdered that boy."

"But you didn't fail."

"That's not the point!"

Gherrim scowled. "You're condemning me for having such faith in you, such belief in your strength, that I would go to extreme measures to prove it?" Each word stabbed at Ehra. "Most people would do anything to have someone who believes in them that much."

"I know, Gherrim, it's just..." What could she say? She was still upset at him, but guilt overwhelmed her. How often had she wished for someone to have such faith in her? She'd never dared to dream it would happen, and yet here she was. Gherrim believed in her so much he'd been willing to risk another man's life. It might not have been circumstances she'd have chosen, but if she pushed him away now, would she ever find someone to believe in her again? "I'm lucky to have you," she whispered.

He nodded, taking the key from around his neck and draping it over hers. "From now on, you'll use the teshneh to do your healing. This key will give you access, and I'll instruct the guards to let you pass. I won't let you drain yourself day in and day out when you can use the power available up here."

Ehra took a deep breath, reveling in the power flowing through her. She felt so strong, so full of magic, yet the monster remained silent. No temptation to take the extra life for herself. No worry about losing her humanity. Just power and magic, and it was all hers. "You'd do that, for me?"

"Of course."

Ehra grinned. "You really do love me, don't you?"

He squeezed her shoulder. "The magic might be overwhelming at first, but we can find ways for you to expend the excess." His hand fell from her shoulder, sliding down her breast and over her hips.

Ehra's eyes fell to the ground. That hadn't been the reply she'd hoped for, but perhaps that just wasn't his way. He didn't use emotions to show his love—he used other, more physical ways. But he gave her this power, this escape from the monster. Shouldn't that count for something?

She looked back to the teshneh. So much power. So much magic. In her hands, it could do amazing things.

But in the wrong hands...

Her father's war, and the plight of her homeland, came crashing back upon her. The Star-Blades would be coming for this. They were convinced they could use it to rid the world of magic once and for all.

Yet how could it, when it brimmed with magic itself?

"Where did it get all that power?" she asked.

"The teshneh draws magic from the land. Every day we adjust it to expend some back into Temhet-Sakh."

That must be what the Star-Blades had planned for it. Take it to Kuriza, to Hatife, and pull all the magic from the land. If they didn't expend it, there would nothing but what magic-users could draw from it manually, the way Ehra just had. And if there were no magic-users in the land, that power would remained trapped. Forever.

They had to make sure the Star-Blades never got their hands on the teshneh. Her father had said he trusted their judgment on how to act once they found the device.

Well, Ehra had found it. And she deemed it safest that it stay right here, under Temhet-Sakh's guard. Where it would feed the city its intoxicating magic.

Ehra inhaled, dizzy with magic. She would stay here, too. To protect the teshneh, and allow it to feed her as well.

irta had to pry Mariq from Turien's bedside. He lay there broken, unconscious, and irreversibly attached to this voidstone thing. Mariq couldn't help but shudder each time she looked at it. The thought of leaving Turien alone with it… what if he woke while she was gone? How could she let him find out what had happened to him from a stranger?

But in the end, Nirta insisted. And she was right. Mariq could do nothing for Turien while he slept, and she needed to speak with the patriarch. If he had answers, she needed to speak with him.

She followed Nirta, weaving through people and merchants and camels on instinct. Her eyes rarely lifted from the ground, despite the wonders she sorely wished to explore. *These people must have a way to help us. They broke us out of Temhet-Sakh and their entire lives are spent in the magic. Anyone who could make an oasis like Haven in the middle of the open desert must have some power we can use.*

Nirta spoke to her, something about nomads and water and the city that had almost stolen Turien from her. *They are Temhet-Sakh's enemies. Does that mean they've perfected ways of thwarting them?*

Finally Nirta stopped them in front of a building. It was no larger or grander than any other, but the deference she paid it told Mariq everything she needed to know. She ducked into the cool darkness and found herself at the top of a dimly lit staircase. She descended and entered a large, open space. Torches of clear, smokeless flame lined the walls. Lush furs softened the floors. In the middle of the room stood a large table, knotty wood polished to a shine, and a dozen chairs. A man roughly a decade older than Cendim stood near one.

He looked nothing like a leader should—short and scrawny, with the knobby knees and elbows of a lad not quite grown into himself. Weak and watery eyes, hands that shook ever so slightly, heritage tattoos no more extensive or elaborate than everyone else's. But the confidence and wisdom that exuded from him were unmistakable. Everything about him proclaimed that he'd earned the title of patriarch, and held it because of wise leadership and a just rule.

Of course, her father portrayed the same aura when he chose to, as well.

Mariq inclined her head and gave a small bow. It wasn't the prostrating greeting she'd been taught in Kuriza, but she was done with that. If this man would take offense to Mariq standing tall, then he was in for a rude awakening.

Mariq met his eyes, daring him to object to her brashness. He inclined his head in return with no hint of emotion or other reaction. "We must be a pleasant sight after the prisons of Temhet-Sakh."

She nodded, not quite sure how to respond. He had allowed his people to rescue them, and to nurse her and Turien back to health, but it wasn't a welcome. "Your city is a marvel," she replied. "It would be a welcome sight to anyone."

"So it would," he replied, sounding neither pleased nor honored by the compliment. He turned away. "I wonder, though, how one not attuned to the voice of the world would view it."

"I don't understand."

"You are not a magic-user. Magic is the voice of the world, a guardian guiding us on the path of wisdom and strength. Without it, one wanders the world blindly. How do the works of the sighted seem to you?"

"The works of the sighted?" Mariq didn't try to hide her indignation. "You see us the same way Temhet-Sakh does? Inferior? Unworthy? Pests to be disposed of? If that's the case, I'll thank you for your rescue and remove myself and my companion from your care before you decide to slap some other magic parasite on us and leave us for dead."

The patriarch turned back to her, his face revealing almost no emotion at all. "You misunderstand. You may be blind, unhearing of the voice of the world, but that does not make you worthless. You are as essential to this place as we are, as everything is. I would no sooner destroy you than I would one of my own people."

Mariq believed his sincerity, but she didn't relax her guard.

"My scouts saw you approaching Temhet-Sakh. We tried to stop you," he said, "but the guards are always on the lookout for sojourners. Those with magic are welcomed, coddled even. Those without... well, you know all too well what they do to your kind."

"And what about you?" Mariq asked, trying—and failing—to keep the suspicion from her voice. "What will you do to 'our kind?'"

"I have already told you neither you nor your companion will be harmed. What more do you ask of us?"

"Not harming us is one thing. Helping is another."

"Quite true," he replied. "That issue is yet to be decided."

"I see."

The patriarch turned back to her. His slumped shoulders made him look lazy, unfocused, but Mariq could see the intensity in his eyes. He stared at her as if she were a puzzle he could unravel if only he focused hard enough.

For her part, Mariq squared her shoulders and stared back. If he even hinted she and Turien weren't worth saving, she would strike hard and fast and be out of here before he could recover.

"You do not ask the questions in your mind," he said. Still his eyes bored into hers. "You challenge me, refusing to show weakness, while inside you scream for answers and cry for help."

Mariq's strength faltered. How had he seen through her, to the frightened little girl inside?

The patriarch smirked, but gave no hints to how he'd known her true thoughts.

"I..." Mariq's voice caught in her throat. She breathed deeply, burying her fears, and summoned her strength once again.

Tried to summon her strength.

No matter how hard she tried, the shield she'd placed around her emotions wouldn't rise. All the fear, the insecurities, the weariness, refused to be ignored any longer. Mariq squirmed that this man, who held her and her friends' lives in his hands, witnessed her breakdown.

When she met his eyes, though, she saw no condemnation in them. No judgment, or condescension, or anything. Not even curiosity. Just... eyes. On her.

And somehow, against all logic, she found herself compelled to be truthful with him.

"One of my friends is unconscious, with some kind of horrid magic stuck to his forehead, and the other was taken from us in Temhet-Sakh. I have no idea what happened to her. I don't need to be coddled here, accepted but ignored. I need to be helped. I need allies, Patriarch, and so far you're the only one I've seen who would even consider that proposition."

He raised an eyebrow at her, but that was the extent of his expression.

"Our world is being torn apart. Where I come from, there are people trying to eradicate magic. Here, they're working toward the opposite. If either of them succeed none of us will have a world to live in. My friends and I are trying to stop that, but without them I can't find the object we're after and save both of our peoples from themselves." She took a breath and stilled her trembling hands. "So if you aren't willing to help, I must be on my way."

Still, the patriarch's expression showed nothing.

Mariq sighed and turned away. She would get Turien and carry him out of here if necessary. Then she would figure something out.

She'd begun to climb the stairs when the patriarch spoke. "Wait."

Mariq paused, tempted to leave anyway. But she turned, certain he would see the defeat in her eyes she couldn't stave off any longer.

The patriarch still stood where he had, his face as unreadable as ever. "Tell me about your friends."

He sat at the majestic table and waved at a seat next to him. Mariq sat, facing him. She had to take another deep breath before speaking. "Turien is... he was a slave. The people we're fighting used to own him, but he escaped them to help us. He thinks he's worthless, but he's smart and brave and has a good heart."

"He is precious to you?"

Mariq's heart thudded in her chest. "He is," she replied. She hadn't known quite how much until he'd been taken from her, then returned on the brink of death, but yes. He was quite precious to her.

"And your other friend, the one lost in Temhet-Sakh?"

"Ehra is the daughter of a sheik, a good man who leads our cause. She is also precious to me."

"She is a magic-user."

Mariq nodded. "Her abilities are… considerable."

"Yes, I heard. Many people witnessed her miracle during the battle that day."

Mariq's hand went to her side, where the spear should have claimed her life. Had claimed her life? She still wasn't sure on that. No scar marked the place. "As soon as we entered Temhet-Sakh, they took her away. I don't even know where to start to get her back."

The patriarch nodded. Mariq found herself wringing her hands and willed them to stop, though a slight tremble remained.

The patriarch was silent for a moment, his eyes leaving Mariq and drifting off to a distant corner. "And your other friend's magic. What does it do?"

"Turien doesn't have magic," Mariq replied. The patriarch's eyes snapped to hers, the intensity almost suffocating. "He'd been given a potion that would give him the ability to use magic for a brief time. He used one in the prison. It… I've never seen anything like what he did."

"Tell me," the patriarch said.

"Blue streams of light flowed from the air into him. He stood still and cold as a statue, only moving to breathe deeply. The light sucked into him when he did. Then he began to glow, and the walls… they just started to… unmake."

"Then what?"

"The walls remade themselves. The guards came and took him away before he could do any significant damage to them." Her voice caught at the memory. "The next time I saw him was when Nirta rescued us, and by then he had that voidstone on him."

The patriarch nodded, stood, and began pacing the room. Mariq remained seated, watching him. She could practically hear his mind sorting through everything.

After a few moments, the patriarch turned back to her. "A

voidstone is a blackened, petrified human heart—a heart that has been purged not only of its magic, but its very life-essence. Everything that once made it a piece of a living being has been drained from it."

Mariq cringed. The thought of something like that in contact with Turien's skin made her stomach churn and flop.

"It is now a pit of complete non-magic. They are leeches, latching onto a source of life and feeding on its magic. We've only ever seen one removed when the person wearing it died. And even then, it did not come off easily."

"Why would a place full of magic-users have such things?"

"Even the threat of a voidstone is often enough to keep the population in check. Should anyone grow too unruly, threatening the status quo or causing trouble, their punishment is severe, permanent, and far worse to a magic-user than death. It's proven to be a very effective tactic."

"Fear usually is," Mariq muttered.

The patriarch returned to his seat, fixing his eyes on Mariq's again. "I have never heard of a voidstone being attached to someone without magic before. Neither have I heard of someone becoming a magic-user for only a few moments. Your friend's situation is unique, and one that leaves me baffled.

"Your other friend's situation is only slightly less complicated. Many inside the city are as imprisoned as you were, though their cells are made of magic and elegance rather than glass and rot. Your friend would be no more able to leave than you were. Though whether or not she wants to leave is a different question. So much magic flows through Temhet-Sakh it's no longer safe. Magic that potent is addictive, and that addiction is very real and very dangerous. Too long lost in its power can corrupt even the strongest of hearts." He paused, and Mariq reminded herself to breathe. "It seems you truly are in need of help."

She nodded, her heart twisting into painful knots. She'd known her situation wasn't favorable, but having the patriarch lay it out so bleakly left her feeling bereft.

"Please, Patriarch," she whispered. "I can't do this alone. I'm dealing with things I have no clue about and I just don't know what to do anymore."

He nodded, but ignored her plea. "This object you're seeking. What is it?"

"It's a device dating back to the Night of Bloody Sands. Supposedly it can infuse people with magic or take it away from others. The Star-Blades believe it's powerful enough to alter the balance of magic in the entire world."

The patriarch nodded again. "I know of what you speak. It is called the teshneh. They use this device to make the voidstones."

Mariq grit her teeth. She hated it already.

"Temhet-Sakh has used it for decades to pull magic from the desert itself, tapping into its reservoir to feed the magic that keeps their city alive. By now it's full to bursting with magic, far more than it was ever designed to carry."

"So we can't just destroy it. All that power would escape back into the desert, which already has too much magic to begin with." Mariq straightened, a spark of hope kindling in her chest. "But if we stole it, took it back to Kuriza, and *then* destroyed it… that magic would suffuse our desert. That would restore the balance, wouldn't it?"

The patriarch's brow furrowed. "It would help, certainly. Restore? Not likely. The desert here is flush with magic, and Temhet-Sakh even more so. The teshneh holds a fraction of that power. Giving that to your desert would give you time but little else."

"I'll take time." Mariq stood and began pacing. Stealing something so full of magic wouldn't be easy, but she hadn't dared hope something this good could be possible. Rather than stalling the Star-Blades' plans, she could halt them entirely. Undo some of the damage done since the purge of magic in Kuriza. By giving magic back to her people, she could bring life to them again. Give Cendim time to expand his war, begin healing the balance of magic in their world. It would only take one more theft. The biggest she'd ever done.

"You said Temhet-Sakh used this teshneh to feed the city."

"Yes. Without it I doubt it could stand at all."

Mariq nodded. She remembered the delicate glass-like spires that would have been impossible for normal architecture to maintain. Something that essential to the city would, by no means, be an easy theft.

And she still had Joythief coursing through her body.

Mariq bit her lip, smoothing her fingers over her sarong. It had been weeks since she'd been poisoned. She couldn't even guarantee being able to steal anything, let alone something as valuable as the teshneh. But what choice did she have? This could be their only chance to restore magic to Kuriza. She'd known their task here would be difficult, and Cendim had sent her for her spider-thief skills. Among others, he claimed, but thieving was her function here. She had to at least try.

"Getting to this device, let alone retrieving it from the city, could be the most difficult task of any," the patriarch said.

"That's not very encouraging."

"No, but it is the truth. And hard truths are better than kind lies."

Mariq nodded. She was done with kind lies. "I don't know if I have the skills to steal the teshneh anymore, but I'm going to try. I need to get it and take it back to Kuriza, but I can't do it alone. I need my friends, and I need help. I need *your* help, Patriarch. Thieving and sneaking are one thing, but voidstones and magic addictions? Even if I had all my spider-thief skills, I would be no match for those things."

The patriarch raised an eyebrow, but didn't speak for a few more moments. "You are a very brave woman, to come here and speak these hard truths to me. Braver still for accepting mine."

Mariq's eyes fell to the ground. "I don't feel very brave right now."

"You are afraid, yet you still fight on. That is the very definition of bravery." She lifted her eyes in time to see a smile on the patriarch's face—one that left her speechless. "You said you needed allies, Princess Mariq Ashai Meidani of Kuriza. As of today, you have found one."

Mariq was so relieved she didn't mention her surprise that he knew her name.

"For now, I think we need to visit your companion. I must see this voidstone for myself."

MARIQ tried not to fidget as the patriarch examined Turien. The old man was silent as death as he bent over Turien, his nose inches from Turien's forehead. He very carefully avoided touching the voidstone, though he spent long moments staring at it.

"It is well and truly attached to him," he said. "As surely as if he were a magic-user."

"What can we do?" Mariq asked.

"I don't know. But the voidstone is already doing its work. It is feeding on his magic."

"Turien doesn't have magic."

"He must have some. Otherwise the voidstone would be feeding on his life instead. I doubt he would have lived this long without at least a little magic in his blood."

Mariq's stomach dropped. She could picture it—the stone growing fat on Turien's magic until what little he possessed, probably a remnant of Cendim's potion, was used up. Then what would happen? He would shrivel until nothing of Turien remained. Her hands squeezed Turien's until his fingers paled. "We have to get it off."

"There's no way," Nirta said from behind the patriarch. "Voidstones only release their victims when there is no life left in them."

"He's not going to die!" Mariq shouted.

"We can heal his injuries," Nirta said. "But there's nothing we can do to remove the voidstone. Turien isn't the first to come to us with one. We've tried many, many times to free people from them. Until it claims his life, it will not be moved."

Mariq hid her face in her free hand. This mission had gotten so complicated. They were just supposed to go into the desert and figure out what the Star-Blades wanted. Now they had to rescue Ehra, find a way to remove an impossible-to-remove circlet from Turien's head, and figure out what to do about a corrupt city robbing the world of its magic. And get the teshneh. And return, before she lost the abilities that would allow them to succeed. Before Hatife fell to war with Kuriza and the Star-Blades. And before the imbalance of magic tore the world apart. How could she rise to this challenge?

Yet how could she not? Failure meant the death of everything, and everyone, she loved.

Fear and sorrow so overwhelmed her she barely registered Turien stirring. He groaned, shifting toward her, and she pulled herself from her misery. "Turien?"

He stared at her blindly for a moment, seeming at peace, before he grimaced in pain and rolled away. He tried to vomit, though nothing came forth.

Nirta approached with a cup of water, which Mariq took from her hands. She helped Turien sit and held the cup for him while he sipped.

When he finished drinking, he looked around blearily. He didn't speak, though his eyes asked a hundred questions.

"You've been unconscious for days," Mariq told him. "These

people rescued us. They're going to help us find Ehra and get the teshneh."

Turien's forehead crinkled. "The what?"

"The device Cendim sent us here for. It's called a teshneh."

Turien tried to nod, but he swayed at the motion.

"Easy," the patriarch said. "You're already weak from your imprisonment, and the voidstone will only exacerbate that."

Turien looked at him for a moment, fear and horror in his eyes. Then his hand rose to the voidstone on his forehead.

As soon as his fingers touched it he shuddered and dropped his hand. "I'd hoped that was a nightmare." His voice was rough and scratchy, as if he'd screamed it away. Mariq's heart broke—more than likely that's what had happened.

The patriarch shook his head. "I'm afraid not. Temhet-Sakh is not known for being kind to their prisoners."

Turien nodded once, turned green, and vomited up his water.

Mariq's heart ached for Turien. What had they done to him? Would he ever be whole again?

"I'm sorry to put you through this so soon," the patriarch said, "but we must know why they put a voidstone on you."

"I understand," Turien replied. Mariq held him close to her, her sorrow physically painful. He leaned into her, seeming grateful for her strength. If only he knew how much she relied on him right now, too.

He closed his eyes, took a few deep breaths, and then began speaking. Mariq was impressed with how steady his voice sounded. "They beat me. Chained me to a wall and whipped me, hit me with fists, clubs, anything they could find. They asked me about my magic, why they couldn't detect any in me, how I'd done what I'd done. I wouldn't tell them about the potions, so they beat me until I lost consciousness." He closed his eyes, swallowed, and drank a little more water. "When I came to, they started again. And again, every time."

The patriarch's eyes shone with infinite sadness. "When did they resort to the voidstone?"

"They couldn't deny I'd done some kind of magic, but they couldn't make it show itself. They even bribed me with a house and job if I'd tell them how I'd unmade the walls. When I refused, they decided I was a traitor to Temhet-Sakh." Turien's trembling redoubled. "They made sure I couldn't fight or run away, and then…"

Mariq rested her head on Turien's shoulder, trying to lend him strength. He shook so badly now he couldn't hold his voice steady anymore.

"It felt like a great, icy emptiness being pressed to my soul. Not evil, just… nothing. A horrifying, nauseating emptiness, freezing and excruciating, and it wouldn't stop sucking me into it. Even now, I can…" He shuddered and fell silent.

Mariq squeezed him gently. She couldn't begin to imagine the horrors they'd put him through. Her heart broke again and again to see him like this, to feel him shake, to hear the pain in his voice. Knowing she could do nothing to help was even worse.

"Why didn't they just kill me?" Turien whispered. "It would have been so much easier. But they just kept torturing me, and now this? Why?" His eyes were wide and haunted when he looked up at the patriarch.

"I cannot fathom the depths of madness in evil men's minds, and I would not wish to. But I do know the voidstones give them power over their people. There are rumors the voidstones even give them actual power, that the magic leeched from the person is siphoned into the teshneh and then controlled by the sultan. But to put a voidstone on someone without magic… I do not understand."

"But they thought he was a magic-user," Nirta said.

The patriarch nodded. "They did, but they had to have an idea all was not as it seemed."

"It doesn't change anything," Mariq said. She tried to keep the frustration from her voice, but failed. "They tortured Turien and nearly killed him. They put this *thing* on him. We have to get it off, and then we have to make them pay."

Nirta sighed. "You cannot get it off," she said, clearly exasperated at repeating herself. "He must die for it to be removed."

Turien looked at her, despair in his eyes.

"Even if he did die, I wouldn't allow it. I'd drag Ehra out of Temhet-Sakh myself and make her bring him back."

Mariq froze. Was that their answer?

She locked eyes with Turien, her heart stirring at the faint hope she saw. "Ehra brought me back to life," she said. "If she did that for me, she must be able to do it for you." Perhaps Turien wouldn't be lost to her after all.

She wished for a smile to break out on his face, but she saw fear more than anything. Understandable. Yet she could see his resolve as well—even if it killed him, it would be better than living with the voidstone.

"You are suggesting he choose to die," Nirta said. "Keeping the voidstone might be unpleasant, but it seems you can live with it, at least for a while. Would you risk that time in hopes of removing something we've proven cannot be removed?"

Mariq and Turien locked eyes. If it could get the voidstone off, they would risk it. What other choice did they have?

"Where's Ehra?" Turien asked.

"You can't be serious," Nirta said.

"I am. If that's what it takes to be free of this thing." Turien's voice sounded stronger than it had since he'd woken, enough to silence everyone in the room.

"As far as we know, Ehra is still in Temhet-Sakh."

"My people can find her," the patriarch said. "Give us time, and we will help you win your freedom."

Turien smiled then, little more than a shadow of happiness in the expression. Mariq let him have his moment of hope, feeble though it may be. She didn't want to spoil that with just how hopeless the rest of their situation was.

ays passed while Turien and Mariq waited for news from the patriarch's spies. Turien spent much of that time resting, healing, regaining the strength he'd lost in his ordeal. He still had trouble sleeping, and his entire body felt jittery. He jumped at the slightest sounds, and strange movements in the shadows made his palms go sweaty and his heart race. They'd been rescued only a handful of days ago. Perhaps with time, his anxiety would fade. Until then—if it ever happened—he tried to relax and enjoy his surroundings.

When he'd returned to consciousness and been taken outside for some fresh air, he'd hardly been able to believe his eyes. They were at the bottom of a small canyon, yet everywhere he looked was green and glittering with water. Even the walls boasted drapes of plants, and cubbyholes in the rock hinted at even more to Haven above and beside them than just this narrow track. Mariq had tried to explain this place to him, but she seemed just as awed by it. Perhaps one day he'd learn how they'd done this, but for now he just reveled in the peace and coolness and moisture of the place.

He walked with Mariq now, as they often did, following the water and paths in the grass. She hadn't left his side since he'd woken. He figured much of it was for his benefit—the sadness and pity in her eyes wouldn't let her deny it—but he suspected part of it was for her, too. Since he'd woken she hadn't spoken of the Joythief, but every time they'd been in negotiations with the patriarch he could see it in her expression and the set of her shoulders. She was terrified of what would happen when she tried to use her skills again.

He glanced over at her. She'd hardly said a word since they'd begun walking today, which was unusual for her. Oftentimes she chattered aimlessly, as if afraid to leave silence between them. Again, he figured she did it for his benefit.

He didn't mind. He enjoyed every word she spoke to him. Every moment spent with Mariq was a moment of enchantment, of contentment and friendship Turien never believed he could have. Especially not with a woman like Mariq. Intelligent, articulate, witty, so full of life and dreams he couldn't help but reach for his own. Even just walking with her, arm in arm, was a dream come true. At first she'd held his arm to help support him, but now that his strength had returned he didn't need the aid. They still walked together, though, and they'd never gotten out of the habit of linking arms. Turien didn't mention it for fear she'd pull away and stop resting her hand on his arm.

"You're quiet today," he said, noting the set of her shoulders and the grim expression on her face. "Is everything all right?"

"Hmm? Oh, I'm sorry. Just thinking."

"About what?"

She hesitated. She'd told him several times she didn't want to burden him further, that he'd gone through enough and didn't need the added pressure. Her eyes flickered down to his slave-hole, now empty, and then to the voidstone, so much heavier than the barbed wire band had ever been.

"I've told you, I'm fine. You don't need to protect me, Mariq. I don't want to be coddled."

His voice still grated when he spoke loudly like this, but he hoped Mariq would focus on the passion in his tone rather than the hoarse nature of it. Turien might have been damaged by his ordeal, but he hadn't been broken. If anything, he'd come through the other side harder and more determined than ever. He had to make sure everyone saw that.

"I'm trying to figure out a way to convince the patriarch to give us more help when we get Ehra and the teshneh," she said.

Turien nodded, flexing his wrist a few times. So far the patriarch had been reluctant to commit to helping them more than what he'd already done. Despite their mutual hatred for Temhet-Sakh and their agreement the city should not abuse and control the teshneh as they did, the patriarch still seemed to see their mission as something removed from him and his people.

They had another meeting after midday. Perhaps it was time for both of them to try to make the patriarch see they needed each other.

They passed the time in an idyllic walk, stopping for lunch at their favorite spot by a pond fed from high above by a bare trickle of water. A cool breeze had picked up, bringing with it the scent of moisture and the sound of grass susurrating around them. Turien could have stayed there forever, away from rescue missions and voidstones and all the horrors the Mad Desert had presented to them thus far. Here, at least for the next few hours, he could pretend nothing else was required of him.

Somewhere in the distance, an alarm began to wail.

Turien's peace of mind shattered like a dream. His heart raced, sweat broke out on his palms, and his thoughts screamed and panicked. He needed Mariq's arm again for the first time in days.

Nirta raced up to them, half-shrouded in her desert garb. "What's going on?" Mariq shouted over the alarm as she slowed before them.

"We've spotted a large group of people approaching Temhet-Sakh. Too organized to be Feral and too well-armed to be sojourners."

"An attack?" Mariq asked.

"That seems likely."

Turien's stomach soured. The Star-Blades. Who else could it be? His former master had come for the teshneh, and to release the weapon against the magic-users. But he hadn't expected them to move this quickly! They must have mobilized from Kuriza almost immediately after Turien and Mariq had left from their ill-fated adventure.

They had to move, and move *now*, but their plans were far from finalized. They'd only spoken briefly of ways to use their skills to retrieve Ehra and the teshneh, and they hadn't been able to get the patriarch to give them anything other than a few scouts to watch Temhet-Sakh. He'd shied away from promising any help when the time came to infiltrate the city. They couldn't hope to outmaneuver a fortified city of magic-users with just the two of them and a vague idea of how to achieve their goals.

But neither could they afford to wait. The Star-Blades had come for the teshneh, and if they reached it first there would be no taking it from them. As unlikely as success seemed against Temhet-Sakh, against the Star-Blades it would be all but impossible.

"We need to see the patriarch," he said.

Nirta nodded and waved them to follow her.

The patriarch's chambers swarmed with people and buzzed with conversations, some whispered, others shouted. Haven was clearly well-accustomed to defending itself—though chaotic, everyone seemed to know what they were meant to do and did it with as much efficiency as could be expected.

"Why can't we just let them attack?" a man asked the patriarch, both leaning on the large table in the middle of the room. "We're talking about Temhet-Sakh, after all. None here would lament the loss of that abomination."

The patriarch paused and nodded his head ever so slightly.

"You can't let them take the city," Turien said, moving through the crowd to approach the patriarch. "This isn't any attack. Those are Star-Blades, the best-trained thieves and assassins in the Scorched Lands. They're after the same thing we are—the teshneh—and trust me, you don't want them to get it first."

"What do you suggest we do, then?" the patriarch asked. "Send what little army we have out to stop them? My people are survivors. Very few are warriors, yet the enemy you suggest we stop is, by your own admission, full of the best-trained killers known to our lands. We cannot stop them, and even if we could, we could not risk these Star-Blades discovering Haven."

"But if the Star-Blades get the teshneh—"

"I understand, but I'm sorry. Our resources must go toward protecting our people."

"We aren't asking for an army. Just a few people to help us get in and out unseen. If we can secure the teshneh before the Star-Blades, then they can war with Temhet-Sakh as much as they want."

By now many of the room's occupants had grown quiet, listening. Now they looked to the patriarch expectantly. Silence weighed on Turien's shoulders.

The patriarch hesitated a few moments longer. "I will grant you scouts to get you in and out of Temhet-Sakh, on one condition. When you leave that city, you leave it in pieces."

Turien recoiled at the brutality in the patriarch's voice. He held no love for Temhet-Sakh after what they'd done to him and his friends, but this hatred went beyond that. The patriarch would sooner destroy the entire desert than allow that city to remain standing. "Between the Star-Blades and removing the teshneh I don't think there will be much of Temhet-Sakh left," Turien said.

"The Star-Blades will wreak havoc on the people, but it's the city itself that's the abomination. Removing the teshneh will hurt it, but we want to ensure Temhet-Sakh is razed. That city must be wiped from the map. If you wish to restore balance as much as you claim to, you'll ensure there's nothing left of Temhet-Sakh to rebuild."

Turien hesitated, exchanging a nervous glance with Mariq. The kind of destruction the patriarch demanded would mean countless lives lost. Even if they managed to find a way to do it, could they bear the consequences of such a desperate, devastating act?

They'd have to. If they wanted to retrieve the teshneh, restore the balance of magic, and save their world from being torn apart, it would have to come at the cost of Temhet-Sakh.

Turien clenched his fists and nodded. "Agreed."

Mariq had been silent through the entire exchange, and even when they left the crowded room she didn't say a word. Turien could see the worry on her face. He knew the loss of her skills to the Joythief tormented her—they would need her to steal the teshneh, after all—but with the way her brow furrowed and her fingers rubbed the silk of her sarong like she tried to wear a hole through it, he suspected more than simple concern drove her motions.

"It'll be all right," he said. "We'll make it work."

She looked up at him as if he had startled her. She nodded, her thoughts clearly on another matter.

"We'll find Ehra too." Another mindless nod, neither agreement nor disagreement. So something else entirely. "What is it, Mariq?"

She didn't look at him. If anything, she crouched further into herself.

He put his hand on her shoulder, gently pulling her to a stop. It took her a moment to turn toward him, and even then her eyes went past his face and to his arm.

Turien withdrew it, as if pulling the bare skin out of sight would hide the reality of his station. With everything they'd been through, all their easy conversations while they recovered in Haven, he thought they'd gotten beyond this. Mariq had always treated him as a human being, a man unto himself, but since coming to Haven it had seemed like they'd been something more. He had almost dared hope their friendship might have led to…

He should have known better. The haunted look she gave that slave-hole, empty though it may be, told him everything. She would never see him as more than what his arm proclaimed him to be. Heritageless. Slave. No One. Meanwhile she was daughter of a sheik, a Star-Blade spider-thief, beautiful and intelligent and deserving of so much more than a nameless slave. How dare he even dream she might choose him.

They stood facing each other, not looking at one another, for a long, awkward moment. Then Mariq knelt, pulled her knife from a sheath, and cut a narrow strip of brightly patterned silk from the bottom of her sarong. She stood and held it for another moment, the shorn fabric fluttering in the light breeze.

"We're putting ourselves in a lot of danger," she said, her voice quiet and unsure. "And now that the Star-Blades are here… I can't imagine what they would do if they saw you without your slave-band. If they caught you, unclaimed, they'd be free to take you back and do whatever they wanted with you. So…" She held out a hand, the one not holding the silk. "If you have no objections, I would like to…" She faltered.

Turien hesitated. Was she suggesting she take ownership of him?

The thought made his entire body go stiff with disgust. He would never be owned again, not by anyone. He was a free man, as much as the hole in his forearm and the voidstone on his head would allow him to be.

"I'm sorry," Mariq said, as if reading his thoughts. "I don't mean it like that. I just… if someone should find you, I want them to know you aren't property to be claimed."

She dared to meet his eyes and he saw nothing but fear and compassion in them. Some of Turien's disgust melted. She didn't want to take ownership of him. She wanted to protect him.

"I'm sorry," Mariq repeated. She lowered the silk and took a step back, her eyes on her feet. "I just want you to come back to me." She turned and started away, head down, hands clutching the silk before her.

Something twisted in Turien's gut. This had nothing to do with his station and everything to do with them. Their friendship. Perhaps even more. He hadn't been imagining it.

Mariq didn't want to lose him. She worried about him and wanted him to remain with her. A simple band of silk might make an enemy think twice about taking him, claiming him. *That* would be a return to slavery. Allowing Mariq to take ownership of him? That felt more like a taste of true freedom. So why did he fight it? Turien would never leave her, slave-band or no.

"Wait," Turien called. He stepped forward and grabbed Mariq's arm before she fled out of reach. She stopped and glanced back at him, fear and sadness in her eyes.

Before he could stop himself, he reached up with his right hand—his slave-hole between them—and wiped a tear from Mariq's cheek. Her skin was soft and warm. His hand lingered, brushing her skin, caressing back to stroke her hair.

No, he wasn't going anywhere. He was already hers, more fully, more willingly, than he'd been anyone else's.

She looked down, her fingers rubbing the silk she still held. Turien lowered his arm and held it between them, palm down, slave-hole exposed. They both stared at it for a moment, the thick band of white scars screaming at him to remember what belonging to another person really meant.

"I pledge my service to you, Mariq Ashai Meidani, Princess of Kuriza," he said. The slave's oath burned on his tongue, yet no bitterness tainted his soul.

A tear fell from Mariq's eye and landed on his forearm. She reached out and threaded the silk through the hole between his bones, winding it around his wrist, and back through. Over and around, always meeting in the middle. The sign of infinity. The symbol of forever.

Mariq's voice cracked. "I pledge my service to you, Turien. Welcome to the house of Kuriza."

She'd changed the response. Slave owners pledged nothing. They demanded service. Yet Mariq had sworn a servant's oath to him in return. She had, in essence, made them equals. She'd made herself a slave to him, and made him family to her.

Turien reached up again, the silk soft on his wrist. No barbs. No constant reminder of his status. Just warmth and softness, like Mariq's skin beneath his fingertips.

They both jumped as Nirta raced up to them. "We don't have much time. The Star-Blades will reach Temhet-Sakh by first light tomorrow. We must be out with the teshneh and your friend before then."

"It took us over a day to run here. How will we get back in time?" Mariq asked.

"We don't have two weak, injured people in tow," Nirta replied. "You'd be surprised how much faster we'll go this time. Is there anything you need before we leave?"

Turien shook his head. Their possessions had been taken in

Temhet-Sakh. Other than his many-pocketed belt around his waist and her harnesses, they had nothing left.

Nirta led them to the staircase ascending to the desert, where a few other scouts milled about. They handed him and Mariq thick, dull robes which they wrapped themselves in. Shrouded as well as his former masters in their shadowcloaks, they returned to the scorching desert and started making their way back to Temhet-Sakh.

irta had been right—Mariq couldn't believe how much faster they reached Temhet-Sakh this time. Her legs were still rubbery and sore, her entire body ached with exhaustion, but they made it to the walls of the crystalline city as the sun lit them with its last, brilliant rays. They hadn't seen any sign of the approaching Star-Blades, but the scouts assured them they were out there, ready to strike as soon as morning came.

Mariq shook her head. These were assassins and thieves, accustomed to working in the dead of night. They wouldn't wait for the light. If they were out there now, they'd be in the city well before dawn.

One of Nirta's scouts melted away from the walls of Temhet-Sakh as they approached. He gave a brief report to Nirta, then turned toward Mariq and Turien. She had no idea how he'd recognized them, covered in so much fabric. Perhaps their wearied panting gave them away. "We think we located your friend," he whispered.

Mariq's heart leapt. Finally, something worked in their favor.

"What about the teshneh?" Turien asked.

"Still no word. We have a few leads, though, and I have people checking them out as we speak."

Not the best of news, but at least they could rescue Ehra. They'd have to figure out what to do from there once she was safe.

The scout led them to a hole burrowed beneath the walls of Temhet-Sakh, which connected to a series of tunnels. The roots of the crystalline city formed pillars, breaking her line of sight, but she could tell this complex was vast. Their whispers bounced around like they had a life of their own, and light and shadow played along every surface. The scout wove between pillars and paths, never pausing to gain his bearings. He walked more quickly than simple familiarity accounted for.

"I hate this place," Nirta muttered beside Mariq. The scout grunted his assent and sped up even more.

"Why?"

"Can't you feel it?" Nirta asked. Mariq and Turien shook their heads, though Turien paused for a moment before doing so. "Temhet-Sakh is an abomination. The people pull every bit of magic they can from the desert and force it into this city. They've chained it to their will and given no thought to what is best for it—only what is best for them."

Mariq looked at the pillars again. She couldn't feel what Nirta and the scout clearly could, but she could see a bit of blue light running up the crystal. The same kind of light that had poured into Turien when he'd taken that potion and unmade the prison walls.

She glanced toward him at the memory. He stared at the pillars far more intently than she had been. She paused beside him. "I think I can feel it," he whispered. He sounded almost pained.

Mariq wasn't sure what to say, whether she should be alarmed he could feel it or concerned she could not.

"And I think..." Turien paused and reached his hand out to rest on the pillar. "I think I know how to destroy Temhet-Sakh now."

Mariq looked around the cavern. Magic ran through these pillars—these thin, narrow pillars that looked far too delicate to support an entire city above them. If Turien used more of Cendim's potion to take away this magic, the entire cavern would crumble. And the city above with it.

"That will be dangerous," she whispered.

Turien nodded, still staring at the pillar as if seeing far more than Mariq could.

Nirta rounded a corner, returning from where the scout had led them out of sight. "Come on, we don't have time to linger."

"We have to catch up," Mariq said, tugging Turien away from the pillar and after their guides.

They walked for long, silent moments through the tunnels until the scout stopped. A few horizontal grooves had been carved into a pillar here, haphazardly enough not to be noticeable but spaced to make climbing fairly easy. "This will place you in a back alley near where we believe your friend is staying. Take the second left, then right, forty paces and to the left."

"Come back here when you've got her. By then we should have word of where the teshneh is," Nirta added.

Mariq nodded while Turien started up the ladder. When he reached the top, Mariq ascended after him. Moments later she surfaced into a stuffy alley, the walls surrounding them bright with magic like the pillars below had been.

They followed the scout's directions to a modest building—if anything in Temhet-Sakh could be called modest. Crafted from glimmering stone, with curved walls and corners, the entire structure seemed to flow directly from the desert. Given Nirta's description of the way Temhet-Sakh used magic, that was more or less accurate.

Mariq crept up to the house, feeling as awkward in the shadows as Turien had looked the first night they'd been introduced. If there had been anyone in the streets to witness them, she'd have been ashamed.

She peeked into a window—a generous living area, comfortable and well-equipped, just shy of being lavish.

She tried the next window. A bedchamber, strewn with pillows and thin sheets. A hulking man lay amongst the pillows, his features bordering on cruel even in sleep. Ehra nestled against him, barely half his size. His arm around her looked more like a cage than a loving embrace.

The darkness covered her blush as Mariq ducked back down. Ehra had taken a lover? Under different circumstances she'd have been happy for her—the poor girl deserved some happiness, after all—but too many worries kept her joy at bay. If this man had lived here for a long time, addiction to the magic of Temhet-Sakh must have corrupted him by now. Could she trust a man like that to care for Ehra? Was he kind to her? Something told Mariq she wouldn't like the answer to that question.

All the more reason to get her out of here.

Mariq heard Ehra stir, so she peeked back into the window. "Ehra," she whispered, as loudly as she dared.

Ehra lifted her head. She tensed when she saw Mariq, eyes wide and mouth open, but didn't alert her lover. She slid from his embrace cautiously, as if afraid to wake him, and motioned Mariq toward the other room. Mariq followed, standing beside the window looking into the living space. Turien stayed around the corner, watching for anyone approaching.

Ehra came to the window a moment later, wrapped in a thin silk robe. "Mariq! You're all right! I tried to find you but no one would say anything about what had happened to you. I didn't find out you were in prison until you escaped. And even then I couldn't be sure you weren't hurt or lost."

"The people who helped us escape have taken care of us. But it's time to go."

"What?"

"We came for you. Turien needs your help, and then we're getting out of here."

Ehra glanced back toward the bedroom, biting her lip. Suddenly she looked the same way she had when Mariq first met her—keeping herself small, nervous, afraid. She hesitated, looking between Mariq and the bedchamber. "I… I don't think I want to go."

"Ehra, please. Turien's had a voidstone put on him, and if we don't do something it's going to kill him."

"What's a voidstone?"

Mariq paused. Ehra hadn't heard about the voidstones? Interesting. "I'll show you. Just come with me."

"I can't," Ehra replied. "Gherrim wouldn't like me wandering off in the middle of the night."

Mariq's eyes narrowed. Fear, not affection, kept her close to him. "Is he your bed partner or your wet nurse?"

Ehra's eyes widened for a heartbeat, then fell to the floor. She knew. She *knew* he didn't treat her well.

"Why are you still here, Ehra?" Mariq whispered.

She took a long time to reply. When she did, her voice held a strange mixture of resignation and ferocity. "He's seen my monster, Mariq. He watched me abuse my magic and he still accepts me. Who else do you know who has ever done that?"

"I have," Mariq said. She looked Ehra square in the eye as she said it and watched her friend be shocked into silence. "Turien has, too.

We've seen your power, Ehra. The only reason I'm alive right now is because of it. We both know what you're capable of, and we came here to rescue you before Temhet-Sakh corrupts you."

Ehra stiffened.

"Have you been ignoring that, too?"

Mariq hadn't intended the words to be so harsh, but Ehra flinched as if she'd been struck. The haunted look in her eyes grew deeper and she held herself as if afraid she would break apart if she let go.

Mariq *had* to get her out of here.

"Please, Ehra, just come with me. See what they did to Turien, and if you can help. Decide then." Mariq paused. "There's no one else who can help."

Ehra looked at her for long moments, still seeming torn. She looked back to the bedchamber, and for a moment Mariq thought she wouldn't come.

"All right," Ehra said at last. "For Turien. After that, I'm coming right back here."

Mariq nodded. It was a start.

A few moments later Ehra emerged from the house, properly clothed and looking for all the world like a child sneaking out from her bedroom. She glanced behind her every few heartbeats, hunched within herself, every muscle tense and ready to flee.

At least she was out.

Mariq led her around the corner to where Turien waited. Ehra gasped when she saw the enormous black stone strapped to his forehead, recoiling for a heartbeat before inching forward for a closer look. Turien bore the scrutiny in silence, dread and hope warring in his eyes. His fists balled at his sides, he twisted his silk-wrapped wrist around and around as if reminding himself the barbs were gone. As if that freedom comforted him, for whatever it was worth.

Long, silent moments passed. Mariq tried not to fidget, to keep from distracting Ehra in her examination, but she ached to get more information. What did she think? Could she get it off? If Ehra couldn't do anything for Turien, she had no clue what they would do next. If they *could* do anything. But the other option was to leave that accursed stone on him until it killed him, and Mariq could not allow that.

Finally Ehra spoke, her voice a thread of a whisper in the darkened alley. "I've never seen anything like this. It's like a hole in the magic, in life itself." She reached toward the voidstone, but stopped well before touching it.

"The patriarch said it's a human heart so drained of magic it's become the antithesis of life."

Ehra shut her eyes, suppressing a shudder. "This thing shouldn't exist. It's…"

"It's what Temhet-Sakh makes to punish those who don't do what they want," Turien said. His voice was quiet, but the hatred in it hit both women like a blow. Ehra faltered in her examination, hands freezing over Turien, eyes locked on his. He met them fearlessly. Ehra looked away first, shoulders slumping. Yet more evidence this place was a nightmare. Mariq hoped Ehra saw that.

"We need your help to remove it."

"I don't understand how I could help," Ehra said. "I'm no more skilled in areas like this than you are."

"The patriarch said voidstones will only come off when the person wearing them dies."

Ehra turned to Mariq, eyes wide. "Oh." She turned back to Turien, her attention more directed, more focused. Even Mariq squirmed under that attention. It felt too personal, too intimate. Too *hungry*.

"Perhaps," she said, her eyes never leaving Turien. "If I could hold his life closely enough… But I can't do it alone." Her hand drifted toward a chain around her neck.

Turien broke his gaze with Ehra to meet Mariq's eyes. "Alone?"

She nodded, turned her head up to look to the top of the palace, visible even from this narrow alley. "I'll need a lot more magic. Come on."

23

The sun was still an hour away, and Turien shivered against the bone-chilling breeze. He didn't even bother to pretend it was entirely because of the cold.

In a few moments he would allow himself to be killed. He couldn't fool himself into thinking the possibility of never coming back didn't scare him.

The writhing blue magic in the teshneh drew his eye again and again, calling to him. He didn't know why. He'd only touched magic that one time. Once the effects of the potion had worn off he'd had no more powers than he'd had before he'd taken it. So why could he sense the magic swirling around the teshneh now? Same as he'd felt in the tunnels below Temhet-Sakh. It wasn't obvious, or even easily felt, but it was there. Insistent. Pulling him toward it, even though he could do nothing with it.

Mariq didn't seem to feel anything. After a single look at the teshneh she hadn't cast it another glance, spending far more time staring over the desert and muttering to herself. From the few snippets he'd been able to hear, she was trying to plan their escape.

Ehra, however, could obviously feel the magic too. She fidgeted, moving and shifting like she overflowed with energy. Her voice was animated, almost manic, and her eyes practically glowed with madness. "Are you ready?" she asked. Thankfully that madness wasn't present in her voice. He'd never seen her so calm and confident.

Turien laughed as he lay down on the cold glass, less than an arm's reach from the teshneh. "Am I ready to die? Of course not."

"Don't worry," Ehra said. "You won't be gone long."

The hesitation she'd shown in the alley was gone, replaced by such surety Turien couldn't help but believe her. Or maybe it was easier to believe her than dwell on the alternatives.

Mariq came to kneel beside him, her ivory knife held in her right hand. Turien looked away before the sight of that sharp blade made him bolt.

"This feels so wrong," she whispered.

"It's all right," Turien replied, though he agreed with her wholeheartedly. "It'll be worth it to get this thing off me." He forced a weak laugh. "Besides, if this does kill me, at least the Star-Blades won't be able to get me back."

Mariq tried to smile, but her eyes welled with tears and she looked away. He reached for her free hand and she grasped it, a small but comforting touch.

"I'll be all right," he whispered. Though he wasn't sure who he comforted any longer.

Mariq and Ehra shared a glance, then both looked down at Turien. Ehra's eyes landed on their intertwined hands, her expression… longing? She tore her eyes away an instant later, and the excitement in them swelled. "It's time."

He squeezed his free hand into a fist, fighting against nausea and terror and instinct telling him to run. He took a deep breath, held it, and let it out slowly. "Do it. Before I lose my nerve."

Ehra leaned over him, eyes alert and magic thrumming through her. Mariq hesitated, but raised the knife. She released him and placed her hand on his chest, pointing the blade at his heart. She shook almost as much as he did.

Turien closed his eyes.

The knife struck, rending muscle and scraping bone on its way to his heart. He felt the moment it hit home—an unbearable pressure and intense pain choked him. Then the blade punctured. He felt his heart burst and blood pour into his lungs. He was too weak to scream. He could only choke on his blood as the world went black.

EHRA didn't blink as the blade drove into Turien's heart. Dizziness surged through her as life and magic flooded the rooftop. Her hunger rose, the monster reared its head, but Ehra took in the power flowing from the teshneh and silenced it.

Red mist floated from Turien's wound, his life-force growing faint before her eyes. She grasped it, warm and soft as velvet, holding his life closely in case it dissipated too quickly. The blood was already slowing. Turien's face grew pale and sweaty and waxy, his breath a gurgling rasp.

"Not yet," Mariq said. She'd dropped the bloody knife at her side and ripped a section from her sarong—now several inches shorter than it had been—to wrap around her hand. She leaned close to Turien, her eyes glued to the voidstone.

Ehra couldn't bear to look at it. Especially now, wrapped in magic and life, the emptiness of the voidstone pained her. Like the vast *nothing* of it clawed at her eyes and sucked at her soul.

Mariq's strike had been true—Turien's life slipped away far faster than she'd anticipated. At this rate she might not have time to heal him before his life-force became too weak for even pure magic to resurrect. "I can't wait for long," Ehra said. "There has to be something left of his life for me to heal him, and it's dissipating too fast."

"We have to wait. The voidstone hasn't come off yet."

"If it takes too much longer he'll be gone for good."

"We can't give up yet." Her voice was hard, but Ehra heard the torment in it. Mariq couldn't feel Turien's life, couldn't see it hovering over him. She couldn't take comfort in gauging how much time he had left the way Ehra did.

Then again, with how faint and wispy his life already was, Ehra didn't gather much comfort from it either. He only had a few heartbeats left. If the voidstone didn't come off before that, Turien would die.

No. She couldn't let that happen. She'd bring him back, voidstone or not. He wouldn't die while Ehra was there to save him.

Mariq reached out, but recoiled from the voidstone before her fingers even brushed it. It showed no hint of loosening.

Ehra clung to the last shreds of Turien's soul, already transparent as a vapor. "Mariq, we're out of time," she whispered.

Mariq pulled at the voidstone with her cloth-wrapped hand, but it wouldn't release its hold on Turien. "Just a little bit longer? If we can't get the voidstone off, all this will have been for nothing!"

A final, deep exhalation gurgled from Turien's throat. His body relaxed, his head lolling to the side. The blood pouring from his wound slowed, then stopped altogether.

The wisp of Turien's life faded in Ehra's grip. She tried clinging to it, but it evaporated between her fingers like mist. When death came, she'd been just as powerless to stop it as everyone else.

Ehra stared at her empty hands. There was nothing left. No life remained, nothing for her to infuse with magic to revive Turien. He was gone. Without that thread of Turien's soul, she could do nothing.

She'd failed, and Turien was dead because of it.

Mariq reached down and ripped the voidstone from Turien's forehead. His body bucked and convulsed as the stone reluctantly parted from him. The skin beneath the stone was seared and raw, an angry shade of red.

And just beneath it, a tenuous link between Turien and the voidstone. The tiniest thread of life pulsed in that ruined skin, so faint it would be gone in a blink.

Ehra grasped that bit of life and held on with all the considerable strength her magic gave her. She would *not* lose this. Not if it cost her everything.

She pulled as much of her magic as she could and channeled it into the spot where the voidstone had ravaged his skin. She nursed that faint pulse, feeding it more magic than she'd ever fed anyone before. Turien would come back. Ehra would find a way to bring him back.

Cool blue magic poured into Turien. The tiny vapor of his soul wavered, no larger than a hair, no longer dissipating but not growing stronger, either.

Turien was still dead. She didn't have enough magic. Not enough power to make that thread of life grow.

But there was more than just her magic up here.

One hand holding what little remained of Turien's soul, Ehra reached her other hand toward the teshneh. She stretched until the caress of magic became a torrent, until her hand broke into the brass sphere and plunged into the current of pure magic balled within. Invigorating power swept over her in an all-consuming wave.

Gherrim had warned her not to get too close to the teshneh's magic. Ehra had just plunged Turien and herself into it.

The pure magic burned her hand and made her blood boil with power. For a moment Ehra lost herself in the magic, unable to separate her own power from that of the teshneh. She *was* magic, able to gift her healing to the entire world. Or take it all in the blink of an eye.

No. Ehra didn't need to heal the entire world. She just needed to heal this one man.

Ehra turned herself into a conduit, pulling searing power from the teshneh and pouring it into Turien as life. She ached, body and soul, with the sheer power coursing through her. The magic threatened to overtake her, but she refused to allow it. If she lost herself, or the magic overwhelmed her, Turien would die. That would not happen. He would survive if she had to drain the entire teshneh to do it.

TURIEN opened his eyes.

Light and pain and exhilaration and hope and fear assaulted him. *Life* assaulted him, in all its excruciating glory.

He could still feel the wound that had killed him and the creeping chill that had encompassed him in those last moments. But something else suffused him now, giving him warmth and life and something so much greater.

Magic.

What he'd felt when he'd taken Cendim's potion had been a taste—a single mouthful compared to the feast laid before him. So much more than he'd ever dreamed, so vast he could barely comprehend it. Magic was within everything, an inextricable part of the entire world.

Even when Ehra stopped pouring it into him, Turien felt magic in his veins, as natural and essential as blood.

He lay there for long moments, awed by the magic and grateful to be alive to feel it. He only summoned the strength to move when he heard Mariq asking if he was all right.

There was almost no pain. His chest ached and his body felt weak and lightheaded, but he sat up with very little effort. Once he met the worried-yet-relieved gazes of Ehra and Mariq he gathered the courage to raise his hand to his forehead.

The skin was bruised and raw, painful to the touch, but the voidstone was gone. He caught a glimpse of it off to the side, as if it had been flung away from them. Even from a distance it radiated icy, soul-devouring emptiness.

Mariq and Ehra followed his gaze. Several heartbeats passed without a sound, with hardly a breath.

"We can't leave it here," Mariq said, sounding disgusted by the thought of going anywhere near it. "It's too dangerous to let anyone else find it."

Turien agreed, but he didn't move toward it. That thing had taken enough from him already. He couldn't bring himself to touch it again.

Mariq approached the voidstone as if it were a venomous snake. Turien flinched when she reached down with her silk-covered hand and picked it up. She quickly unwrapped the silk, transferring the cloth from her hand to the stone and tied the bundle shut, then hiked up her sarong to inappropriate levels and tucked the entire thing into a pouch in her harnesses. He shuddered at the thought of it in such close contact with her, but the fabric and leather protected her from its vast hunger. He hoped it would be enough.

"We have to go," Ehra said. She sounded tired but exhilarated, similar to how Turien felt. "No one can find us up here. You both have to disappear, now."

"What about you?" Turien asked, getting to his feet and gesturing toward the teshneh. "We're taking this thing and going back to Hatife. Aren't you coming with us?"

"You can't take the teshneh! Temhet-Sakh needs it to survive. I…" She glanced at the teshneh, longing in her eyes, before falling silent.

"It's the only way," Mariq said.

"We can protect it. The Star-Blades won't get through Gherrim and the guards. It's safer here than it could ever be in Hatife."

"Ehra, the magic in that thing is enough to restore the balance. Leaving it here won't do any good—it'll just keep Temhet-Sakh drowning in magic, making the division between the lands worse. But if we take it, we can release the stored magic in Kuriza. We could give my people their magic back. It will force the Star-Blades to come up with a new plan. In the meantime, it gives us a chance to breathe and lets Kuriza recover a bit of its magic."

Ehra shifted, wringing her hands and stealing glances at the teshneh. Now that Turien could feel its power, he understood why.

"You'll never be able to get it out of here, let alone to Hatife. Temhet-Sakh has people who can track it. They'll never let you escape."

"They won't be able to organize much resistance if their city is in pieces," Turien mumbled. "We'll just have to deal with whoever does end up following us. There's no choice. Either we take the teshneh to Kuriza and release the magic there, or the world tears itself apart from the imbalance of magic."

Ehra's voice was barely a whisper. "Do you understand the danger to Temhet-Sakh if you take the teshneh from here?"

Mariq nodded. "I do."

"Then you realize what you're asking me to allow."

She nodded again, solemn. "But we're also asking you to come with us. We didn't come here just for the teshneh, Ehra. We came for you. Let whatever fate Temhet-Sakh deserves fall upon it. We're going home."

Long moments passed in awkward silence. Then Ehra sighed, looking out over Temhet-Sakh. "I have a home. And it's here, within the magic." She gestured to the swirling, glowing magic. "There's the teshneh. Take it and go, but I won't follow you. At least some of Temhet-Sakh must survive you stealing it."

"We can't do that," Turien said. "The only way we could get help to make it back in here—the only way we can restore the balance of magic to the world—is to ensure Temhet-Sakh is destroyed."

Ehra's eyes grew wide and glassy, but she didn't react otherwise.

Mariq took half a step forward. "If you stay, you'll be destroyed with it."

"I don't care," Ehra whispered.

They stood in uncomfortable silence as the sun crested the horizon. It painted Temhet-Sakh in glittering colors below them, intricate and mesmerizing in its beauty. Mariq and Turien spared it little more than a glance, but Ehra's gaze locked on the city and stayed there.

"If you aren't coming with us, are you going to stop us?" Mariq asked.

Ehra shook her head, still not tearing her eyes away. "Whatever I feel for Temhet-Sakh, my father is still right. Magic must be restored to Kuriza and Hatife, and if this is the way to do it... I can't stand in the way of that." She paused, wiping a tear away with her sleeve. "Tell him I love him. He might not understand, but he should know I don't want to abandon him."

"Ehra, you can't be serious."

"You don't understand what it's like, Mariq. I've found a place I belong and someone who loves and accepts me. I can use my magic and do what I've always wanted to do. I've never had anything like this before. I can't leave it just because you say it's bad."

"Look around, Ehra! You would see it's bad if you'd just open your eyes."

Ehra's eyes darted around her. She studiously avoided looking at Turien.

"I can't just walk away from this," she whispered. "It's not perfect, but it's the best thing I've ever had. I'd never forgive myself if I abandoned it without a fight."

Mariq clenched her fists at her side. "Fine. Stay here and die with this damned city, then. Go back to that brute sharing your bed that you're so afraid of. Let the world tear itself apart and fall to chaos, leave your father and your friends behind. Throw away everything you've ever believed in. I hope your beloved magic is worth it."

Mariq turned away. Ehra stood there, looking hurt and confused, for a brief moment before she began making her way to the stairs. "I won't stop you from taking the teshneh. But you can't get it out through the palace. You'll be stopped before you get halfway down the stairs."

"Then I'll go over the wall."

Turien's heart raced at the thought, but Mariq didn't meet his eyes. She looked out over the desert, as if that would hide her fear. The Joythief had taken so much from her already, and she hadn't had an opportunity—or the resolve—to test her skills further. Did she still have the ability to scale a building, let alone one as tall and sleek as this monstrosity?

Then again, what choice did they have? Ehra had made it clear she wouldn't come with them, and Turien had to fulfill their promise to the patriarch and ensure Temhet-Sakh's destruction. That left her and what little remained of her spider-thief skills to handle the teshneh.

"I'll do what I can to help you get a head start," Ehra said. "But once they realize what you've done, I'll be powerless to keep them from pursuing you. And there will be no mercy if they catch you."

"We understand."

Ehra hesitated, eyes large and sad, but stubborn determination set her jaw. "You'd better come with me, Turien," she said, turning away from them. "I can get you out of the palace. But after that, you're on your own."

Turien hesitated. He had to follow Ehra, to make good on his promise to the patriarch. But he hated to leave Mariq like this, facing an essential and dangerous and potentially deadly task. Everything rested on her and the skills the Joythief devoured.

"Go, Turien," Mariq said. "I'll be all right."

There was so much more to say, but they had no time. He flexed his wrist, feeling Mariq's soft silk threading his slave-hole. He just had to hope they had time to say it later.

He took a step toward Ehra. For a heartbeat he saw through her mask of strength and stubbornness to the pain inside. It killed Ehra to leave them behind, to choose death with Temhet-Sakh over them.

He stepped closer to her, leaning in to speak quietly. "If you change your mind, head south from Temhet-Sakh. The people of Haven will find you."

She hesitated, only a heartbeat or so, but didn't acknowledge him. When she moved away and started down the stairs, her steps were heavy.

Turien turned back to Mariq one more time. "Be safe. I want you to come back to me."

She nodded, a tiny smile breaking through her otherwise tight expression.

Then he followed Ehra off the roof and left Mariq alone with the teshneh.

24

ariq stood on the roof of the sultan's palace for a few moments, trying to ignore the puddle of blood where Turien had died. Each time she saw it a shiver went down her spine. It had been so close. If they had been any later removing the voidstone, she doubted even Ehra could have brought him back. What would she have done then? Turien had become so much more than No One. She couldn't imagine going back to Hatife without him.

Then again, she couldn't imagine going back without Ehra, either. Yet that seemed like what she'd have to do.

If only they'd found her sooner. Would she have come with them then? Could Mariq have protected her friend from the addictive magic, from the bastard sharing her bed, if they hadn't wasted so much time in Haven? Or was Ehra, desperate for acceptance and magic, doomed from the moment she entered Temhet-Sakh?

The best thing Mariq could do for her was get the teshneh away from here. Perhaps Ehra would come to her senses once this thing had left the city.

Mariq turned toward the contraption in the center of the rooftop, studying it for what seemed like ages. She used swathes of her desert garb to fashion a sling of sorts for it, grateful it was small enough for a single woman to carry, but what about the glowing bits? Would a few layers of simple cloth keep that light and magic inside? She hoped so. This theft would be difficult enough without any added complications.

Mariq glanced back over Temhet-Sakh, so very far below. She tore her gaze away before she lost her nerve and reached for the teshneh. She had to jump in order to reach it, but she grasped one of the brass rings and hauled it down without much effort.

The metal cage felt cold against her hands and surprisingly light. Blue streamers of light weaved around her arms, undeterred in their dance through the teshneh. She felt nothing, even as they passed through her arms and hands. No connection to the magic whatsoever. After everything she'd seen magic do, the terrors and the wonders, Mariq was relieved to be ignored by it.

The sling muted the teshneh's light, but it continued to glow even through the fabric as she'd feared. Still far too easy to see in the first meager light of dawn. Nothing she could do about that but move quickly and pray for a bit of luck.

The teshneh wrapped in her sling and secured to her back, Mariq moved to the edge of the roof. Eighty feet or more down a building nearly as slick as glass, with only a few balconies between her and the ground. Then over a dozen wide streets to traverse with a glowing bundle of pure magic at her side. A far greater challenge than anything she'd faced in Kuriza. Even if she knew she could rely on her skills, it would have intimidated her to try it.

She'd tried not to think about the Joythief. But it never left her, the worry that she would never be a spider-thief again, the fear of failing because she'd lost her only means of success. She tried to tell herself it wouldn't happen, that her skills would last long enough to get the teshneh back to Hatife. After that, she could deal with the loss. Not before. Not here, when everything rested on her shoulders.

Mariq knelt and placed her hands on the short wall surrounding the roof. Thoughts and worries wouldn't help her. She needed to focus. Scale the wall. Get back to the tunnels. Stay out of sight.

But first, she pulled out her remaining ivory dagger. There were no tiles on this roof, just smooth, glass-like stone, but Mariq chipped away a corner in a few moments. She hadn't earned this treasure, not like her others, but it was still something. If nothing else, she will have earned it when she reached the ground.

Now she needed to focus. Scale the wall. Get back to the tunnels. Stay out of sight.

Her legs trembled as she lifted them over the edge of the wall.

There's a balcony twenty feet below me. If anything happens…

No. Don't think like that. She was a spider-thief. She didn't need doors.

The walls weren't quite as slick as she'd feared, the surface pocked with innumerable tiny divots from wind and sand and all-too-rare rain. Mariq made do with the tiny hand- and footholds, her arms quivering as she lowered herself down the wall. Dawn had quieted what little wind there had been earlier, so at least she didn't have to worry about being buffeted off the wall. She grappled for each hold, squeezing fingers into tiny depressions and chipping away bits of loose stones with her toes in order to make room for her feet.

Terrified as she was, Mariq couldn't deny the exhilaration racing through her. This feeling encompassed everything it meant to be a spider-thief—defying expectations, social mores, even what people thought possible for a human body. Clinging to a wall like a spider, owning a piece of the sky like those who remained forever planted to the ground could never understand. For a moment Mariq felt free again. She felt like a spider-thief.

Her muscles protested each movement, but her confidence grew with each successful transfer from one hold to the next.

Over halfway to the balcony, her foot slipped. Her fingers weren't strong enough to hold her entire weight, especially on such a miniscule ledge, and her grip gave out. For a horrifying moment, Mariq was airborne.

She hit the balcony hard. Her shoulder flared with pain, followed by her hip a heartbeat later. The jolt jarred her entire body, every inch of her screaming in an instant. Dazed, she lay still for several moments, breathing and trying to gather her bearings. She'd fallen, but it was far from the worst outcome possible.

She was still well over halfway up the palace. The teshneh was undamaged. It didn't seem like she'd done serious damage to herself, though she knew better than to call herself uninjured. She'd be near immobile by morning.

Then again, she still had to get out of the city with the teshneh. Her chances of returning to Haven were dwindling fast.

She couldn't try to climb again. Even if she trusted herself not to fall a second time, which she didn't, her body was in no shape to try it. Just struggling to her feet took a monumental effort.

She had to go through the palace.

Suicide, she thought. *There's no way I can get through unseen.*

One more look over the edge of the balcony. Sneaking through the palace might be suicide, but trying to scale the walls again would be certain death.

Weight on the balls of her feet, Mariq ducked low and slipped through the door.

The room wasn't as dark as she'd expected, the teshneh casting blue streaks of light across the walls even through its shroud. The glow made her cringe, but what could she do about it? She couldn't contain magic itself. This thin scrap of material only held the physical teshneh—the magic it stored wafted in and out as if the barrier was no more substantial than a breath.

Mariq turned away from the glow and crept across the room, some kind of office or library, pausing with an ear to the door. She listened for several heartbeats, hearing nothing. She reached up and pulled it open.

The hallway could almost have been mistaken for ordinary. Subdued earth tones, very little decoration, like every other hallway in every other building throughout the Scorched Lands. Still, as Mariq glanced around to ensure she was alone, light threaded through the crystalline walls, pulled upward from the earth. It danced in patterns like the magic from the teshneh, but sluggishly—as if drained of energy. Or trapped.

Mariq stepped out and headed to her right, hoping to find a staircase. Shadows disappeared as she moved, reforming even heavier once she'd passed. Within a handful of steps it was bright enough Mariq could make out every detail. A few more and she had to squint.

The light—the magic holding up these impossible buildings—congregated around the teshneh. Around *her*.

Heart in her throat, Mariq bolted. She raced down the corridor, unsure where she was going, not caring as long as it got her out. She could already hear people beginning to question, taking note of the traveling light. No doubt they could hear her pounding steps, her thumping heart. Any moment someone would poke their head out of a door and spot her.

She found a staircase and barreled down it, heedless of her safety. Already she could hear footsteps behind her, not running yet but still getting closer. They'd be on her any moment.

Her body screamed as she pushed it down the stairs, bruises from her fall protesting this cruel treatment. Sharp pain built in her skull, her lungs, her joints. Breathing grew harder as her body struggled to keep up with the demands she placed on it.

The building quaked and groaned, the staircase shaking beneath her feet. The teshneh pulled the magic sustaining this structure to it. Without a continual stream of magic, the entire building was beginning to fall apart.

Shouts echoed in the ensuing silence, shouts every thief feared more than anything. Calls to arms. Orders to search, find, stop. Kill if necessary. And they were close—far too close for comfort.

Mariq ran as fast as she could, skidding around corners and ricocheting off walls. Anywhere to find an exit. Anywhere to get away from the guards and get the teshneh to safety.

She dashed through another corridor and forced open a half-ajar door with her shoulder. The impact made her stumble a few steps. She regained her balance, then skid to a stop.

Guards, half a dozen or more, stood before her. Every weapon in the room pointed at her in the span of a heartbeat.

She turned to dash back the way she'd come, but several of the guards leapt forward and grabbed hold of her. She struggled against them, striking with knees and elbows at anything in reach. She managed to knock the wind from one guard and force another back when she stomped on his foot, but a third grabbed her by the hair.

Mariq didn't allow herself to think. She brought her knee up and pulled the ivory knife from the sheath on her calf. Turning as much as the man's grip allowed her she swung the blade behind her.

The man ducked, but didn't let go of her hair.

That was fine. She hadn't been aiming for him in the first place.

The sharp blade severed her hair just below the base of her neck. She stumbled forward again, off balance from the sudden release, and dashed forward.

She'd almost escaped out the door when another guard grabbed her from behind. She shook him off easily enough, but something else slipped from her shoulders along with his grip.

The teshneh.

Her momentum propelled her forward, and she used it to barrel down the corridor and around a corner. She ducked into a shadow, panting, trying to remain as still as possible. A handful of guards ran past her, screaming about a thief, but the majority did not pursue her.

She had to go back for the teshneh. If she left it here, all was lost. Kuriza would never get its magic back.

She crept back around the corner, but the remaining guards were already gone. Only a faint light bobbing down the hallway showed where they went. Likely on their way to return the teshneh to the roof. Mariq followed.

They paused, speaking quickly, fear in their voices. Tension lay thick around them, a sense of impending doom. The last of the glow around Mariq faded as the spot ahead pulsed with light and magic.

A heartbeat later an enormous crack filled the air, and the ceiling above them split. Mariq dove to the side just as a huge chunk of the ceiling caved in, bringing down several walls with it. Dust filled the air and debris peppered Mariq, cutting several gashes in her skin and clothes. Had she not moved fast enough, she'd have suffered much worse.

The entire corridor, the doorway separating her from the guards and the teshneh, was a pile of rubble. No way through.

Mariq cursed. She'd never be able to find a way around in time. Each moment she spent in this place made it more likely to crumble on top of her. Already more rumblings shook what remained of the building.

She had to escape before her luck ran out or the next collapse buried her. She could find another way in and sort through the rubble for the teshneh. A wretched option, but she could do no good to Turien or Cendim dead.

More guards raced past, organizing evacuations, ordering reports, commanding the thief be caught at all cost.

The guards would suspect anyone fleeing, frantic, or exhausted. If she could blend in with the commoners, perhaps take a circuitous route out of the palace, she could slip away. Find Turien. Figure out how to salvage this disaster.

Time was against her. Steeling her nerves, she rose from the wall and continued down a new hallway, toward the guards organizing an evacuation. She tried to keep her steps sure, but her heart hammered. Heading toward the people who hunted her had to be the dumbest idea she'd ever had.

Walking without a limp grew more difficult and pain thrummed in her head. Just a little while longer and she could find her way out.

Mariq grew more nervous the farther she went. Her steps came faster as she grew more desperate for escape. She was going to be caught. It was only a matter of time before someone realized she didn't belong, that she wasn't just another person escaping a collapsing building. Then what would happen? She'd have lost the teshneh *and* herself. What would Temhet-Sakh do to her then? Throw her back in prison? Slap one of those accursed voidstones on her? Then again, if they got ahold of her and found no trace of magic on her they might just kill her.

That might be the best option of them all.

Mariq tried to shove the thoughts away, to focus on her escape, but her entire body trembled and her mind raced with terror. This was taking too long. She still hadn't found a way out of the palace, let alone the city gates. She should have been long gone by now.

Renewed shouts, pounding feet, calls to arms. The guards hadn't given up. They still pursued her, intent on finding her.

Some theft this turned out to be.

Finally Mariq came across a hallway busier than the others, with a hint of cool desert mornings lacing the air. She turned toward the scent, restraining the urge to break into a sprint and bolt for the door. Almost out. Almost free.

The fresh air of the streets of Temhet-Sakh hit her like a drug, intoxicating and liberating. Mariq breathed easier, her steps growing more sure as she darted away from the palace. Now to lose herself in the city, reach the passage leading back underground, and get out.

"You! Stop!"

Mariq glanced behind her. Several guards pointed at her, pushing through the crowd to get closer. She ran.

Another group waited just beyond the next turn, but these weren't Temhet-Sakh guards. They wore black from head-to-toe, and Mariq even caught sight of a few nighttime cloaks like the one that haunted her dreams. Ebony knives flashed and blood glistened in their wake.

Star-Blades.

She took a sharp turn and dashed down an alley, hoping to lose both groups in the shadows. If they turned to fighting each other, it would stall them long enough for her to reach the tunnels and escape.

Shouts and clashing weapons spurred her forward. At each turn she forced herself to slow and check for more enemies ahead, no matter how desperately she wanted to barrel forward to safety. Most of the guards of Temhet-Sakh seemed to be behind her, but Star-Blades had infiltrated the city. They lurked in every shadow and crawled across rooftops like cats. Mariq was certain she'd been spotted at least a few times, but the Star-Blades wouldn't be concerned with civilians. Not until they got what they came for.

It seemed to take an eternity to reach the passage back into the tunnels. Even as she slipped down the ladder she heard footsteps in the street behind her and more fighting—guards and Star-Blades, a single turn away from catching up to her.

One of Nirta's scouts ushered her into the safety of the tunnels and sealed the entrance behind her. It took all her self-control to not crumple to the ground. She'd never escaped this narrowly before.

Then again, she'd never bungled a theft quite as badly as this one, either.

She'd abandoned their one hope of restoring the balance of magic. Everything she'd tried she should have been able to do with ease. Yet it had been one disaster after another.

Mariq pulled out the stone she'd chipped from the roof of the palace, turning it over in her hands. It was smooth and almost clear, though the colors weren't quite as vibrant as they'd seemed when the magic flowed through the building.

She could no longer steal. She couldn't climb, or sneak, or pick locks. The Joythief had taken all of her skills.

Mariq swallowed her tears and dropped the stone. She hadn't earned it. She'd done nothing to claim this treasure.

She was no longer a spider-thief.

TURIEN could feel the desert screaming. It had grown louder and louder the deeper he went. Now, at the roots of the city, it was unbearable. The strain these magic-users had put on the land made his soul weep even as its cry thrummed in his chest and made his joints ache.

No wonder Nirta and her scouts hated coming down here, or that the patriarch called Temhet-Sakh an abomination. Now that Turien could feel what the city did to the magic, he couldn't say less.

He could easily see where the magic-users had started their work. Under his feet, the rock was solid and natural. Above him it curved into unnatural arches, far too smooth and engineered for even the most graceful of caves. He could even see massive veins of precious metals and gems being forced upwards to become buildings. No matter how beautiful their sparkle, Turien sneered at the arrogance of these magic-users. To glean from the bounty of the desert was one thing. To take all her goods by force was quite another.

Turien glanced around. He was no engineer, but even he could see this place could not stand by itself. Magic alone held these foundations up. What kind of idiot built a city that couldn't stand on its own?

One so arrogant in their power they never paused to consider they might need to survive without it.

At least he knew how to keep his promise and bring down Temhet-Sakh.

Nirta and the other scouts shifted and muttered behind him. They'd been reluctant to show him here in the first place, so far below the tunnels they'd used to enter the city, and now the strain on the magic made them all edgy. It grated against Turien like sand on his skin. Had they been feeling this the entire time? Or was it even worse for them? Turien might be more attuned to magic than he'd ever been before, but that didn't mean he was a magic-user in his own right.

At least, not yet.

Turien pulled out one of Cendim's glowing blue vials. The pure magic inside it called to him. He could feel it coursing through him, up his arm and into his heart. He hadn't even ingested it yet, and already the pull of the power around him grew. He could almost, *almost* reach out and touch it.

"You'll want to get out of here," he said to no one in particular, rubbing the smooth crystal vial between his fingers.

"We aren't going to leave you," Nirta said. He could tell from her tone it was as much a reprimand to her people as a reminder to him.

"You can see this as well as I can," Turien said, gesturing to the unnatural cavern around them. "Once I remove the magic, this entire place is going to collapse."

"And you think we would leave you to be crushed?"

He hadn't thought much beyond his initial plan, but he nodded his thanks at Nirta and remained silent.

With one final inhalation, he opened the vial and downed the potion.

Breathe.

Jagged knives of power sliced through his veins as the magic coursed through him. He forced himself to soothe the tension in his muscles and take a breath, bringing air and power into his body.

Accept.

Turien had braced for a fight, for the revulsion that had filled him last time. It had been a struggle to accept the magic. This time he was ready for it.

Only no fight came. The magic slid into his blood as if they'd always been together, as if their pairing was the most natural thing in the world. For the first time in his life, Turien felt whole. Like he was no longer No One—that he had finally become Someone.

Devour.

The demand of the magic silenced Turien's thoughts. He pulled streams of magic into himself, consumed them like a river emptying into a cave. His appetite was insatiable, and he took in as much magic as he could.

The desert continued screaming, and the foundations of Temhet-Sakh remained firm.

Turien struggled against the pull of the potion and reached into the pocket he'd rigged into his belt. His hands shook, but he managed to grasp another glowing blue vial.

Cendim had warned him not to take more than one vial per day. He'd said it with absolute urgency, making it clear the ramifications for overdose were severe. But what choice did Turien have? He couldn't tear down the magic like this. Temhet-Sakh was stronger than him. He needed more magic. He had no other option. If it killed him, so be it. Temhet-Sakh had to fall, whatever the cost.

He pushed his emotions aside and downed the potion. It burned through him, sweeping through his body like a flash flood. A burst of power rushed through him, nearly knocking him from his feet.

DEVOUR.

The demand was insistent, urgent, eager as a dying man's grasp on life itself. He couldn't even begin to refuse. He drank in more magic, his vision blurring behind streamers of color and power.

The pillars supporting the city trembled and dust fell onto his head from above. The screams of the desert were deafening.

It still wasn't enough. He trembled and sweat, his body well past aching and into searing pain. But it wasn't enough.

He downed a third vial.

DEVOUR.

Turien's consciousness faltered, and he became lost in the demand for magic. More. More. He couldn't get enough. He pulled it in by rivers, by torrents, each lungful not even enough to whet his appetite. He forgot why he did this or who he did it for. It was for the magic, only the magic. He needed it all. Wasn't that reason enough?

Turien was vaguely aware of screaming, of quaking walls and ominous groaning. But the magic overpowered it all—roaring power stampeding through him, the cavern, the entire world. He felt it to the very core of his body, of his soul. Melding with him. Claiming him.

Just as Ehra's magic brought him back to life, this magic *became* his life.

Hands on his shoulders. Voices shouting his name. Magic cocooning him until he needed nothing else.

Turien succumbed to the magic, to the darkness, when Nirta and the others dragged him out of the caverns as they started to collapse around them.

Let the world fall to chaos…

Perhaps it would. Her world. But then again, their world— her father's world—would be saved because of this. She could be content with that.

Though dawn had barely lit the sky, Gherrim stood outside his home with arms crossed and anger clear in his every muscle. His eyes locked onto Ehra the moment she came within sight. He strode toward her, closing the distance in a few long steps. "Where were you?"

"I had some healing to do," Ehra said. She tried to keep herself calm, to hide her guilt behind innocence. She wasn't lying, after all.

"So I gathered. That was quite a flare of magic from the teshneh."

"It was a very severe injury."

Gherrim grunted, his glare deepening rather than lessening.

Ehra scowled. "You allowed me to use the teshneh to heal. I didn't think I'd need your permission every single time something came up."

"I don't like being wakened by strong magic, only to find my woman gone."

Of course not.

A tremor rippled through Temhet-Sakh. It felt ominous, laced with magic—and then a sudden lack of magic hit her like a punch to the gut, as if the air had been sucked from her lungs between one breath and the next.

Gherrim's shoulders tensed and he spun toward the palace. Right about where she expected Mariq to be, fleeing with the teshneh.

Ehra's heart pounded, her stomach churning. It had started. Mariq and Turien were destroying Temhet-Sakh. This was her chance… likely her last chance to escape before the city fell.

She took one step back, but Gherrim reached behind him and locked her in place with a hand around her arm. Tighter than it needed to be. She squirmed, but his grip didn't break.

Another tremor, deeper and longer, shook the city. Furniture rattled inside the house and cracks spread across several of the walls around them. People screamed, flooding into the streets to escape the shattering structures.

Gherrim grew still, his nostrils flared and eyes focused on a spot in the distance. Then his face grew hard, his gaze cold, and he growled. His grip tightened even more on Ehra's arm. He strode forward, fast and determined, dragging Ehra behind at a near-run.

She struggled against him, if only to escape the chaos growing in the streets. Gherrim led her into the worst of the damage, where people screamed and cried, frantic. Already some of the more delicate structures had toppled, showering the streets with glass and magic. The sheer overwhelming strength of the loose power made Ehra dizzy… and hungry.

Her eyes locked onto a young man, hardly more than a boy, whose leg had been crushed by a fallen building. His blood painted the street beneath him red.

Another sudden lack of magic swept through the streets, allowing Ehra to tear her eyes from the tempting life.

Gherrim dragged her through several streets, finally pausing just outside the palace. It was even more chaotic here, pockets of battles between Temhet-Sakh guards and people dressed in black, ebony knives glistening with blood. Star-Blades. Here?

Of course. They'd come for the teshneh as well.

Gherrim skirted the front entrance of the palace, where most of the fighting took place, and ducked into a small hidden entrance on the side of the building. Ehra had to sprint behind him by the time they met a group of guards surrounding a glowing pool of magic. The teshneh. Mariq had succeeded in getting it off the roof, only to leave it here. What did that mean? Was she hurt, captured? Ehra saw no sign of her friend, but that didn't ease her fears. Not at all.

"Return that to its proper place," he commanded. "Its magic is unstable, so be careful."

Gherrim relaxed when he saw the teshneh being taken to safety, but then he turned as if staring through the walls. "I can still sense the thieves," he said, his voice distracted. "They're below, but fleeing. Southeast." He pointed. "One feels just like the teshneh."

Ehra tried to still her rapid heartbeat. That had to be Turien, and she could only hope the other one he sensed was Mariq. Please, don't let him find them.

Long, tense moments passed. Then he turned to her. "You were at the teshneh tonight, and you weren't alone."

Her heart stopped. "What?"

He released her arm and grabbed her around her waist, ensuring she couldn't wiggle away. His grip was still far too tight. He stared into her eyes and sniffed at her. "Those people... I can sense them on you, too." His voice grew cold, his eyes hard, and his hand on her waist became a vise. "What have you done?"

"I…"

He pulled her after him, hauling her away from the remaining guards and into an abandoned hallway. Part of the wall had crumbled, and she stumbled on debris. "You were a part of this, weren't you?" He shouted into her face. "What did you do?"

His patience ran out as she stammered, searching for a response. He raised his giant hand and brought it down with all the force he could muster—which was considerable. Ehra staggered as his slap burned her cheek. She would have fallen if he didn't hold her upright.

"Tell me what you did!"

Hot, horrified tears scorched her face. They were the only response she felt capable of making.

He growled at her and threw her to the ground. She landed among dust and rubble and shards of glass. Blood bloomed on her palms and knees. By now so little magic suffused the air Ehra hardly noticed the power spread before her.

"Mariq was right," Ehra raised a hand to her stinging cheek. She didn't care that she smeared blood all over it. "You are a brute."

"And so you defy me? You betrayed me just because some bitch called me names?" His eyes were so fierce Ehra feared to look in them. She quailed, an apology on her lips.

… for a heartbeat.

Ehra swallowed her apology. Mariq had been right to call Gherrim her brute, her wet nurse. What kind of woman had Ehra become, to let him do this to her? She'd never been the kind to give in. She was a princess by birthright and a goddess in her magic. She didn't have to answer to anyone.

She got to her feet and met Gherrim's eyes. "You will never hit me again."

Gherrim ground his teeth, balling his fists at his side. He enunciated each word through clenched teeth. "Did you have anything to do with this?"

She would not look away. She would not let him cow her. This had to be done, and Ehra would not allow Gherrim's rage to make her apologize like she was ashamed of her actions. "Yes."

He grabbed her by the shoulders and slammed her back against the wall, so hard she cried out. "How could you? Do you have any idea what you've done?"

"Temhet-Sakh is straining the world's magic," she said, forcing conviction into her voice through the fear and pain. "It had to be done."

"We've taken you in, made you one of ours. This city is beautiful beyond anything else in the world. You know that. Now look at it." When she didn't look away, he took her jaw in his hand and forced her face toward the destruction around them. "Look at it now! How could you do this?"

Ehra choked on her tears. It was beautiful. She loved Temhet-Sakh, as much as she loved anything in the world. But her father was right. Mariq and Turien were right. "I don't have a choice. If I hold onto what I love, the entire world is going to suffer for it."

Gherrim released her jaw and shoved her away. She turned tear-filled eyes to him. "I'm still here. I'm giving up everything to stay with the city. Until the end, whatever that means. If it means rebuilding from rubble, then I'll pick up stones and build walls until my fingers bleed. If it means dying with Temhet-Sakh, then I'll do that too. As long as I'm here." She would have added *with you* at the end of that, but with her head pounding from his strike, she held her tongue.

"The teshneh is still here. Temhet-Sakh will not fall." He said it like nothing else mattered.

"Gherrim, I stayed. Doesn't that mean anything to you?"

Gherrim grunted, neither confirmation nor denial, but he'd already started out of the palace, intent on chasing down Mariq and Turien. What else would he do? That magic meant more to him than anything.

Including Ehra.

The palace rumbled, bits of the ceiling falling around her like empty sheets of crystal and glass. The ambient magic had dwindled to the faintest trace. Ehra felt its absence like a hole in her heart, but her thoughts felt clearer than they had in a long time.

Mariq had been right about Gherrim. He was a brute, controlling, even abusive. Ehra hadn't thought he would go that far. But had she ever stopped to think? When he first took her away from her friends, he'd had to drag her. He forced her to leave what she knew, the people she loved. And he'd never relented in his pursuit of her, never taking no for an answer. That's how he'd first gotten her into bed—she'd been wounded, and he'd persisted. He was always persistent, always taking from her… giving back, on occasion, in a time and fashion that suited him.

"You never said you loved me," she said, the admission hurting more than Gherrim's slap had. She'd known it, but had always explained it away. Now, though, the truth was clear as day. He never said it because he'd never felt it.

Gherrim turned back to her, steps away from the door. "What?"

She looked up into Gherrim's eyes. "You never told me you loved me."

"We're lovers," he said, as if explaining a simple concept to a stupid child.

"Making love and being in love aren't the same thing," Ehra replied. Her heart raced and her entire body shook. A sharp, horrible pain built in her chest.

"I told you, Ehra, your magic calls to me…"

"And that's all it's been about, isn't it? Magic. Never about us. About me."

He didn't respond, but the hardness in his features was answer enough.

A tiny squeak escaped Ehra's throat. "Why?" she asked, keeping her eyes on her feet.

"I wasn't lying about your magic, Ehra. It's more powerful than anything I've ever felt. Only the teshneh can compare. And when we're together…"

"You could share in my power." She'd felt it from her first day in Temhet-Sakh, the sparking of magic between their skin when they touched. The more intimate they got the more intense the sensation grew, until the shared power was a pleasure all its own.

Gherrim could sense magic. Being able to feel how powerful some magics were must have given him a craving for them. By claiming her—and by extension, her extraordinarily powerful magic—as his own, he could siphon it from her every time they were together.

But then even that hadn't been enough, had it? He'd brought her to the teshneh, allowed her to use the pure magic to heal. Which filled her with even more power he could take.

Magic was his drug, and she'd become his source. She should have seen it sooner. Anger surged, drowning her sadness. "You have no idea what you could have had with me."

Gherrim scowled. "You'll be lucky to find anyone else who will take you."

The heaviness in Ehra's heart choked her. "I know. But being alone is better than being with someone like you."

He took a step closer to her, hovering over her. "You don't think I'd just let you go, do you? You're mine."

Ehra leveled her gaze on her former lover. "I was never yours, Gherrim. And now I never will be. But remember this, since you're so in love with my magic: if I ever see you again, I'll give you a taste of it."

Gherrim froze, the color draining from his face. She didn't have to say more.

When she walked away, Gherrim didn't follow her.

STUPID bitch. Who did she think she was, threatening him? Leaving him? She should be grateful for everything he'd given her. A home. Magic. And he hadn't been alone in his enjoyment of their intimacy, physical and magical. She'd cried his name more than a few times during their nights together.

The teshneh's power felt shattered, erratic, only a fraction of its magic feeding into the city. But up close it had been more potent than ever. Gherrim clenched his fists until his knuckles cracked. If that friend of Ehra's had broken the teshneh, there would be hell to pay. He was more than ready to collect that payment.

He could still smell their magic—well, one of them. The other must have been that woman Ehra had saved, the one without magic. She wasn't worth following. The other, though. The one who'd hidden his magic somehow, and who now smelled of the teshneh's magic. Gherrim would not let him get away.

He stomped through the crumbled remains of a wall and into the street outside the palace. Temhet-Sakh lay in ruins. Dust filled the air and debris covered the streets. Huge portions of the palace were missing, several of the surrounding buildings even worse. Some were just gone. The magic that infused Temhet-Sakh was a fleeting thing, little more than a scent on the wind.

Gherrim grit his teeth. He'd given Ehra more than she'd ever dreamed of, and she'd repaid him with this. By destroying that dream. Bitch.

He caught sight of a few scattered fights, guards and commonfolk against people in black. More of Ehra's treachery? Were they here for the teshneh too? Gherrim would sooner die than let them take it from him.

He watched the man—or woman, Gherrim couldn't see their features well enough to tell—cut down the guard with brutal efficiency. Then another, and another. Soon there were no more guards in sight, and the person in black hadn't received a scratch.

Not a ruffian, then, or a well-dressed Feral. They moved as if battle came to them as naturally as walking. Gherrim was no slouch with a sword, but he knew better than to think he could challenge a warrior such as this.

Instead of throwing himself into battle and death he stayed hidden and followed them to another group of black-clad people. He'd be able to find Ehra's accomplices easily enough. This trail, however, would not last forever.

"I don't care what it takes," a man said, pacing and giving orders, "find that device. The war against magic will be lost without it."

So they were here for the teshneh. As he suspected. But they weren't magic-users after the power. He'd said the war *against* magic. They wanted to use the teshneh to destroy magic.

Gherrim couldn't let them have it. Temhet-Sakh needed it.

He needed it.

He looked around at the rubble that had been one of the community squares. Bodies littered the streets, rocks and dust and broken glass everywhere. Even with the magic of the teshneh, Temhet-Sakh was ruined.

He was not. And neither was he a fool. These people, whoever they were, would overpower what remained of the Temhet-Sakh guard. They would find the teshneh and take it from him.

He'd already lost Ehra's magic. He couldn't lose the teshneh's as well—whatever the cost.

Decision made, he stepped from the shadows and approached the man giving orders. "If you want the teshneh, you're going to need my help."

"I doubt that, magic-user. Kill him."

Gherrim held up his hands, but continued to talk fast. Before those approaching blades could find his heart. "Fine. Say you do find the teshneh, and you manage to use it in your war. It will only get you so far. Magic is pervasive. It won't be so easy to eradicate. And then you'll wish you'd listened to me."

The people in black hesitated.

"Pull magic from a land all you want. Kill what magic-users you can find. But our very existence proves you can't get them all. In a few generations it will be as strong as ever, and your war lost."

"Magic-users cannot remain hidden forever. We'll root them out."

"In time to stop them from breeding? Hiding their children from you, seeding the world with magic once again?"

The man hesitated.

"I can help you," Gherrim said. "I can track magic. Any magic. Spare me and I'll not only lead you to the teshneh, but I'll make sure no magic-user can hide from you."

"You would be condemning your own kind."

Gherrim shrugged. "People are replaceable. Magic is not."

"You would condemn that as well," the man said.

"No. You'll have the teshneh and use it to take the magic of the lands—of the magic-users, correct?" That black hood nodded. "That magic would stay in the teshneh, forever, unless a magic-user pulled it out."

"A magic-user like yourself, I imagine."

Gherrim nodded. "You'll need someone who knows how to use the teshneh. I do. I'll take any magic you want, from anyone, without question. As long as you give me the teshneh and all the magic it holds."

"So you can make new magic-users? We aren't quite that stupid."

Gherrim snorted. "Why would I share power like that?"

The man stepped forward, peering at Gherrim through that black hood. "A magic addict, then? I've heard such things exist." He stood before Gherrim a moment before lowering his hood. Not an intimidating face, if you ignored the eyes. Those were almost enough to make Gherrim take a step back. "Very well. A test, then, to prove your loyalty to the Star-Blades' cause. How many people remain in the city?"

Gherrim scowled. Temhet-Sakh was a big place, and he couldn't count individual sources of power among the magic. "The city's magic is depleted, but there's still a lot of it around. I'd say there's still quite a few, but that's the best I can tell."

"A significant portion of the city remains?" The man's sly smile made Gherrim shiver.

Gherrim nodded.

"Excellent."

Gherrim watched as the man turned away and consulted with another black-clad person, a woman from the voice. She pulled something from her robe, something glass and filled with smoke, and handed it to the man. He cradled it like a precious gift before turning back to Gherrim. "Take us to the midst of the densest group of magic-users."

Gherrim spun in a circle then led the Star-Blades north, away from the palace. Those closest to the sultan would have heard the warning, seen the crowds, and joined in his exodus. Farther away, though, they likely had no clue their leader had abandoned them.

When the sense of magic grew from a tickle to a caress Gherrim stopped. The man looked around, pointing to a tall building nearby. "Up there. Get us to that roof."

Gherrim did so, leading the way up a set of nearby stairs. Several weathered pillows and low tables were strewn about, not unlike most other roofs in the desert. Evening tea in the cool of night was a staple of Temhet-Sakh society.

The man stood by the edge, looking over Temhet-Sakh. The damage to the city was evident here, but not quite a dramatic as near the teshneh. It would take time for the magic to bleed out of the buildings. Even now several walls crumbled as they watched.

"It is a beautiful city," the man admitted. "But beauty is often a disguise for evil."

Gherrim frowned, but said nothing. If he wanted the teshneh and the magic it held, he couldn't afford to fail in this.

"Magic enhances passions, yes?"

Gherrim hesitated, confused by the change of subject, but nodded.

The man grinned like a skull. "Excellent. Let's see how it likes the taste of Joythief, then."

He dropped the glass over the edge of the building, watching it until it shattered below them. Smoke drifted from the broken glass—far more than such a small container should have held. The scent of it almost choked Gherrim. This was dark, hungry magic, bitter and single-minded in its black intent.

"You're using magic while trying to destroy it?" he asked, not daring to look at the Star-Blade's face.

"A necessary evil." He paused, once again eyeing Gherrim. "Be glad I'm willing to use unconventional methods. Otherwise your body would already be cool in the street. Many of my colleagues wouldn't have hesitated as I did."

Gherrim nodded. "What does this… Joythief do?"

"It steals magic. Takes away passions."

Gherrim shuddered.

They fell silent when the first screams started. The formerly quiet streets exploded with noise and motion as people burst from their homes, wailing and sobbing. As they watched several people closest to the broken glass collapsed like discarded dolls. Others stood vacant, as if their bodies continued living but their souls had already died.

Their magic… was gone. Just *gone*. Gherrim sniffed but could scent nothing but the Joythief.

"Much more potent," the man muttered, as if taking notes in a laboratory. "A more violent, and hopefully thorough, application than liquid. Excellent."

The man continued watching long after Gherrim had lost his nerve and turned away. He might have agreed to help in the Star-Blades' plans, but that didn't mean he had to like it.

Finally the man looked up, satisfied with his Joythief. "Once we have the teshneh, we'll hunt down what magic-users escape the mass Joythief." Another evaluating look at Gherrim. "Do you object?"

Gherrim looked down at the scurrying people, trying to flee from something they couldn't see, couldn't escape. He could smell their magic being consumed, winking from existence one scent at a time. A horrible, awful way to die. An even worse way to live.

If he refused now, this fate awaited him.

If he refused, he would never again taste magic as potent as Ehra's, as the teshneh's. That would be a fate worse than death.

The man seemed to see every decision on Gherrim's face. "I'll give you your drug, magic-user, but if you betray us you'll wish I'd let my Star-Blades destroy you now."

The teshneh held more magic than Gherrim could consume in a decade. Add to that the power of a land, of the magic-users this man would capture, and he could gorge himself on magic for a lifetime and never run out. He wouldn't need Ehra to siphon power from. He could live in the euphoria of magic, revel in the pleasure it brought every moment of every day. More than he'd dreamed possible. Why would he betray the man who'd give him this?

Gherrim took a deep breath, ignoring the scent of the Joythief and the much-lessened feel of the peoples' magic. "They're taking the teshneh," he said, eyes narrowed as he turned toward the southeast. The same way that damn ally of Ehra's had fled. The one who smelled like the teshneh.

"We cannot let them escape with it," the man said.

Gherrim clenched his fists. "We won't."

26

From the moment Mariq returned to Haven she was ready to leave it. No matter how bruised, battered, or defeated she felt, she just wanted to be gone.

Turien had done his part—Temhet-Sakh lay in ruins behind them. They had barely escaped the tunnels before they'd started to collapse, evading clumps of people fleeing the crumbling city. Ehra had, blessedly, seen the truth and met them out in the desert, leaving Temhet-Sakh behind. On both of their counts the day had been a success.

But Mariq had failed yet again. The teshneh remained in the hands of Temhet-Sakh, perhaps lost in the destruction. So far she had been useless. Turien swore otherwise, that without her both he and Ehra would be lost, that their entire plan to restore Kuriza's magic was based on her idea, but what did that count? They couldn't restore the magic without the teshneh, and Mariq had failed in retrieving that. Again.

At least she'd helped save her friends. That had to count for something.

Mariq paced around Haven like a caged animal. They didn't have time to waste. Cendim expected them back. Who knew how long the world had before the magic became so polarized it would tear everything apart? Would they feel it coming?

If they didn't act soon, it might be too late.

A commotion by the patriarch's chambers caught her attention. She spotted several runners scurrying about with pinched expressions and hasty footsteps, rushing into the room only to dash out a moment later. Nirta appeared next, her weathered face looked more harried than usual. Mariq hurried toward her. "What's happening?"

Nirta hesitated, as if unsure whether to tell her or not. Then something seemed to crumble within the older woman and her shoulders fell as she let out a breath. "Our scouts have picked up several groups approaching Haven," she said, her voice worn and weary. "The survivors we bypassed out of Temhet-Sakh have joined together, and they're heading this way. They're moving slowly, but there's more than a thousand of them."

"Refugees," Mariq said.

Nirta nodded. "Several other groups, smaller, moving much faster, are approaching as well. They're coming from every direction, sealing us and the survivors in."

"Feral?" Mariq hesitated. Feral would make sense, though it was possible one of those groups was Star-Blades. At least some had to have escaped the destruction of Temhet-Sakh.

"We believe so. Only we've never seen so many, moving with common purpose. We didn't even know there were this many to begin with."

Mariq's breath caught in her throat. "What could be drawing them here?" She'd barely gotten the words out when a thought occurred. "The refugees must have the teshneh—Ehra had said they'd do anything to protect it. That much magic would draw out the Feral, wouldn't it?" And the Star-Blades would follow their prize to the ends of the world, if they had to.

"They must. The refugees are converging on Haven, though I've no idea how they learned of our location. Their collected magic is, in turn, drawing the Feral. If those beastmen are allowed into Haven…"

Nirta didn't finish, but she didn't need to. Mariq was all too familiar with the violence the Feral were capable of. Her side didn't hurt—she had no evidence of her mortal injury—but she placed her hand there anyway.

Mariq followed Nirta when she turned and entered the patriarch's chambers. The place was more crowded than she'd ever seen it, with almost no room to squeeze between arguing, frightened people. Mariq spotted Turien against a wall. She wondered if Ehra was somewhere in here, too short to see through the crowd.

The people quieted as the patriarch called for their attention. "The most urgent problem first. How many Feral are approaching?"

A few moments of murmuring and tallying passed before someone dared to admit the truth. "More than we can count, but our best estimates are several hundred, possibly upwards of a thousand."

Haven could never fight off that many. A few hundred people lived in the garden canyon at best, and most had never seen battle. Against the savage Feral, it would be a massacre.

"Are we certain they will find us?"

"They're approaching from every direction. It's only a matter of time."

The patriarch paused as if the news pained him. "How long?"

"Hard to say. The Feral are unpredictable at best, and they might not come directly to Haven. Days if we're lucky, hours if not."

"And what of the refugees?"

"They're coming straight for us. They'll be within sight of Haven before Deepening."

"Perhaps the Feral will go for them instead of us," someone said from the depths of the crowd.

"Good riddance!"

A chorus of cries echoed this, but one voice rose above the others. "How can you say that?"

Mariq spun. Ehra. She'd come after all.

"They're from Temhet-Sakh," a man shouted. "Let the Feral rid our desert of them for us!"

"They need shelter!"

Mariq turned as Ehra pushed her way through the crowd. The tiny woman looked like a vengeful ghost—face drawn and haggard, eyes furious and red from weeping. Men a head or more taller than her backed away, as if she was a wild animal about to attack. Even Mariq found herself bracing for danger when Ehra's gaze swept past her.

"These are *people* you're talking about. Men and women with jobs, passions, lives. You can't condemn them to death just because you don't agree with some of their choices!"

"They would have drained the desert of every bit of magic it held for their own selfish benefit," a woman said.

"Do you think every person in Temhet-Sakh understood that? That all are complicit in this crime? Can there be no innocents in all of Temhet-Sakh?"

The room fell silent as the arguers looked at their feet, shuffled back and forth, or otherwise avoided Ehra's fierce gaze.

"I know what it's like inside those gates. Yes, there is corruption, and deceit, and pain." She paused, her eyes glassy but back straight, head high. "But there is beauty too. Happiness. Love." Another pause, accompanied by a tiny sniffle. "There are good people in Temhet-Sakh who shouldn't be punished for seeking refuge with a community who welcomed them when no one else would."

"We would have." The statement sounded weak, almost pitiful.

"But you didn't. You hid in Haven, secure in your safety. For every one you intercepted, twenty saw nothing but the gleaming gates and welcoming arms of Temhet-Sakh. Can you blame them for taking solace there?"

A few murmurs, but otherwise the room was silent as a grave.

"Whatever they've done or not done, they're still people. You can't leave them to the mercy of the Feral. That's inhuman."

Ehra's chastisement left the room sobered, but Mariq knew they wouldn't relent after one impassioned speech. Too much hatred ran between these groups for one to simply forgive. They'd need some reason, some necessity to force them into peace.

"What if the refugees helped you fight off the Feral?"

The silence took on a different quality. Before it was the quiet of a punished child. Now it was incredulous, scornful. Yet intrigued. Mariq had to swallow and clear her throat before she could continue. "Your people aren't fighters, Patriarch. You said so yourself. But Temhet-Sakh had a military and plenty of people accustomed to using their magic in interesting ways. If they agreed to help repel the Feral from Haven, would you give them sanctuary?"

The expectation and sudden hope infusing the room made it hard to breathe.

"I suppose we don't have much choice," the patriarch said at last. He took a moment to meet the eyes of several people, then he turned his attention to Mariq. "Princess Mariq Ashai Meidani, I formally request you conduct the negotiations on our behalf."

"Me?" The thought made her shudder. Suggesting negotiations was one thing—conducting them was better left to other people.

"We need someone impartial. You, being the princess of Kuriza, would have both the status and the neutrality to see both Haven and Temhet-Sakh in agreement."

"No, not me. Ehra would be much better…"

"Just as Temhet-Sakh would not trust someone harbored by Haven, my people will not trust someone who'd chosen Temhet-Sakh," the patriarch said.

"But no one from Temhet-Sakh would listen to me. I'm not a magic-user." Anything to get out of this. She couldn't negotiate a treaty. She'd rather steal what she wanted than convince the owner to give it to her. She might have been raised a princess, but negotiations and politics had been Lookan's purview, not hers. Those kinds of weighty issues had been men's work, not appropriate for the Princess of Kuriza. Diplomacy was as foreign to her as Temhet-Sakh's magic.

"I am," Turien said, stepping up beside her. He held forward his naked right arm, Mariq's silk slave-band threaded through the hole. "And I am owned by the house of Kuriza, named as family by the princess herself. By all rights I am allowed to speak for them."

The patriarch watched Turien for a moment before nodding. "It is done."

"Wait—" Mariq wanted to protest, but the relief suffusing the room silenced her. They had a plan that might save Haven from the Feral. Even though it cost an alliance with Temhet-Sakh, it was their best chance for survival and everyone knew it. Mariq couldn't take that away from them. No matter how ill-equipped she felt for the task.

Scouts dashed from the room, no doubt preparing to bring news of a proposed truce to the refugees before the Feral attacked. Nirta ushered her and Turien along with them. They had no time to waste—the sooner the negotiations were settled upon, the safer everyone would be.

Before Mariq could gather her thoughts they were wrapping themselves in heavy desert garb and climbing out of Haven. Once out of the canyon the scouts dissipated, Mariq and Turien following Nirta on a more straightforward path toward the ruins of Temhet-Sakh.

"I can't do this, Turien. I'm not a diplomat. I'm a thief."

She'd spoken barely above a whisper, but Turien walked close enough to have heard her even though no one else could. "Cendim believed you could."

"Cendim believed a lot of things," she said. "He wasn't always right, though."

Turien ignored the comment. "Negotiating isn't that hard. Find what each side wants and what they're willing to give up. Make the need greater than the sacrifice and you've won. Given the state everyone is in, the need is already great. Finalizing the negotiation will be more of a formality than anything."

"These people hate each other. Great need or not, there's no way they'll listen to me and look past that. I'll say the wrong thing and get them all fighting on the spot."

"No you won't. I won't let you mess up like that."

Mariq took some comfort in that, but it didn't allay her fears.

"Do you really think the refugees have the teshneh?" Turien asked. He hadn't mentioned it since they arrived back in Haven, no doubt unwilling to point out her utter failure a second time.

"What else could be drawing the Feral here?" Turien grunted his agreement beneath his concealing robe. "They'd better have it. If it was destroyed with the city Cendim's plans are doomed."

"I don't think we'd still be around if the teshneh was destroyed. That much magic releasing into the already magic-saturated desert would have pushed the balance too far."

Mariq hesitated. "Are you a true magic-user now? Without any of Cendim's potions?"

Turien, too, hesitated. "Yes. I can feel it in me."

Mariq didn't know what to say. Turien sounded awed, even proud of his newfound abilities. And why wouldn't he? His entire life he'd never had anything to call his own. Now he'd become a magic-user, and not even the Star-Blades could take that away from him. He could forge a new life with skills that were uniquely his. He would never be No One again.

She was happy for him, no doubt of that. But what of her? Turien had gained everything at the same time she'd lost everything.

At least she'd be able to stay in Hatife. Cendim wouldn't reject her for this failure any more than he'd rejected her for her last. Perhaps she could take up a new area of study, find some way to be of value. Though she doubted anything could be as thrilling as thievery.

Then again, all of this hinged on their ability to survive the incoming Feral and retrieve the teshneh, which seemed more impossible the closer they got.

Mariq groaned and rubbed at the headache forming behind her eyes. "Why can't I just steal the damn thing and be done with it?" It was wishful thinking, far from anything they could consider a feasible plan, but the thought still appealed to her.

"Could you do it?" Turien asked.

Mariq hesitated. No. She couldn't. Before coming here she'd have been able to sneak into the refugees and make off with the teshneh in her sleep. Now, she'd be caught within moments. Theft was no longer an option. Had not been an option for a long time.

Turien seemed to understand this, because he nodded and continued as if he'd heard her thoughts. "Even if you were able to steal it, we couldn't. There's more resting on this than just the teshneh now. The safety of Haven and the remnants of Temhet-Sakh are at stake, too. If we left them to the Feral we'd be responsible for their deaths."

"If we don't get the teshneh back to Hatife in time, we'll be responsible for the entire world's death."

On that sobering note, the scouts returned and announced the refugees were willing to negotiate.

MARIQ had plenty of training in controlling outward signs of emotion. That was the only reason she didn't fidget or flee when everyone looked to her to start the negotiations.

The middle of the desert was hardly a proper place for such an event, but they couldn't afford to be picky. Besides, by the time everyone had gathered almost fifty people lingered in the depression Nirta had chosen. Only the patriarch's chambers in Haven could have fit them all, and he insisted no resident of Temhet-Sakh would find their way into that canyon without a promise of help.

Looking at the two groups glaring at each other from across the depression, Mariq couldn't see how they could get such a promise.

She had thrown back her hood, as had Turien and most of the others from Haven. The sun beat on her exposed skin but she kept her features impassive as she welcomed everyone. "Thank you for agreeing to meet," she began, glancing between the patriarch on her right and the refugees on her left. She wanted to cringe away from the hostility sparking between them.

"Not that we have much choice," one of the refugees said. Even without his gaudy heritage tattoos Mariq would have known him for their leader—the sultan, Ehra had called him. His posture and manner of speaking alone identified him as someone accustomed to power. "Temhet-Sakh and Haven are the only settlements close enough to offer safety. With our city destroyed it's come here or die in the desert."

"If you're so reluctant for our help, you're welcome to the second option," someone from Haven called out.

The patriarch glared back and silenced the tittering that had followed the statement. "We are here in good faith," he said, the reprimand sharp enough to make several people flinch. "I will not allow grudges to destroy this alliance before it can even be forged.”

“Alliance?” the sultan spat. “More like extortion. We have nothing and will surely die without aid, yet you demand recompense for saving our lives!”

“We don’t have time to argue,” Mariq said. “The Feral will be here far sooner than anyone would like. If any of us want to survive, we have to act fast. There will be plenty of time for squabbles once the threat is passed.”

This silenced everyone long enough for Mariq to take a breath and plan her next sentence.

“Any of us alone are easy prey for the Feral.” Excellent. Everyone’s attention had centered on her. She blocked them out and tried to focus. What would Cendim say to get his point across? “We need shelter and a defensible place from which to repel the Feral. Haven offers both. But we also need warriors, soldiers and magic-users to fight off anyone who tries to attack us. Temhet-Sakh excels at this.”

Both groups seemed proud of the praise. Mariq glanced at Turien beside her. He gave a small nod of encouragement.

“Alone, Haven would be overrun, with far too little defense to hold back the Feral. Temhet-Sakh would fight, but with so many Feral and no place to defend your backs, the battle would be bloody and hopeless.”

Looks of consternation, anger, frustration met her.

“Together, though, we have everything we need to defeat the Feral. Temhet-Sakh pushes back the Feral while Haven offers refuge for those who can’t fight and support for those who can. What could go wrong?”

“They could turn their attacks on us!” someone from Haven shouted.

“Haven could use us as a shield and refuse to let us in once they’re safe!” one of Temhet-Sakh’s magic-users replied.

The depression erupted in shouts and accusations. Mariq

grimaced—that had been the wrong thing to say. So much for the negotiation being a formality. It seemed like these people would jump on any excuse they could to continue hating each other.

"Enough!" Turien's voice silenced the crowd as effectively as anything Mariq had seen. Tiny streamers of blue light faded from sight the moment she glanced over at him—he must have pulled on the magic a bit to get everyone's attention. "If we don't start extending some trust the Feral will tear us all to pieces."

Mariq raised her voice into the silence. "I am the Princess of Kuriza, soon to be married to the Sheik of Hatife. If the patriarch and Haven renege on their offer of sanctuary, my lands will consider them the guilty party, and whatever actions Temhet-Sakh chooses to respond with will be supported. Same for Temhet-Sakh. Should they turn on Haven, we will avenge the innocent blood they shed. You have my word." Mariq knew she stepped outside her bounds, promising military power her father or Cendim or both might balk at, but she had to do something to convince them to trust one another. She just had to hope the threat would negate any need to try that promise.

Mariq remained silent while the leaders consulted with their people. She remained poised and calm on the outside, though she hid fear and insecurities so huge they threatened to swallow her whole.

Finally the leaders stepped away from their groups and came to the middle with Mariq and Turien. They eyed one another with suspicion, but Mariq could sense the desperation in them both. They needed each other, and they knew it.

"We cannot deny we need the protection of Temhet-Sakh's warriors," the patriarch said, "but we cannot abide such blatant abuse of magic within our home. We call it Haven for a reason—a safe place for all. Including magic."

"Perhaps it wouldn't be a tiny speck on the map if you were more willing to use what you have," the sultan spat.

"And perhaps Temhet-Sakh would still be standing had you been more prudent."

"This isn't about magic," Mariq snapped. "This is about survival."

The sultan leveled a pitying glare on her. "Of course it's about magic. Everything is about magic, and you would know that if you had any experience with it."

"The experiences I've had with those addicted to magic tell me quite a lot," she replied coolly. "And they tell me putting magic as the focus of everything is a terrible way to live. It corrupts the heart and skews the vision until your humanity is lost as much as the Ferals' is."

"Magic is good," Turien added. "In temperance."

The patriarch shook his head. "No matter how true your words, we cannot trust magic addicts to exercise temperance. It's against their very nature by now. As long as the teshneh is anywhere near them, it will always be a temptation."

Mariq's heart leapt. Perhaps this was her chance. "Then what if the teshneh was removed from the situation?"

Both leaders turned their eyes to Mariq: the patriarch with curiosity, the sultan with anger and deep-seated fear.

"If, to prevent further mistreatment of the magic, Temhet-Sakh surrendered the teshneh, would Haven be more willing to welcome them?"

"Mistreatment of the magic," the sultan repeated before the patriarch could answer. "You can't even begin to understand magic, let alone how to treat it."

Turien took a step forward. "You stand before an entire city condemning you of the same thing," he said. "Temhet-Sakh would still be standing if it wasn't for your abuse of magic."

"Temhet-Sakh stood *because* of the magic."

"And that only condemns you further," the patriarch said.

The sultan turned back to Mariq. "Do you believe they will treat the power any differently? Within a season they'll be nursing magic from the teshneh as much as Temhet-Sakh ever did."

"You won't surrender it to Haven," Mariq said. "You will give it to me."

"To you. Someone with no magic of her own." He spoke the words as if Mariq had suggested he give this almighty power to a scorpion.

"Yes. To me. Your people have already done enough to the magic. I will take the teshneh and repair some of the damage you've done."

"Temhet-Sakh would rather die than turn over the teshneh."

"Temhet-Sakh is already dead. And without the teshneh, so is everyone else."

Deafening silence followed her statement. Mariq looked around, but no one would meet her eyes.

The sultan looked to the patriarch. "Do you support this demand?"

The patriarch watched Mariq for a moment before replying. "I do."

"It isn't bad enough you take our home from us, now you take our magic as well?"

"You still have your magic," Mariq said. "But your power will be limited to what you can control, and what the magic can naturally sustain. That should not be a hardship."

The sultan sneered. "You would leave us at the mercy of our enemies."

"Haven wouldn't be your enemies if you would be responsible with the power given to you."

The patriarch nodded. "This is true. We would welcome your people into Haven, as long as they were no longer driven mad by magic addiction and too much power. But until they are cleansed of that, we will remain apart. You will receive no aid from Haven while the teshneh remains in your possession." His tone made it clear there was no room for argument.

The sultan remained silent for long moments, glaring at Mariq and the patriarch as if he could intimidate them into backing down. But neither of them budged.

A flurry of noise and motion sounded over the dunes, and a scout appeared. "The Feral will be here before Deepening," he said, panting. "We must get everyone to safety and prepare for battle."

Muttering, along with a few whimpers, escaped from the gathering. The sultan glanced back at his people, men and women crowding together for support and protection. They were dead out here, and out of time, and they all knew it. His posture slumped and he turned back to the patriarch. "Then I suppose we have no choice." He sounded more weary than anything. "We cannot deny we need Haven's support now that Temhet-Sakh is gone. If our survival depends on us surrendering the teshneh, better to lose the magic than our lives."

Mariq could hardly believe her eyes as the sultan handed her the teshneh, wrapped in some kind of leather sleeve which allowed very little of the magic out.

"Don't open it near any magic-users," he warned as he released his hold on it. "Since the loss of Temhet-Sakh it has grown unstable, more powerful than ever. The strength of the magic inside will almost surely kill any magic-user in its reach."

Mariq nodded.

The sultan watched the teshneh, deep longing in his eyes, for a moment. Then he tore his gaze away with visible effort and extended his hand toward the patriarch. "If you swear to abide by your promise and offer us sanctuary, I swear my people will protect Haven with their lives."

The patriarch nodded. "If you save us from the Feral, Haven will take you in as our own."

They shook hands.

People began slipping away in small groups, some toward Haven and others spreading out, discussing defenses and plans of attack. Mariq took a few moments to stand still and breathe. It took that long for her to begin to understand what had just happened.

She'd done it. She'd saved Haven and Temhet-Sakh's refugees. She'd gotten the teshneh, and she hadn't had to steal it. Once this final threat passed, she was free to return to Kuriza and repair some of the damage. Complete her mission.

Maybe Cendim had been right about her.

Maybe she wasn't useless after all.

27

Haven felt far too small now. The canyon hadn't been designed to hold so many people, and with so much fear and pain in the air even the coolness felt stifling.

Mariq just wanted to slip away. Take Turien and Ehra, leave Haven, and return to Cendim so they could finish this. Restore the magic balance, stop the war with Kuriza, and start figuring out what to do with their lives. But until the Feral were taken care of, they couldn't risk leaving.

Mariq hated that she wasn't out there fighting. She, Turien, and Ehra were ensconced within the canyon, protected by the people of Temhet-Sakh and Haven's few warriors. She would be worse than useless on the battlefield, but she'd never been good at sitting back and letting other people fight on her behalf.

She'd had enough waiting before the Feral ever arrived. She left the teshneh safely hidden in her room and climbed out of the canyon to take up watch in the hot sands above. It was well inside the protective perimeter, but at least Mariq felt like she was doing *something*. If the Feral did happen to break through, Mariq would be one of the first to know.

Though what she could do about it?

Sounds of fighting reached her, faint at first. Just the call to battle, shouts and grunts and the clash of weapons. Flashes of light, fire, and concussions of sound followed a moment later. Temhet-Sakh's magic-users at work. Part of Mariq wished she could see the battle, watch this incredible power in action. But she knew if she got close she'd want to help. That would only get her, and anyone she distracted, killed.

A spot of black flickered in her peripheral vision.

It would take someone with more skill than Mariq had ever possessed to slip past the scouts and make it to her position, so close to the heavily fortified Haven.

There it was again—only this time, the spot had taken on more shape. Not just any shape—a person. Who could sneak their way here but…

Mariq's breath caught in her lungs. A Star-Blade. In all the hassle of Feral and negotiations, she'd forgotten about them.

That was a dumb, and often deadly, mistake.

Mariq sucked in a breath, ready to call an alarm, when she was grabbed from behind. The same soft black cloak, the same unbreakable grip. She could almost feel the poisoned dagger against her throat again. "Scream and I'll introduce you to pain you never knew existed." Mariq bit her tongue, visions of Turien's barbed slave-band running through her mind. "Not like it would do you any good anyway. One scream among many wouldn't draw much attention."

Mariq struggled against the man, but she only succeeded in making him grip her harder.

"We knew Cendim would be a thorn in our side, but I don't think anyone expected you to be just as much of a problem."

Cold terror swept through Mariq's body. There had been a subtle change in the tone of that voice between one sentence and the next—a lessening of the iron, a hint of wheedling mischief replacing it. Mariq knew that voice. It had guided her much of her life and, near the end, tried to lead her astray. "Lookan?"

He laughed, the disdain he'd directed at her in public now flaunted at her in private. "What's wrong, sister? You didn't think all those lessons of defying expectation and pursuing what you wanted were for you alone, did you?"

"You're a Star-Blade?"

He spun her around to face him. He'd thrown his hood down, revealing his cut and bruised face. Wounds no doubt earned in his escape from Temhet-Sakh.

He raised his right hand between them, crusted with blood from a day-old injury. Mariq didn't want to see it, but it was plain as day: the outline of five knives on his palm, blades pointed outward in a star. Only this one was more elaborate than Cendim's, or any other she'd seen. Smaller blades extended between the main ones, somehow melding into the heritage tattoo that wound around his fingers.

Dear gods. He's not just a Star-Blade. He's the Star-Blade.

My brother is Turien's owner.

"You pranced around with your 'secret' training, feeling so superior, while I was the true secret. I gained all that you did and more, and no one—not Father, not the servants, not even you—had any idea." He leaned in close to her, sneering. "I've climbed to the very top of the organization you believed made you special. I authorized your training and oversaw every step of your progress. When you faltered, your caring brother was there to push you forward. You became a Star-Blade because of *me.*"

All Mariq could do was stare at him. She'd glimpsed this cold, heartless bastard in the hallways of Hatife, when he'd threatened Cendim with war. The same one who'd spoken beneath the nighttime cloak, who'd promised pain and death if she defied him.

Her own brother, whom she'd looked up to and loved for his belief in her, had been the one to poison her.

She should scream, despite his threat. His mere presence here was a danger to everyone. But the sounds of battle had grown ever louder, enough so that no one would be able to distinguish her shout from any other. And she knew he would have his own pair of ebony daggers in that cloak—likely more than a pair—and he would be all too happy to use them. She would be no good to anyone dead.

"I found something to silence that tongue at last," Lookan said, his grin firmly in place. "Had I known that was all it would take, I'd have told you long ago."

"How could you?" she whispered.

"How could I encourage you to be more, to do better, or reach out and become the best spider-thief you could be? I wasn't lying before, Mariq. I'd hoped we could work together. I can always use skilled Star-Blades, and having one I could trust, my own sister? It's more than most leaders could dream of."

"So through it all I was still just a pawn to you, too. You never cared about me like you let me believe. You were just shaping me into a tool for you to use." She shouldn't be quite this surprised—Lookan had always been much like their father, after all—but the realization nearly knocked her to her knees. "I feared you were as bad as our father. But now I see that he's nothing compared to you."

Lookan grinned and ducked his head. "Thank you."

"That wasn't a compliment."

Lookan's gaze turned cold and hard as diamonds. "Watch yourself, Mariq. I'm not quite as harmless as I led you to believe."

Mariq swallowed her comments. No matter what persona he wore—deadly leader of the Star-Blades or simpering heir of Kuriza, she knew better than to push him too far.

"Better," he said. "Though we'll still have to work on your attitude if we want to make you a suitable bride."

"You know Cendim likes me the way I am."

"Yes. The dear Sheik Zahra and his fondness for lost causes." Lookan grabbed her wrist and Mariq yanked it away. "I've decided to annul your *bardiya* with Cendim. There were... unforeseen complications that will make the match no longer profitable for Kuriza."

"You mean the fact I wouldn't kill him."

"And that you decided to join his little crusade," Lookan agreed, "not to mention that we're now at war. I couldn't in good conscience marry off my only sister to a man who is gathering an army to march toward our homeland."

Mariq's breath caught. Cendim had been pushed that far? He'd commit to launching an attack on Kuriza only if it was the last choice remaining to him.

"Luckily there is no shortage of men eager to gain favor and position with Kuriza. It was only a matter of time before one agreed to pay for a bride within the family."

Mariq's heart beat painfully in her chest. "You sold me?"

"Like the whore you are."

Mariq slapped him. Lookan worked his jaw, narrowed his eyes, and punched her. She fell to the ground, dizzy and disoriented.

"I'll teach you propriety if I have to beat it into you every day for the rest of your life," he growled. "Get up. We're going back to Kuriza."

"I'm not going anywhere."

"That wasn't a request." Lookan reached down and hauled her up with a painfully tight grip on her arm. He gave no indication of loosening it. "If you insist on fighting me I'll knock you unconscious and drag you back to Kuriza by your hair. Whatever's left of it, that is." The wheedling, petulant tone was gone, replaced with cold, brutal iron. Mariq suppressed a shiver. "Now. Where is the teshneh?"

By now the Star-Blades she'd glimpsed on the horizon had joined them, four in all—two were practically invisible in the sand-colored robes of Haven's scouts. Even at the peak of her skills Mariq couldn't have evaded them all. Then again, if Lookan was head of the Star-Blades, she doubted she could have evaded just him.

Lookan waved a hand toward the men and one came forward. He was larger than the others, and didn't move with the same grace. Definitely not a Star-Blade.

"Gherrim," Lookan said, and Mariq had to stifle the recognition. Ehra's brutish lover. He'd allied with the Star-Blades? They hated magic. "Find me the teshneh."

Gherrim raised his head, sniffing like a jackal scenting blood. He turned toward Haven and pointed. "Not far."

Lookan jerked his head toward one of the men. "Go with him. Do what you can to remain unseen, but do not return here without the teshneh."

Mariq kicked sand at them as they passed—an impotent gesture, but she had to do something. Her plans were foiled at every step. She'd clawed her way to victory only to face defeat yet again.

She would not let Lookan keep this victory. She might not be able to stop him now, but she just had to wait until they got back to Kuriza and find a way to release the magic. She could sneak in, grab it when they weren't looking...

Mariq shut her eyes. A spider-thief could have snuck in. Mariq was just a delicate princess now.

Still. She could figure something out. She had to.

Lookan grinned as he watched her. "Scheme all you want, sister, but I will win the day in the end."

She glared at him, but didn't answer.

He held out his hand, palm up. "Daggers."

"I stopped carrying them when I lost my skills."

"One more lie and I promise you'll watch every single moment of me bleeding the life out of your friends. A magic-user and a runaway slave—I'll take great pleasure in both."

She couldn't win, could she? "Turn around, then," she said, hiking her sarong up slightly to show they were not in an appropriate place.

"So you can stab me in the back, or run away while I'm not looking?" Lookan asked. "Do you believe I'm that stupid?"

"Yes."

His eyes burned with fury. "The knives. Now."

"I lost one in the desert." She removed the remaining knife from her thigh sheath and handed it over. Lookan didn't press, perhaps glimpsing the empty sheath.

"You see? You can play your little games of rebellion and independence all you want, but in the end, you still belong to us. No matter how hard you fight, or how vehemently you believe otherwise, you'll always be under our control. Because you're our property. Remember that, sister. I made you what you are. You're mine."

He turned away from Mariq as if she meant nothing and started giving orders to his Star-Blades. Mariq stood there, trying to be strong but feeling far from it.

Gherrim and the Star-Blade returned a short time later, carting the leather-shrouded teshneh. It was too much to hope they wouldn't have returned.

The Star-Blades dispersed, disappearing into the sands. Lookan grabbed Mariq's arm and held her with an unbreakable grip. He reached into his cloak and pulled out a glass globe, the same innocuous clarity as Joythief. It swirled in the glass with lazy motions, like smoke.

Mariq couldn't tear her eyes from it, even as her heart plummeted. Turien had said his master had some kind of weapon that sounded like Joythief, one he would use against the magic-users. She'd never imagined he would bring it here.

"Thank you for destroying Temhet-Sakh for me and driving almost every remaining magic-user in the Mad Desert to this place," Lookan said. "You're making my job so much easier."

Mariq wanted to lash out at him, but all she felt was emptiness.

"Take a deep breath," he said, his grip on her arm tightening even further. "Unless you want to lose even more, it'll be your last breath for quite some time."

Lookan threw the globe to the ground, the glass shattering against a rock. Vapors stretched out from it like fingers, spreading far faster and with much more volume than the globe should have been able to hold. Mariq gasped and almost lost her breath. They'd really done it. They'd turned Joythief into an airborne poison. It would only take one breath to destroy a person's passions. How far would it spread? What would it do to the ambient magic of the Mad Desert?

Lookan cackled as he pulled her after him, away from her friends, away from the Joythief spreading toward Haven.

All their work. All their successes. Everything they'd overcome now meant nothing.

Lookan had released the Joythief. Haven and the majority of those remaining in the Mad Desert would be drained of their passion—their magic—within hours. Minutes, maybe. The loss of so much magic would restore balance, no doubt about that. Only the balance would be with virtually no magic left anywhere.

And Lookan had the teshneh. Mariq shuddered to think what that would do to Hatife, or Kuriza, if he stole what little magic remained there too.

Mariq mounted the horse Lookan shoved her toward, despair clinging to her like a cloak. The world may be saved, but they had just lost everything.

MAGIC screamed like it had back in Temhet-Sakh. But where that had been a cry for help, this was a screech of death that sent shivers through Turien's soul. He could barely think through the agony pounding at his consciousness. Behind that, or beneath it, he could hear the great maelstrom of Joythief, consuming everything in its path. Passions. Skills. Magic.

Life itself.

The Star-Blades were here. His former master. They'd come all this way with the weapon Turien had feared from the moment he'd learned of it. Did they know he was here? Would they, as Mariq had feared, try to take possession of him again?

Speaking of Mariq, where was she?

He didn't have time to find her, or even to worry about her. The Joythief was growing stronger, pulling magic from him like sucking marrow from bone. So similar to his own magic but infinitely more hungry. The Joythief would never be satisfied. It would never stop consuming. How many lives would be ruined, or even lost, because of it? After everything they'd gone through to get this far, Turien couldn't let Joythief—and therefore his former master—win.

He had magic of his own now—magic that devoured, consumed, just like Joythief. Cendim had said the potion that originally granted him his magic was similar to Joythief. He felt *connected* to it, somehow. He *was* Joythief. Could Turien devour it?

He had to try.

He closed his eyes and reached for the magic coursing through him. *Devour.*

This time he didn't need a potion. No encouragement to accept the magic. He just opened himself to it, breathed, and took it in.

It filled him like water surging into a dry valley. Turien tasted the sweetness of magic and the sourness of Joythief. He'd expected it to remind him of the voidstone—empty, cold, horrific—but the Joythief was more like lemon or turmeric, bitter and abrasive yet not unpleasant. Something so devastating should not be appetizing.

His magic roared like a tempest, blue streamers of light swooping past him and around him and through him, faster and faster as he fed on the Joythief. He followed the trail of bitterness, leaving the sweet, ambient magic alone as best as he could. His magic wanted to take it all, to destroy everything as surely as the Joythief did. It hurt to rein it in—physical pain that made Turien grit his teeth and clench his fists and fight his own power with as much strength as he could muster.

He heard a woman calling out, his name being shouted, but it was distant. Hard to focus on. The Joythief was here, now, everywhere. He couldn't let anything distract him from it.

Blue light filled his vision. Magic soared toward him, coursed through him, but his hunger only grew the more he took in. The bitter Joythief grew thicker, smoky tendrils mixing with the glowing blue light. Turien grunted and groaned through the pain, through the ever-deepening *need* for more.

He must stay focused. He had a goal, an end he must see through. It grew harder to remember that the longer he fed.

This was his former master's doing. He could not let his former master beat him. He'd thrown off his shackles, become a friend and a magic-user and a member of the house of Kuriza. Mariq had given him a silk band that meant so much more than a simple slave-band. He could do this. For her.

Leave the magic. Just take the Joythief. It had the power to sustain him. It could satisfy his hunger. The magic must stay.

The pain grew. The hunger consumed him.

He was Someone. He was Turien.

He could not allow the Star-Blades to hurt anyone else.

Must. Defeat. The Joythief.

Chaos surrounded him. People cried out, sobbed, wailed. Bestial, animal howls echoed through the canyon—the Feral were caught in the Joythief, too. Turien shut it all away. There was only him and the Joythief.

Time became meaningless, pain became a distant thing. He followed the sour taste of consuming magic like a hound on the scent.

An eternity passed, just him and the Joythief battling for the magic of the Mad Desert.

Finally Turien collapsed to his knees, his magic exhausted. He shook from the exertion, from the sheer volume of Joythief he'd devoured. It roiled in his stomach and scorched his throat like bile. Would it consume his passions, his magic, like it had Mariq's? He hadn't stopped to consider that possibility before.

Not like it mattered. He would make that sacrifice if it meant he'd beaten his former master.

Turien felt at the magic. Threads of sour Joythief still lingered, but they were weak and scattered. Sweet magic remained, not quite as overwhelming as it had been but still very much alive. Turien felt as if he'd been battered by an entire army of Feral, but he'd done it.

He just had to hope he'd done it in time.

EHRA found him a while later, half-unconscious beside one of Haven's soothing pools. She didn't need to ask what had happened—one shared look explained everything. She helped him to his feet and led him back toward their rooms.

"Most of the Feral fled when the Joythief hit," she said. Turien had missed quite a bit while he'd been unconscious or lost in the magic. "The warriors of Temhet-Sakh took care of the rest, though not without a lot of casualties." She said that bit stoically, as if unwilling to allow her emotions near the truth of the statement. "A lot of people were knocked unconscious, but it looks like most survived the Joythief. There will be scars, of course, but without you it would have been so much worse."

"It's really over?" Turien asked. He felt wrung out and exhausted, and he couldn't comprehend that the danger had passed. How could it be? They'd been jumping from one danger to the next every few days for months now.

Ehra nodded. "There's a lot of clean up to do, but for now, yes. It's over. It's safe for us to leave as soon as you're ready."

Turien exhaled in relief. Then he looked around, his brow furrowing. If they were ready to leave, where was Mariq? She'd been anxious to get back to Hatife since the moment they'd gotten the teshneh.

The sourness in his stomach doubled. His master had never forgiven Mariq for turning against him and siding with Cendim, just as he never would when he learned of Turien's actions here. Plus Mariq had the teshneh, full of magic and the potential to give or take it at will. His former master had come all this way for it—and if he had to take Mariq in order to get it, he wouldn't hesitate for a moment.

Dread filled him as he sprinted the final way to Mariq's room. He was dizzy from the effort, his legs hardly strong enough to support him, but he had to find her.

Her room was empty. No Mariq, no teshneh.

"The Star-Blades must have taken her," he said. The words tasted as sour as Joythief in his mouth.

"Maybe she's just out looking for you?" Ehra sounded near frantic.

Turien wished it was true, but his gut told him it wasn't. "If the teshneh was still here, maybe. But she wouldn't have taken it on a whim. She was determined to keep it safe at all cost, and flaunting its power while wandering an encampment of people who would be tempted to steal it back is the furthest thing from safe. No, the Star-Blades must have gotten to her and to it." He felt sick saying it, but neither he nor Ehra argued the point.

Some of the fire that had been missing from Ehra's eyes since Temhet-Sakh returned. "Where will they take her?"

"Back to Kuriza. They wouldn't do anything away from their place of power if they didn't have to." Even as he said it, he shuddered. If he returned to Kuriza, the Star-Blades would see him dead.

If he didn't, Mariq would die in his place.

He and Ehra were already gathering their supplies and heading out the door. Their best hope was to catch them before they got to Kuriza—before they got too far from Haven. If they could stop the Star-Blades out here, alone, they *might* have a chance.

ariq couldn't think of it as going home again. It was returning to prison after a taste of freedom—drowning in a pool of tar after floating in clear, fresh water. Kuriza wasn't her home. Perhaps it had never been.

"You'll want to stop that fighting," Lookan said, his voice dripping with over-the-top cheeriness. "You don't want to give your husband a bad first impression."

"I don't have a husband! You can't make me do this!"

"You forget yourself, sister," Lookan replied. "I can. By all rights as your brother and heir to Kuriza, I can sign any marriage treaty I wish. Whatever I decide for you is the fate you will live with. You might want to remember that."

His words—and the truth behind them—frightened Mariq more than anything else. He'd already proven he could force her into any situation he wished, both as her brother and as leader of the Star-Blades. He'd manipulated her into being his tool from the very moment she was born. He'd tried to marry her off to Cendim and make her assassinate him. If he wanted to change his mind and give her to some beggar off the street, he had the right to do so. No one could argue with him. Not even her.

Her mind raced with escape routes and options, but nothing seemed viable. There were too many guards, and she didn't have the skills to hide any longer. Trying to run would be as futile as trying to pretend her brother would take her feelings into consideration.

Her rooms felt foreign to her, lacking the subtle touches that had made them hers. She washed the dirt and sweat from her body and donned a clean, albeit ill-fitting sarong from the guest wardrobe. She tried to do her hair, but the rough chop from her escape left it hanging raggedly just below her chin. Nothing she could do about that. Gold bangles and chains of coins applied, she looked every bit the useless, delicate princess Lookan was forcing her to become.

She hated it. More than anything in the world, she hated this persona. And yet, it was becoming the only thing that remained of Mariq.

Cleaned but hardly refreshed from their long, exhausting journey, Lookan escorted her to their father's receiving chambers. The man himself lounged at the table, just as he always had when Mariq had been summoned to serve tea. Did he know about Lookan's true identity? No, he couldn't. He would never allow a rival like that into his court.

Her father glanced up at them, nodded to Lookan, then looked to the man sitting opposite him. He waved his hand, presenting Mariq to him like a gift.

He was an overly large man, though the fat piled atop still-powerful muscles. Cruel, hard eyes and pinched lips only accented his brutish figure. His heritage tattoos had clearly been expanded from a wealthy merchant's tattoos to one of royalty. Mariq was certain he hadn't come to the promotion honestly, and multiple scars around his knuckles told her just how he kept people from questioning his rule.

"You see him?" Lookan asked, whispering into her ear as they stood in the doorway. "That's Sheik Karga. A minor ally of the Star-Blades. He hasn't much to offer us, I'll admit, but his price is just enough for a troublesome girl like you. It's a wonderful deal. He gets a new bed toy, we get an ally, and you... well, since you couldn't serve the Star-Blades as an assassin, you can serve us as a whore."

Mariq shuddered.

Lookan pushed her into the room. "Go ahead, dear sister. Surely you haven't forgotten your proper place?"

Mariq glared at him, though her knees were weak and watery. She forced away her grimace, and her fear, and glided into the room as if she'd done this yesterday. The tray waited for her, and she brought it to the men then knelt beside the table, head down. She hid her trembling hands in her lap.

"That's a good girl," her father said, as if placating a hyperactive puppy. "You'll behave for Karga, won't you?"

She looked up at her father, then at the other man. His eyes glittered with hideous cruelty as he leered at her. Mariq pictured his death a hundred different ways.

Sheik Karga drained his teacup, stood, and grabbed Mariq by the arm. He held her still while he inspected her, his lecherous eyes taking her in with sickening interest. He sneered at her short, uneven hair.

Mariq's stomach twisted and she trembled like a leaf, but the grip on her arm never loosened. She would surely have another hand-shaped bruise ringing her biceps by morning. The one Lookan had given her on the way here still darkened a section of her heritage tattoos.

He leaned closer, so close she could smell the tea on his breath.

"You belong to me. Whatever I want is mine to take from you, whenever I want it. You don't get to complain or refuse. Fight if you wish, but know it will only give me more pleasure to force it from you. Your purpose in life, from this moment on, is to serve me. Do you understand?" He watched her, waiting for her response.

She'd expected a gruff, mercenary tone to his voice, but he spoke with the smooth tones of a practiced politician. Somehow that was more frightening.

She wanted to fight him, even though she knew she couldn't win. If she had her knives, it might be a different story, but…

But what good would it do? If her father gave her to this man, she was his. Fighting would only make it worse.

It killed her to do it, but she nodded.

"She'll do," he said to her father. He released her with a slight shove and returned to his seat.

"Then it's done," her father said. "How soon before the details are taken care of?"

Lookan stepped to her father's side. "There are just a few things left to finalize, Father. I'll have them done as soon as possible—a few days, no more."

She looked up when she felt Lookan's eyes rest on her. He grinned, his eyes cold. She could hear Lookan's words echoing back to her: *You're our property. No matter how hard you deny it, you belong to us.*

Sheik Karga set down his teacup, paused for a heartbeat, then cleared his throat. Mariq filled it again. He took another deep drink, his free hand resting in her hair like a man claiming possession of a dog by holding its scruff.

I could stab him while he sleeps. I could poison his tea. Suffocate him with a pillow. Climb out the window, find a caravan heading toward Hatife…

Only she no longer had her knives. Or her climbing skills. And if what Lookan had said was true, Cendim had refused to wait for Kuriza to have the advantage and marched toward them even now. Kuriza braced for war, alert and watching for danger. Even if she could get away, returning to Cendim would be impossible.

Did he even know what had happened to her? Surely Turien and Ehra had noticed she'd gone missing, and with the release of the Joythief in Haven they must have figured out the Star-Blades were behind it. But did they know Lookan was the villain they looked for? Would they know to come back here to find her?

Even if they did, her enslavement to Sheik Karga would be finalized within a handful of days. They wouldn't get here in time to save her.

If she was still a spider-thief, she could have escaped this fate. But the Joythief had stolen that, and now she had nothing. Diplomacy wouldn't free her from this. Negotiations, charm, nothing she'd discovered about herself in the Mad Desert would do her a bit of good here.

urien wasn't sure where, or how, to find his former masters. They'd always come to him.

But he couldn't wait for that this time. Mariq was in danger, and at any second she could become worthless to the Star-Blades. He had to make sure he got to her before that. Before they did something horrible.

Something *else* horrible.

He couldn't stop to think on his actions. If he did, he would realize how stupid it was to go back to the master he'd defied. The master he'd done atrocious things for, and had seen the price they exacted for failure. They wouldn't just kill him. No. If they found him, he would wish for death, and they would be very long in granting that wish.

All in all, this was suicide. But he couldn't turn back. Not now, not ever. Mariq needed him.

They'd lost days in the Mad Desert, avoiding Feral and trying to catch sight of Mariq and the Star-Blades. But they clearly moved much faster than he and Ehra, and the best they could do was hurry and hope they weren't too late.

From the moment they entered the Desert of Plenty it became clear too late had already come and gone. Corpses littered the desert, wearing tattered uniforms of both Kuriza and Hatife. Skirmishes could be heard at all hours of day and night, and by the time Kuriza came into view they and Hatife were already at war.

Turien and Ehra crept toward the walls of Kuriza, careful to avoid the battle as best they could. The heaviest fighting centered near the gates, but the Star-Blades had many hidden ways into and out of the city. Turien had been forced to use them many times in the past.

He led Ehra toward one that would take them close to the palace, where he hoped they could locate his former master. If not... well, Turien just had to hope luck would be on his side.

He'd just about reached the entrance when he noticed Ehra wasn't beside him anymore. She stood several paces behind, her gaze locked on a skirmish taking place a short distance away—far too short for Turien's comfort. "Ehra?"

"There's so much life being lost."

"It's war," he replied. "One we can't get caught up in if we want to save Mariq."

"If I still had the teshneh, I could save them."

Ehra sounded so lost. No one should have to bear the longing and sadness he heard in her voice. Turien hesitated, watching her. She wanted nothing more than to help those suffering people. And why shouldn't she? That was what she did, and did well. She shouldn't be afraid of the thing that made her special—Turien had waited long enough to have something like that. "Even without the teshneh, you're still you. Just like Mariq is still Mariq even without her spider-thief skills."

Ehra broke her gaze from the battle to look at him. "That's the problem," she said, her voice barely above a whisper. "I'm still me, monster and all. If I try to help those people, at least half of them will die for it."

"But the other half would live." Turien couldn't believe he encouraged her. He'd seen the dangers of Ehra's magic. But he'd also seen the miracle and knew how much that returned life would mean to so many. "Some of these are your people, Ehra. Hatife is out here, fighting for magic. If nothing else you can go out there and help your father win this war."

Finally he saw what he'd been looking for: determination. She took a few steps toward the battle before glancing back at Turien, a mix of fear and doubt and resolve in her eyes.

"This is what your magic is made for, Ehra. I'll get Mariq and the teshneh. You help your father's army stay alive."

She took off toward the skirmish without another hesitation. Turien headed toward the hidden entrance to Kuriza—despite his encouragement, he didn't want to be too close to Ehra when she lost herself to the magic.

He crept through tunnels and emerged into the quiet streets of Kuriza a few moments later. The battle outside seemed distant, easy to forget. No one even seemed to care that so many people were dying just on the other side of the wall. Then again, they never seemed to care about much at all.

Turien grit his teeth as he dashed toward the palace. Kuriza was doomed if they didn't get the teshneh and restore magic to this place.

He reached the servants' entrance to the palace and panted, catching his breath, before knocking on the door. Long moments passed before it opened, the same girl who'd been here last time peering out at him. Back when he'd still worn the barbed slave-band.

She gave him a slight nod when she recognized him, then cast her eyes down to his slave-band—the barbs replaced with silk. She regarded the change in silence but didn't comment. "Did the princess call for you?" she asked.

Turien was so stunned it took him a moment to reply. "Call for me... is she here?"

The girl nodded.

Turien had to brace himself against the wall, so much relief washed over him. He would have to thank every lucky star in the sky for this. "Please, I need to see her."

"I'm not sure…"

Turien could hear the hesitance in the woman's voice. Perhaps her orders were vague enough that she wasn't sure what to do with him. Or perhaps she didn't want to follow them. Either way, Turien could use this. He made sure to meet her eyes, conveying all the helplessness and fear he felt for Mariq. "I was ordered to come back to her."

Some of the stiffness left the servant's posture and her eyes darted around anxiously. Almost.

"Please. If they think I've abandoned my mistress, you know what they'll do to me."

The plea worked. The servant's eyes softened as she looked at Turien. She nodded and gestured for him to follow. "It would be best for you to stay out of sight," she whispered as they walked through hallway after hallway. "Sheik Karga wouldn't like another man being close to his new wife."

Turien tripped over his feet, stumbling for a few steps then hurrying forward to catch up to the servant. "Wife?"

"Sheik Meidani arranged it. We've been preparing a banquet for the official marriage for days now."

"What about the *bardiya* to Sheik Zahra?"

The servant's eyes flashed as she glanced at him. "The treaty's broken, if you couldn't tell. We're at war with Hatife. Sheik Meidani couldn't marry his daughter off to that man now."

No, of course not. Not when Cendim had come so close to defeating the Star-Blades, and had succeeded in turning Mariq into a weapon against him. But to have arranged another marriage so quickly? Turien shuddered. If Tufe Kolam knew the extent of Mariq's allegiance and involvement in Cendim's plans, what kind of punishment would he have concocted for her? "When is the marriage finalized?"

"The banquet's tomorrow."

Just in time. They had to move fast.

"Where can I find her?"

"Guest quarters, third floor. Second room on the left is Shiek Karga's. The one beside it is hers."

Sheik Karga. Turien knew the name—he'd met the man a few times in his service to the Star-Blades. If Mariq was set to marry him, he had to get her out. Now. "Thank you."

Turien started down the hallway, then paused and turned back to the servant girl. "One more question." He held up his arm and the silk slave-band. "How did you know this was hers?"

The girl smiled. "She always had such beautiful clothes. I recognize the pattern."

Turien smirked. Leave it to servants to notice, and remember, such details.

He made his way to the room the servant had indicated. The hallway was silent, but not in an innocent way. Turien knew better than to think it had been left unguarded with silence like that, ominous and too perfect, hovering around it.

He turned around without entering the corridor. He'd make it to Mariq another way.

It had been a long time since he'd done any kind of climbing, but the balconies arrayed for guests of the palace allowed him to make it with only a few close calls. He triple-checked he had the right room before ducking into the window. He stayed against the wall, in what little shadow he could find, though he knew it did little good. He'd never excelled at skulking or sneaking. Words had always come more easily to him than actions.

Sudden movement to the side caught his attention and he leapt backward without thinking. Mariq barreled toward him, the finial of a silver perfume jar extended like a knife. Her form was off, even Turien could see that. He side-stepped her attack and evaded the makeshift weapon while Mariq stumbled, overbalanced. Turien caught her shoulders before she could fall.

Mariq struggled in his grasp for a moment before recognizing him. Her eyes went wide as she stared at him. Then she clung to him, desperate, sobbing as if she'd never expected to see a friendly face again. Turien held her until she quieted. When she straightened he reached up and brushed her shorn hair from her face.

Anger roared through him as he spotted the bruises on her arms. He trailed them with his fingers, gently enough to not hurt her further. She refused to look at him, her eyes on her feet, until he tipped her chin up with another gentle touch.

Turien wanted nothing more than to erase the pain and brokenness from her eyes. But the best he could do was wipe a tear from her cheek.

"You found me," she whispered, as if afraid saying the words would shatter the illusion.

"I told you to come back to me," Turien said, a faint smile tugging at his lips. "When you didn't, I had to make sure *I* came back to *you*."

She smiled, the barest hint of the real Mariq—*his* Mariq—in her expression.

"Come on," he said, taking her hand and pulling her toward the window. "We're getting out of here."

"How? Sheik Karga has me under guard, and Lookan checks often to make sure I haven't run. He has the entire palace watched."

"Even the walls? Your brother doesn't know you're a spider-thief."

Mariq fell silent, as ominously as the corridor outside her room had been. "Yes, he does. He's a Star-Blade. The leader of the Star-Blades." She left the rest unsaid. It didn't need to be said.

Turien couldn't breathe. His mysterious master, who'd controlled his every move his entire life, was the Prince of Kuriza, Mariq's *brother*? His position as leader of the Star-Blades gave him more power than anyone should ever hold. To also be heir to the entire kingdom? He might as well be unstoppable.

And if he kept an eye on Mariq, knowing she was a spider-thief, he'd have the walls and windows watched.

Which meant he knew Turien was here, too.

"It doesn't matter. We have to get out of here. Now!"

Still holding Mariq's hand, Turien threw open the door and bolted out. Mariq didn't even hesitate. She just squeezed his hand harder and raced after him.

There were indeed guards in the hallway—even more than Turien had assumed. Huge, scarred men blocked each exit only paces from Mariq's doorway, and at the commotion Sheik Karga himself emerged from his room next door. He looked fuming mad, ready to pummel anything that got in their way.

Turien would not let Mariq stand before him again.

He inhaled deeply, focusing not on the ambient magic but the power within the people themselves. He couldn't take life the way Ehra did. Turien couldn't kill any more than Joythief could kill, but he could devour just a bit of the magic that gave them their passions. A sip wouldn't be permanent, but he knew well enough from his time in Haven that it could be very, very disorienting.

Everyone in the corridor stumbled, clutching their hearts, their heads, or curling in on themselves. Mariq included. Turien cursed himself for his clumsiness and half-carried Mariq around the prone, groaning figures. He may have kicked Sheik Karga a time or two as he stepped over the man as well, just for good measure.

"Wait," Mariq said, pausing as they crossed Karga moaning on the floor. She broke from his grip and stumbled into the man's room. Turien stood just outside the door, watching in case any of the guards stirred.

A few heartbeats later Mariq returned, smoothing her sarong. "I had to get my thieving harnesses," she explained. "Too bad Karga didn't search them, though. I wouldn't have minded seeing what the voidstone would do to him."

Turien shuddered at the thought. He wouldn't wish the voidstone on his worst enemies.

Then again, seeing the hand-shaped bruises on Mariq, maybe he would make an exception.

Turien urged Mariq to get a head start, then gave another pull on the magic to keep the guards from pursuing. His feet skid on the cool marble floors as he raced as fast as he dared to the bottom floor. Mariq was half a pace ahead.

They reached the main hall and Turien turned them toward the front doors, not willing to risk the time it would take to navigate the maze of servants' corridors. People crowded the room, scrambling in every direction as they prepared for a wedding feast, but Turien pushed their way through. He had almost escaped with the bride.

Something tugged at Turien, like a string had been pulled taut around his heart. He stumbled. So did Mariq, and everyone else. His mouth went dry. Something had pulled at the magic, and he hadn't done it. Only two other things could do that, and both spelled disaster for them.

His eyes found Lookan standing on one of the marble steps, the leather-wrapped teshneh in his hand. One corner of the cover had been pulled up, light and magic sucking in through the tiny hole. His eyes scanned the crowd and locked on him and Mariq. He grinned as if he'd been given a priceless gift. "Not only have you brought me the teshneh, but your beloved Cendim has handed over his entire army. In a few moments the entire Scorched Lands will be purged of magic. And it's all because of you." He gave them a little half-bow and smiled. "Thank you for making the Star-Blades' dream possible."

Mariq stood and raised placating hands. "Lookan, if you do this you'll destroy everything."

"Kuriza will be free of magic even if I must destroy it and rebuild from the ashes."

Lookan loosened the ties on the leather bundle and pulled out the gleaming brass and magic it had been concealing.

Freed of its prison, the teshneh did what it had always done: sucked magic from the land. But this land had no more magic left. The stored power swirling around the brass rings drew in tighter, spinning faster and faster like the heart of a dust devil. The teshneh crackled like a thunderstorm, too full of magic yet pulling what little it could find into itself all the same. Turien felt the pull on his own power, making him nauseous and dizzy as he struggled to hold onto it.

Turien suddenly understood why this thing had been called a weapon, and why the people who'd created it needed to be stopped.

Lookan lobbed the teshneh into the air. A strange, shrieking whine followed it as it flew up, higher and faster than should have been possible. It shattered a hole through the ceiling, not even slowing as it sailed upward, story after story until it had made an opening straight to the roof.

Lookan laughed, turned, and ran down a corridor.

Turien and Mariq hesitated. They couldn't let Lookan escape, but neither could they allow the teshneh to continue absorbing magic. This power wasn't like his, like Joythief's. This wouldn't just devour passions and render people unconscious. As unstable, and hungry, as the teshneh was, this would pull so much magic from a person it would kill them.

Even now, it tried. Oh how it tried. It took everything within Turien just to keep himself upright.

Turien and Mariq locked eyes. He'd finally gotten her back, and now they had to part ways so soon.

"I'll go for the teshneh," Mariq said, the same struggle in her eyes as she fought the teshneh's power. "It's too dangerous for a magic-user to go after it."

Turien nodded. "I have a score to settle with my old master anyway."

Mariq grabbed his hands and squeezed. "Come back to me," she said. "And don't let Lookan get away."

Turien flexed his wrist, remembering a lifetime of scrapes and barbs and abuse. "Don't worry. I won't."

30

ot even the monster could ignore the sudden death of magic.

Ehra snapped back to herself, no idea how long she'd been lost to the monster. How many lives had she taken? Had she saved any? She didn't know. But something more awful needed her attention.

The teshneh hung over Kuriza's palace, horrifying in its beauty. The earth quaked as magic sped toward the brass rings from any source it could reach. Plants, animals, humans. Anything alive. Anything beautiful.

There had been so little left when they arrived. Now there would be nothing. Once the magic was gone, what would happen?

Chaos. Death. The entire world crumbling as magic and non-magic tore it apart.

Her vision blurred as she ran toward Kuriza's gates. The entire battle paused as people fell and cringed or stopped frozen in their tracks. Ehra ran forward, the sheer magic in her blood giving her strength to endure the teshneh's consuming power.

Did the monster take life but not return it?

She couldn't think on that now. She had to get to the teshneh.

Time meant nothing as she dashed forward, inhumanly fast. She could feel the magic draining quickly, slowing her with each step. The teshneh was drawing faster. The sultan had said the device was unstable, unsafe for any magic-user to come in contact with. Ehra could feel that with each breath she drew.

By the time she made it through Kuriza's gates and into the palace, she'd returned to normal human speed. Terrified, disoriented people milled about the main hall, many more sprawled unconscious across the marble floor. The magic drain was heavier here, faster, and the power Ehra had held moments ago was completely gone. Her steps grew sluggish as the teshneh moved from draining the monster's stolen magic to Ehra's.

In moments, she was too exhausted to climb the stairs to the roof. She did it anyway.

She didn't stop. She couldn't now, even if she tried. The teshneh drew her toward it, the pull on her magic too strong to ignore. She had to get there. She had to stop it.

THE teshneh's magic still felt shattered. Wrong somehow, both more and less powerful than it should have been. Dangerous magic. Exposure to this kind of power could kill.

Gherrim didn't dare question the Star-Blades. Not if he wanted the magic the teshneh took from this dead land. And it *was* dead, far more than anyone seemed to believe. There was no magic here, no vitality. The teshneh was one of very few magic sources he could sense.

One was the man who smelled like the teshneh. If the Star-Blades didn't take care of him, Gherrim would. The leader of the Star-Blades, Lookan, had made Gherrim promise he would wait until the teshneh had done its work before seeking revenge for Temhet-Sakh. Something about making a point. It grated on his nerves, but the eventual reward would be worth it.

The other magic source was Ehra.

His senses were alive with her magic, powerful and familiar as a lover's kiss. The memory of it awakened a craving in him, a desire to have that magic back despite her rejection. He could convince her to give it to him again. He needed to.

She'd loved him. He could get her back—he would make her come back to him. One way or another, her magic would be his again.

When the scent of her power entered the palace, Gherrim snuck away from the Star-Blades and followed her.

The pull of the teshneh grew uncomfortable, then painful, as he chased Ehra up the stairs toward the roof. He caught up to her just before she reached the top level. He lunged forward and grabbed her arm before she could dash around a corner.

Magic sang through him, spreading like wine through his body. He breathed deeply and reveled in it. This was just a touch. He shivered to think of how much he would feel when he had her again.

Her eyes were wide, almost frantic, when she looked back to him. "What are you doing here?" It took her several tries to get the entire sentence out.

"You of all people should have known I would never let the teshneh out of my sight."

Ehra wrenched her arm out of his grip and glared at him. "Of course not. Magic is the only thing you ever cared about."

She spun and walked away. As if Gherrim was below her attention.

"Don't you turn your back on me!"

"I have more important things to do, Gherrim." She didn't even look back as she spoke. "If you cared half as much about people as you did magic, you'd help me stop this."

She was going after the teshneh. Suicide. The magic up there would be far too intense for any magic-user to survive. She'd never make it, let alone stop it.

But if she did, all of Gherrim's magic went with it.

He sprinted after her, grabbing her arm again and flinging her against the wall. He pinned her there, body against hers, magic surging between them.

She tried to push him away, but Gherrim was far too strong. Her flailing only made him press her harder, trap her more thoroughly.

Her magic flared, sweet and heady and delicious.

And then Gherrim staggered back, nauseous and dizzy. His entire body felt drained, his thoughts sluggish. So tired. So cold.

His head lolled to the side and he struggled to raise it, to focus his vision on Ehra. She'd stepped out of reach. He tried to approach her but his legs wouldn't work and he had to brace himself against the wall just to stay on his feet.

"I warned you. You'll taste my magic if I ever see you again."

"You *bitch*," he wheezed. "I should turn you in to the Star-Blades now."

Her scowl turned even more bitter. "How do you know about the Star-Blades?"

"They wanted the teshneh. I wanted the magic." Some of his strength returned, enough for him to stand on his own now.

"You allied with the Star-Blades." She spoke it like a condemnation. "You would help them murder thousands of innocent people? As they tear the world apart by draining away all magic? You're worse than I thought."

"The magic in the teshneh is *mine*," he said, fists clenching. "If I have to kill you to get you out of my way, I will."

"I believe you." Her magic flared again, and this time Gherrim couldn't stay on his feet. He collapsed, each breath coming with immense effort. "But that assumes I let you get close to me."

Gherrim could sense his magic now, floating between them. Compared to Ehra's it was weak as a newborn. Tiny, insignificant. He'd never been able to scent his own power before.

"I'll kill you," he repeated, the words slurred even to his ears. "I'll take your magic, whore, and kill your friends who stole the teshneh's magic. It's all *mine*."

"I wasn't going to do this," Ehra said. Her words sounded muffled. Gherrim could barely focus enough to understand them. "But you're more than just a brute. You're a monster, even more so than me. And you have no idea. You think you're wonderful, but you're wretched."

The last of Gherrim's strength was pulled away. He couldn't feel anything now. Not his arms or legs, or even the magic. It was all gone. *My magic*, he thought, furious. Desperate.

"Goodbye, Gherrim."

Gherrim's thoughts went black, without even the soothing presence of magic to comfort him.

EHRA hated how invigorated she felt. Gherrim's life had given her strength, restored her boundless energy to fight against the pull of the teshneh. She doubted she'd have been able to continue without that strength. But it had come at the cost of his life. No matter how much he'd deserved it, his death had been at her hands.

And this time she didn't even have her monster to blame.

Horrible as it was, Gherrim's life would help her make it to the teshneh. Would help her save Kuriza, and Hatife, and the world. Guilt could come later.

The rooftop was alive with color and light and darkness and death, all at once. Mariq stood before the teshneh, staring at it in dismay. It hovered out of her reach, power and magic sparking from it like lightning. Terrifying and beautiful and deadly.

"I can't stop it," Mariq cried.

Ehra stared at the teshneh. Its magic called to her, more strongly than it had on the rooftop in Temhet-Sakh. That pure magic, roiling and volatile now, beckoned her.

"I can," she replied.

Even augmented by Gherrim's life, more energetic and powerful than any human had a right to be, Ehra could barely stay on her feet as she advanced toward the teshneh. Her limbs grew heavy, her mind foggy. Magic left her like blood pouring from a wound with every step, leaving her weak and tired. This must be what wading into death felt like. Suffocating, painful. Wrong. The teshneh drew too much magic into it.

So Ehra pulled some out.

Energy and giddiness and joy suffused her. That bit of magic gave her the strength to pull more, and more, until the teshneh no longer hummed with power. Magic coursed through her like blood, life-giving and powerful. She could do anything with this power. She was a goddess.

She looked over the desert, feeling the emptiness of it. This world was dying.

And Ehra could resurrect it.

Ehra pushed the magic out, threading it into the world the same way she infused life into a dying person. The teshneh tried to suck it back in, but Ehra kept pulling magic from it and pushing it out. Faster. More and more, until she replenished the world's magic faster than the teshneh could steal it. The quakes subsided. The shades of death and darkness retreated, leaving color and life in abundance. Up here, on this rooftop, the world flourished.

Ehra cast her gaze to the ground. Down there, death and destruction ruled.

So many bodies. So much blood. So little magic.

So many people hurting, dead, dying.

Ehra could fix that.

She threaded her own magic into the stream of power flowing from her, pouring magic and life back into the world until she was nearly empty.

The energy that had suffused her a moment ago dwindled. Lethargy set in, heavy and suffocating. It took an immense amount of concentration to continue healing the world.

She knew what she was doing. She knew what it cost her.

She didn't stop.

Ehra had been dead since the night Temhet-Sakh fell. Her body had continued to function, but inside had been nothing. The one place she'd found peace, a purpose, and love had turned out to be false. Nothing but a façade of happiness. Pulling back that curtain and showing her the truth had killed her as surely as a knife to the heart would have.

There was no going back for her. Temhet-Sakh had freed her from the monster, but just for a moment. The monster was inside her, always. She'd hidden it, run from it, but Ehra was the monster. Would always be the monster. And some part of her loved it.

She couldn't let that continue.

How many innocents lay dead below her, inside the city and out? How many lives had been lost to control or contain this magic roiling inside her?

She couldn't let that continue either.

Ehra could save those lives—those hundreds and thousands of lives. She could return the world to its balance and undo so many of the mistakes made here today. It would only cost her everything.

The world would be better off if none of this had happened.

The world would be better off without her monster.

Ehra cast one look back at Mariq. Her friend who'd seen her monster and stuck with her anyway. Mariq and Turien had stayed by her side through it all. She had finally found true love and acceptance for who she was. It might not have taken the form she'd expected, but here, at the end, it was enough.

Ehra smiled at her. Ducked her head in acknowledgement and love, hoping the motion spoke the words she couldn't.

Then she turned back and dashed toward the teshneh.

Mariq called to her, terror choking her words.

Ehra leapt up, catching the bottom of the brass rings with her hand. It burned like fire and ice and left her entire body tingling. She dragged the teshneh down with her and, with superhuman strength granted by the flood of magic, pried apart the rings.

An innocuous *ting* sounded as the brass circles fell apart and clattered to the ground.

Ehra screamed.

Magic gushed from the spot where the teshneh had broken, more potent and powerful than anything Ehra had ever felt before. She channeled that magic through her, pouring every bit of power she had—her monster, giver of life and death—over Kuriza. Ehra could no longer see, could feel nothing but magic and pain and satisfaction that at the end, her monster would finally do something good.

Ehra hung there for moments made brief by her exhilaration and unending by her pain. She didn't know how long she poured out her magic. But when she had no more left, the light dimmed enough to give her one last glimpse of Kuriza.

It was green. It was alive. People were stirring. There were still many dead, but many, many more lived because of her magic.

Ehra smiled.

She'd been wrong. Slipping into death wasn't nearly as difficult as reaching the teshneh had been. It was effortless, like falling asleep. Ehra felt herself hit the ground, the world already far, far away. She closed her eyes and released her last breath.

And finally, she found peace.

MARIQ knelt on the roof of her father's palace, not even trying to slow her tears. They obscured her vision, blurring lines and shapes into an unrecognizable mosaic, but she kept her gaze locked on a single splotch of color. The one spot she wished would move, that broke her heart all over again each moment it did not. Ehra. Her poor, tortured, broken friend who deserved so much more than this.

Her brave, amazing, noble friend who'd sacrificed herself to save them all.

A breeze blew against her, cool and sweet with salt from the sea to the east and hot with spices from the west. The Desert of Plenty, made even more so by Ehra. Grass sprouted green and vibrant as far as Mariq could see. Flowers bloomed. People who'd been near-dead a moment before stood, smiled, laughed. *Lived.* So many lives returned.

At the cost of one.

Mariq would never, ever forgive her brother for this.

She climbed to her feet, overcome by rage and grief. It took every bit of strength within her to walk over to Ehra's body and kneel beside it.

"Thank you, my friend," she whispered. "The world will be a poorer place without you."

She wanted to say so much more, but words weren't enough. They could never be enough. So instead she let her tears reveal her heart.

They didn't flow long. Someone had to pay for this. And Mariq knew where the blame lay—on the same shoulders that bore the weight of her poisoning, Turien's enslavement, and this entire war.

It was time for Lookan to die.

31

Turien kept his promise. Even through the dizziness of his magic being pulled away, the all-consuming lethargy that had nearly stopped both he and his former master in their tracks, and the sudden euphoria of having his life returned tenfold, he never lost sight of Lookan's fleeing form.

Lookan slowed his mad dash through the corridors, enough that Turien thought he might finally catch the man. But before he could, Lookan squared his shoulders and strolled into the massive library where Turien had first met Mariq. Turien skid to a stop just shy of the door, pressing himself against the wall. He knew his former master better than to barrel into a room after him blindly—more likely than not he'd impale himself on a dagger.

Besides, Mariq should be here for this. She deserved this chance to stop Lookan as much as he did.

Turien held his breath and peeked into the room, but from this vantage point he could see nothing but a shelf of books. It seemed like so long ago he'd sat here, dining with Sheik Meidani, the barbs of Lookan's slave-band digging into his wrist. Negotiating for the life of the man's daughter like she was a camel.

He'd been No One back then. A slave who existed only to do the will of his evil master.

No more. He was Someone now. He was Turien, a man unto himself.

He couldn't wait to prove that to Lookan.

After a moment Turien heard voices—Lookan's, then Sheik Meidani's. Dread settled over Turien. He held no love for Mariq's father, but he knew Lookan's tone well. After a conversation held in that voice there was almost always blood for Turien to mop up.

His former master had taken enough lives. Turien rounded the corner and entered the room, no clue how he would stop Lookan but determined to do so nonetheless. He could only hope Mariq would find them quickly.

Lookan and Tufe Kolam barely took notice of him. The sheik stood before his son, drenched in sweat, Lookan's ebony dagger poised at his throat. The fury in both of their gazes froze Turien in his tracks.

"How *dare* you threaten me!" Tufe Kolam bellowed, swatting at Lookan's dagger as if pushing away a child's wooden sword. He began reaching for a short blade strapped to his side, but Lookan rolled his wrist around Tufe Kolam's arm, brought his dagger back around, and sliced a line across his father's cheek in one smooth, too-fast-to-follow motion. Blood flowed instantly and the sheik staggered back, aghast. His fury was replaced by disbelief and just a hint of fear. He did not reach for either blade again.

"I am done serving you, father. I am done being your simpering errand boy. Today, you will listen to *me*!"

Tufe Kolam spat at Lookan's feet. "You have no idea what a mistake you're making, child. You don't have the power to take Kuriza from me."

"I don't have the power?" Lookan laughed, incredulous. "I have more power than you could possibly dream of, and more than you've held your entire miserable life."

Mariq's entrance cut off her father's response. Turien's relief at seeing her made him feel momentarily weak.

All eyes turned to her—battered, exhausted, eyes red from crying but filled with rage. Once she caught sight of Lookan her gaze never left him. She looked ready to tear him apart with her fingernails.

"What, no overdramatic threat?" Lookan asked, still holding the dagger at Tufe Kolam's throat. "No insinuations of my parentage or deserved fate before you exact your so-called justice?"

"You aren't worth it," Mariq replied. In contrast to her visible rage, her voice was quiet and deathly calm. That made it all the more chilling. "Monsters like you don't deserve that kind of respect."

Lookan's fury made him visibly tremble. "None of you understand. My power will demand your respect sooner or later. I will free Kuriza from magic. The Star-Blades *will* win this war, and I will have all the Scorched Lands at my feet!"

"You've already failed, Lookan. Kuriza's magic has been restored," Mariq said, her voice cracking. "One of my closest friends died to see to that."

Turien's heart thumped painfully. "Ehra's dead?"

Mariq nodded, eyes hard even as a tear leaked down her cheek. She never looked away from Lookan. "She sacrificed herself to stop *you* from destroying everything she loved. We would all be dead if it wasn't for her."

Lookan shrugged as if it didn't matter. "This plan may have failed, but I have others. The Star-Blades never start anything they can't finish."

"Star-Blades?" Tufe Kolam tucked his chin to peer more closely at Lookan's ebony dagger, still wet with his blood. Details seemed to click together in his mind. "My son is a Star-Blade?" His voice quivered.

"*The* Star-Blade," Lookan corrected.

"You? You're the bastard who's been trying to bully his way into my court?"

"Succeeding, father. You should be proud. I've turned the Star-Blades into a force of nature. We're unstoppable."

"Not if I have any say in it," Mariq said.

Lookan paused and glanced at her. "Then again, there are always bad seeds in any organization. Sometimes they just need to be purged."

Tufe Kolam's brow furrowed, then he looked toward Mariq. His eyes went wide and his mouth hung open. He looked as if he'd just been told his shit was made of gold.

"There's no need for this," Tufe Kolam said, gently pushing the dagger away from his throat. His tone had turned politic, almost simpering. "We can work something out, one leader to another."

"I'm afraid not, father. If I'm to salvage my plans I need more than just a sympathetic ear on the throne. I'll need the power behind it."

"You can have it. I won't give you any trouble."

"You know what, father? You're right."

Lookan moved faster than anyone could react, slicing through Tufe Kolam's neck and shoving the man aside. Blood splattered the colorful mosaic tiles, the tea service, the priceless parchment and leather books. Tufe Kolam didn't make a sound, was barely able to struggle as he died. Lookan watched the entire thing with such dispassion it made Turien sick.

"Now then," he said, wiping the blood from his dagger, "as the new Sheik of Kuriza I have many things to see to. I would command you both to stand down and serve me, but we all know you won't do that. Which means I'll have to subdue you. For the safety of the kingdom, of course."

Turien took a step forward to stand beside Mariq. She clasped his hand tightly. They were both unarmed, both battered, but they would defy Lookan together.

Lookan grimaced. "You never know when to give up, do you? I poured so much into you both, shaping you into such powerful tools, and *this* is how you repay me?"

"By using what you gave us to stop you?" Turien asked, genuine mirth making him laugh despite how dire their situation was. "I can think of no better way to thank you."

Lookan's face grew dark, his eyes dangerous. His grip on the knife tightened. "I'm not about to let a couple of magic-loving failures take Kuriza from me."

"We don't have to take the kingdom from you. You've already lost it," Turien said.

Lookan's eyes narrowed and he raised his dagger. "How dare you. You can't speak to me like this. You're a slave. You're *no one*."

Turien released Mariq's hand and stepped forward, looking Lookan straight in the eye. "No. I'm Turien. And I'm who you made me to be. I finally figured out who that is." He leaned forward, dropping his voice to a whisper. "I'm the man who's going to destroy you."

Devour.

Turien inhaled deeply, pulling hard on the magic within Lookan. Deny it all he wished, magic existed in everyone. Lookan had no less magic in his blood than Turien had, before he'd become this. Living Joythief.

Lookan had crafted Turien into a weapon. How good it felt to turn that weapon back upon him.

Lookan staggered, his eyes going wide as Turien devoured with all his might. He'd hoped Lookan would fall unconscious, making this battle infinitely easier, but Lookan had plenty of magic in his blood to sustain him. Whatever Mariq—or from her words, Ehra—had done to the teshneh hadn't just restored Turien's verve. It had restored everyone's.

When Lookan sagged to his knees, Turien lunged for the sheik's body and drew the short blade from its sheath on his side. It was ornate to the point of gaudiness, but the steel was sound. Enough to fed off any attacks from Lookan's ebony dagger while Turien tried to think of another plan.

Lookan recovered quickly—too quickly—and swiped at Turien with a speed that surprised even him, it seemed. Turien backpedaled, swinging the blade before him. He'd never been Lookan's equal at swordplay. His former master had seen to that. Learn enough to be competent, but never enough to be competition.

Mariq would be far better suited for this.

Turien devoured more of Lookan's magic and his former master took a desperate swing, gritting his teeth against the pain. Turien's magic was wearing him down.

Turien blocked the swing and took a step back, drawing ever farther away from Lookan and closer to the door of the library.

Closer to Mariq. Another step and he could hand off the blade to her.

He glanced back, losing sight of Lookan for less than a heartbeat, but that was all the time his former master needed. Lookan lunged forward with a desperate burst of speed and sliced his dagger through skin and muscle, clean across Turien's abdomen. Hot blood gushed no matter how hard Turien tried to staunch it.

Mariq cried out behind him. As much as he wanted to turn and reassure her, the best he could manage was a slow, agonizing slump to the ground.

Lookan didn't even glance down as he stepped over Turien. His eyes, filled with murderous fury, were only for Mariq.

COME get me, you bastard.

Mariq could never beat Lookan in a duel, she knew that. When she had her skills, yes. Maybe. But now? She wouldn't even present a challenge.

Yet she couldn't flee. She wouldn't. Turien lay bleeding on the floor before her. The horrible wound would have been mortal almost immediately, if they hadn't been bolstered by Ehra's magic. Even so, he wouldn't last long. She had to get him help, which meant getting him out of this room. Away from Lookan.

Besides, Ehra had died to stop Lookan from destroying what was left of Kuriza's magic. That sacrifice had to be honored, and the best way Mariq could do that was to kill the man who'd made it necessary.

No, she would not flee. She would finish this. For Ehra. For them all.

Her brother lunged at her, dagger first. Mariq jumped to the side, avoiding the strike. She'd hoped to get within range of her father's blade, dropped by Turien's side, but Lookan kicked out at her and she was forced away before she could grab it. The motion put her farther into the library. Now Lookan stood between her and the door.

He recognized his advantage as well as she did and used it at every turn. He struck at her relentlessly, forcing her to stay moving, never giving her a moment to catch her breath or form a plan other than survival. He wasn't fighting as well or as quickly as he could—Turien's magic had drained him significantly—but he was still more than a match for her, unarmed, Joythief firmly seated in her blood. Besides, she got the feeling he was having far too much fun for this battle to end quickly.

She spun away from another strike, the dagger cutting a long gash in her sarong.

Weariness made her limbs heavy, her motions slow. Dodging was an acrobatic skill, one that took extreme amounts of energy. After the last several days Mariq could barely stand.

Lookan slashed at her again, and this time the dagger hit flesh. The blade pierced her upper arm, marring her heritage tattoos with gashes and blood. She cried out and pulled back, stumbling to the ground.

Mariq reached her left hand up to slow the loss of blood. The movement made her sarong slip a bit to the side, revealing the empty knife sheath on her harness. If only she still had a weapon—something she could use to weaken Lookan.

Her heart skipped a beat. She did have a weapon. One she could use even in her weakened state.

Lookan leered over her. She didn't try to fight him anymore. Let him think her weak and foolish. Let him lord his victory over her—she knew he would. Lookan was always too arrogant to pass up a little self-important gloating.

Mariq kept her head down, her shoulders slumped. Weak. Harmless. Defeated.

She inched her hand toward the cut in her sarong.

"All that fighting and look where you end up," Lookan said, taking slow steps toward her. "On the ground at my feet, where you've always belonged."

Mariq stifled a remark and shifted as if the words had hurt her. She used the motion to expose the pouch on her thieving harness. One quick motion released the tie holding it closed.

"As much as I'd love to see Sheik Karga put you in your place, you've proven far too unruly to spare. You just refuse to give up and let us win."

That's kind of the point. She reached into the pouch, where the cold vastness of the voidstone waited.

Lookan's words blurred as Mariq grasped the voidstone. Even wrapped in cloth it froze her skin, burned in her blood. She felt weak and lethargic just holding it. She struggled to keep her eyes open, to keep her attention focused on what she was doing.

A shadow fell over her. A voice speaking, the words just out of her reach. A hand under her chin, forcing her face up. Something cold and sticky pressed against her throat.

Mariq loosened her grip on the voidstone. Clarity snapped into place—Lookan kneeling before her, holding her head up. His knife, red with blood, poised to slice open her throat.

She met his eyes. Cold, twisted glee glittered in them, a feral smile on his face.

"Goodbye, sister."

Mariq ripped the voidstone from the pouch. Lookan glanced to the side just in time to see her arm swing up to meet his temple, silk and stone impacting his skull.

Lookan staggered back. Even that brief touch from the voidstone left him dazed.

Mariq used his surprise to push him back, hooking her ankle behind him to make him trip. He fell to the ground on his back, stunned for just a heartbeat. Long enough for Mariq to expose a portion of the stone.

Mariq crouched over him and pressed the voidstone to his forehead. "Goodbye, Lookan."

From the moment Turien had taken Cendim's potion he'd had magic in his blood. Not much, just some. Enough for the voidstone to feed off.

Turien has used much of his power against Lookan. Her brother didn't have a drop of magic left in his body.

Mariq had never heard a scream quite like her brother's. It was pure, raw agony ripped straight from the soul. Lookan's voice broke and grew hoarse, his limbs thrashed as he screamed until his voice failed. Even after it was gone he still tried, eyes squeezed shut, hands curled into claws ripping at the voidstone.

It almost—almost—made her regret doing this to him.

Mariq watched as the voidstone sucked Lookan dry. He shriveled before her eyes, the life draining from him in moments. It was a relief when he finally lay still and the voidstone slid off his sweat-slickened forehead. It clattered to the ground, hints of red streaking through the blackness. Mariq shuddered. The stone almost seemed smug.

She ignored the voidstone, the bodies of her brother and father, and knelt beside Turien. He was pale and covered in cold sweat, but he was alive. She pulled off her father's cloak, wadding it against Turien's stomach and pressing down with all her strength.

Then she began screaming at the top of her lungs.

32

ariq slumped forward in her chair, not caring her posture was far from ladylike. It had been a long season. She was allowed to be exhausted after everything they'd been through.

"Sheikha Mariq," a servant said. "Sheik Zahra of Hatife is here to see you."

Mariq straightened, stifling a yawn. She must have dozed off. "Please, show him in."

Cendim entered the room, looking as old and tired as Mariq felt. His smile was firmly in place though, a bit less expansive and much more weary, but it still made Mariq smile in return.

"It's wonderful to see you, Cendim," Mariq said, embracing him.

"And you as well, my dear. How is Turien?"

"The surgeons say he's healing well. He'll still be down for a long time, but they're confident he'll be up and about eventually."

"Lovely to hear."

Mariq nodded. It had been a close thing. Even now, five days later, it still sent cold prickles down her spine to think of how close she'd come to losing him.

"Congratulations on your new title, my dear. I must say, first Sheikha in the Scorched Lands suits you."

"Thank you. I'm afraid much of my father's court doesn't agree, especially after I rejected Sheik Karga. He still thinks I'm his property, even though my father and brother never finalized the marriage. He refuses to accept I'm sheikha now, and that my word holds the weight of law."

"Men like that are always unhappy. Do beware of him, though. Karga is not a man who forgives."

"I know. I'll find some way to deal with him." Mariq sighed. "He's working very hard to find someone else to rule Kuriza, and he's gathering a lot of support. Everyone is happy to have the rule of Kuriza remain with royal blood until the only blood left belongs to a woman."

"You'll win them over in no time."

Heat rose to her cheeks. Instead of replying, she cleared her throat and spoke the words that were still so hard to say. "Cendim, I'm sorry about Ehra."

His smile faded, and tears magnified the sadness in his eyes. "Don't blame yourself. She died for what—and who—she believed in. I can ask for no more."

"I miss her."

"As do I."

They shared a moment of silent companionship before Cendim straightened. "I believe the scribes are waiting for us. Shall we?" He gestured toward the door with his left hand, where a table had been set up and courtiers from both kingdoms had gathered. He held out his right elbow for Mariq to take.

She did so, her smile returning. "Let's."

The quiet buzz of conversation fell silent as Mariq and Cendim entered the room. There had already been long speeches and celebrations, so there was no need for that any longer. Only two signatures were required on the lengthy parchments laid out before them.

"Today we celebrate the lasting peace between Kuriza and Hatife," Cendim said. Several people cheered as he bent down to sign the document.

Mariq followed and added her signature below Cendim's. "From today forward, our kingdoms are joined by this treaty. We are sister-kingdoms, bound by honor and friendship to protect and preserve each other."

Cendim and Mariq shook hands, and the peace was complete.

Mariq lingered for a while, shaking hands and speaking with politicians from both kingdoms, but as soon as she could she slipped away and went upstairs to Turien's room. "How is he?" she asked the nurse, sitting on the bed beside him.

"Asleep, Sheikha, but the surgeons say he is healing well. A few more days should find him regaining his feet."

She nodded, though her eyes never left Turien. "Thank you."

A while later Cendim entered the room and stood beside her. "So much has changed for you both. Do you think you're ready?"

If anyone else had asked, she'd have lied without a thought. "Not in the least," she replied instead. "But we'll figure it out. Turien watched my brother lead the Star-Blades his entire life. He should have plenty of examples of how not to do it."

"Just as you have much experience in how not to rule a kingdom," Cendim replied.

Mariq glanced back at him. "And some examples of how to do it well."

Cendim smiled. He hesitated, watching Turien sleep, before speaking. "Mariq. I've decided not to reinstate our *bardiya*."

Mariq turned back to him, curious and confused and a little hurt. True, she didn't love Cendim as a husband, but his respect and friendship had gotten her through so much.

"You've helped me accomplish my goal, and although I can't deny the pleasure of your company, that was the main reason I asked for you in the first place." He looked from her to Turien and back, then smiled. "Besides. I think you have better prospects in your future than an old man like me."

Cendim laughed as Mariq sputtered and stumbled over her words. He patted his hand in the air, calming her. "I must head back to Hatife. Should either of you need anything, you know how to reach me."

Mariq sat in silence for a long time after Cendim left, keeping Turien company while he slept. She reached over and stroked the silk of his slave-band. The tattooists had made good headway on Turien's new heritage tattoos, but there was still a lot of work to be done. Mariq wouldn't remove the slave-band until the tattoos were complete enough to make Turien's identity clear. By the time they were done, he would be as highly acclaimed as her own tattoos spoke of her.

Turien had earned every last bit of it.

Finally she returned to her own chambers, the same rooms she'd occupied as a child. She'd spent far too much time here, dreaming of another life, to move somewhere else.

She'd been a spider-thief in these rooms. Now it was time for her to be something else. It was long past due for her to get what *she* deserved.

And though she might have lost her status of spider-thief, she was convinced she could find something far more important now. Happiness. Value. A life of her own.

Mariq was no longer a spider-thief. She was far more than that.

She was Mariq Ashai Meidani. No longer property, no longer a pawn.

She was, as Turien would say, Someone.

Acknowledgments

Writing books is always hard. Anyone who's ever tried it will tell you that. But some books are harder than others.

Joythief was a very, very hard book to write.

The struggle for an identity of your own is something that, to some extent, I think everyone is familiar with. As children, teens, even adults we long for that niche, that place where we feel like our most genuine self. Sometimes we even have to stop halfway through life and realize that our place, whether through tragedy or circumstance or simple evolution of character, no longer fits us. Accepting that and being willing to search for the place we do belong take a lot of courage.

Thanks to everyone who's helped me find my niche, and accepted the genuine "me", flaws and all. Brian, Mum and Daddoo, Rob, Bev, Ashley, RJ, Lisa, Shannon. You guys make this journey so amazing, and I love every single one of you.

Other Books

BY BRENDA J. PIERSON

Soul of the Blade
Soul of the Guardian

WRITING AS BJ PIERSON

SuperDrew and the Secrets of Donhil Corp

"Crafting an Artisan"
in *A Touch of Magic*, edited by Janina Franck